A Plague of Hatred

THE ENCROACHING CHAOS

Jeremiah Cain

VYLETRA LLC

vyletra.com

Published by Vyletra LLC, Mobile, AL
vyletra.com

This is a work of fiction. Names, characters, places, and incidents are a product of the author's imagination. Any resemblance to actual people, living or dead, or to businesses, companies, events, institutions, or locales is completely coincidental.

A Plague of Hatred: The Encroaching Chaos / Jeremiah Cain.
Hardback ISBN: 978-1-7348024-5-0
Paperback ISBN: 978-1-7348024-6-7
Ebook ISBN: 978-1-7348024-7-4
LCCN: 2023901444

First printing June 2023

Cover and interior illustrations © 2023 by Jeremiah Cain

A

CONTENTS

PART ONE

For the Betterment of the World

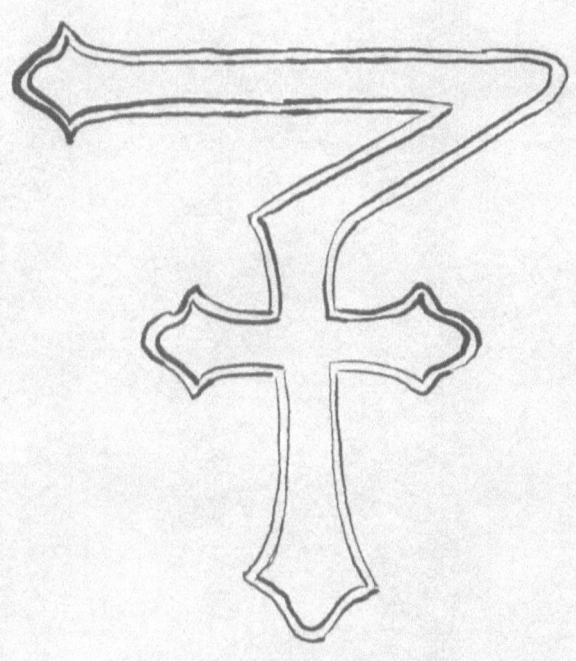

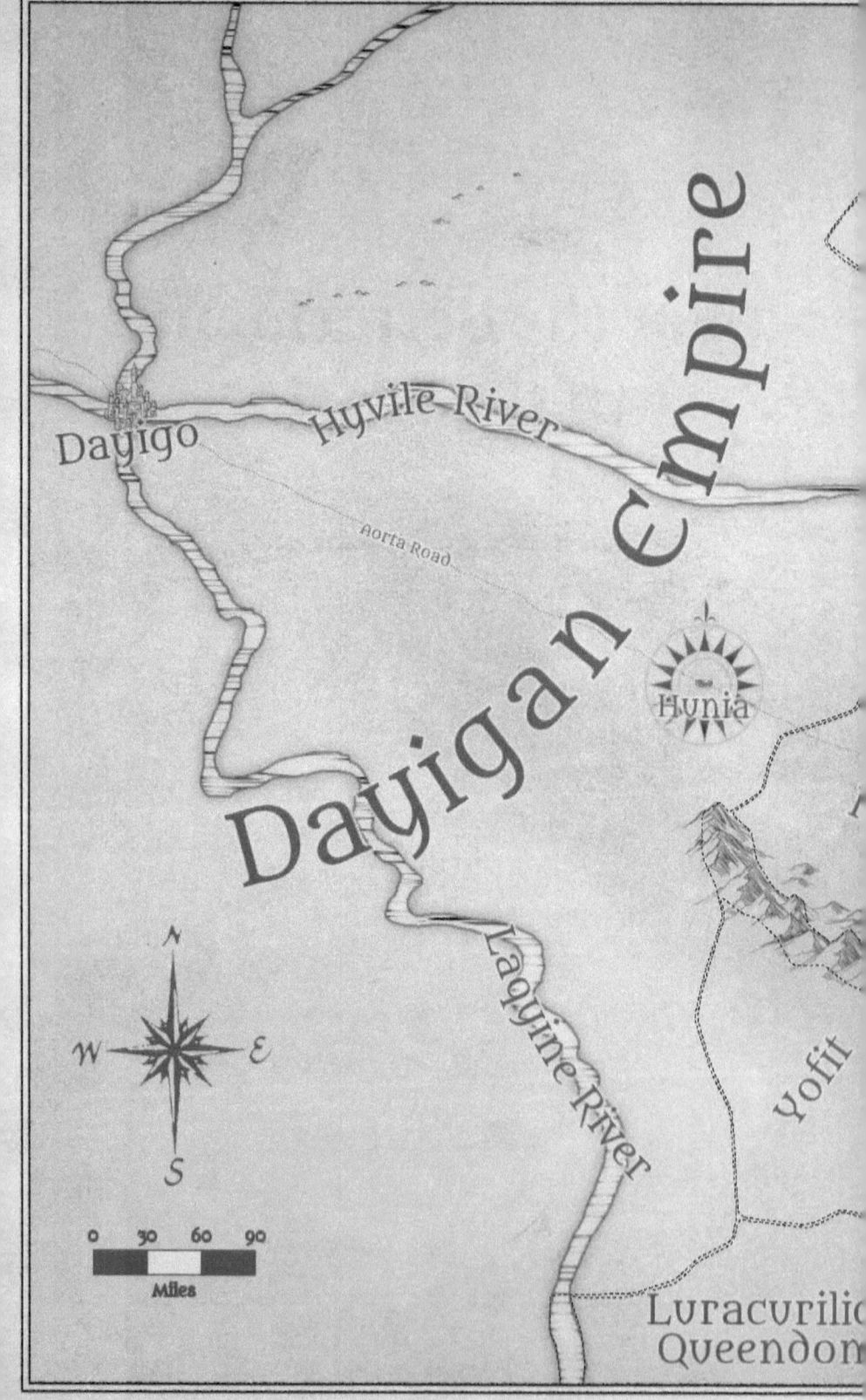

CHAPTER ONE

Octkiés 08, 812

She strolled down the wide road as if the irregular cobblestones were clouds beneath the wooden soles of her
gray shoes. Her skirt, mimicking the color of the sky,
danced around her. Her brown leather bodice was tight over
her white linen blouse. Her face, young and sweet, Roslyn
was a pretty eighteen-year-old girl with bright blue eyes and
long, blond hair braided around a white scarf and blue ribbons.

The sun—the ever-watching Titan Jerah—seemed warmer
on her skin and brighter on this summer day as he looked
over the town of Hunia. The "town," as they called it, was but
a line of wattle-and-daub houses and shops down a single
wide road. In either direction, the road spanned miles, far
beyond the small town. Here, it held only a few dirt side
roads that led beyond the shops to the vast farmlands close
behind.

Roslyn waved to local serfs at the side of the large road,
some of those who sold their vegetables from wooden stalls.

"Good morrow, sir," she said with a smile as she passed by.
"Good morrow, ma'am," she said to another.

"*Roslyn,*" a voice called while approaching. The woman—
Nell—and her husband worked at the baron's mill. From
where Roslyn stopped, she could see inside through the many
arched, open windows of the wide, round stone building. A
harnessed ox walked a slow circle around a large grinding
stone.

"You're not headed out of town, are you, dear?" Nell asked.
"Not on your own?"

"Of course not. Only to the edge. I'm meeting Jon."

"Jon. I should have guessed it with the way you're beaming. I could see those pearly white teeth of yours clear inside the mill. 'Tis not decent for a girl to be smiling like that in public."

Roslyn smiled more grandly as she spun around. "Then let me be indecent," she said with a laugh, "for I cannot contain it."

Nell inhaled sharply as she closed her eyes and set her hand to her breast. "God Karulus, help us all. You be a Faery child, you. You've always been."

"Perhaps I am a changeling." She wiggled her fingers like claws on either side of her head.

"Wouldn't surprise me none."

Roslyn laughed. "I have reason for delight. Jon returns today after three months away. I'm to meet him at noon."

"Is it so? And where's he been off to, then?"

"He wouldn't say. He said it was a surprise."

"A surprise, says he." Nell chuckled. "With that boy, it could be anything. Trouble and trouble, the pair of you both." Nell shook her head. She then laughed. "Well, go on, then. No good standing around here chatting to an old woman when young love's awaiting."

Roslyn looked down at her shadow. "You're right. My shadow's nearly underfoot. God Karulus keep you well."

"And you, dear. Safe journey."

Roslyn's pace increased—not quite a run, but an excited walk—as she hurried toward the western edge of town.

A horse-drawn cart filled with barrels smelling of beer clattered past, wooden wheels thumping on the uneven road.

Roslyn stopped. In the distance, she saw an eighteen-year-old boy, grungy and skinny, the kind of body born of a lifetime of too much labor and too little food. His tangled, fair hair touched his shoulders. He carried a large burlap sack over his back. His brown tunic, just as coarse as the sack, was belted with a rope. His trousers were thin and beige.

He looked around as he walked, scanning the surrounding people, but stopped as he saw Roslyn. A smile grew within the downy patches of his forming beard.

He ran to her and she to him. They met in the center of the street.

He dropped the sack and embraced her.

Roslyn kissed the lips she'd missed so much.

"You," she said, close in his embrace, "were supposed to be at the edge of town."

"I couldn't wait a moment more to see you."

"What if I had passed you?"

"The town only has the one road." He laughed. "'Sides, God Karulus, himself, wouldn't've allowed such a travesty to happen. He would have grabbed us both up and pushed us together." Jon lifted her and spun her around. He kissed her again.

"They'll have us for lewdness," she giggled, "if we continue like this in the street."

"Are we in the street? I see only my lovely Rose."

She groaned. "Go to!" She pushed him away with a laugh. "Awful."

Their hands entwined.

"What?" He feigned insult. "That was sweet, that. Poetic."

She looked into his brown eyes. They shined with bliss. His lips grinned widely. He seemed *too* happy, even for this happy meeting.

"You're not drunk, are you?" she asked.

He released a loud guffaw. "Nay." He smiled. "Nay, not drunk. On drink. But drunk on the news I bring?"

"Pray tell, what news?"

"Come," he said excitedly.

Holding her hand, he grabbed up his bag and rushed her to the side of the street.

"Close your eyes," he said. "And face away from me."

Roslyn grinned with curiosity. "My love, you are too well known as a trickster."

"'Tis no trick, of that be sure. Pray you, turn 'round and close your eyes."

She did as he asked and was immediately a little girl, excitedly and impatiently awaiting a gift. She tried to listen for any clues her ears might detect. Perhaps she heard the rustling of cloth. He was no doubt rummaging through his bag. But there were too many noises on the street to determine any actual information.

"All right," Jon said at last. "Have a look."

Roslyn's smile grew so large that her face ached as she turned. She opened her eyes. Her smile fell. She felt sick in the pit of her stomach.

Over his clothes, Jon now wore a vibrant red tabard hanging just past his knees. Along the bottom, up the sides, and around his neck, amber thread edged it. But Roslyn stared in horror at his chest. There, embroidered in amber thread, was the sun and two moons in an upward-pointing triangle. Below it, a downward-pointing triangle represented the island city, Dayigo.

"Say something," he said.

"Your tricks grow more . . ." she started but lost her words. "Why?" she asked in bitter shock. "Why are you dressed like a Dayigan?"

"We are Dayigans, Rose. Hunia's been part of the Empire for two years now."

"I know that," she snapped. "But why are *you* dressed like . . . *that*?"

"For *us*, Rose. I joined the king's army so we could be wed. I couldn't have you marry a serf, could I? And I couldn't lose you."

"I would have married a serf. I'd *planned* to marry a serf, if ever he'd asked."

"That's all well and good to say now, innit? But would you be saying the same after years and years of toiling away in the fields of the baron, only to use what little free time we have left toiling away on the little plot of land he allots us so we don't starve? And part of everything from our own farm goes back to the baron, too. Plus, there's a charge to use the baron's mill. And the baron's oven and to hunt on the baron's lands. And if there be trouble, the baron's court. *Plus*, another part goes to the Church, as well. I've seen what that life did to me family, Rose. Every year you don't starve to death is a good year, and all."

She turned away, no longer able to look at the tabard. "The king of Dayigo hates us."

He set his hands on her shoulders. "No, not no more. That's over with now. The Blue Sickness has been gone for years, and—"

"Don't call it that." She stepped away from him. "They gave the plague that name to blame it on Karulents, even though it had nothing to do with us." She turned to face him. "And," she sighed, "it affected us just as badly."

Jon nodded sadly. "Your father—rest his soul—was a good man. He worked hard to become a free peasant so you wouldn't have to know the life I lived. And he would hate me from his grave if I brought you back to serfdom."

Again, she stared at the Dayigan insignia on his chest. She wanted to rip it from the body of her love and rip it into pieces. Yet she only stared. Inside her mind, she screamed.

"I thought you'd be happy," Jon said with an uncertain smile. "I'll be stationed here in Hunia. They pay the army well, and more with rank. The baron said I could take up your lease, so you won't lose your father's cottage. And you'll have time to continue your research and your potions. I know how important that is to you."

"What about the war on the eastern border?" she asked.

"The *conflicts* with the Tridulan Empire don't have a thing to do with the Hunian garrison. And if the conflicts did escalate to the point that it did, any man, sixteen to sixty years of age, would be levied to fight. The only difference is that I'd be better trained, paid, and less dispensable." He paused. "I know I'm not as smart as you—with your reading and scholaring—but I did think this through. Oh . . ." He began tugging at a thin hemp rope he wore as a necklace under his tunic. He pulled it up over his head.

From it hung a ring, which he now presented in his palm. The polished steel band was crowned with a blue-painted rose. As he held it up toward her, he looked at her with sad eyes and a downward tilt of his head. "For you."

She sighed. "A Dayigan soldier." She rubbed the side of her forehead. "Karulus help us." She chuckled at the absurdity of it all, combined with his lackluster attempt at a marriage proposal.

Jon smiled slightly, though with a healthy dose of confusion in his eyes.

Roslyn looked away from him and toyed with her hair. "When God Karulus asked the Lavender Lady to be his bride," she said coyly, "he knelt before her and—you know—actually asked."

Jon's smile widened. He hurriedly kneeled on one knee and took her hand in his. "Roslyn, m'love, will you honor me by becoming me bride?"

She set her finger to her cheek as if thinking, though grinning all the while. "I suppose I should. A Dayigan soldier will need someone who can mend him if he's injured."

"And I'll have the best healer in all the world."

"I'm far from that," she said. "I'm not even quite the best in Hunia, despite little competition. But the church has taught me much." She kneeled to him and gazed into his eyes.

"Since the sickness took my father . . ." she started but stopped. She sighed. "Over the last year and a half, Father Hanugfrie has been like a father to me. Pray you, first ask him for my hand. It seems right to do."

Jon nodded. "Of course."

They stood.

"We'll have a good life, you and me," Jon said.

From behind Jon, a man called, "Soldier."

Roslyn looked over Jon's shoulder to see a man in his mid-twenties. Though he was dressed in the ragged clothes of a serf, he was spotless and postured. His blond hair was trimmed short. His horse, Roslyn noted, was quite an expensive charger.

"*Soldier*, says he," Jon said, thrilled by the word. He turned to face the man. "Yea, sir, I am, sir, a freshly trained soldier of the Holy Dayigan Empire."

"Yes." The man remained unimpressed. "Tell me, is this the town of Hunia?"

"The very same, sir, but barely," Jon said. "That is to say, we're barely a town. Hunia has the great fortune of being located on a major road and a day's journey, on either side, between two places where people actually want to visit."

"I seek the inn," he said, seemingly vexed by Jon.

"As does everyone, sir. 'Tis just up the hill"—Jon lifted his hand and slid it forward and up as if ascending a hill—"and 'round a slight bend. The baron's put a wishing pool there, dead center in the road, to make it easier to find."

"My thanks, Footman." The man nodded curtly. "Miss." He nodded to Roslyn.

The man patted his horse's neck and rode away toward the center of town.

CHAPTER TWO

He kept his eyes low, mostly gazing at the piss-yellow ale in his half-empty tankard. His broad shoulders hunched, leaning his upper weight onto his arms; these folded tight on the small tavern table. The hood of his shabby gray cloak was pulled up snug over his muddled hair despite his being indoors.

Swithun, a year past thirty, figured he looked more like a highwayman than a soldier. It was for the best he knew, but he wondered when that became the better option.

He lifted his head a little more than necessary while taking a drink, looking around without seeming to.

It was a small, one-story tavern paneled in grayed planks of wood framed in unpainted logs. The patrons were sparse and well behaved. Little surprise. It was barely past noon, too early for much in the way of drunken foolishness.

A barmaid served stew to a dusty woman with two raggedy children: travelers, most likely, staying in the adjoining inn.

In the corner, two men sat having a drink and a laugh while listening to an older third tell a tale.

Everyone was Human, like Swithun, but he had already noticed that. He hadn't seen another race the whole day since he'd neared this town of Hunia. It was odd to him, he being from a city, but since he'd joined the army, he'd visited many little, back-country towns like this and knew most were segregated.

And with only one religion as well. In the case of this town, the wrong one.

Swithun gazed back down into the shallow depths of his ale.

Most people said war was coming. Many said it had already begun. A civil war. And these decent, hard-working people all around were the enemy. Or, more accurately, they were the enemy of the church that controlled the crown that controlled the army that controlled Swithun.

"Mind if I sit down?" A man's voice.

A blond stranger, mid-twenties and dressed in a well-laundered version of peasant garb, stood across the small table. His hand was on the back of the chair, already sliding it out.

"Sorry, friend," Swithun said. "I'm waiting for someone, all right, and I ain't looking for conversation in the meantime."

"'Twill be but a moment, I assure you," the man insisted, his accent notably higher bred than his clothing. Before Swithun could protest, the young man was sitting down.

"I was wondering," the stranger began, "if they served *Volagroken turnips* in this tavern."

"Volagroken turnips?" Swithun glanced sideways at the younger man. A nonsense: nothing grew in Volagrok but volcanoes and dragon whelps. But it was what Swithun had been waiting for—the first half of a question-and-answer code.

Swithun supplied the second half, saying, "You'd do better to try the lacerated meat pie."

The stranger leaned in. "Sergeant Swithun, I presume," he whispered.

"I am. And what should I call you, sir?"

"Sir is fine. Or *Captain*. Pay your tab and meet me outside. We cannot talk here."

—

Quite casually, Swithun strolled from the tavern to enter the wide, cobbled street of Hunia. Scanning for the nameless captain, he walked among the handful of people strolling between and in and out of the simple wattle-and-daub houses with thatched roofs. A scant few buildings were plank, like the tavern and inn, with thatched roofs. He'd seen only two stone buildings with tiled roofs, both in blue tiles: a mill down toward the town's edge and a stone chapel that sat just up from the inn.

He soon saw the other man just up the way. The young captain, in what was no doubt an attempt to blend, was half-heartedly browsing a vendor's cart of apples.

His father must have money, Swithun thought, *for him to be a captain at that age. Lucky bastard. And whilst most people fight their asses off for rank.*

The captain tossed an apple to Swithun as he approached.

"Have you any clue why you are here?" the captain asked, once away from other ears.

Swithun looked around to assure himself that no one else was near. "Me orders was a place and time, sir. Nothing more. But I can't help but notice this here's a Karulent town."

"Yes," the captain said. "I'm sure you know the world is changing. The Church is increasingly pressuring the king to declare the worship of God Karulus illegal. Many would see Karulents burnt to death alongside Dark Light witches. 'Tis a controversial matter, of course."

"I've heard, sir."

The captain furrowed his brow as he scanned the other man's face. "What do *you* think, Sergeant?"

The question took Swithun off guard. "I . . . I'm a Dayigan soldier, sir. I think what the Army tells me to think. But, it do seem to me like Patriarch Krasil utilizes the army a lot more than any holy man I ever heard of before him. Know what I mean?"

"Yes," the captain said. "Very true. In the last few years since Supreme Patriarch Krasil came into power, the Church has become more wrath than worship. A necessary change, for the betterment of the world. But, of course, you were there when it began. You are from Wendian, yes?"

Swithun nodded. "I been gone a long time, sir."

The captain stopped, and so did Swithun.

They were before the stone steps of a Karulent parish church, and they turned to face the brightly painted blue doors that led through its five-story bell tower under a thirty-foot steeple. The tower stood as an entrance to the small nave that composed the main body of the structure.

"The priest of this parish," the captain began, "a Father *Hanugfrie*, is an enemy to the Church and Crown. You are to seek him out and execute him."

"A priest, sir?"

"A *Karulent* priest, yes."

"Yes, sir," Swithun said, but his eyes drifted to the ground.

"I believe you said you think what the army tells you to think," the captain said flatly. He leaned to Swithun with hushed words. "The Church of Déagar has tolerated the Karulents for centuries, true, but that has ceased. We must learn to view them no differently than we would any other heathen who defies God Déagar and engages in the savage practices of magic. We have given them ample warnings. No longer will they exist within *our* empire. Do you understand, soldier?"

"Yes, sir."

Two plainly dressed women descended from the blue doors of the church.

"Good afternoon, ladies." The captain smiled and nodded.

They smiled back and continued to pass.

The captain paused a breath as he scanned the scruffy sergeant at his side, obviously trying to read him. "My sources tell me you fought well against the Tridulans to the east. You snuck in under the cloak of night and assassinated major targets for our cause."

"They was Dark Light savages, sir."

"This new enemy is no different. Save that we have been too lenient, too long. Surely, you haven't forgotten the Blue Sickness, soldier."

"I definitely haven't, sir." Swithun looked up at the captain. "The bastards killed . . ." He stopped himself, gritting his teeth. "I lost a lot, sir. If the king says they's the enemy, then they is."

"Good." The captain waggled a finger at Swithun in a signal to follow.

The two ambled down the wide street as the captain whispered, "Are you familiar with the Azerents?"

"I am, Captain. Azerent Mages, they're sometimes called. From what I hear, powerful casters what use Karulent magic."

"*Too* powerful. This is why, if we wish to rid the empire of magic, we must cripple the Azerents beyond restoration. Father Hanugfrie is one of them. Ideally, we would like to target a member of their hidden inner order, which unfortunately he is not. But he is a master. You must take him by surprise or not take him at all. 'Tis said he can crush a man's heart from ten feet away."

"Me arrow can pierce a heart from farther than that, sir. If called upon to do so by the Greatest of All."

"An arrow, if you like." The captain stopped and turned to Swithun, again looking him up and down. "The details are yours to resolve on your own. Your record suggests that your success should be no issue. However, you are to wear this."

The captain opened a pouch on his belt and produced a thin strip of copper, about a foot long and an inch wide.

Swithun took it and examined it with confusion.

The captain became annoyed. "Place it against your upper arm."

Swithun complied. The strip snapped like a spring and circled his arm, becoming a seamless band.

"It allows us to track you," the captain said. "And alerts us if you are severely injured. Or dead."

"Thank you . . . sir," Swithun replied uncertainly.

"But do remember, Sergeant," the captain continued. "As far as anyone else is concerned, you act of your own accord. If you are caught, you will be punished accordingly. Once the deed is done, we will find you. Understood?"

"Yes, Captain."

"Very well. I will leave you to it. May the fires of God Déagar guide you."

CHAPTER THREE

Then peaceful song of a choir echoed from inside the parish church as Roslyn followed a waist-high stone wall from the building's side. She opened the wooden gate and passed beneath an arch of fragrant honeysuckle.

Inside the garden, low hedges of boxwoods edged four square plots. Paths of trimmed grass ran between them. A pool—its low circular walls the height of the boxwoods, but matching the stone of the garden border walls—was placed at the intersection of the paths. From its center, a conic spiral of a tin half-pipe ascended, taking the water from the pool to flow upward to a peak before cascading down.

Roslyn listened to the splashing water and breathed deeply, taking in the place's calm.

Three nuns tended to the garden. They wore long, pale gray habits and sky-blue wimples over their heads. There was a tranquility to their silent tasks, and Roslyn imagined they communed with Karulus as they trimmed herbs and plucked weeds.

Roslyn's attention turned to Father Hanugfrie, the elderly man who sat cross-legged on the grass at the wall of the church. He too wore a pale gray habit—though with a masculine cut—but over it, he wore a long, dark blue hooded cloak.

His hands were on his knees, palms upward, and his eyes were closed.

Roslyn hated to disturb him, but she approached him nevertheless.

"Father," she said softly.

He opened his eyes and looked up at her. He smiled. "Is it already time for your lessons, child?"

"It is, Father. Though, I do not wish to bother you."

"'Tis no bother, child. I was simply . . ." He took in a deep breath and released it slowly. ". . . breathing in the divine power that permeates the air."

"The pneuma," Roslyn said, as she helped him to his feet.

"Is it pneuma?" he asked.

She thought for a moment. "No. No, pneuma is what we call it when it is inside of us, the life force that flows through our veins—"

"Arteries," he corrected. "Go on."

". . . flows through our *arteries*, and powers both our vital organs and our soul. Around us in the air," she continued, "it is the spiritual voices of all Karulents in the world unified as one song of worship. But I . . ." She bit her smile. "I don't actually remember what that is called."

He chuckled. "'Tis no matter. Such things are more the concerns of mages and the like. An abundance of pneuma, you know, allows magic. Your lesson today will not be so arcane."

"First, I have wondrous news," she said. "Has Jon come to see you?"

"No, should he have? I can check with my wife." He looked toward one of the nuns and raised a hand to beckon.

"No." Roslyn stopped him. "I doubted he would have. He's been very busy since he returned to town. But he will. Soon." She smiled. "He is going to ask you for my hand in marriage. I thought it proper it should be you."

"I would be honored to fill the role in your father's place."

"Wonderful. You *will* act surprised when he asks, won't you?"

"*Roslyn*," he faked shock, "are you asking a Karulent priest to lie to your future bride-groom?"

"Perhaps." She grinned.

"But this is, indeed, wondrous news," he said. "And well-timed, for I have a gift for you without cause. And now I have a cause for a gift. Come."

—

Roslyn entered Hanugfrie's study—a small circular room with a worn wooden desk filling most of it. A few cluttered shelves were built into the stone walls. Centered on the wall behind the desk was a crossed version of the number seven in gold-painted wood.

"I confess I am concerned, Father," Roslyn said. "About Jon. He's joined the Dayigan Army."

Hanugfrie stopped. "So you wouldn't need to marry a serf, I assume."

"Yes."

He turned to her. "Your father was a good man, and you took good care of him in his final days."

She shook her head. "I could barely do anything for him. It is why I so desperately want to learn the ways of healing now, so I'll never again be so helpless."

He looked her in her eyes. "You did what you could, Roslyn, which was very brave in the face of the Great Pestilence. He was proud of you and would be proud of how much you have progressed in your studies. But he was wary of Jon. Not that he did not like the boy. He was wary of the hard life inherited by a woman who weds a serf. 'Twould seem Jon has done the only thing in his power to remedy your father's concerns."

She nodded.

"I must admit," he said, "your father's concerns were my own until you told me of Jon's decision."

"But the Dayigan Army."

"Admittedly, it would not have been my first choice," Father Hanugfrie said. "Or fifth. But, as I understand it, Dayigan soldiers enlist for seven years. What is done is done."

She sighed. "Yes, Father. You're right, of course."

"Now," he said in a lighter tone, "I believe I mentioned a betrothal gift."

He neared a shelf near the back of the room and selected a large book.

"For you." He gave it to her.

Roslyn, carefully taking the book, barely contained her excitement. She ran her finger along the embossed symbol on the leather cover. It showed a large five-pointed star with a five-petaled flower nearly filling the star's interior. In the center of the flower was a pentagon holding an eye.

She opened it and flipped through the beautifully handwritten pages with detailed drawings of herbs, roots, and anatomy.

"I had it shipped from Vilana," Hanugfrie said.

"Is it Azerent?" Roslyn asked as she flipped.

"Not exclusively. But the Azerent Healers compiled it and use it. It, of course, does not include any of the magical methods known only to the Order, but it is quite extensive in secular medicine and some low-level magic."

She set the book down on his desk and grabbed him in a tight hug.

"Roslyn," he said. "We do not bear-hug members of the clergy."

She stepped back. "Forgive me, Father." She sighed. "I will memorize every word."

"I believe you will. Karulus has given you exceptional talent, Roslyn. I—as a mage, not a healer—have taken you as far as I can. But this book"—he set his hand atop it—"will give you the knowledge to make your talent shine."

CHAPTER FOUR

With a pail in hand, Roslyn approached a goat grazing in front of her cottage. It was a cozy place, her cottage, framed in dark wooden beams with wattle-and-daub walls and a thatched roof. A fenced-off area to the side held a variety of vegetables with a small medicinal section. Apart from the cleared area near her house, woods surrounded it for most of the quarter mile back to town.

Roslyn petted the goat's back. "Are you going to give me some milk?" she asked. She paused before saying, "Good girl."

The goat jerked, startled. It looked up the path through the woods.

Roslyn looked, too.

A man was running toward her. He was a Dayigan soldier who Roslyn recognized as Jon's lieutenant. Behind him, two other men carried a fourth.

Roslyn threw down the bucket and ran toward them.

"Jon's been injured," the lieutenant called. "A training exercise. He insisted we bring him here."

Roslyn passed the lieutenant and hurried straight to Jon.

He was barely conscious and clutched his chest. Blood soaked his tunic.

"Inside," Roslyn said to the guards who carried him. "Quickly."

"Yes, miss."

She hurried beside them. "Jon, can you hear me?"

He nodded weakly, with a jerk of pain.

"I'm going to take care of you," Roslyn said, "but I need you to stay with me, all right?"

He nodded.

Roslyn grabbed Jon's wrist and set her fingers on his pulse. To a guard, she said, "Tell me what happened."

"He was practicing swordsmanship against a militiaman. Jon was blocking, but his sword slipped, and the opponent's sword struck him."

"A cut or a thrust?" she asked urgently.

"The side of the blade, miss."

"Thank Karulus for that."

Roslyn threw open the door to her cottage and dashed to a nearby bed. She grabbed a blanket and threw it out on the plank floor.

"Set him here, and take off his belts." She rushed to a table at the side of the room and grabbed a pair of shears. She returned to Jon.

"I need you to stay still," she said to Jon, "so I do not cut you. But keep pressure on the wound." Looking up at a guard, she added, "Set your hand atop his to help him."

Roslyn began cutting downward from the neck of Jon's tunic. "Pray you," she said to the other guard, "go to that table under those drying herbs, just there by the side wall. There's a clay pitcher of water that's been boiled and cooled. Get it for me. And the clean cloth beside it. And the basin."

"Yes, miss."

Roslyn peeled back the blood-soaked tunic. "I need you to let go now, Jon, so I can see the wound and irrigate it."

Jon called out as she exposed the site. Blood oozed up.

Roslyn grabbed the pitcher and the cloth from the guard and began carefully pouring water as she brushed the area with the cloth.

Jon called out again.

She washed away the thick blood and revealed a deep, five-inch-long cut.

"God Karulus," she prayed as she poured more water, "God of water and of healing, purify this wound of all that would harm this man."

She set the dry end of the cloth on the cut and pressed it.

"Jon, are you still with me?"

He nodded weakly.

"You have a five-inch incision to your left pectoralis major. That's your chest. I will need to suture it, but it doesn't appear to have affected anything internal. You're going to be fine."

—

The soft, flickering firelight imbued Roslyn's cottage with a warm and cozy ambiance. A rickety ladder stood on the right side of the front door, leading up to a loft where a meager bed sat among dusty items in storage. Below, in a short section of the first floor, a trunk sat at the foot of a rough-hewn bed with bark-covered posts.

There, Jon slept soundly on his back, clad only in thin beige trousers. A gentle breeze flowed through an open window beside him, carrying the scents of the night-cloaked woods outside.

Beyond that area, the ceiling opened up to reveal sturdy wooden rafters supporting a thatched roof. In the center of the back wall stood a stone chimney with a crackling fireplace at its base. Three old benches were placed before it, providing seating for warmth and comfort.

To the left of the room stood two sturdy wooden cupboards and three narrow counter-height tables along the side wall. Above them hung rectangular racks suspended from the rafters, holding an array of herbs that hung upside down to dry.

Roslyn stood at one of the tables, grinding a mixture of herbs with a small mortar and pestle. She paused for a moment to take in her home and look back at Jon sleeping. She smiled contentedly.

She poured the contents of the mortar into a small wooden bowl of honey and stirred it with a wooden spoon as she approached her soon-to-be husband.

"Jon," she whispered tenderly as she sat on the bed beside him.

He opened his eyes and smiled, attempting to sit up but wincing in pain. He looked down at his chest and gently touched the wound she'd stitched up with her hair.

"You sewed my heart back together, then?" he asked with a grin. "Nice work."

She smiled. "Actually, your heart is much more central than people think. Much of it is behind your sternum." She tapped the flat bone in the center of his chest.

Her fingers lingered, touching his skin. She slid her fingertips downward to his stomach, pausing a moment as her pulse increased.

Roslyn caught herself and withdrew her hand.

"This," she said, averting her eyes from him as she stared straight down into the wooden bowl, "will help with the pain and promote healing."

She scooped a large spoonful of the thick concoction and spread it carefully over the injury.

"I've barely seen you since you returned home," she said casually.

"'Tis just this last phase of training, that's all." He folded his arms under his head. "In just over a week's time, you'll be seeing me more than you can stand. And soon after that, every day, right here in our house. What's up that ladder there?"

"The loft. It used to be my bedroom."

"We'll *fill* it with children. A dozen."

"A dozen?"

"Two dozen."

"We'll need a bigger ladder."

He laughed.

Roslyn began spreading the paste of herbs and honey with her fingers, working it between the stitches.

"That already feels much better," Jon said. He sighed and turned serious. "In truth, we should move our own bed up there. I'll build an addition for children later on. This area right here could be a shop, a right nice shop for potions, and all."

"I suppose the dozen children could all be clerks." Done with treating the wound, Roslyn sat back and wiped her fingers on a cloth.

"I'm serious now. A proper shop for you, right here. I'll build you a counter and some shelves."

Roslyn glanced around the area and could almost see the faint image of his daydream.

"I would like that," she said, and returned her eyes to Jon. "How does your chest feel now?"

He sat up and began kissing her lips deeply.

She dropped the spoon. The wooden bowl fell to the floor. Roslyn wrapped her hands around Jon, touching his bare skin in ways she'd never been allowed to before.

"So, your chest feels better, then, yes?"

He laughed and fell back against the bed, lying flat. He looked down at himself with a look of alarm.

Roslyn followed his eyes. The front of his pants had begun to swell. "You do that all the time," she said dismissively.

"Yes, but never when we've been so . . ."

Alone, she realized. There was no one within a quarter of a mile to judge them, to tell them to stop, or to remind them to wait. Only their mercurial convictions halted them in this heated moment.

Roslyn's heart pounded in nervous intrigue as she looked back at the swelling in his pants. There were no buttons, just an open fly tied at the top. She could glimpse the skin of the forbidden thing as it grew just beside the hole, pressing its lengthening shape against the thin beige fabric.

She looked back into Jon's eyes. So much want and anticipation. She knew her own eyes must look the same.

Roslyn tentatively slid her fingertips down his slim stomach, watching his muscles react in twitches and jolts.

His breathing had become slow and strained.

She pulled the tie at the waist of his trousers. The bow slid apart. She tried to make it playful, casual—just a silly little game. It was not. She crossed so many lines in such a minor action. Her heart pounded, and heat rushed down her.

Jon pushed down his pants and kicked them off him. In a frenzy, he pulled her to him and climbed on top of her.

He kissed her deeper still as he pressed their bodies together.

"I talked to Father Hanugfrie," Jon said breathily.

"Please don't say his name right now."

"No, I mean . . ." Jon jumped up and to the floor, firm prick slapping his stomach. He pulled Roslyn to her feet.

He kneeled and took her hand in his.

"You haven't answered yet," he began. "Roslyn, my neverending love, will you be my wife?"

"Yes," she said. "Forever and ever."

—

Swithun paced his room in the inn. The small room was mostly taken up by an unimpressive bed with four-by-four corner posts. The straw-stuffed mattress had seen its share of travelers. At least the sheets were clean. The room had un-painted plank walls and, besides the bed, held a small side table topped with a large earthenware bowl of water for any washing up he might need. The inn offered candles but at a price beyond Swithun's means. Luckily, he had a window, and he kept the wooden window panel slid to the side, allow-ing in moonlight and a summer breeze.

"Fucking za," he cursed in indecision.

He slammed his hands down on the windowsill and looked out to the empty main road of Hunia.

Centered in the road before the inn, a low stone wall edged a pool of water where Karulents sacrificed silver coins to their God. Just up the road, Swithun could see the parish church.

Swithun had spent the last few days getting to know the small church, familiarizing himself with the layout, its flow, and a few unused areas and rooms. Locks were scarce, its doors welcoming everyone without fear.

From his window, he now stared at the church, hating it and blaming it for what it would soon force him to do. He had no choice, he told himself. It was for the betterment of the world.

Nevertheless, with every blatant smile Swithun had given the townspeople from the inn to the church, and back again, he'd felt remorse. He could think of nothing more than: *I'll soon murder your beloved priest. It needs to be done.*

It was for the betterment of the world, Swithun kept telling himself. The captain was right; the Karulents were dangerous. They'd killed countless people with their plague.

In recent years, his own priests had often spoken of the evils of Karulents. From the pulpit, they shouted out:

Magic is the realm of the Gods alone! Only the wicked dare trespass!

Swithun could not allow the Empire to return to the horrible plague times. It was for the betterment of the world. Murder was not murder when done in the name of God Déagar, he assured himself. It could not be sin or wrong. To question this, however, was.

He left the window and sat on the bed. He set his head in his hands.

"The Karulents are the enemy now," Swithun whispered. "They are vile savages worthy of death."

Yet, the soldier couldn't recall the Déagrian priests ever saying they were evil before the new patriarch came into power.

—

"I have to go back soon," Jon whispered. He lay on his back with one arm under his head and the other around Roslyn. She lay with her head on his chest and her arms and legs wrapping him. Both were bare beneath a bedsheet, and she savored the slick warmth of his skin.

"You can't go out," she purred. "'Tis long past curfew."

He chuckled, rocking her with the motion of his chest. "I wish it was true, but curfew don't affect soldiers. The night watchmen answer to me."

"Do they?" she asked, impressed.

He nodded. There was a slight sound of sadness as he added, "All eight of the town guards do. Me and the lieutenant are the king's men, but the militiamen are the baron's." He sighed. "'Twas stupid me getting injured."

"It was an accident."

"A stupid accident. I keep trying to push meself, you know, prove meself. I'm supposed to be this great Dayigan soldier, but almost all the militiamen are better fighters. And they all have more experience. I keep feeling like they're all wondering why the baron released me from serfdom 'stead of them."

"Can't they just join the army, too?"

He shook his head. "Even if the baron would release them, the garrison's just two slots here. Normally, they might could join the Great Ordinance and fight in the conflicts to the east, but the king's put a stop to Karulents joining the army at all. It delayed me a whole day when I got to training, whilst they figured out if I could still join."

Roslyn sat up, holding the sheet to her breast. "Why has the king stopped Karulents from joining his army?"

"Fucking za, I shouldn't have said. You're not going to get like you get, are you?"

"If the king is—"

"For all I know, there's certain times every year when Karulents can and can't join." He reached up and pulled her back into his embrace.

"Enough talk about work," he said. "I don't have much longer 'till I have to go back."

Roslyn snuggled up next to him.

"We'll have to confess all this," Jon said, "to Father Hanugfrie. Won't we?"

"*No,*" Roslyn groaned playfully. "No, no, no. We'll plan a trip to the next town over when we get a chance and do confession there."

"Smart, you."

"Tomorrow is Sabbathday, though," she said. "Will you stand with me in church?"

"Sounds nice," he said. "I'll meet you out front, and we can walk in, hand-in-hand."

"Wonderful." She squeezed him tighter. "I'll wait for you out front."

CHAPTER FIVE

T he day arrived. Swithun had chosen Sabbathday morning for the deed, and the chapel was filling up with most of the town.

On almost every Sabbathday since his birth, Swithun had done this same thing, filed through the doors of a church among a crowd of people who greeted each other. On the steps, some paused in temporary groups of conversations before continuing inside.

So very like a Déagrian church.

But today, Swithun walked stiffly. He'd tied three arrows to his calf. He leaned his weight onto a simple wooden crutch, with the upper part shoved into the armpit of his faded blue tunic.

At first chance, he slipped away from the crowd. Just inside the main door, he crept up a narrow, creaking staircase. It led up the side of the bell tower, where, even now, a mighty tolling called the flock to mass.

Swithun did not continue up to the bell. He had already chosen a small area about halfway up the tower, a closet—cramped, dusty, and dimly lit—stuck in at the apex of the great open nave.

But a closet with a view: a small circular window letting a thick chain run through to droop out along the high-up ceiling. The chain passed through a large iron ring and then turned downward to hold a great iron chandelier suspended over the many churchgoers gathering below.

From here, Swithun could see the priest. A clear shot. All he had to do was wait.

As the service began, Swithun dislodged a long section of his crutch. This four-foot band of strong, flexible yew was designed to be a bow. He quickly proceeded to string it, forming a simple bow with a limited draw. It would get the job done: one swift arrow into the Reverend's unarmored chest.

No one would know what had happened until they saw blood. Saw the priest fall. Their beloved church leader. It was for the greater good. The Patriarch of the Church of Déagar conveyed Déagar's will, and this he commanded.

The sight would remind the strayed congregation who they should be worshiping. And Swithun, he'd rush out within the panic, never to be noticed.

Swithun felt remorse as he watched the priest through the small circular window. Father Hanugfrie, in his regal blue robe, gave the sermon. Swithun wanted him to say something iniquitous or rebellious, to speak out against Déagrians. Or the king. Or the Supreme Patriarch.

No. His words were of love and peace and charity.

Swithun closed his eyes and murmured, "Praise God Déagar, eldest of the Gods, protector from the Dark Light. You're the Greatest of All. I praise your name, majestic and holy, without ending. I pray you *guide me*, my God. Is this truly your will? For me to kill this servant of your brother? I know it ain't right questioning the Crown and Church—they're your vessels 'mongst us lowly mortals—but I figured I should double-check on this one, right?"

He listened for a reply. He opened his eyes and glanced up for a sign.

Nothing.

Taking a lack of response as leave to continue, he sighed and nodded. "I better get to it then. I pray you'll guide me arrow to completion. Astha'will-maybe."

—

Roslyn sat halfway up the seven steps to the church, waiting. The road was empty, except for three pigs that cleaned it by eating any garbage. Everyone Roslyn knew had passed by her, and she'd assured them Jon would arrive soon, and she'd assured them she'd be inside soon.

And yet, here she sat.

A part of her grew angry that he'd forgotten. A part of her worried there'd been another injury, or a complication to the last. Surely, she reasoned, she'd be the first to know, his healer.

"He forgot," she sighed.

Last night had been so wonderful, and she'd happily counted the moments until she'd see him again.

And then the moment passed.

And more moments passed as she faded from gleeful anticipation to dismal disappointment.

Somehow, the fact that they were soon to be married on these exact steps made the matter all the worse, as if it portended something. Every reasonable part of her knew it did not. But still.

Roslyn looked up to see Jon, in his red Dayigan tabard, running to her.

She stood up without approaching him.

"Forgive me," he said, out of breath.

"You're extremely late. Mass has already started," she huffed. "We'll have to stand near the back." She turned toward the door.

"We've been called away, Rose."

She looked back at Jon. "What, right now?"

"Early this morning. They had us up packing our kit before sunrise. Bandits have been causing trouble about three leagues southwest."

"Bandits? There's always bandits . . ." She sighed and nodded. "When are you leaving?"

"The regional commander had already wanted us to be out of town. But I had to come here to tell you."

"I suppose I'll have to get used to this, marrying a soldier. You will be safe, won't you? You have nothing to prove to those militiamen."

"Don't you worry. I'll be home, safe and sound in a day or so."

"Next week," she said firmly. "Right here. *On time.*"

"Next week." He smiled. "On time."

Jon made a handsome soldier, Roslyn thought, as she looked at him. For a moment, she imagined him older and bearded, still wearing that same Dayigan uniform. He was in the apothecary he'd built for her in their house, three children running about, as he talked of some bandit he'd thwarted.

"Right, then. I must be off," he said, pulling her from her daydream. "Love you, Rose."

"I love you too, Jon."

He kissed her quickly on the mouth and hurried away.

She shouted to him, "Be careful of your injury."

"Right," he called back. "If it starts bleeding, I'll rub dirt on it."

"No. Do not rub dirt on it, Jon. And remember to drink plenty of water. 'Tis the hottest part of summer."

He paused and turned back. "Yes, my lovely healer."

Roslyn smiled as she watched him run down the street. He rounded the curve, and he was gone. Her smile faded as sadness washed over her. She looked at the ground.

"Be safe, my love," she whispered.

Roslyn turned and entered the blue doors of the church.

Just inside, the small room, called the narthex, held little more than a wooden font of holy water.

She neared it, ready to dip her hand inside and cleanse her spirit before entering the proper church.

She stopped.

The door up to the bell tower stood ajar.

A strange feeling came over Roslyn as she neared the simple door. She was afraid. She was intrigued. She knew that Father Hanugfrie wouldn't want the door open. Or for anyone to go up there.

Roslyn hesitantly neared it and opened it. She looked up the narrow, shadowed staircase.

"Is anyone there?" she called.

She paused.

Roslyn ascended the stairs.

—

Swithun watched the priest in a bright blue robe trimmed in gold. The priest was praying, "Praise be to Karulus, spirit of truth, and of compassion."

The entire room repeated each line of the prayer. An entire town with voices united in a chorus of worship.

Swithun nocked his arrow. "Guide me, Déagar."

"*Guide us, Karulus,*" intoned the room. "*You are our God and our savior.*"

He drew the bow.

"Heal our hearts, although we are wicked," the room continued.

"This is the will of Déagar," Swithun whispered aloud, trying to overcome his writhing brain while his entire being screamed out that this was wrong.

". . . and by your light, guide us safely to Laqyigo."

His heart was a kettledrum.

"It ain't a priest." The bowstring cut into his fingers. "'Tis just some vile savage."

Below, Father Hanugfrie lifted his hands to the heavens. "As is thy will, may it be."

It was a perfect shot. With the priest's arms lifted, his entire center mass was exposed.

"The will of Déagar." Swithun began to release the string. "By your fire, guide me."

A motion sounded behind him.

A young woman in her late teens entered.

Swithun jumped, releasing a blind shot while turning. He sprang to his feet and looked back.

She said something.

He could not hear her. Or anything. His ears were deaf and ringing. It was so hot here. His heart, beating so fast.

Had he just killed a priest? He didn't know.

He grabbed the woman and, without thinking, pushed her against the wall.

All he could hear was his heart. And a damned ringing in his ears. All he could feel was fire rushing through his veins. His muscles ached with the need for violent release. His stomach churned with sick.

She struggled. Tried to scream.

His hand clamped over her mouth.

She didn't seem to be a sister of the church. She was dressed as a normal townswoman; her blond hair flowed free without cover.

"Stay still," Swithun hissed in her ear.

Whoever she was, she was now his problem.

"You make one more fucking sound or try to get away, I break your fucking neck. You hear me?"

She stopped struggling, but he could feel her shaking in his arms. A profound, tense shaking, as if her bones, themselves, rattled. She breathed quick and staggered breaths through her nose. The occasional teary sniff.

"Fucking za," Swithun cursed. "I should rip you apart for coming here."

He pulled her to the wall and looked out the eyelet into the sanctuary.

Father Hanugfrie was alive and well and preaching of forgiveness.

Wherever the arrow had gone, it had gone unnoticed.

Swithun held the woman from behind, tight against his body, one hand across her stomach clad in soft brown leather.

His blood still coursed. His thick hand gripped her mouth. His breathing, feral. He hated her for being here. She seemed so innocent. And pretty, too. It would only make it more difficult to do what needed to be done. No witnesses.

Swithun focused on the sermon below, hoping it would hurry and end, and the people would leave so he could flee this place. He had two more arrows, but knew better than to try another shot. Not with this woman here.

He blinked away the salty sweat that stung his eyes. It was so hot here.

Hanugfrie would have to die later.

The intoxicating scent of the woman was all Swithun could smell with each breath. Not the scent of a lady, not rose oil and waxy cosmetics, but the unadulterated odor of a warm peasant female body. The wondrous aroma vibrated through him.

He ignored it, focusing on the muffled sermon below. They seemed to be near the end. Then, Swithun could figure out what to do with this unfortunate witness. Break her neck, he'd said, and that very image took form in his brain as he held her tighter.

Her proximity was maddening, but he needed to hold her from escaping. He glanced down her slender neck to bare shoulders, to rounded breasts covered by the thin fabric of an off-white blouse, these supple mounds propped atop a brown leather waist cincher. His mind rushed with thoughts.

"Fucking temptress," Swithun snapped behind her ear. "You ruined everything."

"Please." She sniffed. "Please, let me go."

He threw her aside and glared at her as she stumbled backward and fell to her butt on the floor.

"Be glad I'm a good Déagrian and beyond your lustful temptations, whore." He drew a dagger. "Now, stay there. And stay quiet."

Again, Swithun peered out into the congregation.

They were leaving. At last.

"What . . ." Her voice from behind him, small and full of fear, cut through the rampant, gushing thoughts crashing through his brain. "What do you plan on doing to me?"

He turned back, scanning her again. "I . . . don't know," he said. "Whatever God wills me to do." Then he looked away.

What should he do, he pondered. Kill her? Some random teenage girl who happened to be in the wrong place at the wrong time. But did he have another option?

"I planned this out perfect, right," he said vacantly. "Every detail of it. And I'd be done and gone if you ain't come here."

He gazed down at her trembling form, the fear in her eyes bright as wildfire. And he was the one who lit the blaze. To see that terror directed toward him, branding him as a monstrous villain, twisted his insides.

Yet, he knew what must be done. The defenseless woman, sitting here on the verge of tears, must die, then the priest. It was for the betterment of the world, he assured himself.

But he could not leave a corpse here; he resolved. He might need this place again. And a living woman would be easier to remove than a dead one.

"Where d'you live? Near here?"

She nodded her head stiffly, those puffy, wide eyes locked on him. Unblinking. "I live in a small cottage just outside town."

"Stop looking at me like that!" Swithun commanded, as he raised his hand as if to strike her.

She clamped her eyes shut and turned her head toward the floor. Now she looked as if braced for assault. It made him feel even more like a villain.

"I'm the good one here," he growled. "Don't forget that. On a holy mission from our God Déagar, I am."

She said nothing and remained braced.

"Is anyone at your house? A husband? Father?"

"I—I . . . live alone. My father . . ." She stopped. Panting. Her eyes searched for a place to look.

"He what! Left town?"

"*Died,*" she confessed with pain. "I'd been taking care of him. I have jewelry there. Not much. A few heirlooms. You can have them if—"

"I ain't no robber. I am a . . . a agent of God! These are holy things I do. Now, take me to your cottage. And if you do a thing to draw attention to us on the way, I'll cut you open 'fore you can scream." The words from his own lips sounded so vile, even in his own ears. He felt nauseous but suppressed all signs.

He yanked the woman to her feet.

And they continued down the righteous and glorious path set forth before him.

CHAPTER SIX

A perfect plan: Kill the woman in her home and make it look like a robbery. Even take the jewelry she mentioned: It would look more convincing, he rationalized, and why shouldn't he be compensated? No one would ever associate her death with matters of church and state. Father Hanugfrie would have no reason to be on guard.

It should have been so easy, too. Swithun had killed before. But not like this—not a frightened, innocent woman begging for life.

He stood over her as she writhed against the ropes tying her limbs to her simple bark-coated bedposts. He held a dagger high above her soft stomach, ready to thrust it downward deep into her core.

"Are you testing me, my God?" Swithun whispered to the roof. "Are you trying to see the limit of my obedience? I've faith you'll guide me down this path you've started me on. But give me some sort of sign how to go on. Astha'will-maybe."

—

Swithun awoke on the floor of the woman's one-room cottage. A new day. He stood and stared at the living, breathing woman tied to the bed.

Her continued life was a symbol of his unfaithfulness, his failings as a man and soldier, his disobedience to his God. Swithun's heart burned with shame. He could still kill her, even now. So simple. A lamb tied to the altar.

He was still.

"Why do you look at me so?" she asked. "Leering like a dog."

Yesterday's fear was gone from her, just as yesterday's beast was gone from him. And she seemed almost relaxed. It unnerved him, as if some measure of the control he'd had was lost.

"I'm deciding what I should do with you."

"You mean whether or not to kill me?" she said flatly, her eyes meeting his. "I have no fear of death. True, you took me by surprise at first, but I've come to terms with my fate. I know God Karulus will guide me safely to the paradise Laqyigo."

Her words angered Swithun. "'Tis only by the divine mercy of God Déagar that a soul can pass to Laqyigo. Not by Karulus."

"The *True Light* is the only way," she said. "And both Karulus *and* his brother Déagar are True Light Gods."

He turned away from her and rubbed his eyes. "That *were* true. Least, I thought it were. But things have changed now, haven't they." His voice deepened in anger. "There's no room in the True Light for witchcraft."

She looked at him for a moment, taking in his words. "That's why you're here, isn't it?" Her tone changed to that of realization. "Father Hanugfrie is a worker of great and holy miracles, and the Déagrians fear such things."

"Fuck you, whore. Our stance don't have a thing to do with fear. We do what's right and true because 'tis what must be done. Magic is perversion of nature. But . . . why I'm here? That's nothing to concern your pretty little head with, right?"

He scanned her again and was unable to see her as anything but a defenseless woman tied up by a monster. Someone he should be saving.

He could no longer look at what he'd done. "I need to go outside for a bit." He forced a harsher tone and added, "I'll leave you alive, for now, but if you call out, 'twill be the last sound you make."

He turned toward the plain door leading outside.

"I am Roslyn," she said to his back.

He froze but said nothing.

"I will pray for you," she said. "I can tell you are confused and don't want to do this. I will pray you find the right path."

He continued away.

—

He thought himself a fool for leaving the woman—*Roslyn*—alive. A greater fool for leaving her ungagged. But Swithun could not do what was needed. He hated the feeling, a lingering impotence. He would have to hold faith in terror to keep her quiet, a fear that he was just outside listening for her screams. He wasn't. He needed to return to the church. He needed this matter with Father Hanugfrie resolved so he could leave this wretched town of Hunia.

"Father," Swithun interrupted politely. He stood at the front edge of the church's open nave.

Here, Hanugfrie prayed before a large stepped rack of votive candles, each of the many wicks flickering from within blue glass.

The priest did not respond or even look but raised a finger as if to say, *please wait.*

With his head bowed, he continued to face God Karulus atop a pedestal beyond the candles.

The wooden statue was as large as a living man and was brought further to life by detailed paintwork, coloring his skin pale blue. He dressed like a king in dark blue. His right hand, high above his head, held a staff topped with an orb topped by a crossed version of the number seven. Gilded wings stretched wide from his back.

Karulus, here, looked barely different than he had in Swithun's hometown basilica. It would be difficult for him to fully see this God as an enemy.

Hanugfrie finished his prayer and turned to the stranger. "Yes, my child."

"I need advice, Father. Can I schedule a time to meet with you?"

"Schedule?" He chuckled, a serene sound matching his manner. "You must be from a city, child. Come. I can talk with you now, if you like."

He led Swithun to the back of the great room and into a small circular study with stone walls. He took a seat before a modest desk of scuffed wood, while Hanugfrie took a chair behind it. The wall to the priest's rear held a large crossed version of the number seven in gold-painted wood.

This version of the seven, the Septenar, unnerved Swithun, as it was just as much the symbol of his own church as it was of the Karulents, and it made this priest look all the more priestly.

A moment elapsed when they were both quiet, the older, gray-haired man sitting back in his chair. Waiting to listen. Swithun shifted forward, thumbing a loose thread at a thigh-level seam of his tunic while he tried to look anywhere but at the priest.

"You said you needed advice," Hanugfrie finally prompted.

"That's right, Father. I'm conflicted in me duties to the True Light. I been called upon to do a holy task, right. For the betterment of the world, but . . . the closer I get to finishing it, the worse I feel about what I have to do."

"I see. Sometimes the Gods call upon us to do troublesome things. *However*, sometimes men call upon us to perform tasks in the *name* of the Gods, which are not anything to do with divine will. Do you know, absolutely, that you have been called upon by the True Light?"

"Yes, Father, I'm certain of that." Swithun glanced downward. "I think I'm certain. But me heart aches with conflict, right. And I feel more like I betray the Light than walk its path."

"I see." Hanugfrie nodded. "You must first verify the origins of the mandate. I can help you with this. I know an ancient ritual in which I can guide you through a transcenden—"

"Magic?" Swithun's eyes widened. "No. Forgive me, Father. I shouldn't have—This were a fool's act." He stood up.

"You are a Déagrian?" Hanugfrie said calmly. "That is why you tried to kill me today? A fear of magic?"

Swithun froze as the words rang through him. Was his dread apparent, he wondered. According to the nameless captain, the priest could crush a man's heart from ten feet away.

"Sit," the priest offered as pleasantly as if inviting the soldier for tea.

Swithun complied, though he wondered if he would ever stand again.

"Magic has come under scrutiny these last few decades or so." Hanugfrie leaned forward in his chair and folded his hands on the desk. "Although the plague has all but ended, it has frightened people, you know. Blame has a way of finding targets. Meanwhile, the dark sorcerers of the Tridulan Empire to the distant east grow more powerful, and wicked magic has become the only magic of which the common people hear. Your new patriarch has used this fear to rise to power and—"

"You dare speak out against Patriarch Krasil!"

"Someone has to. Do you honestly think he speaks the will of Déagar? On tides of hate and unfounded accusations, Krasil has risen, his bony finger aimed at *us*, a quarter of the Empire's population *no less struck by the plague than the Déagrians*."

Swithun glanced downward.

"It seems very likely," Father Hanugfrie continued, his tone even, "that Krasil's campaigns have nothing to do with God Déagar at all."

"Fucking horseshite! All of it. His Holiness acts to stop you Karulents 'cause magic is evil."

"Some of it, yes, but not all."

With a flick of Father Hanugfrie's fingers, a small orb of light—sapphire blue and the size of an egg—formed above his hand, which he positioned, palm upward, beneath it.

The soldier watched in horror, expecting it to fly at him and rip through him. Instead, it remained above the open palm of Hanugfrie.

"Magic, my son," the priest began, "can be evil, yes. Dark Light sorcerers call upon the power of infernal Gods and Demons to do insidious works and to forge weapons of war. Even True Light magic can be twisted. However, we Azerents invoke only the powers of His Divine Infinity, *Karulus*, spirit of truth, and of compassion, God of the Sapphire Ib. And with his divine guidance, we use our gifts to gain the knowledge and strength to better ourselves and mankind, both spiritually and in various aspects of everyday life. We strive to learn the inner nature of the soul and the universe, to heal the sick, and to produce better crops. Are these innocuous workings of the Order of Azerents what you detest?" The orb glowed brighter. "Personally, I find this little orb works wonders as a reading light." He chuckled.

The orb flew at Swithun.

The soldier tensed but had no time to move before the light struck his chest. It did nothing but dissolve.

The words, the arrogant defiance to the Church of Déagar, angered Swithun. A deep and boiling rage rumbled in his gut.

"Magic ain't a torch for reading," he snapped, staring hate into the elderly eyes. "'Tis a child playing with fire and a man's proud attempt to enter the realm of Gods."

"I am well aware of the will of the Gods, child. I regularly commune with the messenger of Karulus. And I also know that the patriarch of your church is a hatemonger."

Swithun leaped up, slamming his fists on the table. "Enough of it! I don't care if you are a fucking priest."

"I do not appreciate your language or tone." Hanugfrie's words remained calm. "Ask yourself this, Déagrian: why have they sent you to kill me? I am no conjurer of violent things. I cannot summon an aetherial army or rip down the walls of Fidelumair Palace. I cannot even will a fly to die, except by swatting.

"But I *am* dangerous," the priest continued. "For I have knowledge. And nothing frightens false church leaders more than that."

"I won't hear your blasphemy. His Holiness, Supreme Patriarch Krasil, is the prophet of the True Light. What he says is truth."

Swithun set his hand on the dagger on his belt. *"Can't hurt a fly, eh?"* he muttered.

Swithun drew the blade and swung, aiming for the neck, but the priest lunged backward in his chair, sending it—along with himself—falling backward to the floor.

Without pause, Swithun hurried around the desk to pursue, dagger held firm, and eyes filled with zealous hate.

Freeing himself from the overturned chair, the old man stumbled back toward the wall. He managed to return to his feet and backed away, his arms blocking his face.

Swithun swung the blade, cutting deep into his crossed arms.

The priest pressed himself against the wall of his office. Blood streamed from his arms.

Swithun approached steadily. This time, there would be no questioning of his divine mandate. This Father Hanugfrie must die now to save the world from lies and sickness.

Something hit Swithun in the back of the head. He grabbed his head and turned to see a large book floating behind him. The impact had been only an annoyance—no injury done. But it hit him again.

He grabbed the treacherous tome and flung it across the room.

He turned back to the priest.

Father Hanugfrie was gone.

With a grunt of hate, Swithun slammed his dagger into its sheath. He then smashed his fists into the wall. And again. Checking for any unseen passage.

It seemed solid.

"Fuck!" He slammed his entire body against the wall and hit it with weakening, frustrated strikes.

"Forgive me, God Déagar. I've failed you."

CHAPTER SEVEN

S withun stormed into Roslyn's house and slammed the door behind him.

She was still tied to the bed where he'd left her.

"What d'you know about Hanugfrie?" he shouted as he rushed to the bedside and towered over her.

"What do you mean?"

"Where would he go to?" he slammed his fist into the bed-post, making the whole bed shake. "He escaped from me. Does he have a house in town? Some hiding place?"

"I won't help you," she said angrily.

"Karulent whore!" Swithun jumped on top of her, strad-dling her as he pulled her up by the shoulders. He shouted into her face, "Tell me!" He shook her.

A small fist struck his face. A sucker punch. He recovered, but saw one of her hands was free and grabbing his dagger. Before he could grasp the sight, she thrust the blade into the thick muscle of his upper leg.

Swithun roared in pain as he released her to drop back on-to the straw mattress. He slapped her hard with the back of his fist and then rolled off to the floor.

"I know you know where he is," Swithun growled, clutch-ing the bleeding wound in his leg.

She grasped the dagger, rushing to cut herself free.

He stood and grabbed her hand with the dagger, pulling it away from the rope, even as she tried with all her might to stab him again. He squeezed until she dropped the blade to the mattress.

"You Karulents can't be trusted." He gripped her thin arm while she struggled against him. "You act like you walk in the Light, but you're no better than the filthy savages to the east."

He threw down her arm and grabbed his dagger. He stabbed it through her skirt and ripped off a long strip of fabric. Then another. She futilely struggled against the remaining rope. He could see much of the beautiful pale skin of her slender legs, and he was very tempted to keep cutting fabric.

She stopped her struggles and looked away from him, straight up to the ceiling, and began speaking softly: "Praise be to Karulus, spirit of truth, and of compassion."

"Stop that!" he commanded. He put a wad of cloth against the gash on his leg and held it in place. "Tell me where Hanugfrie went to. You was in that room where I found you, so you must work at the church." He wrapped a longer strip of cloth around his leg to cover the wound.

"You are our God and our savior."

"Stop it! Now." Again, Swithun slapped her with the back of his fist, harder this time, causing her head to twist limply to the side.

She gave a slight whimper and panted for a moment. Her eyes watered, but she did not cry. A trail of crimson rolled down from her nostril toward her ear.

"Heal our hearts," she continued in the same calm, faint tone, "and by your light, guide us safely to Laqyigo. As thy will, may it be."

Swithun's anger doubled as she defiantly kept her calm as she prayed her insolent, iniquitous prayers. He grabbed her skirt and ripped it again, this time deliberately sending the tear higher, closer to her hidden regions.

"'Twould be so easy, you know, to take you here and now and get some payment for me pains."

She swallowed dryly but remained calm, staring up. With a voice shaky but firm, she said, "The Sapphire Scripture tells us, *'Sin is a wicked thought, and the feats begotten by a wicked thought. Yet whosoever is given no option, truly and wholly, in his deeds, hath not sinned, himself, but hath fallen victim to the sins of another.'* Whatever you do, I will still be pure."

He threw down the sections of her skirt, but glared at her with hate—hate so pure and intense it throbbed through his entire body.

"I am the good one here," he mumbled. "The *pure* one." He tied the final knot in his bandage. "What I do, I do for the betterment . . ." He stopped, letting silence fall as he looked at her, an injured beauty reflecting his villainy.

Her eye had already started to swell, and a red line had stained her cheek.

Despondently, he moved to sit on the side of the mattress. He leaned forward, his hands folded, with his elbows on his knees. His thoughts were so heavy that he couldn't keep his head upright. In silent lamentations, he kept staring at the rough, uneven floorboards.

After some amount of time, Roslyn spoke up, gently asking, "Why do you hate us so much?"

"I don't hate. Hate's a sin. But our empire must be free of what you and that false priest are. The Dayigan Empire"—he looked back toward her—"is the greatest nation in the world."

"I *am* a Dayigan," she said. "I've lived here, right here in this town, all my life. As did my parents and grandparents, and those before them for generations. We did not ask to be swallowed up by your empire, but we were."

"The Dayigan Empire," he restarted, "is the greatest nation in the world and founded by the divine right granted to us by our God Déagar. Yet, we *let* Karulents live here, free to do as you like. And you betray that freedom by not following our rules."

"Your rules changed," Roslyn said softly. She turned to him. "This isn't just about Father Hanugfrie. I've heard the rumors. His Majesty plans to make the worship of God Karulus illegal."

"'Tis necessary." Swithun looked down. "We won't let the Empire fall back into the plague times."

Four firm knocks at the door made him jump.

Swithun snatched up the dagger and held it to her throat. "*Shh.*"

"Open up in His Majesty's name!" a voice commanded from outside. "We have reason to suspect a dangerous person might be in the area."

"Get rid of them," Swithun hissed.

Again, the soldier pounded on the door.

"There's," Roslyn spoke up hoarsely, her eyes wet with tears, then cleared her throat. "There's no one here but me." Her voice cracked. "But thank you for calling."

Silence.

Swithun just stared at the wooden planks that separated him from who knew how many guardsmen. Though part of the same army as he, they would not know of him or his mission. They would not understand that this was for good, for Déagar.

"Rose, 'tis me," said the voice outside. "We're going to need you to open the door."

Again, silence. Swithun barely breathed. He looked at the thick rope holding one of Roslyn's arms in place and then to a window by the bed.

"This is for God Déagar," Swithun whispered blankly as he looked around, lost. "Keep silence, and you might still be forgiven," he said, panting.

He looked at his beaten victim and was sick with himself. "We won't return to the plague times," he muttered.

Swithun dashed to the window and slid the wooden shutter aside. He looked out into the thick woods lit in the dim, patchy glow of the setting sun filtering through the canopy.

"Rose, please," said the voice beyond the door. "We've given you fair warning. We'll have to break down the door."

"Help!" she screamed. "He's here!"

Swithun scrambled out the window, landing as softly as he could. He began creeping away, his stomach churning as he anxiously balanced a conflicting line between quiet and quick.

"There's someone behind the cottage!" a voice echoed, not too far behind him.

No longer caring about noise, he ran. Or at least tried. His leg was injured, and the woods were thick. No paths. Everything was shadowed from the light. Obstacles surrounded him, slowing him every time he gained ground. He ducked under branches and shoved some aside. Others reached out to rip his clothes and scratch his arms.

He kept changing direction, trying to confuse all who hunted him. But the noises from his movements were so loud—so much cracking of leaves and sticks that it seemed anyone could hear.

After half an hour into his twisted, hurried escape, Swithun tripped over a sinkhole holding the rotting, pulpy remnants of a thick stump. A once-mighty tree, now fallen, lay beside it, equally decayed and smelling of mulch.

On hands and knees within all the dead, brown and black things of the woodland floor, he stopped and listened.

It was properly night now, the moonlight barely reaching him.

Tears escaped Swithun's eyes. Not tears of fear but of horror. Horror at his own actions. Grief for his own victim. "Forgive me," he whispered, not to Déagar, but to Roslyn.

He listened.

There were no sounds save for the pounding of his heart and the droning of insects.

Had he lost the guardsmen, Swithun wondered. Or had they been close enough to see him fall?

Perhaps they were circling now.

Keeping low to the ground, Swithun scanned the moonlit trees and climbing vines and shrubberies, searching for any sign of his pursuers. There was no one he could see.

Despite a dire need to pant to ease his burning lungs, Swithun barely breathed, keeping his quiet.

He wished he knew how many he dealt with. Dayigo, the capital, had a garrison with hundreds of men. But this little town would have nothing comparable.

A twig snapped.

Swithun turned to see boots beyond the undergrowth.

Like a snake, Swithun slithered back into the sinkhole and moved behind the stump.

The boots approached in a winding, slow course. They searched.

They drew closer.

Swithun could now make out the same tabard that he, too, would wear when in uniform. A simple red tabard emblazoned with the crest of the Dayigan Empire. Despite its color, the color of God Déagar, the local guardsman was most likely from this little town and allegiant to Karulus. Even if Swithun could explain his mission, he could expect no sympathy.

The boots were only ten feet away.

If Swithun attacked now, he would have the surprise. But there could be a dozen more soldiers searching nearby, ready to rush toward any sounds of skirmish.

He controlled his breaths. Waiting. Hoping the soldier would continue on.

The boots were so close now that Swithun could spit from here to polish.

The boots jumped back, as if the wearer had seen a snake. He had: Swithun.

Drawing his dagger, Swithun leaped from the ground but froze as he took in the full sight of the guardsman. Or, more accurately, *guardsboy*. To wear the uniform at all, he had to be at least sixteen, but he could not be far beyond. But the uniform itself curbed Swithun even more than the age of the wearer. He'd never stood before it, his own tabard.

He looked at the crest of amber stitching to which he'd vowed allegiance: the sun and two moons connected as a triangle above a triangular depiction of the island capital city.

Clad within this symbol, this boy, though they had never met, was a brother.

Either in bravery or stupidity, the boy did not call out for reinforcements, but raised his sword and fretfully charged toward Swithun.

Sword against dagger was usually no fair contest, but the boy's swings were sloppy, his parries, undisciplined. Nevertheless, Swithun saw potential in the young soldier, and in the back of his mind, he thought how he should like to tutor him in swordsmanship.

But no, he realized. For he would have to kill him. And soon, before other guards heard and joined the fight.

Their blades locked, and Swithun stared into the boy's eyes. They held the same stare Roslyn had given. Such fear. As if Swithun was some sort of monster. As if a holy quest was inconceivable to them.

"You have a name, boy?" Swithun asked through his teeth, their faces so close he could feel the boy's quick, panicked breaths on his throat.

"Jon, sir," he whimpered.

"If you got unconfessed sins, Jon, resolve them now. You have about twenty seconds left to live."

Swithun counted down. "Twenty, nineteen . . ."

The boy's eyes widened with utter mortification. His mouth, agape. The strength left his arms, making it even harder not to kill him.

For the last ten seconds, the boy didn't even fight. His arms fell limp to his sides. His sword fell to the leaf-carpeted ground. He seemed on the verge of fainting.

The two soldiers stood before each other, older brother looking down on the younger.

"One."

"Please, sir. I—"

Swithun's dagger thrust hilt deep into the boy's gut, then sliced a sideways gash to quicken death. Blood coated Swithun's blade, his hand, and his forearm. He stared into those fear-filled eyes that faded blank.

Swithun caught him as he fell. He lowered him to the ground and kneeled beside him.

He cradled the boy's limp head with a gentle hand as he stared into the empty eyes.

Swithun's eyes watered. A tear trickled down his dirty cheek.

"Forgive me, boy," he whispered, though it was more of a whimper. "But this is still for the betterment of the world." He looked down at the young soldier—Jon—he had ripped from life. "We can't ever return to the plague times."

PART TWO

A Plague of Hatred

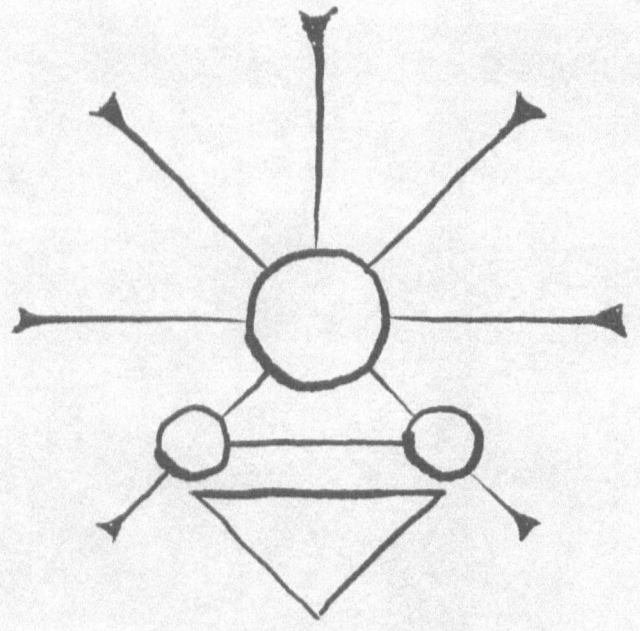

CHAPTER EIGHT

Septhiés 4, 808: Five Years Earlier

He shouted furiously as he snatched away the flag, crumpling the red cloth while shaking it violently. "We won't allow this *flag* to be displayed over Wendian!" Swithun yelled. Rage ran down his spine as he gripped the cloth.

The boy he'd snatched it from stared up at him with a dumbfounded look on his face. He was a skinny, dirty, twelve-year-old boy in an ill-fitting tunic and with uneven hair. The man recognized him as the son of a nearby baker.

Swithun felt a right fool, he a grown man in his late twenties shouting politics at a boy just older than his son. The boy had most likely been paid next to nothing to hoist this flag in front of the castle, and he was probably now more concerned about getting in trouble and losing his shitty salary than anything Swithun had to say.

Ignoring the boy, Swithun looked up at the thick wooden mast on the opposite side of the building's entrance. From a horizontal rod near its peak, an identical red banner hung.

It displayed, in gold stitching, three circles depicting the sun and two moons arranged in an upward-pointing triangle. Below, more gold embroidery depicted a solid, downward-pointing triangle representing an island city.

People had gathered in the large open dirt patch that the city called the "square," despite its irregular shape. Some neared and whispered. Others stared as they stood back near the perimeter—a wall of shops with gray stone first stories and gray wood upper stories.

A few of the vendors in their wooden stalls stopped their shouts and haggles to gawk at Swithun. It seemed that even some of the roaming chickens paused their mindless pecking to take a gander at him.

The boy just kept staring with his mouth agape, and his eyes perplexed. "Sir?" he finally asked.

Swithun was in it now, he realized, but what exactly he was *in*, he wasn't sure. Grabbing the flag was just an angry impulse. A rightful impulse, he was certain, but he hadn't thought to the next moment.

Turning to the people, Swithun raised the crumpled flag. "Will you stand by while they raise the flag of Dayigo over *our* city? Our alliance with Dayigo ain't nothing but a trade agreement. *Not this.*" He shook the wadded flag.

The crowd was unmoved, and Swithun didn't recognize most of them. For the last couple of weeks, the city had been filling up with visitors crowding the inns and taverns. These travelers now whispered among themselves, scrutinizing him with the detachedness of holidayers. Swithun was a local street show, he realized. They'd certainly talk of the flag-snatching fool when they returned home.

A man hollered out, "You tell them, Swithun. We're Wendian, not Dayigo!"

Praise God Déagar, Swithun thought, *a local*. He gained some courage to continue.

Two men began pushing their way through the murmuring crowd. Each was armored in chain mail, covered in a belted white surcoat. Emblazoned on the chest of each surcoat was the crossed number seven in green.

The body of the thick, green seven was stylized as a perpendicular cross, with each section the same length and ends flailed out, making the whole number resemble a fancy square. It was a symbol Swithun recognized—the mark of the Knights Silthex.

As the knights neared, one asked, "Is there a problem here?"

"Here's your problem." Swithun shook the flag again. "Our king wouldn't've *ever* tolerated the Dayigan flag over Wendian."

"The king of Wendian is dead," the knight said, voice deepening around the words as if they angered him, yet the anger seemed more aimed at his needing to remind Swithun than at the information itself. "A quarter of all royals, nobles, and clergy in the Dayigan Trade Agreement are dead. Dayigo attempts to preserve order before the lands fall to savagery."

"Wendian's a righteous city," Swithun maintained, "untouched by the Pestilence. You don't have authority here."

The soldier set his palm on his sword. "We are Silthex knights, the army of the Church of God Déagar. Our *authority* has no boundaries. Return the flag to the boy."

The whole square was watching without a whisper among them.

Swithun's heart pounded with a numbing mix of rage and dread. Mostly dread. Nevertheless, he stood resolute.

The knight drew his sword halfway from its scabbard.

The other knight did the same.

Someone grabbed Swithun from behind. He jumped in reflex.

"No problem here. No problem here." It was Laurence, the tailor—Swithun's employer and friend. "Everyone's just a little on edge with all the unfamiliar faces in town. Right?" he asked of Swithun.

Laurence reached out his hand to request the flag.

Swithun looked at it for a moment. "Right," he said, and slammed the contemptible cloth down into his palm.

"See?" Laurence shook out the flag with a snap. "Right as rain." He handed over the flag to the boy.

The boy looked no less stupefied as he held it, glancing at Swithun, glancing at the knights, and glancing at the pole soon to hold the flag.

"Come on, then." Laurence set his arm around Swithun's shoulders and led him away.

—

Just west of the square, Swithun slammed his hands down on a low stone wall at the side of a short bridge.

"Were you planning to fight two Silthex knights unarmed?" Laurence's tone was light, as if they should have a laugh about it now.

But Swithun's anger stayed. "I had to do something, didn't I?"

Swithun looked beyond the rail, where a stream flowed down to join the Hyvile River. The large city docks, once active from dawn to well past dusk, were now blackened, charred ruins. The river, once bustling, was now empty water, ten miles across to a distant unseen shore.

"I miss working the docks," Swithun said absently. "Made good money working the docks. Simpler times."

"Unfortunate as it is, the king was right to burn them. They say the Pestilence comes from the river. That's why all the port cities got hit first. *Most* of the port cities. Luckily, our king acted quickly."

"Little good it did *him*," Swithun said. "Or the queen—rest her."

"Yes." Laurence sat on the wall next to him. "I can't think what possessed them to travel in times like these. Tragic, really." Laurence lowered his head. "They would have been fine in Wendian."

"Are we fine, though?" Swithun asked, turning to the tailor. "The Pestilence is closing in around us. Travelers tell tales of more bodies than people know what to do with. And towns wiped off the map. Monasteries, too, completely emptied out. Meanwhile, we might be safe from all that, but me wife and son are half starved to death. I wouldn't mind if it was just me, but them . . ."

"I pay you as well as I can."

"Forgive me. I didn't mean no insult by it. I know you're struggling, too. Can't sell much fancy clothes to a city when its largest gold-earner lies in ashes, right?"

"Quite right."

Another man Swithun recognized as Edgar, a local potter, approached quickly, looking back as if he thought himself followed.

He was one of the winged people who made up about five percent of the city, which meant he had two large feathered wings from his back. In Edgar's case, the feathers were brown. Besides that, and being a bit scrawny in Swithun's opinion, he looked Human. His leather apron was coated in blotches and smears of dried clay.

"You plan to do something about this, right?" Edgar whispered to Swithun. "You're still the leader of the city's militia, king or no."

"I'm a dockworker turned tailor's helper," Swithun said. "Only the king can call the militia together, and I don't reckon he'll be doing that anytime soon."

"Either way," the potter said, "me and the men will follow you. I hear there's talk of an empire."

"Nonsense," Laurence joined. "The flags are only for the visit from the leader of *your* Church. They'll come down once he's gone."

"I heard the talks, too," Swithun said gravely. "The *Dayigan Empire*, they're calling it."

"But . . ." Laurence began. "But there has never been a True Light empire. The word itself is unholy. They wouldn't do that." The tailor paused. "Would they?"

Silence fell over the three as the question weighed them.

The potter set his hand on Swithun's shoulder. "You'll do something, won't you? For Wendian and His Majesty—may his soul be at peace."

Swithun nodded absently.

"Good. May the fires of God Déagar guide you." The potter ran back toward the square, forbidden by law to fly in the city.

"I don't believe it," Laurence said as he stood. "I *won't* believe it. 'Tis but ridiculous rumors, and I must say, I, for one, am glad to have all these visitors in town. I've sold more in the last two days than in the last year. Your boy's minding the shop now."

"Ord's minding a *dress* shop? Fucking za," Swithun cursed. "That ain't no place for a boy."

"'Tis not as if I have him working as a seamstress. Besides, I make men's clothing too."

Swithun scanned him. Laurence wore a vibrant blue cap to match his vibrant blue linen tunic trimmed in bright purple with embellishments in gold thread. His tights were yellow and crisscrossed with blue ribbons. It was a far cry from Swithun's coarse, dirt-colored wool tunic and mud-colored trousers, and not anything he'd consider men's clothes.

"Right," Swithun said.

Laurence gave him a mild glare. *"Nevertheless*, your boy's only there whilst I pop down to the church for afternoon prayer. If you're done with your deliveries—and with starting a rebellion—you may come with me if you like. It might calm you down. Those crates that need moving at the shop can wait a little longer."

The commotions of the street silenced with the double thump of the large basilica doors. Inside, Swithun could almost feel the thick silence pressing in around him, as if he shouldn't breathe too deeply lest he disturb others.

Within the foyer, Laurence and Swithun both approached a font centered in the small room. The font was in the shape of an immense stone chalice engraved around its upper section, with faded purple-leafed trees bearing white circular fruit.

Together, the two men dipped their hands into the font and into the holy water within. They prayed their silent prayers of forgiveness—Swithun to God Déagar, Laurence no doubt to *his* God, Karulus.

Afterward, they passed through a set of open doors into the basilica proper. Its mighty stone walls towered thirty feet, enclosing a room that was twenty feet wide and twice as long.

As a boy, Swithun had thought the place was breathtaking. As an adult, he should be used to it, but no. He still found it amazing, with the added wonder of appreciating its greatness.

He and Laurence walked side by side down the center of the gray tile floor. Though he'd seen them countless times, Swithun marveled at the frescoes painted on the upper wall. They showed the glory of God Déagar and the wickedness of the Dark Light Gods and their Demons.

A few small, translucent glass windows were between the paintings, allowing distorted daylight to shine down.

The broad floor was empty except for five people stationed sporadically. They kneeled in prayer. Beyond them, seven steps rose to the chancel, centered with a wooden altar. Behind it, the wall held a seven-foot, crossed version of the number seven—called the Septenar—made of wood and painted in a thin coat of gold.

When Karulents began moving to Wendian—Swithun would have been about ten at the time—there was some debate about whether the city should build a second house of worship. He barely remembered the details, but recalled that, in the end, they deemed a second building impractical. Wendian's bishop invited the Karulent priest to share. Services would be separate, of course—a Déagrian service by the Déagrian bishop, and then a Karulent service by the Karulent priest. The Holy Brothers, God Déagar and God Karulus, were both True Light Gods, but their worshipers maintained different perspectives.

Laurence and Swithun now divided, moving to opposite sides of the vast room.

Swithun paused and looked back toward Laurence.

The tailor walked with his head already bowed as he approached an arched alcove set midway into the side wall. In it, a semicircle of stone, at table height, held countless blue candles. Some flickered and dripped wax to the stone; some waited, new and unlit. Beyond them on the altar, a pedestal held a life-sized stone statue of God Karulus.

The thin God with sky-blue skin had navy hair to his shoulders. His face was beardless and appeared as if he were near thirty. Folded at his back were wings painted in gold. He wore a carved robe, painted royal blue, and belted in shells.

His right hand, high above his head, held a staff topped with an orb surmounted by a crossed version of the number seven.

Laurence took a few coins from a purse on his belt, put them into the slot of a wooden box, and lit a candle with a long reed.

He seemed worried as he kneeled, praying. Swithun thought it odd to see him this way, so pensive when he was accustomed to seeing Laurence so jovial. Perhaps Laurence fretted about the plague closing in around them. Perhaps he fretted that the city would not recover, even if the plague let it be. Or perhaps Swithun was just projecting his own worries onto Laurence.

Swithun, indeed, worried.

Swithun turned away and walked to what was nearly a reflection of the altar Laurence prayed before. But this, on the right side of the room, held red candles, and the God standing atop the pedestal was God Déagar.

This God wore intricately carved, full-plate armor—from helm to sabatons—all painted in gold. His cape was long and left the color of pale stone. In his right hand, he held a sword with its copper-plated blade resting toward the floor. His lowered golden shield bore the number seven, filling the entire circle.

Swithun tossed some coins into the box, lit a candle, and prayed.

"Praise God Déagar, eldest of the Gods, protector from the Dark. You're the Greatest of All. I praise your name, majestic and holy, without ending. By your fire, guide us safely to Laqyigo. All I ask is that you keep me wife and son safe, healthy, and fed. Astha'will-maybe."

Laurence waited in the center of the floor. When Swithun approached him, he looked at him and sighed.

"How certain are you about this empire business?" Laurence whispered.

Swithun shook his head. "Could be rumors, like you said."

Laurence glanced back toward the blue God and then returned his worried eyes to Swithun. The tailor whispered, "The king of Dayigo holds no love for Karulents."

The words were unexpected and left Swithun silent. He'd never thought of anything like that mattering before. Swithun almost reminded him there was a grand Karulent cathedral—their own separate cathedral—in Dayigo, but it seemed a daft thing to say. Besides, the cathedral predated the current king by decades. Before Swithun spoke another word, Laurence had already headed toward the exit.

—

As Laurence and Swithun crossed the square, Swithun glanced back at the Dayigan flags. They were both up now, one above either side of the castle door. The bright red cloths flapped in the wind as they towered over Wendian.

"Long live Wendian," Swithun muttered to himself.

He turned back to where they headed, to Laurence's shop. A crate propped the wooden door open. The shutters of the large window were folded to the sides. It allowed a breeze on this hot day, but equally important, it showed off the displays inside.

Even Swithun could recognize the quality of the dress on a form just inside the window. Laurence had dressed the queen before her death, and this dress appeared fit for royalty. Fine fabrics draped over racks at the right of the window.

But the crowd drew Swithun's attention. The chatter grew louder as the two approached, peaking as they entered the shop.

A woman recognized Laurence and called out his name, drawing the attention of others in the crowded space.

"You simply *must* dress me for the patriarch's visit," she said. "Tell me you still have space in your schedule."

"If it is off the rack," Laurence said. "And with minimal alterations."

Swithun pushed past as people crowded around Laurence, shaking his hand, hugging him, and giving him kisses on his cheeks.

Finally, in the empty area behind the counter, Swithun breathed before approaching his eleven-year-old son.

"'Tis a madhouse, this," Swithun said.

"That it is," Ord replied. "But I don't mind much. These rich fucks—"

"Mind your tongue, boy, or your mum'll be scrubbing it clean."

"Yours and mine, both." Ord laughed. "But these rich *folk* have more coin than they know what to do with. They give me some just for handing them a dress or something."

"It is called a tip," Laurence—now behind the counter—said. "And you can earn yourself another one by getting the knee-length, emerald green, fine linen tunic trimmed in white silk from the fourth rack in the back. Take it to *that* man." He pointed.

Ord hurried toward the back.

"After that," Swithun spoke up over the noise, "you make your way home. And give all them tips to your mum."

Ord muttered something that was probably best unheard by his father and hurried to the back.

"Have you heard anything about the bard?" Laurence asked. "He's supposed to be here today. I wanted light singing, along with the strumming of a lute."

"I don't know nothing about him, but if we try to cram one more person in here, the walls'll bow out."

"Well, not to boast, but I am the only tailor in the city of any real fame. There *was* Eadwine, as well, but he never returned from Vilana." He leaned in and whispered, "They say the Pestilence took him, poor thing, but the family's not saying much."

"Vilana's fallen to the Pestilence?" Swithun asked, a little louder than he'd meant.

A man, now holding the clothes Ord had gotten and standing at the counter, gave a shocked look.

"No," Laurence assured them both. "Vilana has not fallen." Then, to the man, Laurence kindly said, "I see you've already settled your account. I thank you for your patronage."

The man nodded and was away.

"You know the mages' hall is there—in Vilana," Laurence said to Swithun. "And a good thing, too. The city's an island—like Dayigo, but not nearly as large—so the river's all around it. The Azerent Mages will have a barrier up to keep the city safe."

"Magic," Swithun said, disgusted by the word. "I know your people practice it, but it ain't right. God Déagar says it ain't right. I mean nothing against you personally—I know you don't do that. But *other* Karulents."

"Yes?" Laurence looked to the floor. "Others." He turned away. "Either way, I . . . I'm certain poor Eadwine found his end *en route* to Vilana, not there."

"I ain't mean nothing 'gainst you, friend," Swithun said.

"Put it out of your mind." Laurence motioned to a nearby woman. "Ma'am?"

"Baroness," she corrected as she approached.

"Forgive me, my lady." He produced a large smile. "And forgive me for being unable to come to you privately, but as you see . . ." He waved both hands high to the surrounding crowd.

"'Tis no bother," she said. "I wished to see Wendian. I have never been here before."

"It is a beautiful city, my lady. Your valet provided me with all your specifications, and the dress I created for you . . . *will amaze*. We'll simply need to do a quick fitting. Swithun, go—"

"I saw you before," the baroness interrupted as she stared Laurence up and down. "Yes, you attacked a boy in the square earlier. I remember all that *blue* you are wearing"—she shook her head—"and whilst your city prepares for a visit by His Holiness, the Supreme Patriarch. I said to my valet, 'They are always causing trouble.'" She turned to a thin woman just behind her. "Did I not say that very thing?"

"You did, my lady." The thin woman gave a slight bow.

Laurence's smile faded. His eyes narrowed. With forced politeness, he said, "With all due respect, my lady, I believe you may have mis-seen the event."

"Never mind all that," she said. "They warned me you would be a Karulent before I came. I suppose it is to be expected."

"Swithun," Laurence said, "rack two, if you would."

Swithun paused, looking at Laurence and then at the woman. He almost said something to her, but he didn't. Instead, Swithun left for the back.

CHAPTER TEN

L aughter and conversation filled the crowded streets of Wendian as Swithun twisted his way through. It was a sober excitement—ale and the like had gone the way of the tournaments and whorehouses in an attempt to create a more virtuous city. Virtue, the Church said, could thwart the wrath of the Great Pestilence.

However, the city was quite charged. Bards, with either lutes or flutes or other instruments, stationed themselves throughout the city. All the gray shops and houses displayed some sort of red flag, from expensive banners with the number seven in golden thread, down to squares of faded red cloth.

With some effort, Swithun squeezed around a group of chatting visitors and entered the square.

"'Tis done up real nice, ain't it?" Swithun said to someone passing by and paused, smiling with pride.

The city had carpeted the entire area in fresh straw, not that Swithun could see much of the ground with all the people crowded in. Ropes, starting at the tops of the shops, stretched above the whole square to the castle on the other side, and from them hung large thin cloths of vibrant red. The Dayigan flags, of course, flew high on poles at either side of the castle doors.

Swithun acknowledged the flags, but didn't let them bother him.

A stage now stood just to the side of the castle door. On it, a boys' choir sang out solemn, beautiful praises to God Déagar. On the stage, beside the choir, the great and the good—most of whom were most likely dressed by Laurence—sat on fine, padded benches.

Center stage, back from the rest, stood a ten-foot-tall rectangular mirror. Its frame consisted of elaborate foliate designs of gold. The mirror itself was a smooth panel of gold polished to a reflective gloss. Never had Swithun seen anything grander or cleaner than this mirror, and the sight of it awed him as if it were something otherworldly. A red carpet spanned from the mirror to the front of the stage.

Swithun moved toward Laurence's shop, and there he approached his son, Ord, who was waiting.

"Where's your mum?" Swithun asked over the noise.

"She can't come. The tavern's called on her to work today. One of the other barmaids took ill."

"Fucking za," Swithun said. "Took ill? Fucking lying, I bet. What'd they say was wrong with her?"

Ord shrugged. "Did you see the mirror?" he asked excitedly.

Swithun nodded as he looked back at it. "'Tis a holy thing, that."

"But what is it for?"

"I figure 'tis for looking at. That what rich folks do, go around getting fancy things for looking at."

"Right." Ord nodded with a touch of confusion.

He slapped Ord's back. "Come on, then. They've given me a spot near the front on account of me being head of the city's militia."

—

With Ord just behind him, Swithun squeezed his way to the front of a sectioned-off area, right up to the thick rope spiraled with red ribbon.

A Silthex knight standing guard just beyond the roped area glared at Swithun for a moment, and Swithun realized he was one of the knights from the flag incident.

Swithun looked away quickly, as if he'd been caught doing something. It made him feel even less like he should be here, here with the well-to-do, well-dressed, and well-scented.

"Stand up straight, boy," Swithun whispered to Ord.

"Bet you wish you'd let Laurence lend us some posh clothes now, don't you?"

"I wish I'd at least made you take a bath."

"And you," Ord retorted with feigned insult. He pointed. "At least we're not up there."

Swithun slapped his son's hand down—the boy knew better than to point like some old curse-casting witch—but Swithun looked where he pointed.

The stage was not five feet away, and the people seated there made the people standing around him and his son look like field workers.

Suddenly, the gold mirror flashed a brilliant light. And where before its pane had reflected the packed courtyard, it now showed a large, bright room of white marble. In the room's center was a low wall, like around a large fountain, but instead of water, a great fire burned.

"Fucking za!" Ord exclaimed. "Is that the afterlife?"

The woman next to Ord shifted uncomfortably before glaring at the boy, as if he were something between a rat and a slug. "'Tis not Laqyigo." She left the words *idiot child* unspoken, save for a roll of her eyes. "It is the Fidelumair." She looked at Swithun, as if he should know.

Swithun shook his head.

"The palace," she said. "In *Dayigo*." She huffed and looked back toward the stage.

A man took a position before the mirror and at the edge of the red carpet. He announced, "I present the Sacred College of Ocelli."

Two rows of five older men approached from within the white room beyond the mirror. They wore bright red, wide-brimmed hats and bright red, floor-length tunics. The tight, white, long sleeves of their under-tunics covered their arms.

The crowd gasped and was, at once, in a flurry of whispers as the surface rippled, and each man passed through with the ease of stepping through a doorway.

Ord gripped the rope in front of him and leaned forward, as if trying to examine the sight as intently as possible.

"'Tis a trick," Swithun said dismissively to a stranger next to him. Still, he watched the men who'd exited the mirror.

The men neared the benches on the stage and took their seats.

"It has to be a trick." Swithun glanced back toward the man at his right, but the stranger said nothing.

"It just has to be," Ord agreed. "But how?"

Swithun realized no one but he and Ord spoke in their roped-off area. The others maintained their composure. But their eyes, locked on the sight, betrayed them. This was new to them, too.

Eight monks in coarse black robes exited the mirror in pairs and stood on each side of the carpet.

The announcer spoke up again. "I present His Most Reverend Eminence, Ocellus *Krasil*, Dean of the Sacred College of Ocelli."

The other Ocelli were no spring chickens, but this new arrival—dressed similarly to the rest—looked to be a hundred years of age. However, he seemed unimpeded by his years. He stood tall, his gait strong. He waved to the crowd as he exited the mirror. Afterward, this man, whom the announcer had called Krasil, stood to the mirror's right.

The announcer called out again, "I present His Holiness, Supreme Patriarch *Leofric*, Bishop of Dayigo, Great Pontiff of the Church of Déagar, Archbishop of the Dayigan Kingdom."

The crowd cheered, and even those around Swithun clapped.

Ord began jumping up and down.

The Supreme Patriarch, a thin man in his early fifties, exited the mirror and walked the carpet to the edge of the stage. He wore splendid white robes of layers of fine fabrics with gold stitching, a golden sash, and a matching pointed hat—a miter—that stood a foot tall atop his head.

He waved gracefully to the excited masses.

"Today," Patriarch Leofric proclaimed, "I stand before a good and moral city, one that has escaped, unscathed, from the demonic Pestilence that has ravaged these lands. God Déagar is with you, Wendian. And in his hallowed name, I bestow his blessing on all who have come to welcome me."

Patriarch Leofric raised his hands to the heavens. "Praise God Déagar, eldest of the Gods, protector from the Dark. You are the Greatest of All. I praise your name, majestic and holy, without ending. By your fire, guide us safely to Laqyigo. In your divine name, I bless Wendian, and pray you keep it safe. Astha'will-miabé."

And the people repeated, "Astha'will-miabé."

"You may have heard," Leofric projected loudly and precisely, "the king of Dayigo wishes to forge the Dayigan Trade

Agreement into an Empire. The rumors are correct. And I support and encourage King Tanimaros in this divinely inspired endeavor. However, I know some amongst you bear your concerns. You." He pointed at Swithun. "Come here, upon this stage."

Frightened and confused, Swithun stared up at the Supreme Patriarch of the Church of Déagar, his holy hand reaching out toward the common man.

Swithun looked around at the people near him—*surely he means someone else.*

"There is no reason to fear, my child," Leofric said kindly.

"Go on, then!" Ord said excitedly and began pushing his father forward.

Swithun ducked under the rope and climbed onto the stage. Every single person in the entire square was silent and watching his every movement.

Swithun stood beside the Supreme Patriarch and lowered his head.

"Your name is Swithun, yes?"

"Yes, Your Majes—Holiness." He bowed his head more. "Your Holiness."

"I am told you are the leader of the town's militia."

Swithun nodded. "That's right, Your Holiness."

"This man," Leofric announced over the crowd, "tried to impede the hoisting of the Dayigan flag." He motioned his hand to the red banner overhead. "Is this true, Swithun?"

Swithun looked up at the flag, as if the patriarch might have meant another flag, different from the one he'd snatched from a child just feet from where they stood. "'Tis true, Your Holiness."

Leofric addressed the people, saying, "Do you know what this man is?"

The crowd gave each other looks and whispers.

Someone shouted out, "A heretic?"

"No, no," Leofric said, with a gentle raise of his hand. "This is a brave man, a man with valid concerns. Concerns many of you share. Swithun, why did you attempt to obstruct the raising of the Dayigan flag?"

Swithun looked up at it again. It was like someone he'd wronged towering over him and demanding an apology.

"I . . ." Swithun began. "Well, it just ain't right, is it? Your Holiness. I mean, Wendian's Wendian, and . . . all I heard of empires is bad."

"*All I've heard of empires is bad,*" Leofric repeated. "So true."

The crowd began sporadic nods as they turned toward one another.

"Truly," Leofric continued, "the empire that ruled these lands long ago was indeed a wicked place, a place ruled by demonic creatures. However, it has long fallen—centuries ago—and we only know of it through infamous legends. Yet here and now, in the ninth century, the eastern brother of that same empire—the Tridulan Empire—remains strong.

"We are crippled, my children," Leofric said somberly. "Wendian is but one of many cities, towns, and estates whose rulers have died, with no heirs remaining. People, *like you,* are unprotected from the bandits in the wilds. People, *like you,* are starving in one land, whilst in other lands, fields go unharvested because no workers remain. All the great nations that comprise the Dayigan Trade Agreement suffer because of the Great Pestilence.

"Yet," Leofric neared the edge of the stage, "the *evil* Tridulan Empire would choose these difficult times to move its malevolent forces against us. Whilst we are down, they attack our eastern border. Whilst we are down, they plan to come here. And to *your* town." He pointed toward the crowd. "And to yours." He pointed again. "They plan—in their unholy crusade under wicked Dark Light Gods—to kill your friends, your family, and your *beloved children.*"

Leofric folded his hands at his waist and took a somber breath. "Therefore, we must unite, my children. Thus, I charge you, in the name of Almighty Déagar: when you return to your respective cities, towns, and estates, you must call upon your leaders and friends to support King Tanimaros of Dayigo in his divinely inspired strategy to fortify our lands, to strengthen us, and to unite our lands into one nation under Déagar! Long stand the Holy Dayigan Empire!"

Thunderous cheers sounded from the invigorated crowd.

"Forgive me, Your Holiness," Swithun said to Leofric. "I didn't understand before. 'Tis definitely something that might be good."

He gave a kind nod. "Say it to the people, my child."

"I was wrong," Swithun shouted to the people. "Forgive me." He began to say more, but a knight tapped his shoulder.

"This way, sir."

The knight began to lead him away.

A scream sounded over the roar of the crowd. At first, Swithun thought it to be an overexcited reveler, but the crowd began pushing and shoving out a hole around the unseen epicenter.

More screams, more panic.

The knight and Swithun stopped, staring.

"What is that?" Swithun asked.

The knight said nothing as he stared. He drew his sword.

CHAPTER ELEVEN

As the panicked crowd scrambled beyond the stage, Swithun stared at the growing gap from which they fled.

Hesitantly, Swithun drew a dagger from his belt. His eyes remained locked on the disturbance until the crowd pushed back far enough for him to see.

A man was hunched over on his knees. He looked frail and was no apparent threat. It took Swithun a confused moment to process why the people fled him as if he were a Demon.

The man vomited blood, splashing on the straw-coated ground.

"The Pestilence is here!" called the knight at Swithun's side. "Protect all on the stage!"

Swithun looked down at Ord—so afraid—and leaped from the stage, fighting toward him.

Silthex knights formed a barrier as the Church fled toward the mirror.

"Ord!" Swithun called as he shoved his way through panic.

The Silthex knights kicked down people who tried to claw their way to the stage.

Swithun hurried to the rope and yanked it down—the short gray corner pole shifting diagonally as the rope snatched free.

Swithun grabbed Ord, holding him tightly.

A man's voice, calm but firm, rang out from the stage. "Surely, His Holiness will not leave his flock in this hour of need."

Swithun turned back to see the old man, the Dean of the Ocelli, Krasil. He stood tall at the front of the stage, and Swithun thought him like a watchtower within a hurricane.

Swithun looked to Supreme Patriarch Leofric, a step from the mirror, and the word "coward" flashed through Swithun's mind.

Leofric glared at Krasil as if he would rip him apart. The look was brief, however, before the Supreme Patriarch gained a graceful smile and stood tall.

He approached Krasil, passing him, and called out over the crowd. "I would never dream of leaving these good and decent people. Calm yourselves, my children. *Calm yourselves.*"

The people ended their shouts and visible horror, yet it was a tense calm, forced. Swithun felt as if every muscle of his body flexed as he held Ord's head to his chest, but he stood still.

"The Church of Déagar is with you," Patriarch Leofric said. "God Déagar is with you all. Go calmly to your homes and inns, and pray for protection. We will remain with you in Wendian."

—

Away from the town square, and thus away from the eyes of the Supreme Patriarch who'd called an end to panic, panic returned.

Frantic, everyone looked for someone. Likewise, Swithun searched for his wife.

Gripping Ord's wrist as if the boy were again five years old, Swithun pushed his way through the narrow streets bound on either side by the walls of closing-down shops.

Someone blocked Swithun, asking, "Do you live here?"

Swithun impatiently looked beyond him, eyeing the tavern where his wife worked. "Yes."

"They said the Silthex are rounding up the sick. Please, do you know where they are taking them?"

"Them?" Swithun's eyes widened. "No, I can't help you."

Swithun pushed past the stranger.

Inside the tavern, the main hall was only a slight degree less chaotic than the streets.

The tavern keeper was standing on a counter turned podium as he tried to address the demands of the gathered tenants.

"We are working to secure carriages out of town as soon as possible," the tavern keeper proclaimed above the noise, "but the streets are impassable."

"My family has its own carriage," a man called back. "We just need access to it."

"Do you not understand? The streets are impassable," the tavern keeper called back. "Please, go to your rooms. This situation is very new, but we will resolve it soon."

He climbed from the counter, but the people swallowed him up like a tide around a shell.

Swithun shoved his way to the tavern keeper. "Have you seen me wife?" he shouted.

"She left—in the middle of all this shite. And you tell her I'll be having a word with her about it, mark that."

"Where'd she go?"

"Where do you think? To the square to find the two of you."

"Fuck it all," Swithun griped and turned back, dragging Ord toward the door.

—

The city square was empty and wrecked. Swithun passed an overturned vendor cart; a large wooden wheel spun slowly. All the merchandise had been stolen, and the merchant lay stabbed to death atop blood-drenched straw.

The stage was empty. The mirror, gone.

But more importantly to Swithun, his wife was nowhere to be seen.

Swithun turned to Ord. "Hurry home, you, and if your mum's there, the two of you stay put. I'm going to check the church for her, but I'll be home after."

Ord nodded stiffly but said nothing. There was fear in his eyes, little boy fear Swithun hadn't seen in a while.

The father set a consoling hand on his son's shoulder. "You're eleven years of age now, son, too old to be afraid, right? Take me dagger and use it if you need to."

Swithun handed him the weapon, and Ord stared at it.

"Now, go on."

—

Two Silthex knights stood guard at the doors of the basilica. Swithun looked a moment at the large green, squared seven on their white surcoats. The seven—the *Septenar,* of which this was a version—was the symbol of the True Light Gods.

God Déagar help us, Swithun thought, looking at it. He approached.

"The basilica's currently shut to the public," one guard said sternly, barely glancing in Swithun's direction.

"I just need to check if someone's inside," Swithun said. "You remember me, right? The patriarch had me up on his stage with him earlier."

"Be quick," the same guard said.

—

A quick scan of the large hall told Swithun that his wife wasn't there. He nearly cursed, but remembered where he was.

Yet there were *some* people there—some workers—and they grabbed his attention. A large wagon, like would be drawn by a horse, was parked right in front of the statue of the blue God Karulus.

They'd tied the God up with ropes threaded upward through wooden pulleys from what looked like four gallows.

Six men pulled and heaved at the ropes as another man held his hands steadying the statue.

"What are you doing there?" Swithun's words echoed in the large room.

"Orders, sir," a worker called back, with a strain in his voice. "The statue is to be removed."

"Whose orders?"

"Mine," another man spoke up from behind the wagon. He approached. He was the rather old man who'd exited the mirror right before the patriarch.

Swithun bowed his head.

The man—Dean Krasil—stopped a few feet before the newcomer. "Swithun, yes?"

"Yes, Your . . ."

"Most Reverend Eminence."

"All that, really?" Swithun asked, but caught himself. "Forgive me, Your Most Eminent Reverent."

Krasil chuckled. "You do not intend something like the flag incident, do you?"

"No, Your Most—"

"*Eminence* is fine."

"Yes, Your Eminence. I mean *no*, I'm not planning nothing. I was just wanting to know why; that's all. If I can ask."

"Is it not obvious? Karulus has been nothing but an overstayed visitor in the house of God Déagar. These men will remove this idol and return it to its worshipers. Only then will this basilica be right to act as the temporary residence for His Holiness."

Swithun turned to the bound God and thought of Laurence. He'd be so disappointed.

Krasil neared Swithun, standing at his side as he also viewed the statue.

"Most people say the Pestilence comes from the river," Krasil began. "In truth, no one is certain. It is a strange coincidence, though."

"What's that then, Your Eminence?"

"Karulus, he is a water deity, you know."

"I did know that, sir. I have a friend that's a Karulent."

"Do you? Then, you must also know what lies across the river?"

"Everyone knows that, sir. 'Tis the Karulent Alliance, there. 'Tis like our Trade Agreement."

Krasil nodded. "The magic-using worshipers of a water deity live just across the river that people think spawned the Pestilence. Yes, it is a . . . *strange coincidence*."

"You're not saying the Karulents caused the—"

"I'm surprised at you, Swithun," Krasil cut him off, "making accusations. What would your friend say, I wonder?"

"He's more my boss, really. But he's not like the rest of them."

"No," Krasil grinned. "Of course not. However, if you are correct—and you seem to be a *smart man*—we might have quite a problem on our hands."

Krasil paused before taking an authoritative tone, "Organize the Wendian militia. We must restore law and order. However, if there are any *Karulents* amongst your volunteers, exclude them, at least until we know whether your concerns about them are true."

"Yes, Your Eminence. We're at your service."

"At the service *of God Déagar*," he corrected. "As are we all. Now go. You must be quick in your tasks."

Swithun turned and stepped away, but stopped. "You're a brave man to stay here, Your Eminence. And to convince His Holiness to stay, too. You're truly a man of Déagar."

"Yes. May the fires of God Déagar guide you."

CHAPTER TWELVE

Day seven since the Pestilence had come to Wendian—
Sabbathday. Swithun should be in church, listening
to a sermon with his wife and child at his side. Ord
would be rocking on his feet, complaining about having to
stand still for so long. Ord's mother would tell him to, "Hush.
Pay attention."

Instead, Swithun, with five men of the militia, patrolled
the streets. Somehow, being part of the militia made the
tragedy seem separate from Swithun. He and his men were
not completely part of it, but were observers walking
through. Never mind that he could hear the sounds of desperate wailing echoing all around him. Never mind that he
could smell the thick smoke of burning animals that had fall-
en sick. Never mind that everything happening to the people
around him was happening to him as well because, right
now, he was on task: maintaining order.

Nevertheless, every so often, something would grab him
by the heart and remind him of the reality in his city.

He paused as he saw an older woman, skirt muddied from
the street in which she kneeled. She clasped her shaking
hands together as she pleaded to the misty, smoky sky.

"Praise His Divine Majesty, Déagar," she said, "God of fire
and lightning, eldest of the Gods, protector from the Dark.
Please, God Déagar. Help us, O Greatest of All. Help us." She
collapsed, her hands falling into the mud. "Help us." She
started sobbing.

Swithun suppressed the pain of seeing her. He and his
group passed her by. They'd seen the same too many times in

the last week. The townspeople all looked like they didn't know where to go or what to do. It was as if the anguish was so great that they had no choice but to vomit it out through shrieks and dismal wails.

But Swithun walked on. He tried not to feel, to think.

A boarded-up shop caught his attention or, rather, that it was no longer boarded up. Someone had pried back the planks and kicked in the door.

He was certain it hadn't been like that on his team's last pass of the area.

Swithun signaled to the others with him and drew his sword. "Go on to the square without me," he said. "I'm going to investigate this."

Swithun carefully approached the opening as he scanned the area for trouble.

No signs of anyone outside.

Sword in hand, he slowly ducked through the broken entrance, making sure not to make a sound.

Inside, utter blackness hit until his eyes adjusted. The smell of sawdust tickled his nose. The dusty rays of daylight beamed through the shutters and broken door, showing a woodworking shop. Little figurines of people, horses, and boats lined the shelves.

He realized where he was. He'd been in this toy shop before. Ord had wanted to come in. Swithun had told him they couldn't afford such things, but Ord just wanted to see, pleaded to see.

Swithun crept further in, toward the workbench in the center of the room. If a thief were in this small shop, he'd need to be hiding there.

Swithun caught sight of a small barrel against the wall. The hilts of a dozen wooden swords stood above its rim.

That's what Ord had wanted: a wooden sword. He'd begged, as if it was so very important.

"You want us to starve, do you?" Swithun had shouted back. "We can't buy toys with the docks burnt down." He hadn't meant to be so angry. And now, the memory pained him.

Now, a man leaped from behind the workbench.

Swithun sprung forward, grabbing for him, but his distraction from the memory delayed him.

The thief bolted for the door. Swithun pursued, bounding through the broken entrance into the street.

A quick search. Swithun saw him running. He followed at full sprint.

The thief made it to the square.

Swithun grabbed him and threw him to the ground. Swithun was on top of him, straddling his stomach.

All the sorrow of all that was going on ignited into anger and burned through Swithun's veins. He punched him in the face, again and again. Each strike became angrier, each impact, bloodier.

"Swithun!" one of his men called to him. It was the winged man, Edgar, the potter. He grabbed Swithun's shoulders.

Hot and panting, Swithun stopped and looked up. He nearly struck Edgar just for touching him.

"You got him," Edgar said in a calming voice. "You got him."

Swithun looked down at the thief. His face was bloodied and swollen. He shook with eyes of fear.

Swithun crawled off the beaten man and kneeled beside him, his head bowed low as the anger pounded through him.

"Why's this happening to us?" Swithun growled.

The thief clutched a wooden horse; its legs now snapped off and scattered on the man's chest. "I would have paid," he cried. "There was no one to pay. I needed it for my daughter. She's very sick."

"Go." Swithun stood.

He watched the thief gather the broken legs of the horse and scurry away.

Swithun's eyes turned to the dead laid side by side within the square. These gruesome, uncovered, stinking things that had once been people lay in five rows of nine.

A dozen men in tattered skirts walked barefoot in a gap between the rows of corpses. They whipped themselves with leather and intoned in unison:

"Praise God Déagar, eldest of the Gods, protector from the Dark. You are the Greatest of All. I praise your name, majestic and holy, without ending. By your fire, guide us safely to Laqyigo. Praise God Déagar, eldest of the Gods, protector from the Dark . . ."

"Who are they?" Edgar asked.

"Flagellants." Swithun watched the wretched procession. "They're a sort of monk. The Church don't fully condone them, but they've told us to leave 'em be."

Blood poured down the flagellants' backs, staining their grayed skirts, trickling down their legs to bloody footprints. Yet, they continued to beat themselves.

Swithun said, "They think they can pay the penance for the sins of the cities and towns they visit and cleanse away the plague. But they're wrong. Wendian's a moral city, loved by God Déagar. He didn't do this to us."

A woman screamed out, "No!" grabbing Swithun's attention.

City workers on the farthest side of the square were snatching up the corpses and heaving them into a large wagon.

"Poor souls," Edgar said.

Swithun said nothing. He watched the young woman who had shouted. She wept over a deceased man as the workers neared.

"God Déagar wouldn't do this to us," Swithun said. "But someone wicked is to blame."

When they tried to take the dead man from the woman, she began frantically hitting a worker with side-fisted blows against his chest.

"You can't take him!" she cried. "You can't."

Swithun and Edgar rushed forward, twisting around the dead.

Grabbing the woman, Swithun pulled her back.

"You can't take him to the river," she screamed as she flung out her arms and tried to reach the workers. "Please!"

"The patriarch's consecrated the Hyvile." Swithun gripped her wrists. "We have to get the dead out of the city. Bad air attracts more Pestilence."

"It ain't right," she maintained. "Blessed or not, the river's not a decent burial."

Swithun grabbed her by the shoulders and turned her to face him. "If the Church says 'tis decent, 'tis decent. Right?"

"Heartless *bastard!*" She slapped him.

"Me wife's in that river!" he barked and threw her to the mud. The words from his own mouth, spoken so angrily, ripped through his shield of disassociation.

"Me wife," he whispered as he started panting. "We should be in church right now. Fuck me. We should all be together."

Edgar approached Swithun. "I didn't know."

"I ain't said it out loud 'fore now."

The woman sat on the ground and looked up at Swithun with sad eyes.

"Get out of here!" Swithun shouted as he drew his sword. "I ain't your fucking show."

She ran off, tripping over her feet.

"You're not yourself," Edgar said. "No one is right now, in truth, but you—"

"I'm all right."

"I heard your boy's being treated in the church. Is it true?"

Swithun said nothing.

"Take a day off—the militia will be fine—and go visit Ord . . . before you're mourning him, too."

CHAPTER THIRTEEN

Swithun paused as he entered the nave of the basilica. The smell of incense hung thick in the air. It was a visible haze, meant to ward off the bad air that was said to bring the plague.

The high-up windows dimmed with sunset. Straw covered most of the vast floor with the many sick and dying laid out upon it. Swithun couldn't help but compare it to the dead laid out in the square. The sights were too similar, and he knew many of these here would soon be there.

And then in the Hyvile River.

Swithun walked the paths between the beds of straw and watched the monks in black robes navigating too. The monks moved solemnly from patient to patient, helping them drink from small clay bowls, praying over them, and comforting them.

Very few people recovered from the Pestilence. Hardly any. This was the thought Swithun tried not to think, but was the very thought he thought as his son came into view.

Ord looked so small on his straw bed in the vast room. His mother had brought him a bedsheet to thwart the draft, and he lay under it with it pulled up to his neck.

He wasn't moving, Swithun realized. The fearful father walked faster, trying not to sprint, dreading the worst.

A monk stopped him. "He's only sleeping," he said calmly, barely whispering.

"You sure?" Swithun watched his son.

The monk nodded.

Swithun took a deep breath and released it slowly. His heart pounded. Still, he watched Ord, trying to find any proof of the monk's words.

"He's been asking for you," the monk said. "And for his mother."

"You didn't—"

"No. No, that's your news to share, if you like."

"I told him she'd been moved to another part of the church," Swithun said. "'Twas true at the time. Don't see how it'd do him any good to know different 'til he's better. Is he? Better?"

The monk glanced at the floor and shook his head. "Your son continues to suffer from a serious imbalance of the humors. He is very hot and wet, so we are administering regimens of both cold and dry. We would like to get him started on leeches to remove the bad blood, but regrettably, leeches are quite expensive."

Swithun glanced at Ord and back to the monk. He whispered, "I don't have much, but if you can help him, I'll . . ."

The monk gently raised his hand. "It is not up to me. Or the Church. The leech mongers have set up shop in the southwest corner of your city square. If you can procure them, we will administer them, gratis. May I suggest bartering your services as security? I believe they would accept."

"My thanks." Swithun nodded and looked at the floor.

"Send your thanks to God Déagar." The monk set his hand on Swithun's shoulder. "Prayer is still our best option. The leechers are shut for the day, but will open at sunrise. In the meantime, we'll continue with chamomile."

Again, Swithun nodded. "I'll head there first thing."

"May the fires of God Déagar guide you." He patted Swithun's shoulder and walked away.

Swithun approached his son and kneeled over him.

"Ord?" he whispered.

The boy cracked his eyes and rolled his head toward his father.

"How you feeling, son?"

"Tired. And itchy. And me fingers feel . . . weird. They're all black." He pulled one of his hands from beneath his sheet and lifted it toward Swithun.

Above the second knuckle of each finger, the skin of each of the boy's fingers was waxy black and shriveled. The fingernails looked as if they might crack off.

Swithun set his hand atop his—the boy's fingertips were cold as death—and lowered it to his side, keeping his hand there to comfort.

"I'll let you get back to sleep soon, son. I just wanted to visit a bit."

"How's Mum, then?" Ord asked.

"Now, you know she wouldn't want you to worry about her, would she? 'Tis *our* job to worry about *you*. I got you a present here. See?"

Swithun pulled a wooden sword from his belt and held it up for him to see.

Ord smiled weakly.

"You wanted it, remember? From the toy shop." Swithun laid it on Ord's chest. "And when you get well, you can play with it every day."

Ord grasped it in his blackened fingers as best as he could. "I love it." He drifted back to sleep.

Swithun stood up but continued to stare down at the sleeping boy. Never in his entire life had Swithun felt such worry, such consuming sadness. Such helplessness.

"Swithun," someone whispered behind him.

Swithun looked back to see Laurence at a distance.

"What are you doing here?" Swithun whispered as he approached him. "Karulents are meant to stay in the area we fenced off for them."

"Yes," Laurence said, with some annoyance. "The militia has made that very clear."

They hurried to the wall, away from the others.

"It was orders," Swithun said. "From the Silthex knights. I tried telling them you ain't like the rest of 'em."

"You don't even know the rest—" He stopped himself. "No. That's not a conversation I'm here for. I just wanted to check on your family. I brought these." He lifted a tin pitcher, holding ten lilies.

Swithun looked at them, and his mouth curled slightly upward in a faint smile. "How'd you manage to get flowers in times like these?"

"I admit it was difficult, but I had to do something. They'll keep away the bad smells that attract the Pestilence. I've got a second pitcher by the door, so I can divide out half for his mother. Where is she?"

The slight smile vanished as Swithun looked down. "Best give them all to Ord. Me wife won't be needing them."

"No. You don't mean she's . . ."

Swithun nodded.

Laurence sighed. "She was a good woman."

"That she was."

"As you said," Laurence began. "I cannot stay." He handed Swithun the pitcher. "I'll be praying for you and your son."

Laurence looked to the alcove, at the half-circle stone table that had held the statue of God Karulus. It now held various jars and items meant for treating the sick.

"Our God is a God of healing," Laurence said. "And Wendian is in need of much of it."

He turned to leave, but Swithun grabbed his arm.

"Can you heal Ord?" Swithun demanded. "With your magic?"

"You know full well, I do not practice magic."

"But you must know someone." He gripped him tighter.

"Despite what Déagrians seem to believe," Laurence became cross, snatching his arm from Swithun, "very few Karulents actually practice magic. At least not on the level you'd require. You need an Azerent Mage, specifically an Azerent Healer, and there are barely any south of the river."

"You can't just do *nothing!*" Swithun shouted as he threw down the pitcher of flowers.

The pitcher clanked and bounced and rolled on the gray tiled floor. Water splashed, and lilies scattered.

Many of the monks turned to the disturbance, casting disapproving glares.

"Forgive me," Swithun spoke up to the room as he raised his hands passively. "Just having a chat; that's all. Slipped out of me hands."

Laurence leaned in to Swithun. "If I could do anything to help that boy, you wouldn't need to ask, much less demand."

With that, Laurence moved away, and Swithun stooped to collect the spilled flowers.

A man burst into the nave and paused, panting as if he'd run. "Everyone, there's important news of the patriarch! Quick, anyone who can, gather outside."

Swithun dropped the flowers back into the tin and hurried toward the doors.

—

Just outside the basilica, in an open area through which a cobbled path led from the doors, a man rang a handbell as he called people to, "Gather 'round. Gather 'round."

About forty people had already gathered 'round, but they didn't face the man. Instead, they circled two iron torches stabbed into the ground beside an old oak tree.

Swithun realized, as he neared, that there was a small, overturned crate between the torches. Two Silthex knights escorted the Dean of the Ocelli, Krasil, into the torchlight.

Krasil stepped onto the makeshift podium. "People of Wendian," he announced. "In these uncertain times, we seem to face one tragedy after the next. Tonight, I, unfortunately, must share another." He paused, staring over the crowd. "The Pestilence has struck down our beloved Supreme Patriarch. He is now with God Déagar in Laqyigo."

The crowd gasped. Some cried out, "No!" Some wept. Swithun merely stared, too overcome to move.

"Forgive my jumping to the point so hastily," Krasil said, "but as you might imagine, we have much to do tonight. Many of you may already know that we have lost two of the ten Ocelli to the unnamed plague and now this, but we will not be defeated. The remaining Ocelli have appointed me as Interim Patriarch, and I vow, by Almighty Déagar, to stand strong in the face of this evil terrorizing our lands.

"As I said," Krasil continued, "I must be quick. But as my first duty as Interim Patriarch of the Church of Déagar, I must acknowledge what most of you already ask. How can this pestilence be a punishment from the Greatest of All when it strikes down so many righteous men like our great Patriarch? I say it cannot. Thus, I officially name this plague the *Blue Sickness* and, in the name of Almighty God Déagar, charge the magic-wielding *Karulents* with its conjuring and proliferation."

Swithun's heart pounded in anger as he listened to Krasil's words. He had suspected as much, but to hear the charge decreed by Déagar's chosen representative enraged Swithun beyond thought. Karulents had murdered his wife. Karulents were murdering his son. Karulents had destroyed his town.

Then Krasil asked the question that sliced through Swithun's helter-skelter, swirling brain like a heated sword:

"Have any of you seen any Karulents near the church to-night?"

Heat swelled within Swithun as his heart pounded faster. He clenched his fists as he scanned the surrounding area. Then, he saw him, Laurence, standing at a distance, watching from the shadows of a shop.

Laurence saw Swithun see him. Even in just the light of the moons, Swithun thought he saw him mouth the words, "Please, no." Laurence shook his head.

"There!" Swithun pointed.

Laurence darted, but the Silthex knights rushed him. They grabbed him.

Swithun ran to him. "Tell me," he shouted through heavy breaths, "you didn't use a visit to *my son* as cover for your wicked, Karulent deeds."

"Swithun, you know me," Laurence cried. "I would nev-er—"

"Take him away," Krasil, beside Swithun, commanded.

As the Silthex dragged Laurence away, he maintained his pleas. "Swithun, you know I couldn't!"

Swithun turned to Krasil. "Forgive me, Your Holiness, I should have . . ."

Krasil raised a finger. "Your apology is unnecessary. This time. You only erred because you are a godly, trusting man. We now know the Karulents tricked us all."

Swithun continued to watch the screaming, struggling Karulent as the knights dragged him away.

"D'you also support this empire idea, Your Holiness?"

"I do."

"Good." Swithun still stared. "We have to unite against the wickedness that would destroy us."

CHAPTER FOURTEEN

The small barred window through the thick stone wall of his cell told Laurence it was morning.

He hadn't slept. He kept trying to tell himself they wouldn't kill him—surely, things had not escalated to that point. But he wasn't sure.

Last night, when the Silthex knights dragged Laurence into the castle, he could see the hate in their eyes. They shoved him and yanked him, even as he cooperated and followed their commands.

They pulled Laurence down into a storage cellar where vegetables, no doubt once belonging to the now-dead king, rotted on their shelves and in their wicker baskets. The smell of putrefaction gagged him.

The knight punched him in the gut for making the slightest gagging noises. Laurence almost cried out but was afraid, so he gritted his teeth and held in the pain.

They yanked open a thick door on the side of the cellar and threw Laurence down with angry force. He hit the floor, scraping his legs and palms on the stone.

The door slammed and was locked.

Laurence stayed in place, his every muscle tight, his every limb drawn guardedly into his body. He feared that they watched him and that even breathing too loudly might bring them back with reasons to beat him.

For hours, Laurence stayed thus. For hours, he could see nothing but an image burned into his mind of their eyes. Eyes with hate so severe that he knew better than to reason with them. Hate of men who would kill him, then and there, with the slightest justification.

Frozen in his cell, Laurence ached to cry like a little child, but he feared what making a sound would bring.

Yet, for all the horrors of the night, a greater dread rose with dawn. Laurence watched the high-up window grow brighter, as if it were an hourglass timing down to some unknown fate. The light filling the room was like the sands pouring over him, burying him, suffocating him.

When, at last, the cell door began to open, Laurence trembled like a mouse.

"Please," Laurence uttered into his clasped hands. Tears streamed his face. "God Karulus, help me."

A Silthex knight—dark shoulder-length hair and beard, well-built, mid-thirties—entered the cell and stood tall, peering down at Laurence. "I am Seneschal Brynistan," he said. "I will be assisting in the investigation to prove your guilt. Stand up."

Laurence stood shakily. "Forgive me, sir, but I do not quite understand what you've charged me with."

"You've pissed yourself, haven't you?" Brynistan asked with a sneer. "'Tis no matter. Remove your clothes. Everything. And be quick about it."

Nodding wearily, Laurence complied as Brynistan, with the rigid posture of a soldier, watched. Finally, Laurence set his clothes on the floor and stood naked and slouched, with his hands folded in front of parts he wished to keep private.

Brynistan motioned to someone just outside the door.

Two monks in green coarse wool robes rushed in and began yanking at Laurence's arms and legs as they searched his skin.

"Pay special attention to the armpits and groin," Brynistan commanded. "That is where the marks of the sickness appear."

They yanked his arms upward, examining him roughly. They spread his feet apart, nearly causing him to stumble.

"He bears no marks, Lord Commander," a monk reported.

"Very well." Brynistan swiped two of his fingers, and the monks stepped back, folding their hands at their waists as they bowed their heads.

Into the adjoining cellar, Brynistan shouted, "He is clean, Grand Master."

Despite all of Laurence's fear, his terrifying surroundings, and his dispirited state, he was taken aback by how extremely old the new arrival appeared. If the new Déagrian Patriarch looked to be one hundred years of age, then this man looked ten times that. And there was decay to his decrepitude. His white hair drooped brittle and thin, his skin hung loosely from his bones, his eyes had yellowed, his teeth had rotted, and his spine hunched.

Laurence did, however, take some pleasure in the craftsmanship of his attire. His surcoat—a masterwork of art within this nightmare—was of fine, white, Vohcktaran silk with a delicate silver brocade woven throughout. Above his thick black belt was a squared version of the number seven—like with the Silthex knights—but his was embroidered in exquisite needlework of vibrant green thread. His floor-length cloak was flawlessly white ermine fur.

"What a pathetic creature thou art," the man said as he peered down his nose at Laurence. "Thou appearest as if a sickly bird stripped of feathers and prepped to be jugulated."

Laurence slouched as he crossed his arms across his body.

The ancient man chuckled before turning to one of the monks. "Go thou and fetch a cloth, so our unsightly guest may wrap his nether self. Blue, I think. Yes. Vibrant, contemptible blue." He turned his murderous eyes to Laurence. "Wouldst thou appreciate that, criminal?"

Laurence nodded stiffly. He could not speak. Nothing leading up to this moment terrified him more than this strange man. His calm, sinister demeanor was akin to a snake about to devour Laurence alive.

"Good." The ancient man grinned. "I would not wish thee to think me unkind. I am Blastilv, Grand Master of the Knights Silthex. If thou dost simply confess to the charges against thee, I will continue to be kind. Yet, know thou, the new Supreme Patriarch—now official in his title—hath named me an Archbishop. Thus, if thou dost attempt to be untruthful in thy words, thou dost, too, give false witness to the Church, itself, and blaspheme against the True Light."

"I don't even understand why I'm here."

Blastilv took a long, labored breath. He nodded to Brynistan.

Brynistan rushed forward, drawing back his fist.

Laurence saw a flash of light as knuckles struck his face. He staggered back, head spinning. His hands fell to his knees as he tried to keep from falling to the floor.

"Play not the fool, base criminal," Blastilv said harshly, yet calmly. "Thou knowest well why thou art here."

The monk returned with a blue cloth and tossed it at Laurence, who caught it gracelessly. It was coarse hemp fabric and poorly dyed, but Laurence wrapped his waist and tucked the end to keep it in place.

Blastilv continued. "Eight hundred people, both residents of Wendian and its honored visitors, have been smote dead by insidious magic in this city over the week past. The Church of Déagar hath charged thee with their murders."

"You cannot truly believe that," Laurence uttered. His hands fell to his knees as his head spun. "The Pestilence comes from the river."

"The *Blue Sickness*," Blastilv said, "is the immoral act of Karulents. So hath the Church of Déagar proclaimed, so is the truth. Dost thou, foul criminal, dispute the Church?"

Laurence opened his mouth to speak, but his chin quivered without a word. He breathed quickly in and out and in before he cried, "'Tis from the River!"

Blastilv nodded to Brynistan.

Brynistan punched Laurence to the floor and kicked him twice in the stomach.

Laurence focused his blurred eyes on the bottom of Blastilv's surcoat, where the garment circled the tops of his black boots. The tailor who'd made it had used a unique stitch with green thread. Beautiful.

Brynistan slammed his boot into Laurence's upper arm. It cracked.

Laurence's swollen eyes watered and blood trickled from his nose. He felt as if he'd vomit or perhaps pass out. He focused on the surcoat, the beautiful masterwork, his solace in the dark.

"Whither went the Karulent priest of Wendian?" Blastilv asked cordially, as if he sought nothing but directions.

"He left," Laurence groaned. "After the icon of our God Karulus was taken down, he traveled to Vilana to report."

"Thou dost admit your connection to Vilana?"

"'Tis no secret. The Karulent Church is based in Vilana."

"Vilana is home to the magic-using Order of Azerents, yes?" Blastilv asked. "Tell me, is thy priest an Azerent Mage?"

"No," Laurence said wearily. The side of his face was set on the cold floor as he stared out to blurry nothing. "Like the Silthex, the inner working of the Order is secretive, but their membership is not. If our priest were an Azerent, the entire city would know. 'Tis a great honor."

"Stand him afoot," Blastilv commanded.

The two monks in green robes hurried to Laurence and pulled him up by the arms.

Laurence, slouching and cradling his injured arm, stared warily at Brynistan, fearing he'd knock him right back down again.

Brynistan smirked as he popped his knuckles. He thrust a slight air punch toward Laurence.

Laurence flinched, despite the distance.

"As you three here can bear witness," Blastilv began, "the criminal hath confessed willingly that the Karulent priest of Wendian blatantly maintains ties with the Order of Azerents, an order known to practice sorcery. Furthermore, the Azerents reside in the island city of Vilana, situated in the Hyvile River. Lo, the criminal hath confessed, twice over, that this same river is the source of the Blue Sickness."

"Stating facts," Laurence groaned, "as if they are accusations, do not make them iniquitous. And torturing me will not gain you anything more than what I've told you."

"Torture?" Blastilv chuckled, a deep, throaty sound that chilled Laurence to the bone.

The Grand Master neared the captive and cast his cold, yellowed eyes directly into his.

"I have yet to *torture* thee, criminal. Yet, it doth await thee, be assured. And harken well: for thy crimes against all who are righteous, thine agony shall be *exceptional*." He grinned, bearing rotten teeth. "And when thou—at long, painful last—

cry out in confession of thy wicked deeds, thou wilt, within the fires of Déagar, burn, screaming before the city thou didst betray."

The words held Laurence breathless. He shivered in place as his eyes drifted to the floor. He nearly fell from the weight of the man's warnings.

The ancient man stepped away.

"This ..." Laurence tried. "This is a nightmare. A nightmare. A ..." He could not say more. He could not think more. His mind felt numb, unable to process the unreal reality unfolding around him.

Dizzy, Laurence set his fingertips to his mouth, chewing on his nails. "I did nothing," he breathily spoke through his trembling fingers. "No one did anything. Nothing was *done!*"

"Pray you," Blastilv said pleasantly to the monks, "go you and fetch the chair I had delivered from Dayigo. You will know the one of which I speak. It is covered in iron spikes. Fear not, though it is heavy, it hath wheels."

"Please," Laurence cried. "How can I make you believe this is all ridiculous?"

Blastilv turned toward Laurence and scanned him up and down. He grinned. "Lo, thou dost tremble like a leaf. Do I frighten thee, criminal?"

Laurence nodded.

Blastilv chuckled. "Honest. Yet pitiful."

The Grand Master turned away but paused. "Bite thy fingers whilst thou canst, criminal. I shall *chop* them off anon. Come, Seneschal, let us depart whilst we await the chair. Our guest requires time alone to fantasize of his fate."

"Yes, Grand Master," Brynistan said.

"Swithun," Laurence blurted. "He will speak for me?"

Blastilv and Brynistan turned to the prisoner.

"Swithun?" Blastilv asked.

Brynistan replied, "The leader of the city's militia, Grand Master."

"'Twas mine understanding," Blastilv began, "that the militia leader reported him to us. Is it not the case?"

"It is, my lord," Laurence said hopelessly. "But he was angry before. Confused. He will speak for me. I know it. Long have we been friends. I beseech you, please bring him here. And he will set this right."

Blastilv paused. "I admit, I am curious to see how this unfolds. Go, Seneschal, and fetch this Swithun."

Brynistan gave a curt, single nod. "As you command, Grand Master."

CHAPTER FIFTEEN

In a cellar stinking of rot, Swithun stared at the door he was soon to enter. The rest of the room seemed to darken as he focused on the iron ring, old and rusted, which was the door's handle.

"You, of course, know Grand Master Blastilv," Brynistan said, as he approached from behind Swithun with the man he mentioned. Two monks in hooded green robes followed.

Swithun glanced back, nodded absently, and returned his gaze to the iron ring.

Brynistan passed by Swithun and unlocked the door.

The five entered.

The cell was dim, lit only by a single, small, high-up window. Swithun was more interested in its inhabitant, who was lying on the floor.

Laurence looked up as they entered. "Swithun," he said with some relief as he pushed himself to stand. "You came." He was quite beaten up, but he managed to smile. "Praise be to Karulus, you are here."

Swithun said nothing, and he certainly did not return the smile. Anger rushed through him, throbbing in his head and pounding in his heart. He only stared at the prisoner, who, with barely a rag to cover his body, still wore the color of the treacherous Karulus.

Laurence's smile faded. His eyes averted to the floor.

"The criminal," Blastilv said, "believes thou canst speak on his behalf. What sayest thou, Swithun?"

"Yes." Swithun nodded. "I can talk about this man. After the docks closed down, he hired me on to work in his shop. I did odd jobs—loading and unloading, moving things, fixing things, and making deliveries."

"It was a dress shop?" Blastilv asked.

"Mostly dresses, m'lord."

"Did anything *suspicious* occur whilst thou wert employed?"

Swithun looked in the general direction of Laurence, but not at him, more at the stone wall, and even that was blurred. "Right before the patriarch's visit—the former patriarch—Laurence were boasting how he were the only good tailor left in Wendian, right. The other top tailor—a good Déagrian man—had dropped down dead. The Blue Sickness. It were peculiar 'cause the other tailor had gone to Vilana, and Vilana ain't have the plague there."

"'Tis ten days away," Laurence spoke up. "There are plenty of places between here and there where—"

Brynistan clubbed Laurence in the gut, causing him to cry out as he curled forward, grabbing his stomach.

"Prithee, continue," Blastilv coldly prompted Swithun.

Swithun nodded, staring at the opposite wall. "Laurence told me the Vilanans can't get the Sickness, cause they's protected by magic."

"Magic," Laurence said, "that the Karulent Alliance would share if the Church of Déagar didn't block them."

Brynistan lifted the club.

Laurence fell to the ground before its impact, his shaking arms blocking his face.

"Please, Swithun," Laurence cried. "They plan to kill me."

"Ain't think nothing of it then," Swithun said blankly. "But now, I think maybe Laurence needed to be the only one dressin' all the well-to-do. 'Cause maybe he was sewing hexes into the cloth or something. Know what I mean?"

"No," Laurence wept. "None of it even makes sense. Do you hear yourself?"

"An interesting theory," Blastilv said. "We will need to investigate this further."

"Swithun, you know me. We've been friends for years. I know you were upset, but please tell them I would never—"

"I don't fucking know you." Swithun turned to address him directly for the first time. "I thought I did. Guess it must have been good to have the militia's leader tricked, right?" He charged Laurence and kicked him.

With fury, Swithun's boot struck the Karulent's stomach, sending the prisoner to the floor.

Laurence began dragging himself toward the wall, trying to escape, despite no means.

Swithun kicked again.

"After you visited my Ord," Swithun growled, "he died." He kicked him again. "'Twas you!"

"I'd never." Laurence pushed himself into a corner, like a trapped mouse. With weary words, he said, "You know I'd never do that to Ord. Or anyone."

"Don't you fucking say his name." He lifted his boot to kick again, but Blastilv set his hands on Swithun's shoulders.

"Thou wert brave to come here," he said as he turned Swithun from the prisoner, "to stand before this villain who hath bereft thee of thy kin. Very brave indeed."

Swithun nodded, trying to calm himself.

"'Twould be unkind of me to subject thee to any more of these *unpleasant things*," Blastilv said. "We now have all the information we require."

He led Swithun toward the door.

"Be assured," Blastilv said, "we will avenge thy son. As is often said, '*The True Light is the only way. All others will perish.*'"

Laurence screamed, "They will kill me! Please!"

Swithun ignored him. As he approached the door, three more monks in green wheeled in a chair. Its back, seat, and armrests were covered in sharp iron spikes. Thick boards, also bearing spikes, crossed each section of the chair with cranks to press them into the seated.

Laurence was screaming Swithun's name and crying, *please*. "They'll kill me," he wept.

Swithun passed the chair, staring at it a moment, and paused.

"Grand Master," Swithun said and glanced back to Laurence, who cowered in the corner. "Hurt him."

Blastilv chuckled. "O aggrieved Swithun, takest heart, for thy most twisted of nightmares could not foresee how *thoroughly* I will grant thy request."

Swithun nodded. He exited the cell.

—

Swithun stood on the short bridge just west of the square, his hands on the thick stone railing. He looked north toward the burnt docks.

There was an uproar in the square. People, torches in hands, shouted angrily.

Swithun ignored it.

He felt numb. Lost.

The pale blue glow of the larger moon combined with the lavender-tinted glow of the smaller moon. They lit the blackened docks just enough for him to make out silhouettes of ruins.

"You worked down there?"

Swithun turned to see Seneschal Brynistan standing a few yards to his right.

"Right there, mostly." Swithun pointed to two parallel rows of burned wooden poles sticking out of dark waters. But even as he did so, he knew it was unlikely Brynistan would determine the exact distant point.

"Pier C," Swithun said. "Simpler times."

"Now that the Church has determined the cause of the Blue Sickness," Brynistan said, "I doubt 'twill be too long before the ports are rebuilt—here and in other cities and towns. Do you intend to return to that work?"

The question annoyed Swithun. He turned to the knight. "Truth be told, sir, I ain't thought that far ahead."

"I have a better offer if you're interested." Wet blood coated the seneschal's hands and splattered his white surcoat.

Swithun paused. "Go on."

"The king—the Dayigan king, soon to be the high king of the Dayigan Empire—wishes to establish a standing, empire-wide army. A *salaried*, standing army."

Swithun scoffed. "You offering me a job, sir?"

"I doubt your present employer will require your services any longer."

Past Brynistan's shoulder, Swithun could see a large bonfire flame up in the city square. Even from here, he could hear Laurence screaming.

"His Majesty," Brynistan continued, "thinks it best to recruit from the local militias to form the backbone of his new army. They will maintain order in their respective towns."

"Under the rule of you and your grand master, I'm guessing."

"No. The Silthex Order is a *Church* military order. We will, of course, work in tandem with King Tanimaros's secular army, but we do not answer to the king. However, the Grand Master and I will not personally be here to witness the birth of the Empire, or its army. He and I are set to leave the continent."

"How's that? There's just seas 'sides Bikia."

"Men keep to Bikia and West Bikia, but there are more lands. We have a mission to sail southwest to a continent called *Klikate Forest*. But before we set out, I would like to be able to tell King Tanimaros that the Wendian militia is willing to join the Dayigan Army. You won't need to leave your city. Dayigo will need men to maintain order here."

"I'll have a talk with the men for you, sir. But ain't nothing at all left for me here now."

"I see. The garrison's only one option. We also need soldiers to march east and fend off the Dark Light soldiers of the Tridulan Empire."

Swithun looked back toward the docks. Beyond them, the moonlight glistened on the Hyvile River.

Brynistan said, "The new army will need good Déagrian men, like yourself, if we are to forge a mighty empire."

The screams of Laurence had died away, but the fire blazed strong, its smoke stinking of burned flesh.

Swithun threw a pebble far out toward the ruined docks. "Tell your king—*our* king—I'll join up with him." He turned to Brynistan. "But only if he gets me as far from this fucking place as possible."

PART THREE

The Eve of Lies and Injustice

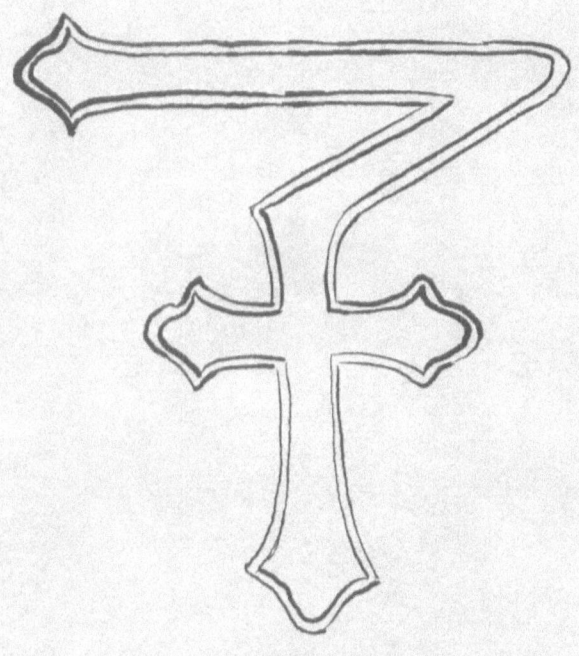

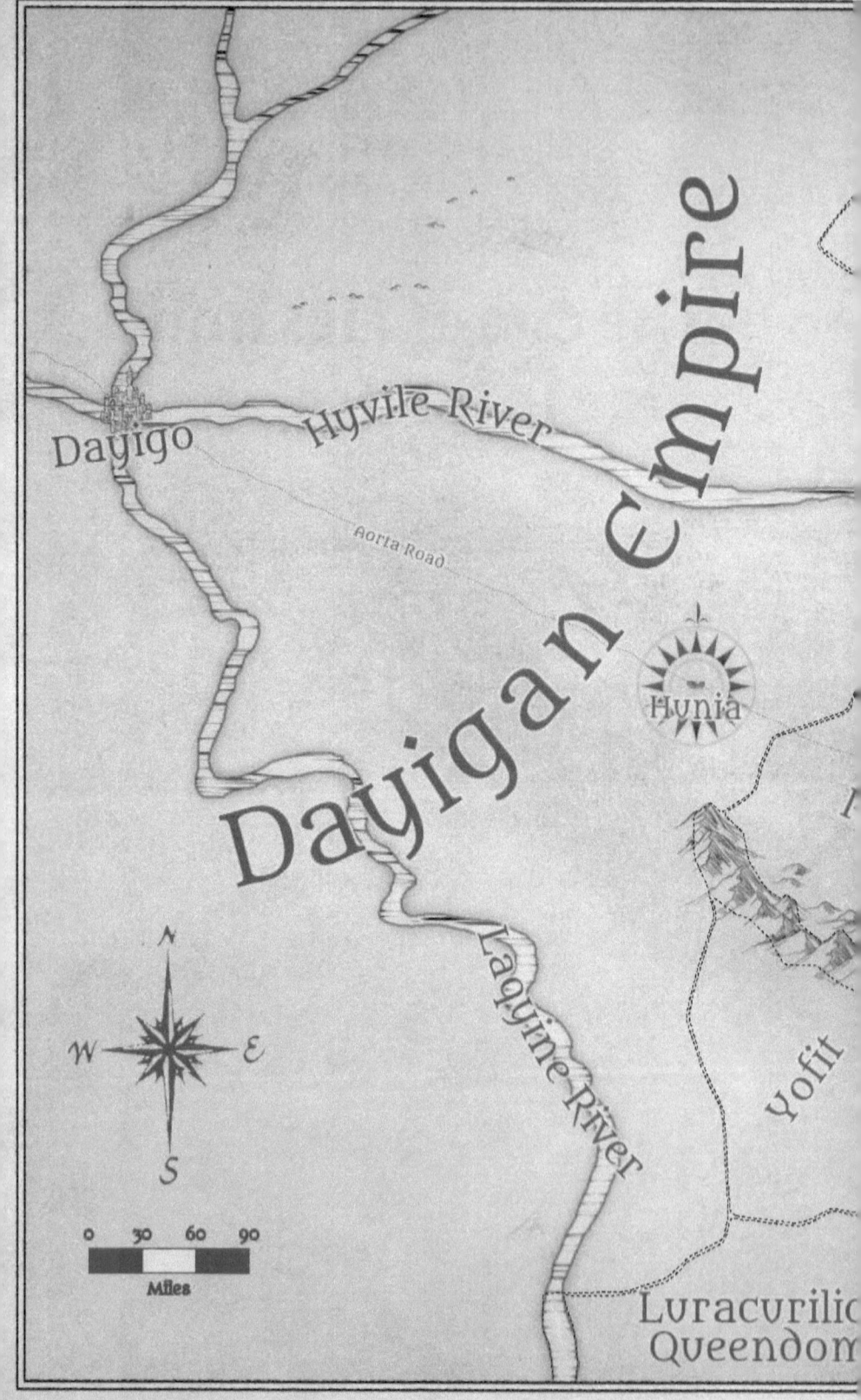

CHAPTER SIXTEEN

Octkiés 15, 812: Four Years Later

Swithun, locked in torment, continued to hold the limp body of the young soldier he had killed.

He thought of all the anger he'd felt when he'd joined the king's army and the path of blood that had brought him to this point. He was certain it was justified, all of it—mostly certain. "We can't return to the plague times," he whispered again.

He kept staring at the boy.

"You monster!" Roslyn screamed as she came from no-where. She ran up and grabbed the boy's fallen sword, holding it clumsily with two hands. "Get away from him."

"It had to be done," Swithun said dejectedly, staring at the lifeless boy within his arms. He looked up at Roslyn. "The boy would've called out to the other guards."

"Other guards? No one else is here, you idiot fiend!"

Swithun turned back to the boy. He laid him on the ground and continued to kneel. "My son would've been his age now." He folded the boy's arms across his chest. "But your people killed him."

"I said get away from him!" Roslyn screamed as she swung the blade around to chop into the side of Swithun's neck.

Blood splattered out, speckling her face and clothes.

She withdrew for another strike, but her amateur aim sent her second blow sideways. The side of the blade struck hard against his head.

The invader fell atop the young soldier as deep red flowed.

She fell backward to the ground and clutched the red-painted sword in her red-painted hands.

Shaking, Roslyn watched the stranger, whose name she'd never known, lie still. A copper band on his upper arm glowed with the green outline of the symbol of the Silthex. *Did it alert the knights of the death?*—she wasn't sure. She couldn't care.

She threw the sword aside and gathered herself. Rolling the villain off Jon, Roslyn kneeled over the young soldier—her love, her intended husband.

"Let me save him, God Karulus," she pleaded to the night sky. *"Please."* She pressed her fist to her forehead. "Let me save him." She moved her hands a few inches above Jon's wounds. "Praise be to Karulus, spirit of truth, and of compassion." She concentrated on her words. "You are our God and our savior. I pray you, let me heal him, my God. I beseech you, give me power over his injuries so he might again live for you."

She could feel the stickiness drying on her skin and wanted to vomit and pass out.

Jon remained still.

"Please!" she screamed. "Let me help him."

She wiped her forehead with the back of her arm—blood smearing blood.

"Please." A whimper.

She let her hands sink to Jon's blood-soaked tabard as she wilted.

Despondent, her eyes stared almost as blankly as his.

"I will save . . ." she whispered. "I will save you, my love. I must save you."

She stood up and grabbed Jon under his arms. She heaved him up from the ground.

—

Clutching her love under his shoulders, Roslyn dragged Jon toward town. The heels of his boots scraped ruts into the woodland floor. Blood sprinkled their path.

Roslyn stumbled, tripped, fell. She dropped Jon. She screamed in bleak frustration.

"Karulus," she wept. "Help me."

Roslyn stood up, grabbed Jon up again, and continued.

—

Down the dark main road of Hunia, lit dimly by the melancholic moons, Roslyn dragged Jon. She could think of nothing but her task—*keep going.* Her muscles ached. *Keep going.* She wanted to give up and fall to the ground. *Keep going.*

Roslyn pulled him up the steps of the church and laid him on the landing.

She kneeled over him and, with teary eyes, gazed at his sweet face—so pale. She brushed his cheek—so cold. She kissed his lifeless lips.

"'Twill be all right, Jon. We're here."

Roslyn reached just under the neck of his layered tabard and tunic and pulled out his necklace up and over his head.

"We're here, Jon," she whispered. "The steps of the church." She stared at the ring on the thin cord necklace—a steel band crowned with a blue rose. Blood coated it.

"I do," she whispered with a sad smile. "Forever and always."

Roslyn placed the ring on her finger, smearing red down her skin.

She looked up toward the blue doors of the church. She banged against the wood.

"Help us!" she screamed and banged harder. "Help us!"

She set her shaking hand on Jon's chest.

"Someone, please," she shuddered.

A blue jay attracted her attention, as it flew down to alight on the other side of Jon.

The bird, still as a statue, stared at Roslyn. Its eyes were black beads, but in a moment, they became pale blue, like the larger moon. They mesmerized her and comforted her.

Suddenly, Roslyn was in a field of tall grass under an afternoon sun. Never had she seen a sky so clear. Jon was gone; the bird was gone; she was alone.

She stood shakily, looking around the marvelous place. The field appeared to stretch infinitely, with nothing but tall grass scattered with blue wildflowers.

The bird returned, descending from azure sky, but when it neared, it faded to pale blue smoke. Twisting, it grew larger, changing form.

Soon, standing where the bird had been, was a man in his early twenties with dark brown skin and short black hair nearly to his scalp. His ears curved up to prominent points, and his eyes were pale blue. At his back, he folded large white wings, like a dove's. His upper body, thin yet muscular, was bare. Below, a belt of gold held a long skirt of shimmering blue silk.

Afraid, Roslyn hurried to hide within the tall grass. She crouched lower as the otherworldly man walked leisurely toward her. She didn't know why she hid. She knew he'd seen her. But she felt like an unruly child before this demigod.

"Prithee, fear not, O virtuous Roslyn." His words were mighty, yet soothing in tone. "For, with an earnest heart, thou didst cry out unto His Divine Infinity, Karulus, God of the Sapphire Ib. And he hath seen favor with thee. Thus, hither was I dispatched. Behold, I am Q'kah Isaiah, messenger of Karulus."

She stood cautiously, yet with her head bowed and eyes averted. She clasped her hands at her breast. "Have you come to heal Jon?" she whispered. "We were to be married and have children and a shop. We were to have a . . ." She sniffed. "A lovely, lovely life."

He reached out his hand and softly touched her cheek, turning her to view his beautiful face.

"Alas, no," he said, "for already his spirit hath departed."

Roslyn inhaled sharply as she set her hand to the base of her throat. She exhaled a stammered breath as she nodded stiffly. "To Laqyigo?" She crossed her arms, rubbing them.

"At present, Xanorael guideth thy love, Jon, to the Hall of Truth. There, the Lavender Lady, Ashatra, will determine where his life hath led him. Perhaps to Laqyigo, in the Plane of Light. Perhaps to Zasenloniartes, at the core of the world."

Roslyn gasped. "Please, not za. He's a good Karulent man. He wasn't perfect, but . . ." She started crying, unable to speak further.

Isaiah gently brushed his thumb beneath her eyes to wipe away her tears. "Be thou calm. I assure thee, Zasenloniartes— what thy people called 'za'—is not what thou doth think. It is a place of reform and reflection, where souls wait before they continue their journey."

"Continue their journey?" She shook her head. "I don't understand."

"There are mysteries unknown to the multitudes. Yet thou wilt know, in time. Hark, wisdom shall be thine, O Roslyn. For now, worry not of thy love, for he is in the hands of the

Gods. Forsooth, there is a dark path as well, reserved for the rare few who are truly vile and irredeemable, but I know, without doubt, this is not Jon's path. Yet, as I said, it is the Lavender Lady's place to judge."

Roslyn sniffed. "May she be merciful and kind." Her voice cracked. "And just."

"Praise Ashatra," Isaiah said solemnly, raising his hands to the heavens. "She is truth and justice." He looked at Roslyn. "Yet in this bleak hour, we stand upon the eve of lies and *injustice*. Lo, a great war sets on the horizon. And generations to come shall be bloodstained and haggard. Prithee, wherefore hast thou come hither?"

She looked at him for a confused moment. "Why have I come here? I just . . . *became* here suddenly."

"Wherefore art thou here, Roslyn?"

"I . . ." She paused, thinking. "I come before our God Karulus because . . . I want to help people. I want to cure the sick and the injured. I want to never standby helplessly again as I watch a loved one die."

Isaiah nodded. "Thus, His Divine Infinity, God Karulus, calls thee to his service."

She looked down at the tall grass swaying in the gentle wind. She whispered, "You mean, he wishes me to be an Azerent?"

"The decision is thine. To serve is to choose a road of hardship and forsake thy previous life. To become an Azerent Healer is to surround thyself in endless study and sickness."

She wanted to run away, flee back to her life and wrap it around her like a familiar blanket. She wanted to never think about these last days again.

But she knew she could not. That life was gone.

"I . . ." She looked at the Q'kah, a messenger of the Gods standing before her as real as any person she had ever seen. "I don't know. I don't—'Tis all too much, all of this."

She lifted her hands as if to shield herself as she backed away.

Isaiah folded his hands before his chest. "When thou art ready, thou knowest where to seek answers."

———

Roslyn awoke under the night sky, on the steps of the church. Her head was on Jon's chest. The usual muffled beat was absent. The warmth, absent.

The blue doors opened.

Father Hanugfrie gasped. "Karulus help us." He turned and called back into the church, "Cyneburga, come quickly. Bring others."

Hanugfrie hurried to Roslyn and stood her up. She resisted. She clung to her love, but she felt weak, hollow. She let go.

Hanugfrie walked her away, down the stairs to the street.

Roslyn glanced back a moment to see Hanugfrie's wife, with another nun and a monk. They lifted Jon and carried him into the church.

Hanugfrie pulled Roslyn close, and she set her head on his shoulder.

She did not cry. She wanted to. The sorrow twisted around her insides as it strangled her heart.

"He is gone." Roslyn said finally, calmly.

There was a strange calm throughout her, a shaky, ill calm, a calm not unlike a still pond able to be undone by the mere casting of a pebble, but a calm. She stood on her own.

"What happened, child?" Hanugfrie gently asked.

She shook her head. "A man," she whispered. "A man wanted to kill you. We stopped him. And the messenger of God Karulus came to me."

"Q'kah I?"

"He called himself Isaiah."

"*He?*" Hanugfrie gave a perplexed smirk. "Well, that *is* quite a change."

"He wants me to be an Azerent."

He nodded. "As his will, so may it be. I will contact the Order."

"I haven't said yes, not yet. Will they even allow me to join?" she asked, her words hollow. "I am a woman."

"I may be old, Roslyn, but I had noticed."

Roslyn acknowledged his attempt at humor with a nod, but gave no smile.

Hanugfrie continued. "The Order of Azerents is not the Karulent Church. We are not concerned with your physical body, but with your soul, which is both man and woman combined, as it is in everyone. 'Tis a part of the deeper mysteries we withhold from common knowledge so as to not confuse the laity. If God Karulus, via his messenger, says you have the spiritual force to be an Azerent, it must be so."

"Pneuma," she whispered, still in shock, staring at no point in particular.

"Yes." He nodded.

"Good. Because I will not watch another person die."

"Then you will join us?"

Drums. Perhaps Roslyn had heard them somewhat before, but now they crept into the range of proper hearing.

The drums were coming closer.

"Do you hear it?" Roslyn asked.

"Hear what, child?"

Roslyn walked toward the road, looking in the sound's direction.

CHAPTER SEVENTEEN

Trumpets joined the rapping of the drums as ten Silthex knights—their white surcoats emblazoned with green Silthex Septenars on their chests—rode their horses up the main road of Hunia. Behind them, about a hundred men in black tabards—these bearing the same green symbol on their chests—marched, many with torches in hand. More followed, twice as many Dayigan soldiers in red, marching to the rhythm of the drums.

Roslyn was not alone in wanting to see the occurrence, and others hurried outside to join the growing number of townspeople edging the road. Excitement filled the bystanders as they watched the parade. Some lifted their children on their shoulders to better see.

Because Hunia was set on a major thoroughfare, such a sight was not out of place. The people would assume the soldiers were passing by. Tonight, the soldiers would surely fill the inn. Tomorrow, the shops. The people of Hunia had no reason to react any differently than they now did—with elation at the visitors.

Roslyn knew better. At least she thought she did. She wasn't sure. Fear wrenched within the pit of her stomach.

Father Hanugfrie stood beside her and whispered, "We must go inside the church now, child."

Staring at the formation, she shook her head. "I'll be fine, Father. They can do nothing with so many people around."

The formation stopped about fifty feet away, just before the inn. A Silthex knight dismounted and stepped forward toward the pool centered in the street.

"I've seen him before," Roslyn whispered to herself. He'd been the young man dressed as a peasant, though clean, with neatly trimmed blond hair. He still had the same expensive horse. Right after Jon proposed, he'd asked Jon for directions.

Roslyn remembered how happy Jon had been that day and how happy she'd been to have him return home. She gazed at the bloody ring on her finger. It was already a distant world.

The knight spoke up, saying, "People of Hunia, a grave act has occurred on your soil. A murder."

The people gasped and began astounded whispers.

"The unfortunate victim," the knight resumed, "was an honored Dayigan sergeant who fought bravely against the wicked Tridulan Empire in the conflicts to the east. He risked his life, day after bitter day, to assure the safety and protection of all of you in this town and all lands across our Empire. And yet, whilst on a peaceful holiday to recuperate, he was struck down dead in this ungrateful town."

Jon's lieutenant, with three of the local militia, approached the knight. "Greetings, sir knight. I am the leader of the local garrison. Me and my men pledge ourselves to your investigation. We will find the man responsible, I assure you."

The knight paused, looking the lieutenant up and down. "You are a Hunian?"

"I am, sir. Yes."

The knight punched the lieutenant in the face.

The militiamen drew their weapons and stepped forward.

"Stand down!" the lieutenant, hunched over and cradling his face, commanded.

"If you are a Hunian," the knight shouted to the crowd, "you, too, are guilty. For *all in this infernal town* have been convicted as complicit in the murder of a great hero."

The chatter of those lining the streets turned to anger and dread.

Roslyn began forward, but Hanugfrie grabbed her arm.

"I must go to them," she said. "If I tell them what happened—"

Hanugfrie continued to hold her. "They do not care what happened. Do you think they gathered all those men so quickly?"

"I've mistrusted the army, true, but they won't attack us without cause," she maintained. "They are charged to protect us. We are Dayigans."

"Not as far as they are concerned."

The knight shouted, "In the name of God Déagar, I sentence the entire town of Hunia—*to execution.*"

"No." Roslyn looked back toward the knights. "Unthinkable. They wouldn't possibly . . ."

Hanugfrie tried to pull her away.

"Silthex, attack!"

Hundreds of swords unsheathed as the formation shouted as one. They spread out like a fire unleashed, attacking all who had gathered. They stormed into the shops and homes. Swords ran through the men and women. The soldiers snatched up the children, capturing them.

Roslyn struggled, but Hanugfrie held her tighter.

"I have to talk to them," she pleaded. "Let me go! I can stop this."

"You can't, child. Listen to me. You cannot do anything at all. They will not listen."

"How can I be the woman you want me to be, that God Karulus has called me to be, if I run from this?"

Hanugfrie released her. He looked into her eyes and nodded. "You are braver than your own good, child."

"Perhaps," she said. "But you will see, Father. I can set this right."

Hanugfrie touched his hand on the side of Roslyn's head. "Sleep," he whispered. His eyes flashed blue.

Roslyn felt her body grow heavy with a throbbing numbness. Her eyes closed. The shouts of the soldiers and the screams of the town echoed away. She felt Hanugfrie catch her.

—

Roslyn heard boiling liquids before she opened her eyes. Alarmed, thinking she'd left a pot on a fire, she sprung up but found herself in a place she didn't recognize.

The cot on which she sat was but taut leather between two poles on a stand. The room was windowless, with rough stone walls. The edges were crammed with tables and shelves. She marveled at the collection of strange, bulbous glassware and the strange liquids of all colors that filled them. Some of the liquids glowed. Others bubbled over flames.

She could not help but be envious of the vast assortment of herbs hanging upside down from a rack above. Some herbs—despite her expertise on the subject—were unknown to her. And filling the shelves, there were more in labeled blue glass jars of various sizes. There were books too, about two dozen, and old rolled-up pages next to them.

Amazed, Roslyn tried to stand, but was taken dizzy. With one hand to her forehead, she thrust her other down on the cot to keep her balance.

Mother Cyneburga, Father Hanugfrie's wife, entered from a low door framed in thick beams of grayed wood. The plump woman in her mid-forties wore a long, pale gray habit, and a sky blue wimple covered her hair.

"By Karulus," Cyneburga said, "I leave for five seconds." She hurried to Roslyn and set her hands on her back and shoulder. "'Twill be a minute before you can stand, dear."

"Where's Jon?"

"Oh." Cyneburga placed her hand on the breast of her gray habit. "You don't remember, dear?"

"That is to say, where is his . . ."

"Upstairs, dear. We were preparing him when the soldiers came."

"Upstairs?"

"We are in the church's cellar, Rose."

"But the church doesn't have a cellar." Roslyn sighed. "Well, I suppose it must have. I need to see him."

"I'm afraid that's impossible, dear. The entire town is overrun with knights and soldiers. They're searching everywhere."

"Then I must help the townspeople. This is *my* fault."

"No." Cyneburga shook her head. "No, 'tis not your fault. Not at all. This has been a long time coming. Han said he saw trouble in the stars, but we never imagined this."

"Where is he?" Roslyn asked.

"Just there, dear." She pointed behind Roslyn.

Roslyn turned on the cot to see Father Hanugfrie sitting cross-legged on a blue velvet cushion. Seven glowing blue crystals circled him. Above him, on the wall, hung a large square of velvet showing a large, white, five-pointed star with a five-petaled flower—periwinkle in color—nearly filling the star's interior. In the center of the flower was a pentagon holding an eye with a blue pupil. Roslyn recognized this as the symbol of the Azerents.

"Meditating?" Roslyn asked.

"More than that," Cyneburga said. "He's left his body. He's up there now." She pointed.

Roslyn's eyes followed Cyneburga's finger to the ceiling. "Laqyigo?"

"The town, dear. We *are* underground, recall. He should return shortly with information."

"Forgive me, of course. My brain is still a bit foggy. But we are just to wait here?"

"Han has guided as many townspeople as he could to the hidden entrance to the cellar. They're just beyond that door." Cyneburga motioned to the door through which she'd come. "Some are injured. Nothing major, but I'm sure they'd appreciate the help of a wonderful healer."

"I would agree, Mother Cyneburga, but there is a greater need above ground. And if Father Hanugfrie is not here—"

"I'm here. I'm here." Hanugfrie stood up. He set his hand to his head as he staggered. "What is the difficulty, child?"

"I must go help the people of our town."

"Cyne dear," Hanugfrie said, "I've led a few more people to the cellar entrance. Pray you, would you go let them in?"

Cyneburga looked at Roslyn and then at her husband. Concern marked her face. Nevertheless, she nodded and left through the door.

"What is happening in the town?" Roslyn asked.

"They're rounding up everyone," he said solemnly, "and have killed a lot in the process. They're locking the children in cages. I'm not sure why. 'Tis horrible, truly. I've only managed to rescue the twenty in the adjoining room."

"That leaves hundreds above ground," Roslyn said. "Let me go save the children, at least. Surely you have some magic we can use against the Silthex."

"I'm not some Dark Light battle-caster, Roslyn." It wasn't much of an outburst, but Roslyn had never heard him say a cross word and wasn't sure how to react.

"Forgive me," he said. "It is all extremely frustrating. Azerents are about gaining knowledge, understanding the universe, revealing the nature of the Gods, and knowing ourselves. Truth be told, the healers, more so than us, are the ones who use practical magic. Currently, the primary focus of my practical research has been producing a more productive strand of wheat." He cradled his forehead in his hand.

Roslyn stared at him for a moment, absorbing his words with sadness.

"Father," she maintained, "I *will* go save the children. You have been like a father to me and a mentor, but in truth, you have no authority to make me stay here."

He nodded. "You have always been willful, Roslyn. Just like your father." He paused, glancing to the side. "And kind like him, too. I will help you."

"My thanks, Father."

He looked toward a cupboard and paused. "I believe I do have a potion or two that might be beneficial."

R oslyn cracked open the main doors of the church as narrowly as possible. She squeezed out into the night. Darting to a crouch, she set her hand on the leather satchel at her waist and crept down the stairs. She barely breathed. Her heart pounded. Roslyn scanned the area to see sporadic fires throughout the town. No soldiers. Yet, she knew better than to be relieved. They were somewhere. Close. She knew it.

Hanugfrie was at the base of the steps. Invisible to all but Roslyn, he stood normally in the open, a stark contrast to her cower. He appeared monochromatic in shades of translucent blue, with his actual body back in the cellar.

"This way, child," he said, with no need to whisper.

Roslyn followed him slowly, while looking all around for anyone who might attack her. She assumed the soldiers had no reason to hide. Presumably, there was no Silthex ducked under a bush. But she simultaneously knew that such an assumption, if wrong, could get her run through by a sword.

She spotted someone, not a soldier. The someone was lying out on the side of the street. She'd already passed a few bodies, but she saw some minor movement in this one.

He rocked ever so slightly in pain as he clutched his leg.

She crept toward him.

"Roslyn," Hanugfrie called, "*this* way."

She ignored the priest.

"I will help you," Roslyn said to the injured man.

He looked about forty and appeared weak but responsive. Roslyn knew him as a serf on the estate, who maintained a seasonal vegetable stall in town.

"Can you describe your injury?" she asked.

"'Tis me leg. Took a sword in it. Fucking Silthex—excuse me language, miss. He left me for dead, the bastard."

"Roslyn," Hanugfrie called, "someone is coming."

"How far out?" she whispered back.

"You have a little time, but not much."

"Talking to yourself?" the injured man asked.

"'Tis complicated," Roslyn said. "Can you walk?"

"Tried. I go all dizzy and fall."

Roslyn quickly checked him for other injuries. "You've lost a lot of blood."

"*Roslyn*," Hanugfrie shouted, "you have to move now. Don't respond. He'll hear. Just go."

Roslyn looked back to see a Silthex in a black tabard meandering toward her.

The soldier stabbed a corpse, no doubt checking for life.

On her opposite side, Roslyn could see a grouping of three large barrels right outside a crockery shop.

"Keep pressure on your wound," Roslyn whispered. "We must go."

The injured man nodded.

The soldier had stopped and looked away as he kicked, side to side, a tin cup on the road. It clanked noisily against the cobbles, piercing the silence.

Roslyn pulled the injured man up, bearing most of his weight as they scurried toward the barrels.

"You there!" the soldier shouted.

Roslyn threw the man behind the barrels and jumped behind. She froze.

"Stay there!" Hanugfrie called out. "I don't think he quite saw you."

Roslyn pressed herself down as small as she could as she bit into the side of her finger, trying not to breathe.

Boots slapped the cobbled road as the soldier neared. They slowed, searching.

Roslyn could hear Hanugfrie: "Praise be to Karulus, spirit of truth, and of compassion. You are our God and our savior. Heal our hearts, although we are wicked, and by your light, guide us safely to Laqyigo. As thy will, may it be."

The soldier's steps drew closer.

Grabbing up a pebble, Roslyn eyed the broken door to the crockery shop. She wasn't sure how far away the soldier was. She ached to look around the barrels and sneak a glance, but every part of her mind screamed how stupid she'd be to take that chance.

Taking a slow, silent breath, Roslyn threw the pebble at the shop door.

The soldier ran again, passing but a yard from Roslyn as he slammed open the shop and charged in.

Roslyn patted the shoulder of the injured man—to comfort him or comfort herself, she wasn't sure.

A loud crash and an ensemble of shatters clattered inside, as if the soldier had overturned a table of pottery. Roslyn nearly shrieked; she nearly jumped; she seized her entire body to avoid either.

More sounds: a sort of sliding and then more shattering. Footsteps crackled on broken shards. Next came the sound of kicking or punching of wood. More pottery shattered.

More boots pounded on the street. Another soldier ran toward Roslyn. He passed her close enough to share a breeze and hurried straight into the shop.

"Quit mucking about in here and get back in the road."

"I saw someone run in here."

"There's no one here, look. Get back to your post."

"There!" a soldier shouted.

"Stop in the name of His Holiness, Patriarch Krasil."

A man screamed, followed by repeated calls of *no* and *please*.

Eyes watering, Roslyn clamped her hand over her mouth as she listened helplessly to the scuffle.

"Take him to the inn," a soldier commanded.

Past the side of a barrel, Roslyn saw two soldiers drag the struggling potter out of the shop. It was a momentary glance before they were but receding footsteps.

Roslyn lowered her hand from her mouth. "Please forgive me," she cried, barely audibly. "I didn't know you were there." Her breaths were quick, panicked.

She wiped her eyes and returned to the injured farmer.

The injury was a deep gash across his outer mid-thigh.

Roslyn could hear the potter screaming as her shaking hands grabbed a knife from her belt. She cut off the trouser leg at a point just above the wound.

Roslyn opened the flap of the leather satchel strapped over her shoulder. The inner lining displayed two rows of clear glass orbs, each with a corked neck at the top. They held various colored liquids.

She took a flask of clear liquid, uncorked it, and poured some on the wound.

The man winced in pain.

Normally, Roslyn would have warned beforehand. Instead, she stared at nothing in particular.

The soldiers only entered the shop because I led them there, she thought, as she ripped up the trouser leg with her knife.

Roslyn wadded a long section of cloth and set it firmly on the wound. She used other strips of cloth to bandage the area.

Afterward, she just stared.

Hanugfrie stood beside the barrels. "The soldiers are gone, but more are coming. We must return to the church."

Roslyn looked up at him but said nothing.

"Are you all right, child?"

She shook her head.

"We'll go back to the church, all right?"

"No," Roslyn whispered. "We go on. To the children."

She looked back at the farmer. She thought she should say something comforting, but no words came. She crept away.

CHAPTER NINETEEN

Ducked behind a wooden handcart filled with straw, Roslyn watched the inn, at a distance up the road. Many Silthex had returned. They shoved struggling Hunian men and women through the inn's front door.

In a flash of blue, Father Hanugfrie appeared at Roslyn's side.

"What are they doing?" she whispered.

"They have collected as many people as they could find from the town and surrounding farms. I'd say there are over eight hundred people in there now. The soldiers nailed all the shutters and doors closed, save for that one in the front."

"But why?"

Hanugfrie sighed. "Honestly, I'm not quite sure. I moved around the soldiers and listened for details, but they mostly spoke of unrelated things. Evidently, a good many of the soldiers are hungry and vexed that their unit commander hasn't given them time to eat since noon."

"Those monsters," Roslyn said. "Is that all they can think of whilst they do *this*?"

"If I had to guess," Hanugfrie resumed, "I'd say they'll hold our people overnight in the inn. Tomorrow, there will be an elaborate trial—a proper show of power, you know. Afterwards, I expect the town will have a hefty fine levied against it."

"I'll go there next," Roslyn said. "And get them out?"

"You will not," Hanugfrie said firmly. "I checked inside. The people are frightened, but calming. The tavern has made stew and is rationing it out free of charge. I do not foresee any reason for the Silthex to enact any more bloodshed."

"They had no reason before," Roslyn said, watching the soldiers shove more people through the entrance.

"You must understand. It is political, Roslyn. A quarter of the Empire is Karulent. They will be able to rationalize away what they've done thus far. 'Twill anger and subdue our people, yes. But if news spread that they attacked an inn full of compliant Karulents, it could start a civil war. And neither the king nor the Church of Déagar wants that."

Roslyn nodded, yet stared, no less fearful for the people in the inn. She wrung her fingers together, bending and twisting them around one another. Finally, she sighed. "To the children, then."

"Yes. I searched the area," Hanugfrie said, "'tis clear of soldiers. But you must hurry."

Roslyn crawled to the back of the handcart.

From her new position, she could see a large cage barred in squares of flat, riveted iron. It was set atop a hefty wagon with fittings for horses. About two hundred girls, ranging in age from babies to fifteen, were crammed inside.

"How many cages are there in total?" Roslyn whispered to Hanugfrie.

"Five, spaced throughout the area. Divided boys and girls."

Roslyn hurried to the door.

She recognized most of the captives. Some of the older girls were her friends. A few whispered her name.

"Pray you, stay quiet," Roslyn said. "I will free you."

Roslyn opened the flap on her satchel.

"That one," Hanugfrie pointed. "'Twill flash oxidize the iron. That is, rust it. Extensively."

Roslyn set her hand on a flask of gray, milky liquid.

"*Not that one*," Hanugfrie blurted. "That is essence of basilisk. 'Twill stun the girls still as stone. You want the light blue one."

Roslyn grabbed the correct flask and held it up, ready to throw. "Stand back as far as you can," she said to the girls.

They pushed themselves back away from the door. Not far, but as much as they could manage.

Roslyn took a step back.

"The potion has an evaporant added," Hanugfrie explained. "It will instantly transmute it into gas with contact with air. I will need to contain the gas; otherwise, 'twill disperse, hitting everyone and everything. When I say three. *One*."

Roslyn pulled back her arm.

"*Two. Three.*"

Roslyn threw the flask at the lock.

The glass shattered, and the liquid vaporized.

Hanugfrie cast out his hands and pushed slowly inward, as if contracting an unseen sphere.

The blue mist contracted, too, flowing around the lock and the surrounding bars. The metal rusted and turned brittle.

After a short time, the mist faded.

Without waiting, Roslyn grabbed the door and began pulling as hard as she could. Some girls pushed from the inside.

The door would not open.

"Someone is coming," Hanugfrie said.

Roslyn continued to pull. "If he sees the rusted lock, he'll call for others and we'll lose our chance." She pulled harder. "Distract him," she strained.

The lock cracked.

Roslyn could see the soldier. He wore a white surcoat—a knight. More than that, she realized he was the young captain of the unit.

She pulled harder. A metallic thud sounded. The lock broke, and Roslyn stumbled back, gripping the door as it swung open.

Regaining her balance, Roslyn rushed to help the girls down.

Hanugfrie appeared behind the commander. With a wave of his hand, the priest blew sand up from the road to hit the back of the knight's neck.

Frantically, Roslyn helped girl after girl out of the cage while working as quietly as possible. "You must get out of town and run. Run as far away as you can."

The knight turned in response to the sand. More sand hit his neck. Again, he turned.

The ridiculousness of it made Roslyn want to vomit. *Is this what the Empire's afraid of?*

The knight looked toward Hanugfrie, almost seeming to see him. More sand hit him, but he continued to look toward the invisible priest.

Hanugfrie moved to the right, but the commander turned to face the general direction. He squinted his eyes, straining to see.

The commander lunged forward and thrust his hand up, grabbing Hanugfrie by the neck. The priest went limp, his monochromatic image blurred. He hung like a rag-doll.

"No," Roslyn gasped. She handed a baby to a teenager a few years younger than herself. "Run. Get the other children to safety."

The commander stabbed his other hand at Hanugfrie's side. He thrust again and again, as if trying to grab something he could not see.

Finally, he grabbed it: a cord, which became visible as he clutched it. It led from Hanugfrie's navel and continued to materialize along its length, snaking through the air up the road.

"Let's see where you are hiding," the captain said, as more of the cord appeared.

Roslyn fumbled through her satchel and grabbed the flask of milky gray liquid. She dashed toward the commander.

He watched the cord as it passed the inn. It wouldn't be much longer until it pointed to the church with all those hidden in the cellar.

Roslyn threw the flask at the cobbles at the commander's feet.

It shattered, and the potion vaporized as gray mist.

"No," Hanugfrie choked. "I can't contain it."

It was too late; the cloud grew larger, enveloping the commander and Roslyn as well.

She could feel her skin grow increasingly tighter all over her body. She could feel her muscles lock in place until she couldn't move an inch, despite her desperate efforts.

The mist cleared.

Roslyn's skin grayed, as did the fabric of her dress and her hair, all except her face—now, like a flesh-colored mask on a sculpture. She saw the same effect on the captain.

Hanugfrie vanished.

"That was foolish," the captain said. He faced away, frozen with his hand held up as if still grasping Hanugfrie's throat. "We would have put those children in a church-run orphanage. They would have learnt to fear God Déagar."

"You've already done enough to teach them to fear Déagar," Roslyn said. "I would rather they learn the love of God Karulus."

"You sound young," he said. "Another little girl poisoned by a twisted church."

Two other Silthex knights ran up to their commander.

"Captain Rothgar," one said. "Are you all right?"

"Don't be daft, man. Release me."

The knight set his hand on Rothgar's chest. "In the name of God Déagar, he who is Greatest of All, I cleanse you of magic."

The gray faded from Rothgar's skin and clothes, and his arm lowered to his side.

"Did you see where the cord of light ended?" Rothgar demanded.

"It was nearing the inn, sir. Surely it must have been headed there."

Rothgar looked toward the inn and then looked past it. "You searched the church?" he asked.

"Yes, sir. More thoroughly than anywhere else, sir. If the priest is alive, he must be in the inn."

Rothgar looked for a moment more. He then turned to Roslyn and approached.

"You *are* a little girl, aren't you?" He began circling her, looking her up and down.

Roslyn tried to move, but she could not so much as feel her own body. Only her eyes darted, straining to see the commander. Inside, she trembled, fearing what he might do.

Rothgar continued, saying, "No, you are definitely a woman. An attractive woman. But a fool."

He turned to his men. "Bring her."

The two knights toppled her stiff body and lifted her by her shoulders and ankles.

Roslyn could not even struggle—not in the slightest. They carried her like a statue toward the inn.

"Put her down there," Rothgar commanded.

The knights lifted her slightly higher, and she heard splashing under their feet.

They set Roslyn upright, centered in the wishing pool in front of the inn.

"Does she not make a lovely statue?" Rothgar joked loudly. "Just what the fountain needed."

Laughter broke out. Roslyn couldn't tell how many men were around her, but there were many voices at once.

Rothgar stepped over the pool's wall and splashed toward her.

"I know you cannot move your head," Rothgar said, "but if you turn your eyes downwards, you can see we've stacked lard-coated straw along the walls of the inn." He grinned. "You, little girl, will soon have the *honor* of bearing witness to the wrath of our fire God."

He began to move away.

"Wait!" Roslyn called. "You have no reason to do this. *I* killed the soldier. Just me, all alone. No one helped me or conspired or even knew."

Rothgar stopped. He approached Roslyn again, drawing so close that his nose nearly touched hers.

"You?" he asked. "You killed an honored sergeant of the Dayigan Army?"

"I vow by the staff of God Karulus, I alone am guilty of his death. Take my life if you need vengeance, but I pray you, free those in the inn."

Rothgar scoffed. Then he chuckled. "Those in the inn are guilty, too. *All* Karulents are guilty of betraying the Light. The True Light is the only way; all others will perish."

He walked away.

"Please!" Roslyn shouted. "Those people *are* True Light. Déagar and Karulus are brothers."

"Archers!" Rothgar commanded. "*Ready, arms.*"

Roslyn darted her eyes, trying to see what was happening. No soldiers were in her sight.

"*Take, aim.*"

"Get out of the inn!" Roslyn screamed. "Get out now!"

"*Loose.*"

A barrage of flaming arrows shot at the inn, striking the straw stacked at the base of the walls and striking spots throughout the thatched roof. The flames spread quickly, snaking across the inn.

Roslyn began screaming. She heard the people inside screaming too and banging to get out. She fought against the enchantment that bound her, willing with all her might to move. Nothing. She could only scream and watch.

"Silthex," Rothgar commanded, "we're finished here. *Move out.*"

Unable to turn away, Roslyn just kept watching as she listened to the nightmarish sounds of hundreds of men and women burning to death. She felt tears stream down her face. The inferno grew larger, enveloping the entire building.

The heat enveloped her, slapping her face with continuous fury.

The beating on the walls from inside the inn grew louder, more panicked, more desperate. Cracks protruded from the thick wooden siding—birthing desperate, reaching fingers—but none were anywhere wide enough for escape.

Smoke, billowing out toward Roslyn, surrounded her, burning her eyes as she could see nothing but massive red and orange arms of violent heat dancing within the milky haze.

Roslyn choked, coughing deep, painful hacks from the aching depths of her lungs.

Finally, she saw a bloody fist punch its way through the siding. The blackened arm reached futilely to freedom yet grew limp. Fire surrounded the area, swallowing it up.

After what seemed like an eternity of torture; after watching the inn flame up, blacken, and collapse in on itself; after hearing the twisted choir of the agonized dying fade to silence; the spell wore off. Roslyn was able to move.

She collapsed to her hands and knees in the black water and stared at the scorched ruins. She'd seen no one escape. Eight hundred people, Hanugfrie had said, nearly all of the town, massacred.

The smell lingered, the smell of burning wood and burning flesh. It had permeated her skin, hair, and clothes—inescapable.

Horrified and shaking, Roslyn crawled out of the filthy pool and neared the ashes.

She could see some of the people, contorted and exposed, within the thick burnt beams and rubble. Their blackened skin had cracked open to the blackened bones. Some had huddled together in their demise. Roslyn knew she knew them all, but there was not enough left to determine identities.

She wanted to scream, but had no voice left.

Instead, she just stared.

Trembling.

The Veiled River

Karulent Alliance
Dayigan Empire
Ruins of Vilana
Dayigan
N
W
E
S
0 30 60 90
Miles
Port Lytel
Mount Triumph
Kingdom of Syklisier

CHAPTER TWENTY

Efflorel 6, 826: Fourteen Years Later

She kept walking, continuing unhurriedly down the thin dirt road through the dark woodlands. Her legs ached from the extensive journey, yet she could not risk a carriage driver knowing her destination. Nocturnal insects provided the only sound she'd heard in hours. A hooded cloak, long and forest green, hid all that she was. The constant need to hide had become a crucial necessity.

For over a decade, the Church of Déagar had stood as the one and only legal church within the Dayigan Empire. The worship of God Karulus, her God and savior, was punishable by death.

Nevertheless, Roslyn would not bow.

And so it came to be that, on this cool early spring night of her thirty-second year, she arrived in the shadowy yard of a moonlit cabin.

She knocked five times on the simple wooden door and waited five seconds. She knocked twice more.

A square panel at eye level opened within the door, and a young man peered out. "Bit late, innit, miss? Who may I ask is calling?"

She drew back her hood, showing a thin face with delicate features. Sadness lingered in the blue of her eyes and a frown crossed her lips. Her hair, dirty blond in both color and state, hung limp, retreating into her cloak.

"My name is Roslyn." Even as she talked to him, she did not meet his gaze. Instead, she kept her eyes, as well as her head, lowered, as was proper. "I've come to sail the Veiled River. Will you allow me passage?"

"Sorry, miss. If such a river did exist, 'twould be unsafe to travel." He began to close the panel.

"But yet, I have my ticket here." She removed a folded note from a purse on her belt and held it to the hole.

The man pulled in the page and closed the panel door, leaving her in dark silence.

Roslyn waited. As nervous as she was, she remained calm. In the unlikely event that she was being watched, the observer should see nothing but an unsuspicious woman at an unsuspicious door. Luckily—or sadly—she'd had much practice in this sort of thing.

Finally, the door opened and the same young man showed her in. "Welcome to Port Lytel, miss. Lord Karhelm will see you."

By flickering candlelight, he led Roslyn down a slight, tight hall.

"In here, miss." He opened a final door but did not enter with her.

This room was better lit. A fireplace cast a glow supplemented by a tin candelabra on a simple table. Its tallow candles streamed thick lines of black smoke.

A tall, well-built man in his mid-thirties stood in the center of the room.

Even as Roslyn entered, his face gave no sign of salutation.

"I was told you wished to see me, my lord," she said, keeping her head at a downward tilt.

"You are the Azerent Mage sent by Father Hanugfrie."

"Azerent Master *Healer*, my lord. I primarily perform the magic of my specialty and have taken a vow to do no harm. But I trained under Father Hanugfrie for three years and studied at Azerent College for five. Afterwards, I served God

Karulus as a healer in multiple ports, during which time I received accolades for skill and merit from both the Order of Azerents and the Karulent Church. Also, I received multiple awards from the Veiled River Commission for bravery as a healer and as an evacuation coordinator, both under life-threatening conditions. I am pleased to join your port, and I know I will be an asset to your team."

"Quite a mouthful." He paused without expression and looked her up and down. "At least your appearance is adequate," he said. "They warned me you'd be a woman. You should know, I find it obscene. A woman casting magic."

"The Déagrians would say the same of *all* who practice magic."

He crossed his arms. "I assume that was meant to be humorous. It wasn't."

"Actually, I meant it to be accurate, which it was."

"Regardless," he said, "you are here. Let us hope God Karulus keeps you strong, for in this desperate time, we have no other choice than to utilize your gifts."

"My thanks, my lord, for allowing me to serve our God."

"I prefer that you call me *Lieutenant*."

"An army rank? Are you a soldier?"

"Once, at twenty, I was an honored Dayigan soldier with a royal commission and on my way to commanding thousands. But in an hour, I became a despised criminal. I continue to use the rank to remember that the world can change in a moment. You'd do well to remember the same."

"Lessons I've learnt quite well on my own, Lieutenant."

"Why is your cloak green?"

"It is the color of the Silthex, Lieutenant. 'Tis become quite fashionable for many Dayigans to wear it."

"I am aware of that. Why do *you* wear it?"

"A disguise, Lieutenant. Whilst I traveled."

"Surely, there must be some other colors than Karulent blue, Silthex green, and Déagrian red. Brown, perhaps. No one's ever developed any strong opinions about brown."

"Yes, Lieutenant."

"Come. I will show you Port Lytel." He neared the same door through which she'd come. He set his hand on the latch and paused, closing his eyes for a moment. "Lytel," he whispered, and the latch shimmered around his hand. Before Roslyn could question, the moment ended, and he opened the door. "After you."

Roslyn walked toward the open door to see that it led to a passage carved through stone.

She looked back at him. "Are we now underground, Lieutenant?"

"We are in the same place as we were before. Only the door has changed." He lifted the candelabra, shedding light on the entrance.

Roslyn neared and marveled at the doorframe—this butted up against another wooden doorframe leading into the rocky tunnel.

"The spatial compression is amazing," she said. "It is Gellic, yes?"

"'Tis Azerent, actually, combined with divine. We were able to commandeer one of the Dayigan golden mirrors. Our former Azerent Mage managed to break it down into materials he could then reuse."

"You destroyed a Corridor Mirror? They're ancient."

"We didn't do it lightly." His voice rose slightly in reaction to her implied accusation. "The mirrors can transport someone from any point on the continent of Bikia to any other point within the same confines—provided there is a mirror at both ends. We had hoped our new device could evacuate Karulents directly out of the Empire. Unfortunately, our mage found the reach of his new devices to be much more limited. After some effort, he could only extend the maximum reach of the doors to one mile before he, along with our Master Healer, was killed. That was a month ago. The doors currently stand at their maximum reach."

Roslyn touched her finger to the slight seam where the two doorways met. "A mile within a sixteenth of an inch. Still quite impressive."

"If you have finished staring at the doorway, miss, I do have an entire port to show you."

"Of course."

With Karhelm behind her, Roslyn followed the narrow passageway twenty feet before it opened into a cavernous chamber. Torches were mounted throughout, and large, simple chandeliers hung among stalactites.

"'Tis amazing," she said as Karhelm moved to her side. "Forgive my excitement, Lieutenant, but the other ports I've worked in were tiny, the largest of which were little more than converted cellars."

"Yes, Port Lytel is quite a bit more than your average priest hole. God Karulus blessed us with this place four years ago, and we have been truly grateful. As you can see, it started as a natural limestone cavern, but we have made improvements. We have smoothed and leveled as much of the floor as possible, and we have carved stairs where needed. This way." He descended two steps to a lower level. "This is our chapel."

Even without introduction, the area's intent was obvious. Roslyn scanned the vast, empty area. A raised portion at the furthest rocky wall held a pulpit carved out as an alcove amid natural stone spires. Above it, in a smoothed section of the wall, was a chiseled, somber form of the holy Septenar—the crossed number seven. As was often the case, there was no seating for the congregation; instead, the empty nave was checkered in large tiles of blue and pale gray.

"Attendance," Karhelm said, "is, of course, mandatory each Sabbathday. We currently have a dozen priests, sometimes more, so they take turns. Often, as many as four will split up one service. It runs long, but most of the priests passing through haven't had a chance to speak before a congregation this large in years."

"How large? That is, if I may ask, Lieutenant, how many refugees reside at Port Lytel?"

"Technically, they are not refugees, not yet, not until they get to the Karulent Alliance. But 'tis a common mistake. We use the term *passengers*, as will you."

"Forgive me. I misspoke. I've spent some time on the Alliance side of the Veiled River, receiving *refugees* after they crossed the Hyvile River."

"Yes," he said. "Well, let's not make a habit of it. To answer your question, Port Lytel, as the largest port on the Veiled River, currently has over five hundred passengers, but it has had four times that number. The men and women who come to us have all been traveling and hiding for a long time, usually in cramped, fearful conditions. We may not be Fidelumair Palace, but we offer what comforts we can.

"Those tunnels up there lead to the men's ward," he continued, motioning a hand, "which is a labyrinth of barracks and a few game areas. You, of course, know the Veiled River is not an actual river, but here we do have a literal river as well. I guess that makes us an actual port, of sorts." He chuckled, and she returned a polite smile.

"The small underground river," he continued, "runs behind the men's ward, providing a bathing area."

He turned, facing another set of tunnels. "The entrance to the woman's ward was back there, where we started. It too has barracks and an entrance to the river for bathing. Also, they get a special area where they can sew clothes and bedding. You are welcome to join them if you need a break from the infirmary."

She stopped herself from rolling her eyes and instead simply said, "My thanks, Lieutenant," before bowing her head.

"We also have a large kitchen and try to provide at least one meal a day. And, of course, your area, the infirmary to treat the passengers who arrive ill or injured, which is many. We are an extended-stay port designed to allow our brethren time to rest and recover before continuing the long, difficult travel to the safety of the Karulent Alliance."

"You truly do the work of God Karulus, Lieutenant."

"We try." He stood a little taller, pleased with himself, before he motioned her forward. "The infirmary is through here, just beyond the chapel. Most of your staff will be asleep, but—"

"Lieutenant!" a man interrupted as he hastily approached. "Forgive me interrupting, sir, but we've got incoming wounded. Déagrians attacked a carriage full of passengers heading our way. Has the new master healer arrived, sir?"

Karhelm glanced at Roslyn.

"Hello, miss," the man said with a nice but curt nod. Then, to the lieutenant, he asked again if the healer had arrived.

He received the same glance from his superior.

"Do you mean her, sir? A woman?" The stranger eyed her as if he'd never seen a woman before.

"How many wounded?" Roslyn asked, the meekness of her tone having vanished. She threw off her cloak, letting it crumple to the floor.

The man looked to Karhelm, hesitant.

"Well, answer her, man."

"Forgive me, Lieutenant. About a dozen, miss."

"Very well," she said firmly. "I will prepare the infirmary at once. Wake the staff."

Again, the man looked at Lieutenant Karhelm.

"I will thank you to hurry," she insisted. "Time is short." With that, she dashed to the infirmary.

—

Only five minutes passed before the first of the attacked arrived. Workers from the port carried them in through a back tunnel near the infirmary. The rest came in waves, minutes apart, until their number totaled twenty-five injured and three dead on arrival.

Nurses—a combination of trained nuns and laity— separated the living from the dead, placing the deceased in the main cavern outside the infirmary and covering them with sheets. They further divided the living. The most badly injured were rushed to beds. The lesser, to the infirmary floor. The least serious of the patients were left propped against the rocky wall outside the infirmary, as they moaned in agony. Roslyn could only spare one nurse to see to these lesser injured.

The bulk of the staff—seven nurses, two healers, and Roslyn—attended the suffering laid out on the infirmary's ten beds and floor.

The infirmary itself was little more than a slightly modified cave with wooden tables topped with thin cots, a few small tables, and supply shelves. Already, the tiled floor was slick with blood.

Roslyn nearly slipped as she hurried to her next patient, the fifth she'd done already.

"See that this floor is mopped, forthwith," she called.

The patient, barely conscious, had been impaled by a sword just under his ribcage, causing major internal damage.

"There's no hope for this one, miss," the head nurse said sternly just behind her ear. She was an older nun in her fifties, and from what Roslyn gathered in their hasty introduction, she'd been practicing nursing for longer than the master healer had been alive and was not thrilled about working under a woman.

"Not even the real master healer could have saved this one," the nurse concluded.

"I will need to cut him open and heal the damage to his insides before we can treat his outer wounds," Roslyn said, while examining the yawning puncture that was seeping a mix of dark red and pale yellow. "'Tis complex, but I've done it before."

She looked up at the nurse. "Clean the area with a three percent vinegar solution. And tell me as soon as the area is prepared. Quickly. We haven't much time."

Roslyn hurried to one of the other two Azerent Healers. The man in his mid-twenties was pale and clammy as he stood over a patient with a deep shoulder wound. The healer kept his hands out with his palms downward, glowing blue as they hovered over the injury.

He wavered in his stance, as if he were about to faint.

Roslyn darted to him just in time to catch him from falling. "Are you all right?" she asked the healer.

He shook her off him and stood on his own. "I'm fine."

"You're pneuma depleted. Your continued use of magic is tapping into your vital life force. If you aren't careful, it could be fatal."

"I know the effects of pneuma depletion," he said crossly. "*I'm fine.*"

Roslyn paused, letting his anger wash over her before delivering her words firmly yet calmly. "What is your name, healer?"

"Coenric."

"You will switch to secular medicine, Coenric, until you have recovered. You can treat the remainder of his injuries with sutures and bandages. We'll discuss how to address superiors when time allows."

"Miss," the head nurse called as she approached. "The patient is ready, but I still don't believe—"

"My thanks, Nurse," Roslyn said. "I need you to send someone to the sleeping wards. We need a priest and as many others who will come to fill the chapel with prayers for the health of our patients. We need the holy power of God Karulus to be as strong as possible within these walls so we might increase our pneuma. Only with his divine help will we succeed."

CHAPTER TWENTY-ONE

Praise be to Karulus, spirit of truth, and of compassion. You are our God and our savior. Heal our hearts, although we are wicked, and by your light, guide us safely to Laqyigo.

Throughout the rest of the night, Roslyn could hear the powerful prayers of the nearby congregation. Again and again, they chanted in chorus as she rushed from patient to patient. She could feel the power of their God wash over the cave system, filling her with warmth and love that seemed to radiate through her heart, heightening her power to heal and press on, even as she was so very worn.

The other healers were also empowered, and much of their weariness waned. Even the candlelight glowed brighter.

In time, they stabilized all the injured, and Roslyn released some to the general sleeping wards.

Finishing her last patient, Roslyn dabbed her fingers in oil and touched his forehead. "God Karulus, bless this man, that he might be healed."

The oil on his forehead glowed.

"Keep the oil in place as long as it will stay," Roslyn said gently to the patient. "It will focus the power of prayer into your body and help your own life force finish your healing."

"Mistress Roslyn," a nurse called from across the room. "We need your help over here."

Roslyn hurried to where the nurse and one of the healers—Coenric again—stood over a woman lying limply on a cot atop a wooden table. She was a well-dressed woman, near forty, with long, dark hair. No injuries were visible.

"What seems to be the trouble here?" Roslyn asked.

"I . . . I'm not sure," Coenric said, as he hastily examined the woman. "She was responding and seemed to be doing well, but she suddenly fell unconscious. Her heartbeat is arrhythmic and weakening."

He circled his fingers around the patient's wrist, pausing to check her pulse. Finally, he looked gravely at the master healer.

"She's gone," he said.

"Stand back." Roslyn pushed her way past the other healer to the patient. There, she spread her hands out about a foot above the woman's body.

A braided cord of light, formed of many strands, appeared down the woman's core.

"Her soul is still inside her," Roslyn noted. "'Tis dim, but still white. If it converts to death energy, it will leave her body."

For a moment, black strands formed within the white before the cord reverted to its former state.

"'Tis changing," Roslyn said. "Do we have a purified sapphire?"

"Yes, Mistress." The nurse hurried away to a wooden shelf with many tiny jars and bottles. She grabbed the desired object and returned.

Roslyn took the sapphire. It was smaller than she would have liked, but they were blessed to have it at all in this difficult time. She grasped it in her fist and held it over the woman.

Blue light shone down and twisted around the white cord.

The patient's eyes shot open. She released a powerful scream.

"*Calm*," Roslyn whispered in an unnatural voice as she waved her free hand over the woman's face. "*Anesthetize*."

The woman fell into a deep sleep.

To the healer, Coenric, Roslyn said, "I need you to take hold of the sapphire and keep her soul in place whilst I examine and heal her body."

His eyes widened in terror at the request. "Forgive me, Master Healer, but I've never even heard of this method. Much less do I know how to perform it."

"Calm yourself and focus. You're an Azerent Healer, so God Karulus has blessed you with many gifts. I've done the hard part. I just need you to hold it in place and project life."

He nodded, stiff with anxiety.

Hesitantly, the younger healer moved his hand toward hers, and Roslyn carefully passed the gem to him while avoiding any disruption to the patient's soul.

Soon, Roslyn was able to examine the woman on the table. "The patient has suffered severe blunt trauma and shows signs of internal hemorrhaging." She waved her hand above the woman's stomach.

The dress unraveled, leaving the area bare.

Roslyn lifted her hand and touched her thumb and forefinger together. There, between her fingertips, formed an item of blue light—like a sharpened shard of shining blue glass. She pressed it to the woman's stomach, cutting the skin apart in a precise incision. Blood flowed.

"By Karulus, God of healing and fluids," Roslyn intoned, "I command you, blood, flow within your proper courses and not without."

The bleeding stopped. She glanced back at Coenric. "'Tis severe and will take some time, but I can heal her. Just keep that sapphire in place, or her soul will pass away."

—

After an hour of tending to the woman, Roslyn plopped exhaustedly down on a bench at the side of the main cavern hall. The chanting from the chapel had ceased. She slouched with her bloody hands dangling just past her knees. She took a deep breath and released it slowly.

Lieutenant Karhelm approached her. "Long night?"

She sighed. "'Twas already long in just journeying here. The incoming wounded, more so. But we saved a lot of lives."

"Yes. That last woman—They say you brought her back from the dead."

Roslyn smiled. "No, Lieutenant. Unfortunately, I cannot bring back the dead. But she was as close as one can get without passing over. I fear the Reaper, Xanorael, looked on. Yet, with the holy hands of God Karulus, we prevailed. Physically, she is now well, but I had to reattach her soul and will periodically need to realign her spiritual energies over the next seven days. Overall, another victory."

He crossed his arms. "To be clear," Karhelm reproached, "you will not practice necromancy in Port Lytel."

Her smile dropped as she bit her tongue and her eyes narrowed. She nodded. "Of course not, Lieutenant. I would not practice such a thing, even if I was able, neither here nor anywhere else. I assure you, the woman was alive, though just."

"There was also the matter of your being short with the male healers."

"Time was short, Lieutenant. Forgive me for thinking saving lives took priority over niceties."

"Your apology is noted," he said, "but you will need to improve in that regard if you are to be allowed to run the infirmary."

"Did your previous master healer give his orders meekly and with please?"

"It is completely different, Roslyn. You know that."

The head nurse called Lieutenant Karhelm's name as she neared. "Pray your pardon, Lieutenant, but the woman who Mistress Roslyn *resurrected* has awakened and is calling for you. I believe 'tis worth your attention, sir. Mistress Roslyn had better come, as well."

———

Returned to the infirmary, Roslyn hurried toward the patient.

The woman had weakly pushed herself up on her side, her head propped on her arm, but as Roslyn approached, the woman shook violently, falling off her padded table.

Roslyn thrust her hands forward, and an unseen force halted the woman's fall. The woman slowly lifted back up onto her table and rolled gently onto her back.

Roslyn stood over her. "Can you tell me your name?"

"Margaret."

"Margaret, my name is Roslyn. I am an Azerent Master Healer. I need you to stay lying down for me, all right?"

Roslyn turned to the head nurse. "Quickly, I need a purified quartz crystal. *If it pleases you, Sister.*"

"Yes, Mistress."

Again, Roslyn spoke clearly and calmly to the patient, saying, "Margaret, you've been through an attack, but I will get you well. Do you know what happened?"

"Dayigan soldiers happened," she began weakly. "They were looking for me because I have information. They attacked our convoy of innocent Karulents who tried to help me." She turned her head, scanning the injured people on beds across from her. "It . . . it was my fault. I must speak to the commander of this port."

"I am here," Karhelm spoke up, just behind Roslyn.

The nurse returned and handed Roslyn the required crystal.

She held it over Margaret's heart.

Inside her body, a white cord lit up, spanning from the top of her head, down her center, to the base of her torso. Seven points glowed brighter down its length.

"I know . . ." Margaret forced her words through pain. "I know the approximate location of a powerful relic, which the army seeks to use as a weapon. I heard the knights talking. I knew not what else to do, but flee and seek assistance."

"Try to stay calm," Roslyn encouraged.

The palm of Roslyn's other hand glowed blue as she held it above Margaret's head and moved slowly down her center.

"What kind of weapon?" Karhelm demanded.

Margaret winced in pain. "I barely heard them. But 'twas the leaders of the Silthex."

"The *Silthex*." Roslyn gasped. Finished, stepped back.

Margaret sat up on the table. "The Order is certain they can use the relic to wipe out the remaining Karulents in the Empire and conquer the Karulent Alliance as well."

"Conquer the Alliance?" Karhelm asked, perplexed. "Impossible. Our lands and theirs have been allies longer than either the Empire or Alliance has existed."

"The Alliance welcomes Dayigan refugees," Margaret said, "and the Order sees that as blasphemous. Their goal is not only to rid the Empire of Karulents, but to rid them from the entire world of Perdinok."

Karhelm digested her words. "You said they *seek* this relic. They do not yet have it?"

"The way they talked of it," Margaret said, leaning in with severity in her eyes. "If the Silthex had the relic, Commander, you would not need *me* to tell you about it. But time is short."

She began to stand, but Roslyn grabbed her shoulder. "I fear we should already be in pursuit. I know the area. I can take you there."

"No," Karhelm said flatly. "My men cannot care for a woman whilst we confront the Silthex. You will give me directions."

"'Tis no roadside market." Margaret laughed. "I will need to guide you myself. I am glad you like tunnels, because they have a maze of them. As I said, time is very short."

"Very well," he conceded, vexed. "But there will be no room in our kit for cosmetics."

"Lieutenant," Roslyn spoke up, "this woman is my patient, and she requires constant care only I can—"

"By Karulus!" he snapped. "You will both go. Now away to sleep. We leave at dawn, which is but a few hours away. And you better be correct regarding the severity of this relic."

CHAPTER TWENTY-TWO

Fifty men, plus Roslyn, trudged onward along the meandering mountain trail. A single horse-drawn wagon carried their supplies in its creaking bed, and crammed between sacks and crates lay Margaret, her life force stable though her body frail. Everything clattered and clanked—the wagon and the kit hanging from everyone's belt or pack—filling the air with a dissonance that echoed through the forest around them.

Every road they traveled, day after day, seemed to have more of an upward incline. Roslyn felt her limbs weakening and aching with every step, yet the fear that stewed within her was far more taxing. She tried to focus on the rocky woods flowered by spring, but as the group drew farther and farther from Port Lytel, the fear likewise grew.

The Silthex—the ones who destroyed her home so long ago—were no one she wanted to visit. However, Roslyn was aware that the surrounding men, Karhelm included, were looking for any signs that she would be weaker than they. Thus, she hid her fear.

In her time with the Veiled River, she had, of course, faced many challenges, including the occasional run-in with the Knights Silthex. She'd been in units that had charged into Déagrian towns, liberating Karulents from their oppression. She'd defended ports that soldiers had raided. She'd often needed to get others to safety while her own life was in danger.

This felt different: so few against who-knew-how-many Silthex knights.

Roslyn pulled her silver necklace out from under her blouse and looked at the ring thereon: a steel band topped by a blue rose. She kissed it as she walked.

She was certain the men felt fear too, but they had the advantage of knowing one another. They laughed in groups and chatted, thus alleviating, in part, their tension. However, her limited conversations with them often involved unwanted flirtations, which only led her to keep her guard further up. Some offered genuine comfort, while others thought Roslyn should be their entertainment for the journey—it was often difficult to tell one from the other.

She could relax somewhat around Margaret. They shared a tent, and within the first night, the women were talking regularly. However, Margaret remained enigmatic and evasive, even in their private conversations. Roslyn suspected that being new to the River made her uneasy about sharing personal information with strangers, a common trait among Karulents. Although she did not know Margaret's story, Roslyn could assume that she had lived around Déagrians for years and thus had needed to keep all that she was a secret for a long time.

Despite the horrible events surrounding it, Roslyn had been blessed to connect with Father Hanugfrie before the war and thus avoid solitude amid those who would kill her.

Tonight, as Roslyn sat on a large rock jutting from a mild cliff, she wondered where Father Hanugfrie was. A week's journey from Port Lytel, Roslyn was just outside of camp and could hear the peaks in conversations behind her at the fire.

The land had become steadily rockier as the Karulent detachment neared a mountain named Triumph, the place where, according to Margaret, a large faction of Silthex knights lurked in tunnels. Roslyn tried to put it out of her mind.

Father Hanugfrie had often spoken of his love for the mountains. She tried to think of that instead. Once, he and Mother Cyneburga had taken her to a beautiful peak in autumn, where nothing but white aspens grew, the canopy, vibrant gold. There, they'd prayed and meditated for nine days within the beautiful gifts of nature.

Roslyn now folded her legs as she sat up straight. That's what she needed to do: pray, meditate, and renew her spiritual energies. Tending to Margaret the last week had exhausted her, but she'd managed to weave the woman's soul securely back into her body, so it was worth the weariness as far as Roslyn was concerned.

Closing her eyes, the Azerent brought an image into her mind: a large five-pointed star with a five-petaled flower nearly filling the star's interior. In the center of the flower, a pentagon held an eye with a blue pupil.

From this ancient symbol of the Azerents flowed a multitude of voices unified in song. The choir was the spirits of all Karulents throughout the lands. With every passing year, the song grew more melancholic, yet still, it sang out. Roslyn let it flow over her as its power filled her and restored her.

A snap of a footstep on brush sounded.

Roslyn grabbed her dagger from the rock, gripping it as she jerked in the sound's direction.

Grinning, Karhelm raised his hands in mock surrender as he continued to approach. "If I am not mistaken, Azerent Healers vow never to harm another person."

"'Tis for cutting herbs." She lowered the weapon. "But if you hadn't been you, you wouldn't have known I was a healer."

"True." He lowered his hands, setting them on the rock. "Either way, 'tis a daft vow to take in times like these. One does need to protect oneself."

"There's nothing *daft* about it, Lieutenant," she said. She sighed and continued calmly, saying, "Violence, particularly the taking of a person's life, whether or not justified, leaves a scar on one's soul. In addition to the morality of it, these scars hinder the type of magic used by Azerent Healers." She felt no reason to add that she had taken the life of the man who had killed her intended husband—before taking her vows—and that the deed had nearly disqualified her from becoming an Azerent Healer at all. It was none of his concern. She only added, "As an Azerent Healer, if I were to take a life, I would completely lose my healing gift."

"Forgive me," he said. "I never knew. I suppose I never talked much with the previous master healer. In truth, magic has never made much sense to me."

"'Tis not as complicated as people make it out to be. At its most basic core, it is simply a combination of focused imagination and will, both empowered by your inner pneuma. The skill is in strengthening your imagination, will, and pneuma."

He chuckled. "It still makes no sense."

Roslyn opened her satchel, which was on the rock beside her. She took a small, handled mirror from a side pouch. Polished silver formed its reflective pane.

She pointed the mirror so Karhelm could see.

"Can you see that fallen tree?" she asked.

He glanced back, seeing the actual object, and adjusted the mirror's angle. "Yes."

"Can you lift it from here?"

"Lift the tree?" He looked curiously at her. "Of course not," he said with a laugh.

"But can you lift the reflection?"

He set his hand on hers, wrapped it around the handle, and pushed it slightly upward.

She looked into his eyes and smiled. "That is Azerent magic at its most basic. In my mind, I create an image formed of blue light and transcribe that image in the Aetherial Plane. With my will, I lift the aetherial image instead of the object. And with the power of my soul, strengthened by God Karulus, I tie the effect to the object in reality. However, just as important as knowing how to do this is knowing and respecting that the fallen tree is home to an entire ecosystem of bugs, plants, and fungi. Disrupting it could destroy them all. So, I will not."

"You make it seem so simple," he said. "But I know it is not. I spoke to the other healers before we left Lytel. They didn't know how to do most of what you did."

She smiled graciously. "Admittedly, healing also takes years of study to know how the body works, both physically and spiritually. One cannot influence what one doesn't understand."

"Interesting. Although I'll just stick with lifting my sword and willing it forward with my arm. Were you able to study in Vilana before its fall?"

"Extensively." She smiled. "I actually lived on the Isle of Vilana for five years in my early twenties and studied at Azerent College. 'Tis a wondrous city." Her smile faded. "It was. After the city's fall, the remainder of the Azerent Inner Circle moved to Reyigo."

"They should be safe there. The city is deep within the Karulent Alliance."

"Hopefully."

Roslyn looked a moment at Lieutenant Karhelm. He would be a handsome man, if not for his vexing behavior. She lingered her gaze on his rugged face.

He looked at her, pausing before he stepped back. He cleared his throat. "Tomorrow, seven of us, including you, will enter a town in the foothills of Mount Triumph. We have brought just enough pelts to pass as traders. Thus, we will be able to operate unnoticed whilst we replenish our supplies and gather information on any Silthex activity in the area. You will be my wife. I suppose you are pretty enough for it."

"Your proposal, *Lieutenant*, is quick and insulting."

"Play-acting, Roslyn. 'Twill seem less suspicious."

"Yes, I realized that, sir, yet it could have been better asked."

He sighed. "You must think me a horrible brute," he began solemnly. "I do not mean to be. 'Tis the times and commanding such a large port. Some days, it seems that this dire reality is the only reality we'll have henceforth. I had an actual wife once. Have I ever said?"

"No, Lieutenant," Roslyn said sadly. She set her hand to her neck and thumbed the silver chain that led to the ring under her blouse.

"A child, too," Karhelm continued. "A son. The man who killed them was a friend of mine. He attended our wedding and all."

"God Karulus will deliver us from the Dark."

"Yes." He breathed. He folded his hands at his waist as he bowed his head. "Praise be to Karulus, spirit of truth, and of compassion. Heal our hearts."

She returned her gaze to him. "But yes, I'll be your pretend wife tomorrow." She thought of her actual proposal, so long ago.

"You will need to change your poise and manner of speech," he said. "For tomorrow, I mean. Play-acting. I suppose you were a lady before all this."

"No. But my father—before the plague took him—was a moderately well-off town merchant, and I was tutored. And, as I said, I studied at Azerent College in Vilana. However, I grew up not far removed from those you wish me to imitate. I feel I will manage. Perhaps," she sighed, "a day as someone else would be a blessing. And you? You do not strike me as a pelt-monger."

He scoffed. "Hardly. Only a nobleman can receive a royal commission to be an officer in the Dayigan Army. But I have played the part of a furrier before and can again. I will see you at dawn, yes?"

"Aye, m'lord," she said. "But I will think me 'ere just a slight while longer, then go me o'er to yon bed to be sound and rest'd for the trip o' the dawn."

He chuckled. "Well done." He looked into her eyes but turned away. "Although I prefer you as a lady."

With that, he turned, and Roslyn watched him as he headed back toward camp.

"There is a mill like that in Hunia, my hometown," Roslyn said to Margaret, as they sat on crates in a crowded marketplace. Beside them stood an old wooden table scattered with a scant selection of furs.

Three of the men from their unit were playing inept tradesmen, selling low-quality furs for more than they were worth in an attempt to keep the merchandise on the table rather than sell it. A few arguments had broken out from frustrated hagglers, but most had just taken their business elsewhere.

Roslyn's *husband* was away, gone most of the day with two of his men.

"That mill just there," Roslyn again tried. "See it?"

"Most towns have mills," Margaret said, without looking up from her sewing. Roslyn wasn't sure if she was actually trying to make a coat or just keeping appearances, but her stitching seemed skilled.

"No," Roslyn said wistfully. "It is nearly exact." She continued to gaze at the structure across the street. "The same stone, the same height. The same ox walking around a large millstone. Even the same squat cone roof—although the one in Hunia has a blue roof." She paused. "At least it did."

Margaret looked up, following her stare.

Roslyn continued with a sad smile. "I remember when I was a little girl, not long after the mill was completed, my father and I got this *idea* in our heads that we should grow a little plot of wheat. It seemed like it took forever, but eventually, we got a small yield—tiny, a nonsense—and we took it to that mill. I remember Nell, the miller's wife . . ." She glanced downward. "Forgive me, 'tis a silly story. I just miss . . . everything."

"No." Margaret smiled. "'Tis nice. Forgive *me* for being so distant these past few days. I have never even thanked you for saving my life. 'Tis just this whole matter with this *relic*." She leaned in and whispered. "You should have heard the way the knights talked about it, as if the rest of the continent of Bikia *combined* would be no match. Alas, it has me quite fretful."

"Perhaps its strength was exaggerated. It is in the nature of men to inflate their tales."

"Hopefully." Margaret set down her stitching. "Tell me of the flour. What became of it?"

"The flour?"

"The flour you received once you had your wheat ground at the mill. Did you make something special with it? Do tell."

"Actually, yes. We made a fantastic cake—not with all of it, mind you. There was not a lot, but more than a cake's worth. It was a delicious pear cake rich with honey and spiced with cinnamon and cloves. My father and I ate a slice every night for a week." Roslyn smiled. "I gave some to a little serf boy named Jon, and he . . ." Her smile faded. She closed her eyes. A tear rolled down her cheek. "Forgive me . . ."

Margaret patted her leg. "Mayhap we can make such a cake when we return to Port Lytel."

"Perhaps," Roslyn said, disheartened, for she knew, regardless of the outcome of their venture, that the time of cake had passed. And she regretted not taking full advantage of those lost, happy times.

"Behold," Margaret said. "Your *husband* approaches."

Roslyn looked up through the crowded market to see Karhelm approaching with two other men from Port Lytel. He stopped to browse some tumbled stones, chatting casually with the merchant. His face lit up with amusement at something the merchant said, and Roslyn couldn't help but smile in response. Soon, he continued to the fur stand, and the two men from Port Lytel followed closely behind.

"How now, women?" Karhelm bellowed in a thick country accent.

"I'm quite well," Roslyn said.

The two bantered briefly in the accent, attempting not to laugh through their words, yet smiling all the while.

"What say you?" Karhelm asked Margaret.

"I say naught, for I am mute."

"Mute, say ye? You're quite well-spoken for a mute."

"Indeed. But I would rather be mute than speak in such an idiotic manner."

"I see," his voice lowered unhappily, his accent lost. "If it pleases you to be mute, be mute. Regardless, our ruse shall soon end. I have set up a meeting. Come. Both of you."

—

Karhelm guided the women to a spoonsmith, who was busy in his small shop crafting his wares.

"Do we be needin' spoons, m'lord?" Roslyn scoffed, perplexed, at Karhelm.

The spooner gave her an icy stare. "Fie yer mocks, madam! Ne'er b'little the import of a first-rate spoon. Come." He motioned for them to follow. "We be goin' to the back, whither the true quality be kept."

Her confusion unappeased, Roslyn followed as he took them into a small room with walls lined with shelves of silver spoons. He reached for one shelf and pulled it back: a steep, dim staircase emerged from the shadows beyond.

"Down there." The spooner motioned without any more explanation, then stepped past them and out of the room.

Karhelm solemnly led the other two into the shadowed depths below.

—

The small underground room was dirty and dimly lit by a dying hearth. Not that there was much to see. A few wooden benches. Cracked, damp walls of masoned stone. The small table had seen better days.

A man waited therein, standing pensively by the fire. He was, in nearly all form, like a slender Human, yet he was not Human—this made obvious by the two feathered wings folded at his back, these gray like his hair.

Although this race of man, known as Terovae, was much more common in and around the Karulent Alliance than here, Roslyn had met enough in her travels to think little of the difference. It was more the face she noticed. The thin old face, lit by the flickering flames, furrowed with anxiety.

"Welcome back to Port Triumph, Karhelm," he said, forcing cordiality. "I wish it could be under better circumstances—if such a thing still exists. My assistant has informed me of your quest."

Karhelm eyed him a moment. "Should I infer from your demeanor that you have information and it is . . . *unpleasant?*"

The Terovae nodded. "Well beyond unpleasant, I fear. Local legends speak of one particular relic that can be found at Mount Triumph, which may very well be what you seek."

"Pray tell, man. No need for dramatics."

"True." He let out a resigned sigh. With a hint of dread in his voice, he said, "It is said that Mount Triumph is the resting place of Fersivolíel."

Roslyn gasped and stumbled back to lean against the wall.

Karhelm looked at her, seemingly catching her alarm. "For the love of Karulus, I'm no scholar of relics. Could someone please elaborate? What in za is a Fersivolíel?"

"An ancient stone warrior," Roslyn began, her voice shaking. "He was created early during the first calendar to battle the Demons when they infested the world. If he fought alongside the present-day Déagrians . . ." She paused, staring at the rough floor. "No army could stand against them."

"It appears that the woman knows more than I," the Terovae said to Karhelm.

"Yes," Karhelm replied, dazed. "'Twould seem I skipped introductions. This is Roslyn, our Azerent Master Healer. She is among the best." There was a hint of pride in his introduction.

Roslyn looked up at Karhelm. The acknowledgment took her by surprise, momentarily pulling her from panic.

"I thought she could attend to any sick or injured passengers you have whilst we are here," Karhelm concluded.

"A woman?" The Terovae eyed her. "Bizarre. But, as you can see, Port Triumph currently has no passengers."

"Roslyn," Karhelm continued. "This is Port Commander Gaderian."

"Well met," she mumbled absently. She was sick with dread. "Forgive me." She touched her head with a trembling hand. "I need air."

She dashed for the stairs.

—

Outside in the street, Roslyn sat against the spoon shop, her knees up near her chest and her hand on her forehead. She felt dizzy and ill. Her skin felt hot and cold at once. Her stomach churned.

Margaret was soon sitting down beside her.

Without looking at the other woman, Roslyn said, "I know I shouldn't have run out like that. The men already think I am unprepared for this."

"Fuck what the men think."

"Margret, what awful language," she said, more in half-hearted reflex than actual offense. She was beyond caring for social niceties.

"So it may be, but I have grown quite weary of a healer of your talent vying for the respect of those who are, in fact, your inferiors. And pray, call me *Meggy*. All my friends do." She sighed before her tone turned somber. "Methinks you had a good reason to run out, yes?"

Roslyn nodded. "And if the others knew what I know, they would cower here alongside me." She leaned toward Margaret, and with hushed words, said, "Are you, perchance, familiar with the Chrono'qyelseran?"

"I think not. And I certainly hope you do not wish me to pronounce it."

Roslyn cracked a slight smile before biting her lip. She glanced down. "Cro-no-qyel-sair-an. In truth, 'twould be surprising if you knew of it. It cannot be copied. Only a slight few people are spiritually developed enough to read it at all, lest their eyes burn out or they die. Admittedly, I am not in that 'slight few' yet. As we Azerents progress in the Order, we are allowed to hear select recitations from it, yet even this is dangerous, as hearing quotes above someone's spiritual grade could cause one's ears to bleed, deafness, or even death by spontaneous combustion. That said, the Chrono'qyelseran is a set of books—"

"I assume you do not intend to tell me something that could make me spontaneously combust."

"No. Of course not. The Order has carefully given each section of information a grade level, and this—I assure you— is perfectly safe for the laity." Roslyn leaned in, whispering, "The books chronicle the history of the world from the beginning of time to the end of the first calendar. Within ancient tales of warring Gods, Vampires, Demons, divine prophets, and the birth and fall of empires; it tells the tales of the stone warrior."

"Surely, he is not wicked," Margaret said. "You said he *fought* the Demons."

"Fersivolíel fought for the True Light, yes, but he fought under God *Déagar*. If today's Déagrians have found a way to use him—a warrior forged to fight Demonic hordes—as a weapon against us and the Karulent Alliance, we are already dead."

Margret turned pale, and silence lingered a beat. She asked, "You are certain he would fight against the people of Déagar's own brother?"

"Despite what even I, myself, once thought, Karulus and Déagar are not brothers and never claimed to be. They were both born of the Holy Mother, as was all life, but are separate creations, no more related than a Human and a hare." Roslyn stopped a moment, realizing, with mild vexation, that she'd quoted a Dark Light Goddess. It was still true.

She continued, saying, "Their brothership is a modern contrivance. They were allies—nothing more. And that has evidently ended."

"Even still," Margaret said, "I do not believe Déagar would condone this—"

"It is over, Margaret," Roslyn snapped, but breathed before regaining a defeated tone. "...Meggy. This is the beginning of the end, for all Karulent and those who would help us."

A man stepped to stand over the women. "You two are well informed."

"Rothgar," Margaret gasped. She began darting her eyes for some means of escape.

"You have been quite the wicked girl, Meggy," he said with a sneer. "I shouldn't like to see what would happen if you tried to flee again. Stand up. You too. And do not call out."

They stood apprehensively.

"*Run, Roslyn!*" Margaret called as she darted toward the man.

Rothgar lifted his hand. An arc of green lightning shot from his palm to Margaret's forehead.

She fell unconscious.

He grabbed Roslyn by the arm.

She struggled against him.

"I know you," she said.

He neared his hand to her forehead and another arc of green flashed from his palm.

Roslyn felt herself grow limp as sleep overtook her.

CHAPTER TWENTY-FOUR

Roslyn awoke in darkness. The distinct scent of lumber assaulted her nose before she realized rough planks of timber lay an inch from her face. She ran her hands along the cramped confines, feeling the close corners and narrow sides.

A coffin, was her horrific realization. A heart-stopping terror filled her as Roslyn pounded and kicked as much as the constricting limits allowed, desperately attempting to escape.

Dust rained down, filling her lungs with each desperate gulp of breath.

Then a light approached, flickering as dusty rays amid the narrow cracks between the boards.

The lid was thrown open, and Roslyn was snatched out by two men she'd never seen. Each was a burly bearded man wearing a white surcoat adorned with a green, squared version of a crossed seven—the symbol of the Order of Knights Silthex.

The area, a cave or mine, was twenty feet across and twice that in height.

"Fret not," a third man, the man who Margaret had called Rothgar, began. He stood, well postured, a few feet away and held a torch. "The coffin was but to transport you. We do not intend to bury you. Not yet."

The men threw her to the cold stone floor and held her down, a boot slamming against her shoulder. She struggled, but it was futile. Without warning, they clamped a heavy, metal collar around her neck, then fastened the heavy links of iron chain to its ring.

Released by the men but held by chains, she looked up, squinting her eyes toward the man called Rothgar.

"'Twould be in your best interest to cooperate," he said. "Tell me, are you an Azerent?"

Roslyn rose to her knees, shaking, braced to be hit, yet she stared straight into his eyes. "You commanded the knights who destroyed my town."

"You will need to be more specific. I'm afraid I've destroyed a good number of Karulent-infested towns."

"Hunia," she said through her teeth.

"Ah. My *first* town," he said proudly. "Wait. Are you the statue girl? You are. 'Tis been a long time," he smirked. "Good, catching up."

"Your actions will be punished."

Another voice shouted from across the room. "By whom?"

Roslyn looked up farther toward a masoned wall forming the opposite side of the otherwise natural rock chamber. Stairs led up to a slight ledge and door.

There stood a man who, though apparently Human, was older than anyone Roslyn had ever seen before. Amazingly old. She stared, captivated, as he descended.

His crumpled, leathered, ugly skin hung from his bones. His spine bent. Nevertheless, his attire was regal: a long surcoat of white silk with a Silthex Septenar embroidered in green on his chest. His long cape was white fur.

"I asked thee a question, girl." The ancient man neared.

Rothgar stepped aside as the old man came to stand but a foot from Roslyn.

He grasped the side of her face in his cold, wrinkled hand and yanked her head to face upward toward him.

"Thine idol tongue did wag pitiful threats. Regale me, girl. Who will punish *us*? Who will come for thee deep within this mountain, this labyrinth of tunnels? Dost thou assume thou wilt be rescued, girl? Dost thou hope thou wilt ever again have thy freedom?"

Roslyn took a deep breath and forced calm. "You are a Kla, like the Patriarch of the Church of Déagar. No Human could be as old and wretched as you."

Annoyed, he threw aside her face, causing her head to turn downward.

"Of late, some have come to call my kind by that name. A meaningless word by those who know us not. If thou needest introduction, my name is Blastilv, Grand Master of the Knights Silthex."

"I am Roslyn," she said. "I will pray for you that you and your kind return to the True Light."

The Kla grinned yellowed teeth. "Wilt thou? Wilt *thou* pray for *me*, girl? Are we now companions? Thou knowest me, and I know thee. Mayhap I will be more compassionate now I know thee so very, very well."

He pulled back his hand and slapped her hard with the back of his hand—the triangular emerald of his ring striking her and adding to the impact.

Roslyn fell on her hands as blood dripped from her lip.

Blastilv chuckled. "Already, I knew thy name, girl." He leaned down as he hissed into her ear. "I intend to rip out thy soul, Roslyn."

He stepped back.

She shrank from him, every nerve in her body screaming for flight. Steeling herself against his presence, she hissed through gritted teeth, "God Karulus will punish you!" She wiped the blood from her mouth.

Blastilv stood tall, swollen with pride, despite his crooked spine, and peered down at her. "Thy God is naught but a wretched deceiver. Though he may promise salvation, he delivers naught but forsakenness. How I long to stand before him that I might spit in his arrogant blue face. Know thou thine allegiance to him hath brought thee hither."

He stepped away, clasping his hands together, before he continued saying, "Even so, methinks 'tis not thy faith in thine azure deity that gives thee hope. Perhaps thine allies will rescue thee. Perhaps they watched my men box thee and carry thee ahorse into Mount Triumph and deep into these twisting burrows carved by three years' toil. Perhaps they seek thee even now. Do such fantasies give thee hope, girl? Do they strengthen thee? Behold." Blastilv glanced toward the raised door. "Sergeant."

There stood a guard dressed in a black tunic emblazoned with a green, Silthex Septenar across his chest. He nodded obediently before turning to leave the chamber, only to return a moment later dragging a corpse behind him.

He threw it down into the dungeon to break against the rocky floor.

Roslyn stared in horror as she beheld Lieutenant Karhelm's broken form. Hollowness welled within her. The sight was unbelievable, yet indisputable. As far as she was concerned, she had just left Karhelm in the hidden room beneath the spoon shop.

Nevertheless, this bloated, stinking body had been absent a soul for near a week. The remaining blood that seeped onto the rock was thick.

Blastilv addressed Roslyn coldly, "I pray thou wilt save the sergeants the effort and trust that the rest of thy meager group is likewise dispatched. Or shall we have their carcasses delivered as well?"

"What do you want from me!" Roslyn screamed.

"Cry thou not, O gentle girl," he said with cold kindness as his rough hand moved to wipe her cheek.

She jerked her head away.

"Pretty, pretty. 'Twould be a pity to see thee injured. I wish naught but thy cooperation and these horrid things will conclude. 'Tis your own fault, in truth. If the Karulents had not resisted and concocted your *Veiled River*, such means would be unnecessary.

"Prithee," he gently asked of the nearby knights, "loosen the chains. Let our guest stand afoot."

The two who had first chained her moved and adjusted where the chains met the floor.

"Better?" Blastilv reached out a hand to help her up. "See how kind I am to thee?"

She ignored the hand and stood on her own.

He continued as he slowly paced. "Our young empire is strong, yet its quick construction hath, in truth, forced a rather unstable framework. One that is vulnerable to those like thee who would seek to rip it down. Thus, His Holiness hath charged me to fortify it. And so, I shall disinter a warrior who will stand as an indomitable champion before our army, strengthening the Holy Dayigan Empire into an everlasting fortress and ripping our foes apart. Thou knowest, already, of the ancient warrior of stone from the Demonic Era; my sources have told me such."

He stopped walking and faced her as if she should reply.

She stood silent.

"I grow wrathful at thy disrespect, girl. If cordiality suits thee not, we will proceed differently." He turned to the stairs and ordered, "Produce the last insurgent."

Soon, a guard appeared, dragging the hapless spooner, living but enchained and gagged, down the stone stairs to Blastilv. He threw him to his knees.

A cruel sneer lit up Blastilv's features as he drew a blade from his belt and grabbed the spooner by the hair, yanking his head upward. He carved a deep gash across the throat and cast him aside.

The spooner lay there, writhing and choking on his blood, coughing between rasping screams as a warm river of red spread across the dungeon floor.

"No!" Roslyn called, reaching for him even as the chain held her back. "You horrid monster! You are *nothing* of the Light."

Blastilv grinned. "We *are* the Light." He walked unhurriedly toward the stairs.

The others followed.

Roslyn lunged toward the dying spooner, yet he was far too removed from her grasp. She watched in anguish as his body violently twitched and trembled while the pool of blood expanded beneath him. Roslyn's eyes brimmed with tears, but with one final, desperate act, she thrust her hands toward him and unleashed a torrent of blue light from her palms, maintaining a steady stream that blanketed the dying man.

"Praise be to Karulus," she said. "Empower me with your healing light. Empower me, O God Karulus. *Shine through me!*"

The gash across his neck closed and healed.

Amazed by her own abilities, Roslyn stared at her hands before looking back at the spooner. He was shaken, but fine.

"Behold, Seneschal Rothgar." Blastilv watched from the base of the stairs. "Did I not say to thee that I could motivate her? She heals quickly and without touch. Lo, too, she is unwearied by her effort."

Roslyn returned her awestruck stare to her hands.

"Yes, Your Eminence," said Rothgar. "My wife did well in bringing her here."

"Indeed. I will see Lady Margaret is well rewarded. And thou."

Roslyn looked up in response to Margaret's name, but said nothing, pausing before turning sadly to the floor. The betrayal stung, but she could do nothing but accept it, one more kick when she was down.

"As for this Azerent," Blastilv continued, "I will need to run more tests ere I am certain she can restore the warrior Fersivolíel. Yet, I am optimistic."

He turned to Roslyn. "'Tis a pity thou didst study not defensive magics in thy school. Thou wouldst be difficult to confine. Yes, thou art likened to a Faery—powerful yet easily encaged."

With that, the men grabbed the spooner and left up the stairs, leaving her alone with rotting Karhelm.

Once the door had slammed shut and locked, Roslyn froze, listening for additional noises. The muffled voices beyond the door moved away.

After a wait, she hurried to the body of Karhelm. She struggled against her chained collar, nearly strangling herself.

Her fingers, stretched as far as she could manage, barely touched the arm of the broken, putrefying corpse.

Roslyn desperately reached farther. Choking. Gagging.

Finally, she took hold of him and dragged him closer.

Her feelings for Karhelm had been confused, yet he'd been a good man, undeserving of this. Roslyn stared despondently at his desecrated body, stabbed in the gut and broken against the floor. His eyes, open and vacant.

"May God Karulus be your advocate before the Lavender Lady and deliver you safely to Laqyigo," Roslyn said.

She stabbed her hand deep into the large gash in his stomach and dug upward, through rotting meat, behind his ribs, feeling her way through gore as she nearly vomited.

She found the heart. Pulling and twisting at the solid, slippery organ, she tried desperately to pull it free. At last, she ripped it from his body and held it up.

"Forgive me, Lieutenant," Roslyn said, panting and sick, staring at the bloody thing in her bloody hand. "And forgive me again, Lieutenant, for I will need your eye."

CHAPTER TWENTY-FIVE

I
t was not until the second day that they removed Karhelm's rotting body.

Every day thereafter, they came for Roslyn. Blastilv and Rothgar, accompanied by two or three of their guards, brought the spooner down into the dungeon. They inflicted injury after varying injury on the weeping, cloth-gagged man.

Roslyn healed him every time. She knew she shouldn't. She knew she only performed for their depraved, twisted experiments. Yet, she couldn't let him die.

The constant sounds of the spooner's muffled screams haunted her still after his absence. As Roslyn slept on the rocky floor, the sounds echoed through her troubled dreams.

She could tell the spooner had lost his mind by the eleventh day. Scars marked every inch of his naked body. The cries through the nauseating gag sounded bizarre—strange, distorted sobs that twisted horror with laughs of queer merriment. These discordant noises cut into Roslyn's ears, ringing in her brain and ripping deep into her soul.

Roslyn let him die on the twelfth day. She watched with silent tears as he bled out from three large sword-carved gashes across his ribcage.

"May God Karulus be your advocate before the Lavender Lady," she whispered sadly, "and deliver you safely to Laqyigo."

She was near to following him to madness. The torturous deeds, the hellish crypt, the constant use of her power bringing her to soul fatigue—all had made her body weak and mind numb. She longed to rip the skin from her bone, so she might be free of aching nerves.

The spooner was still dying before her. Roslyn had blacked out for a moment. Now, she watched him grow limp and motionless. A part of her wished to call the Reaper for herself.

Blastilv grabbed her and shook her. "Thou wilt heal him!" he commanded.

He slapped her to the floor and kicked her in the gut. "Do as thou art told, girl!"

"I can do nothing for him now," Roslyn whispered, almost peacefully. She was beyond crying. Nearly beyond caring. She knew she bled from the attack, but she ignored the crimson dripping to the stone.

Roslyn watched the body as she lay curled on the floor. "Xanorael escorts his soul far, far away." She chuckled weakly. The laughter hurt her ribs.

Blastilv kneeled over her and rolled her onto her back.

He produced an emerald wand from a pouch on his belt and touched it to her heart.

Even as weakened as she was, Roslyn screamed as the wretched Kla dragged back the wand, thus drawing out a thick braid of white light from her heart.

She continued to scream and writhe against the floor, as her throat felt it would bleed. Never had she felt such agony. The anguish was all-consuming, from the tips of her toes to the crown of her head.

Blastilv pushed his withered hand hard against her screaming mouth as he examined the cord of light.

Finally, he released her soul to return to her core.

Pain, though drastically reduced, continued to throb through her. Roslyn wept softly.

"Her spiritual energy doth remain strong," Blastilv said to Seneschal Rothgar as he stood. "Yet 'tis lesser than I expect from her."

"Will she do, Your Eminence?" Rothgar asked as the two stood over her, looking down.

"That I have yet to determine." Blastilv paused, thinking a beat. "Something is amiss, Seneschal. Yet, I know not what. The experiments will continue."

Blastilv nudged her with his boot. "Hark, Azerent, thou art a murderess. Will thy God forgive thee?"

"'Twas you who killed him," Roslyn groaned, staring upward from the floor, "not me."

"Nevertheless," Blastilv resumed, "due to thy wicked actions, we will now need a *new* subject. Whatever fate befalls it is thine own doing. Let us not need a third."

The two began to move away as Blastilv commanded the guard. "Clear this corpse. The stench of the former lingers still, and I will not have a reprise. And go thou to the nearby town and fetch a child."

"Your Eminence," the guard said, lowering his head, "with respect, I remind you there is but a Déagrian town nearby."

Blastilv glared at the man. "Is there an issue, Sergeant?"

Another man, in the white surcoat of a knight, spoke up, saying, "*I* will complete your task, Grand Master."

Blastilv eyed the man. "Prithee, what is thy name, knight?"

"Beadurinc, Grand Master. I'm part of Seneschal Rothgar's brigade."

"Thine obedience will take thee far, Beadurinc. Kill this insolent sergeant and fetch a child from the town. A girl. One pleasant enough for our defiant healer to keep alive."

"At once, Grand Master." The knight seized the sergeant, who called out as he was dragged away.

Blastilv ignored the scene, instead turning his gaze to Roslyn as he cast an unnerving grin. With that, he left.

Soon, the cell was clear of men and bodies.

The high-up door closed behind them. A clicking of the lock.

Roslyn set her shaking hand to her forehead. She wanted to scream again. She wanted to cry and cry and dissolve into the stony floor.

"Help me," she whispered desperately as she clasped her hands to her breast and looked up to the roof forty feet above.

There, a shaft a foot across ascended some great distance to reveal the blue sky above.

"Praise be to Karulus, spirit of truth, and of compassion. *Make this end.* I don't know why you've brought me to this place of cruelty and torment, but I haven't the fortitude to carry on. Forgive me, my God and savior. Whatever your purpose for me here, I fear I will fail. For how, O God, how can I shine Light when there is naught but Darkness here?

"I beseech you." Roslyn looked at the slight glimpse of sky. "Return me to Port Lytel. There, I will gladly do your works as you have called me to do. Send another to thwart the Silthex. *Please.*"

Her words echoed away into silence as she stared woefully at the tiny glimpse of unattainable sky.

A muffled sound drew her attention: an eerie cry akin to a baby's shriek. It echoed preternaturally.

At first, she ignored it, hoping it would end. Yet, as it grew louder, she realized from where it came. The uncanny call sounded from the wall.

Roslyn jumped up and hastened toward it.

She looked back at the cell door, watching, assuring no one had entered. Listening, she assured that no one approached.

Anxiously, Roslyn slid aside a rock to reveal a slight hole she'd clawed into the cave wall.

No longer muffled, the unnatural noise grew louder.

"You live," Roslyn whispered. "Praise be to Karulus."

She placed her hand in the hole, feeling her way through putrid goo until she found a slimy solid. She grasped it gently and carefully pulled it out.

The grotesque thing continued to cry out in weird wails. It was, for the majority of its small body, a Human heart oozing blood and beating quickly. Two shriveled legs dangled from its ventricles. An eye stared out from dead center. One thin, bent arm protruded haphazardly from its upper right atrium to end at three disproportionate, lanky fingers. Teeth filled a mouth that was a crooked gash into its left atrium. Its single Human ear was like a strange hat.

"Shh," Roslyn whispered with compassion. "They will hear. Forgive me for your pain, but I rushed your creation."

She placed her palm to its mouth, letting it bite into her flesh and suckle of her blood.

The heartbeat calmed.

"'Tis all right," her words were gentle as she set it down.

Closing her eyes and concentrating, Roslyn envisioned a five-pointed star behind a five-petaled flower, which was the Seal of the Azerents. She summoned up her depleted powers.

Roslyn placed her hand above the creature, and a blue light shone down, showering it with warmth. She kept the flow of healing strong, despite the growing agony behind her eyes.

In time, she called out, grabbing her forehead as the light ceased.

"I can do no more. My pneuma is low, and I can't risk tapping into my core life force. Not here."

The strange little thing looked up at her and blinked. As ugly as it was, it made her smile.

"I require your assistance, little homunculus."

CHAPTER TWENTY-SIX

The door clicked in loud contrast to the silence. The lock slowly turned.

Feigning slumber, Roslyn glanced at the homunculus—the slimy creature formed of a Human heart—clinging to the wall just above the door.

The door opened. A guard entered. He held a tin plate of unimpressive food.

Like a large, hideous spider, the homunculus hurriedly climbed down to the portal.

Roslyn's heart stopped as the door began to close. She watched, without seeming to watch, but could see little.

The door slammed shut.

The guard approached, boots clomping on the stone floor. He set down the plate within her reach, and began away.

Roslyn glanced up slightly. She could not see the homunculus. Had it made it? She wasn't sure. Even if it had, it had little knowledge of how to act without her guidance. She had no idea what was beyond the door and feared that the little creature could have encountered trouble.

Petrified, Roslyn counted the protracted moments as the guard, bit by maddening bit, leisurely walked the room. He unhurriedly climbed the stairs. He opened the door, glancing back at her for a moment. At length, he exited.

The door slammed.

Roslyn leaped up and sat cross-legged. Posture straight. She placed the fingers of each hand to her temples.

She breathed.

"Praise be to God Karulus. I pray you, let me see what I cannot see. Hear what I cannot hear. Feel what I cannot feel."

Her eyes glowed blue.

She could see, through the eyes of the homunculus, the tunnels outside her cell. They were simple and tight, carved into the rock with wooden braces set where functional. Iron torches were set sporadically. She could hear indistinct chatter and footsteps.

Roslyn controlled the homunculus as if it were her own form, and through it, she climbed to the peak of the tunnel and crept like a ghastly, oozing lizard down its length.

No apparent plan dictated the arrangement of the tunnels. They crisscrossed, slanted upward and down, led to and fro, and dead-ended without destination. A few alcoves held simple wooden bunks. Some tunnels had collapsed and were boarded off. An unfinished staircase led nowhere.

Roslyn realized, with some panic, that even if she were to break her chains and bound out the door, she would be lost within a maze.

At last, she saw some concentration of activity and willed the homunculus toward it. Looking down from the vantage at the tunnel's peak, Roslyn watched miners hauling sacks and wheelbarrows of rock.

Hoping they'd lead to an exit, she followed the trail of miners. But she stopped.

A sound attracted her. Some exclamation rang out down the way.

She turned the homunculus back to see a sergeant running with excitement.

"We found it!" he exclaimed to another guard. "By Déagar, at last, we found it! Pray, where be the grand master?"

The second guard pointed.

Roslyn knew she could not let them have the warrior Fersivolíel. Changing her course away from her potential exit, she again followed the trail of miners, but now toward their origin.

Down a long, narrow tunnel sloping steadily deeper into the shadowy, rocky depths of Perdinok, she hurried.

A frenzy of activity marked the tunnel's end. Miners and sergeants alike clustered together, all digging breathlessly.

So many eyes were in this area, and Roslyn feared they would see her little homunculus. Yet, the eyes, all of them, stayed transfixed on the tunnel's end.

She carefully crawled closer, keeping to the shadows along the peak of the tunnel as best as she could manage. Nearer and nearer, she crawled, even as she knew she should stop.

At last, within the dust and activity, Roslyn could see it: the upper left quadrant of a man's head protruding from the slanted, jagged tunnel's end. The white marble face had lain unseen for centuries, since fierce Fersivolíel had stood upon a great mountaintop.

Centuries ago, Fersivolíel had stretched his golden sword—entwined with snakes and clutched within his clawed hand—high toward the heavens, as he called out with a roar.

As Darkness swirled above him, the stone warrior drank in the almighty strength of the unified True Light Gods, and through this might, he summoned every Archdemon, Demon, Cambion, and fiend. And he cast them, every one, into Chaos. Afterward, the mountain quaked beneath him and split apart. It crumbled at his feet. He tumbled and vanished into the twisting rocks.

When Roslyn had first heard the tale from the Chrono'qyelseran, she'd been left breathless. Too, she'd grieved for him when he fell. Yet never in a million dreams had she expected to see him. Never in a million nightmares had she expected to stand before him as an adversary.

Through the ear of the homunculus, Roslyn now heard the voice of Blastilv commanding others to "Step aside."

He and Rothgar approached in haste.

The gathered people made way as Blastilv neared and kneeled to view.

"Magnificent," Blastilv breathed. He gently touched the face. "I am elated." The Kla glanced back over his shoulder. "Clear the area. I desire a lone moment with our prize. Seneschal Rothgar, thou shalt remain. Sergeants, take ye note of all responsible for this find. I grant them threefold today's wage."

As the others departed, Rothgar stepped forward and kneeled at Blastilv's side. Nevertheless, he did not show the awe the Kla displayed, but was instead stiff with unease.

"Doth it frighten thee, Seneschal?" Blastilv grinned. "Fear thou not. 'Tis but a beautiful corpse."

"I am not afraid, Your Eminence," he said gruffly. "I trust God Déagar would protect me if his warrior turned against us." He paused, scanning the statue. "Have you determined if the woman is suitable?"

"She vexes me, Seneschal. She is indeed more powerful than the other Azerents we have trialed, yet she is inexplicably drained. 'Tis as if the girl hath, for lack of a better term, a *leak* in her soul. I cannot put her in this body unless I know, without doubt, that she can sustain it. Otherwise, the warrior will crumble around her rejected soul."

"Can we not simply burn her, Your Eminence, like the other Azerents who failed? And find another?"

"She is unlike the others."

"She is stubborn, for one, and disobedient. I confess, Your Eminence, I fear we may lose control over our mighty warrior with the soul of that *woman* in him."

"Fear not. He will be but an automaton under mine absolute authority," Blastilv said. "The Azerent's soul will power him, yes, but her mind and being will be locked away. She will spend eternity staring out of graven eyes yet devoid of the slightest control of the body."

Horrified, Roslyn gasped. Suddenly, she was back in her cell—the connection to the homunculus, lost.

She tried at once to reestablish the link, concentrating and pressing her fingers against her temples. Nothing.

Desperate, she tried again and again.

Finally, she resigned and punched the floor with the side of her fist.

The door burst open.

Roslyn jumped up to see Blastilv glaring down at her from the shadowed entry.

After a long, tense silence, he lifted his hand with the homunculus grasped within. He squeezed it, crushing it within his bloodied fist.

He threw it to splat on the ground.

"Know thou, if I did not need thee whole for my purposes," he growled, "I would rip thee asunder and scatter thy parts across the lands." He then returned to his cold tone. "Why must thou be like this, girl? How pleasant thy final days would have been if thou hadst submitted to me. Yet, that time hath passed. Thy construct was draining thy magic. The *leak*, as if it were so, hath been plugged. With this and the stone warrior found, we may continue with the reanimation."

Blastilv's pompous voice sneered. "Sleep well, Azerent. We have much to do tomorrow morn."

CHAPTER TWENTY-SEVEN

Roslyn couldn't sleep. She lay on her back, staring upward. Far too many thoughts rushed through her mind for her to quiet them for slumber.

How many Azerents, she wondered, had died in Blastilv's cruel experiments? Roslyn did not know all the other Azerents, but the upper echelon needed by the Kla was few, and she knew them all.

Through the craggy shaft in the distant ceiling, she glimpsed the starry night.

How many more Azerents, Roslyn wondered, would die if she managed to escape?

Abruptly, a tiny sound clicked from her door.

She jerked toward it, watching with growing fright.

Never had the guards come as late as this, and she feared her last night in flesh would soon endure the lecherous desires of a wanton fiend.

The door creaked ajar and birthed a shadowed figure, crouching as it entered without a sound. The door closed slowly. Nothing more than a click.

Her heart pounded as her breath bated.

The figure began down the stairs.

A whisper: "Roslyn?"

She said nothing.

"Roslyn, 'tis I, Meggy."

Dread drained, while hurt and hate ignited in its place.

Margaret hurried cautiously to Roslyn, as if too loud a footstep might be heard beyond the heavy door.

The other woman stooped over her. "I could not come sooner, but I can wait no more. They have found the relic. Come, I know a way out of the tunnels, but we must hurry."

Roslyn drew away. "How could you betray us?"

"Ah." Margaret took a seat on the floor. She sighed. "They told you. A slight deception on my part, I'm afraid. You see, I—quite cleverly, I might add—created the *perception* that I had betrayed you and the others. Otherwise, I would not be here now to rescue you. In reality, I told them nothing more than what I knew they already knew. Not to speak ill of the departed, but I am fairly certain that the actual culprit was the spoon maker. Someone has been leading the Silthex to Azerents for about three years. And 'tis just the sort of loose end the grand master would like to clear up if he's found the proper one."

"And yet 'twas you, not the spooner, who, knowing they needed Azerents, brought me here."

"I did nothing of the sort," Margaret huffed. "I led *Lieutenant Karhelm* here, as well as the others, and for the exact reason I told you—to stop Blastilv before he became unstoppable. *You* came of your own accord—and I thank you, as it meant saving my life. But, to be perfectly honest, Roslyn, I'm rather insulted that we are having this conversation. I know we know not each other well, but I would have liked to think you know I am not some sort of . . ."

"Déagrian?" Roslyn offered defiantly. "Wife of a monster?"

Margaret jumped to her feet. "If not for the fact that I *am* a decent Déagrian woman, I would leave you here right now. I put my life at risk even nearing this horrid cell." She turned to face away and set her fingers to her forehead.

Roslyn breathed. She stood and approached the older woman. She placed her hand on Margaret's shoulder.

"Forgive me," Roslyn said. "I didn't wish to believe your betrayal, but I didn't know what else to think."

Margaret gently cupped Roslyn's hand with both of hers. "'Tis an anxious time," she said. "No one knowing who they can trust. I certainly do not. Wife of a monster, indeed."

Staring away, she continued, "He was no monster when I married him. The whole thing was arranged, of course. The nobility has many luxuries, but it does not afford us the chance to meet, fall in love, or any of that peasantry folly. But when I met Rothgar, I thought, by Déagar," she sighed, "I am the luckiest girl alive." She smiled sadly as she turned to face Roslyn.

"We were barely more than children," Margaret recounted, "sixteen and fifteen. Rothgar was a handsome Silthex squire. So smart and strong. Half budding warrior. Half budding priest. A young man truly dedicated wholeheartedly to God Déagar. I realize that means nothing to you but to me . . ." She glanced down. "To me 'twas everything.

"Of course, at the time, I knew nothing of the mysterious Knights Silthex," Margaret continued. "Most didn't. Even today, few know much, including myself, but this was years before the civil unrest. Before Patriarch Krasil gained power over the Church. Before all the hate. All I knew was how very eagerly Rothgar strove to become a valiant *Silthex knight*. Like an excited boy, it was all he ever talked about." Margaret smiled, but briefly. "In truth, his drive was one of the reasons I loved him. I wanted it for him, supported, nay, pushed him, as he trained every day. Often, he left for months with the Order and returned unable to say a single word about anything that had occurred."

"Yes." Roslyn nodded as she recalled her time as an apprentice. "I'm familiar with the dedication and secrecy needed for such things."

"Yes, of course," Margaret said. "The Order of Azerents must have many similarities to the Order of Knights Silthex. And, I fear, many dissimilarities. I remember a few days before my husband was finally knighted—he would have been twenty-one then, a month after Krasil became patriarch. I found him in our home sitting in the dark just..." She paused, turning to the floor. "Just staring at the wall, horrified. I asked him what was wrong.

"He said, 'The Order is not what I thought it was, Meggy.' He would not elaborate. Later, he would deny his having ever said it at all. Claimed I had *misheard* him. I know what I heard. But he never said anything else like that, so I assumed all was well." She shrugged and lightheartedly lifted a hand. "Pre-knighting jitters." Deflated, she whispered, "Was I a fool, Roslyn?"

Roslyn blinked downward. "The Silthex knights are celebrated throughout the Empire. If you were a fool, so are many, many others."

Margret stared as she folded her hands at her waist. "You are kind." She slowly fidgeted her thumbs. "But I was right there," she said gravely, "by his side, encouraging him. And he changed, bit by bit, but so much. He was never unkind to me—I know he loves me even now—but looking back, I realized how much darker and distant he became."

Roslyn neared her, her chain rattling against the floor, and placed her hand on hers. "'Tis all right."

"No." Margaret turned away. "No, we were so cruel to the Karulents. I personally did nothing directly, but I ignored so much. Patriarch Krasil convinced us it was for the 'better-

ment of the world.'" Her words were hollow, spoken sorrowfully. "The Church tended to the sick; thus, when the plague
hit, it hit the Church the hardest. The Karulent Church had
the Azerent Healers, but much of the Church of Déagar—
some might say the best of it—died. The plague touched so
many."

"My father," Roslyn whispered, "was one of the last victims of the plague."

"My condolences," Margaret said. "But perhaps you can, at
least in some small part, understand the state we were in.
Patriarch Krasil rose to power over a fractured Church and a
panicked people. And he filled the many vacancies within the
clergy with men of his choosing. We believed them when they
blamed the Blue Sickness on the practitioners of magic. And
we . . . hated them." She looked into Roslyn's eyes. "Hated
you."

Roslyn was speechless and sick. None of this was news to
her, but to hear it recounted by the agonized words of a
Déagrian stirred deep within her soul. She wanted to slap her
and scream, *How could you allow it!* She wanted to console her
and say, *What could you have done?*

"People began disappearing in the capital." Margaret, aggrieved, began to pace. "Well, across the entire Empire, in
truth, but Dayigo is where we lived, thus where I witnessed it.
One by one, they just vanished. It wasn't the sort of thing we
liked to talk about, but we knew why. Certain shops were
closed down for various reasons, yet the majority *happened* to
belong to Karulents. In time, the Karulent cathedral in
Dayigo was so ruthlessly vandalized that it too closed its
doors. 'Twas a slow escalation. By the time the king declared
the worship of God Karulus illegal, we had already become
accustomed to the idea. Then, news of those *horrible* raids on

Karulent towns." Margaret stopped and set her hand across her mouth as she clamped her eyes shut.

"Did your husband ever mention a town named Hunia?"

"Hunia? No, why?"

"Not even once?" Roslyn asked. "Did he bother to say its name a single time?"

"Not that I recall?"

"Please leave," Roslyn whispered. "I don't fault you, but ..." She swallowed dryly, straining to keep her calm. "Please, just leave."

Margaret neared Roslyn. "We must both leave," Margaret said, reaching out her hand. "Together. This horrible hole is what made me see what was before me the entire time. I glimpsed things here. I heard whispers. I didn't want to believe, but I ..." She looked downward. "The Silthex must be stopped. I realized that. That is why I fled, to seek help."

Roslyn nodded, but did not take Margaret's hand.

She lowered her hand. "Time is short," Margaret said firmly. "We must raise an army of as many as we can quickly gather to come here. Believe me, nothing Supreme Patriarch Krasil, Grand Master Blastilv, or the Silthex have done is the will of Déagar. And I will do everything in my power to vanquish those who use God Déagar's holy name in vain."

"I can't go with you."

"Don't be foolish, Roslyn. I assure you, you have no reason to mistrust—"

"I trust you, Margaret. I do. At least, I think I do. But both you and I have hidden and run too much already. If I leave, Blastilv will find, torture, and kill more Azerents until he finds another who is spiritually strong enough to be put into his warrior. If another even exists."

"Are you truly so exceptional?"

Roslyn nodded. "I'm beginning to believe even more so than I realized. Here, Blastilv's vile experiments pushed me to my limits, and I found those limits far exceeded what I'd thought them to be."

"All the more reason for you to be as far from here as possible."

"No," Roslyn whispered. "I took a vow to do no harm, but . . ." She gripped the chain bound to her collar as she looked up toward the cell door. "But what if, like you before, I do harm by my passivity? What if, sometimes, 'tis more harmful not to fight? To ignore. Countless people need my help. I will stay. And I *will* stop the Silthex."

Praise be to Karulus, spirit of truth, and of compassion."
Alone, Roslyn kneeled on the rocky floor of her cell.
Head bowed. Hands folded at her waist. Night had gone, and she could feel the sun's single ray of warmth through the tiny shaft directly above her.

The vile Kla would soon come, she knew: he had warned morning would be the time of his deed.

"Purify me, O God, make me a vessel for thy works."

She hadn't slept. Roslyn had prayed all night since Margaret had left, and she prayed still.

Death was something for which she was prepared. She assumed that even the most devout Karulents retained some lingering doubt in matters of the hereafter, as did she. However, Roslyn held fast to the near certainty that—when death came and the Reaper, Xanorael, guided her to the Hall of Truth to stand before the Lavender Lady—God Karulus would stand at Roslyn's side and speak as her advocate. Afterward, he would guide her safely to the paradise of Laqyigo.

Yet to have her soul locked—conscious but unable to act—in a stone body for centuries, terrified her.

Roslyn put the fear, as best as she could, out of her head.

She touched two fingers to the center of her forehead. "I call north to Lágeya, Titaness of Light, creator of life, Holy Mother of the Gods; bless me."

She touched her fingers to the base of her sternum. "I call south to Titan Jerah, the all-seeing sun, father of the Gods; see me."

She touched her right shoulder. "I call west to Karulus, God of the Sapphire Ib, spirit of truth and compassion; empower me."

She touched her left shoulder. "I call east to Ashatra, the Lavender Lady, wife of Karulus; enlighten me."

She clasped her hands together. "As is your will, so may it be."

The sound of the door's unlocking echoed through the chamber.

Blastilv entered and stood at the ledge, peering his rancorous eyes down at her.

Roslyn kept calm, meeting his gaze.

"Be thou elated, child," he said. "This morn, thy wicked flesh will be torn apart, and thou wilt be born anew within a holy form of mighty stone. And lo, by thy lithic hands, the world will be purged of all reprobates who would dare defy the Church of Déagar."

Four Silthex knights entered, one holding a white banner with the same crest as emblazoned on their white surcoats. Atop their heads, each wore a white pointed hood.

They descended the stairs toward Roslyn.

One yanked her to her feet, while another unchained her. He commanded her to move.

Up the stairs and down long, narrow tunnels, they joined others and marched in a slow procession. Chanting in unison. Candles on staffs. Incense wafting from a dangling ball.

At last, they came to a large, craggy area nearly a hundred feet across and encircled by the jagged, natural walls of the collapsed mountain. The tallest of this varying barrier towered fifty feet, opened to the gray-clouded day.

Two hundred Silthex knights, all within the white surcoats and conical hoods, stood within a half-circle formation. Three times as many Silthex sergeants, in hooded black, stood at their flanks. All chanted as they faced a great white marble statue.

The statue stood eight feet tall, with his right arm stretching higher. The stone warrior, Fersivolíel, had the feet and lower legs of a lion, yet his muscular upper legs, locked in a powerful stance, were humanoid. A carved skirt of a front and rear panel clothed him. A belt of gold, heptagonal plates circled his waist. His powerfully built torso, too, like that of a mighty Human, led up to broad shoulders. Two large bat-like wings spread at full span from his back. His face, framed in long hair, was contorted in pain, sharp teeth gritting. His thick, bestial right arm was a tower stretched to the heavens and ended at a clawed hand clutched around . . . nothing.

His sword was missing, Roslyn noted, as she recalled the warrior's final moments, as retold from the Chrono'qyelseran. Long ago, the mighty Fersivolíel had stood atop a mountain as he thrust his snake-entwined sword to the sky.

Seeing him, Roslyn realized she'd been a fool to fear that this True Light warrior would have fought for Blastilv. Even frozen in his ultimate moment of battle and pain, his eyes held holiness. But the point was moot, for the soul of Fersivolíel was long away and this was but a corpse.

Grand Master Blastilv raised his hand. The chanting ceased. "Harken, Azerent. I am a collector of many powerful items, like thee and Fersivolíel. I possess the Staff of Infinity. I nearly owned a Wand of Elfhame. As a scholar, thou wouldst no doubt appreciate my acquisitions. Behold this excellent treasure." He motioned.

Rothgar approached from around the statue. He reverently held a wooden box engraved with a five-pointed star behind a five-petaled flower: the Seal of the Azerents. He placed it on a small golden table set before the warrior and opened it.

Inside, atop white velvet, set a spherically cut black gem about the size of a fist. The edges of its facets sparkled with hints of deep purple.

"Dost thou know this relic?" Blastilv asked just behind Roslyn. "'Tis a blackened amethyst."

"Should I know it?"

"Long past, it belonged to the progenitor of thine own cult. King Azerhad slew a Demon and took this, its heart, as his prize. Centuries later, it will now be the key to destroying his Azerents. Thou wilt set thy hand upon it, and thy soul will fly into the stone warrior to be, therein, trapped. I assure thee, thine agony will amplify a hundredfold if thou dost resist."

Roslyn stared, unblinking, at the malevolent thing. "Unthinkable."

"And yet it shall soon be." Blastilv grinned. "A fate far worse than death."

She whispered, "Why me?" Louder she continued, flatly, letting no fear mark her tone. "Why have you chosen me?" She stood postured, turning then to Blastilv as she awaited an answer.

"Thou knowest wherefore."

"I pray you, answer."

He scoffed. "Thou dost waste thy final breaths on errant pride. Behold," he spoke up to all as he lifted his aged, sagging arms, "this is the sin of our enemy."

He grabbed Roslyn by the head and yanked her ear to his mouth. He whispered, "Thou hast more spiritual energy than any other person alive today. And for that, thou shalt be mine." He released her.

Roslyn remained calm. "Yet you think I cannot defend myself."

She blinked, and her eyes glowed fully blue. She swung her arms forward, and Blastilv was thrown back to crash into the wall.

Five nearby knights rushed her as they drew their swords.

She circled her hand three times above her head and shouted, "In the name of Karulus, I conjure protection from those who would do me harm." She pointed to the ground. "Anesthetize!"

A wall of marbled blue light shot upward from the floor and quickly spread in both directions around her, meeting itself as a circle.

The knights who passed through fell unmoving to the ground. The others stopped, yet stood just outside. Many of the others in the area began moving toward her, drawing swords and crowding the wall but not daring to enter.

She ignored them, instead turning to stare defiantly at the fallen Kla, outside the circle against the rocky wall.

He moaned as he tried to push himself up.

"Interestingly," she began, "that, how I threw you across the room, is exactly what happened the first few times I tried to move a patient. Well, I couldn't throw as far then, but pretty much exactly. Luckily, they were just flour sacks for practice. Similarly, you wouldn't believe what happened the first time I dissected a cadaver."

She lifted her hand beside her head, and a small shard of blue light appeared within her fingertips. "'Twas messy."

However, a green light encapsulated the shard, burning it to vapor.

Roslyn turned to see Rothgar braced. His sword, drawn, glowed with green aetherial flames.

He neared, passing unaffected into the circle. "Do you think you're the first Azerent to fight back?"

He swung his sword, and a ball of green fire spun out, hitting Roslyn and burning into the flesh of her stomach.

She cried out, grabbing her stomach, as she buckled to her knees.

Cheers sounded from the knights outside the circle. They stomped and rhythmically clanked their weapons together.

Panting, Roslyn managed to shout over the noise, "You fight to rid the world of magic, yet you use it yourself?"

Rothgar scoffed. "Do you think you're the first Azerent to say that?" He cast another fireball.

Roslyn thrust out her hand toward it, stopping it in midair. She pushed the ball to spiral back toward him.

He dodged, leaping to the side, but keeping his sword ready.

The fireball passed through the circle, hitting another knight. He screamed as he burned to blackened bone.

Again, Roslyn set her hand to her stomach, and her injuries faded away, leaving but a large charred hole in her dress as the lone remnant.

She stood strong. "I don't want to fight you, any of you, but I *will* triumph. For I am a *healer*. And *you*, you are a *disease!*"

Roslyn thrust out her hands and the circle expanded to seventy feet across, knocking more knights unconscious while most fled back.

"The True Light is the only way," Rothgar shouted. "All others will perish."

"We are both of the True Light!" Roslyn screamed as she thrust both of her hands forward.

A wave rippled out, throwing over the golden table and sending the Demon heart rolling across the floor. But Rothgar stood firm as the wave passed around him.

"You may be the best healer in the world," he said, as he stepped forward. "But battle casting is another matter. And I am unsurpassed, empowered by the blessings of God Déagar."

"Do you think God Déagar is served by *him?*" She motioned to where Blastilv had fallen.

The Kla was gone.

Roslyn looked around, seeing no sign of him.

A force struck her, throwing her off her feet to tumble across the floor.

The onlookers exploded in vehement shouts.

Roslyn weakly pushed herself up.

She was nearly to the edge of the circle, and knights gathered, ready to strike.

Rothgar neared as he held his hand forward.

She began sliding backward toward the edge.

"I should thank you," Rothgar said, his hand cast toward Roslyn as waves of force pushed her toward the circle's edge.

Roslyn scratched her nails against the rough floor, grappling for any handhold.

"Ripping apart your little town," he said, "set me on course to the rank I have today. Many good thanks to you, statue girl."

"Five-inch-wide incision, right deltoid!" She cast her hand toward Rothgar.

A deep cut formed into his upper arm. Rothgar grabbed it, as blood dripped around his fingers.

Roslyn jumped to her feet, darting away from the circle's edge.

The crowd jeered.

"Twelve-inch-wide, deep incision, left lateral thoracic!" She waved her hand.

Rothgar shouted in agony as his chest sliced open, showing ribs within a pouring of blood.

Roslyn froze, horrified by her own actions. Every part of her wanted to help him, but she could not.

He set the side of his burning sword against his chest and called out again as the wound closed. A sloppy heal, flesh melded hideously together with blood oozing, but enough to keep him in the fight.

"Twelve-inch-wide, deep inci—"

Rothgar cast three fireballs from his sword, hitting both of her shoulders and her throat, burning into her flesh.

Roslyn called out hoarsely as little more than a hiss. She could not lift her arms. She felt dizzy, but knew she could not catch herself if she fell.

"Cast now, *witch!*" he shouted. "I invite you."

She strained in attempts, but could not.

The crowd roared, and Rothgar lifted his sword victoriously over his head as he circled to face them.

He returned to Roslyn, hunched over as she choked and wheezed.

"I would kill you now if we did not need you alive." He kicked her to the hard floor.

The pain of the impact against the rock caused her entire body to coil.

"Luckily," he said, "the Demon heart will extract your soul regardless of if you are standing or lying broken on the floor."

She began to panic, but kept her wits. She closed her eyes and let her hand fall limply to the floor.

Conjuring all her might, she concentrated.

The walls of the circle spiraled inward, forming a tight coil that nearly filled the entire area within the circle with the same marbled walls of light as the perimeter.

Rothgar resisted the effects, but struggled as the field glowed brighter. He tried to move within the gaps of the spiraled wall, but found the spaces too narrow. Instead, he could do nothing but brace himself, face wincing, as Roselyn's magic flowed through him.

Soon, he touched his hand to his head as he grimaced in pain. Daunted, he tried to dash toward the edge of the circle but stumbled, falling to his knees.

"I can resist your magic, witch," he said, straining. The light continued to waft through his body, draining him. "Not even you can keep up this spell much longer."

She ignored him. "Praise be to God Karulus," she hissed through burned vocals. "Spirit of truth. Empower me and make me strong."

She envisioned her wounds healing. Her throat and shoulders began to glow.

"Praise *Déagar*," she continued, her voice growing stronger, "eldest of the Gods. Give me strength over those who tarnish your name, for they are *your* enemies too."

The spiral of blue ignited as fires of brilliant red.

Rothgar called out, but did not fall.

Roslyn's wounds completed their healing as she stood.

The spiral faded so that again, only the perimeter glowed blue as before.

Breathing deeply, Roslyn watched Rothgar push himself back up to his feet to stand before her.

"You failed," he said. "I remain afoot."

"No," she said solemnly. "I can see the signs and symptoms of your nearing pneuma depletion. Resisting my magic has drained you of your own. If you attempt to cast again, you will drain your core life forces, resulting in multiple organ failures, including your brain and heart."

"I need no magic to defeat you." He held up his sword, no longer flaming.

She swatted her hand, and the sword flew away to clatter against the rocky floor.

"I mourn you," she said. "But I must end this, regardless of what it does to me. Perdinok is a dark world. If you taint the Light, who will be left to save it?"

She raised her hand toward the sky.

A woman called out, "*Roslyn, stop!*"

Roslyn looked to see Margaret crouching against the rocky wall just outside the circle.

"Meggy, leave this place," Rothgar commanded.

"You kill him and what next?" Margaret began. "You kill the hundreds of knights and sergeants in this room? You hunt down the few remaining Silthex after that and kill them as well? What will that do to *you*? In this desperate time, the world needs a healer."

Roslyn's raised hand glowed. "'Tis the only way, Meggy. Blastilv's vile horde threatens the True Light in a manner far worse than the Darkness ever has. Look at what they've already done to the Dayigan Empire. I barely remember peace. What will they do if they grow stronger?"

"There is another way," Margaret said as she glanced down. The Demon heart was right beside her where the floor met the rocky wall. She held her hand just above it.

Both Roslyn and Rothgar cried out to her.

Roslyn could see the pain in Rothgar's face, unlike the worst injury she'd set upon him.

Knights charged Margaret.

"*Stay back!*" she yelled. "Or, by Déagar, I swear I will touch it now." She turned to Roslyn. "If the Silthex puts a soul into the warrior that's not strong enough, it will destroy it, yes?"

"In truth," Rothgar called out, "we know not what will happen. Except you will be dead, for naught. Do not sacrifice *your* life for this depraved Karulent. They are enemies to all that is good and decent."

"I think you believe that, husband. I think that, in your own way, twisted by years under Blastilv's lies, you attempt to do what is just. But I know my young squire would not agree."

Margaret slammed her hand down on the blackened amethyst.

Both Roslyn and Rothgar called out as they dashed toward her.

Margaret screamed with such a horrible blast of agony that it shook the stone walls surrounding the area. Then she was silent.

Rothgar dashed through the blue wall, stumbling as pain hit his depleted body. He grabbed Margaret, holding his limp wife tight within his arms. Through the walls of the circle, Roslyn watched him cry out for her. He kept repeating the word *no*, as if he could undo what had happened with the simple word.

"Heal her!" he commanded Roslyn.

"I . . ." The master healer looked at the body. It was empty. "She is gone."

A rumble, like thunder, sounded from the stone warrior.

Aghast, Roslyn turned to it, as did all of the Silthex.

The clawed hand—frozen in an upward stretch for centuries—moved and descended.

His eyes began to glow a faint red. The head, neck cracking as it moved, turned to look toward Rothgar, who cradled a corpse.

He paused, watching.

The stone warrior then turned toward Roslyn and stepped forward. More breaks crackled up his entire body. Shards popped loose, clicking to the rocky floor.

Most of the surrounding men moved back. Roslyn, however, did not. Her stare stayed locked on his somber red eyes.

The warrior grabbed Roslyn, wrapping his lithic arm around her and pulling her against his chest. She didn't struggle.

He spread his bat-like wings and leaped from the ground.

The cracks in the stone grew deeper and more prevalent. His right leg fell off and crashed to the floor.

One of his wings broke in half, crumbling.

He nearly fell, but grabbed the top of the surrounding craggy wall with his clawed hand, slamming against it, as he held Roslyn with his other arm.

He continued to crumble. Another leg plummeted to the floor, shattering as large chunks of marble tumbled outward from the dusty epicenter.

"Go," the gravelly voice sounded, and Roslyn could hear the voice of Margaret mixed within the inhuman sound. He loosened his grip.

Roslyn struggled to climb up the warrior and onto the peak of the wall. From there, the area looked like the rim of a volcano. She stood on the edge as she stared, transfixed on the glowing red eyes.

"Meggy," Roslyn said sadly. "May the light of truth deliver you safely to Laqyigo."

More cracks formed, marring the warrior's face as his features fell away. The upper arm—strained beneath the claw gripping the wall—cracked and crumbled, breaking from the bulk of the body.

Roslyn watched the stone warrior fall, descending into the hole filled with the Silthex. He shattered against the floor, sending fire exploding out in all directions. It consumed the area within the billowing flames of deep scarlet.

Roslyn turned away as black smoke poured up in scorching torrents.

She remembered the smell of flesh burning. She remembered the sound of people screaming. Again, she was a teenage girl frozen as she watched a slaughter ablaze.

Shaking, she hurried a few paces down the slope before stopping beside a large rock. She turned and stared at the black erupting into the sky. Horrified, she could not suppress the trauma of the past as it twisted in her mind, merging as gruesome, vivid flashes with the horror of the present. She screamed and clawed the rock beside her.

"No," she panted. "No. No, I must keep going." She felt lightheaded from her heavy breaths and smoke-filled air. "I must stay strong, for Margaret."

She stood shakily, holding herself against the rock. "I will remember you, Margaret," she whispered. "In your name, I vow to end the plague of hatred infecting our lands. The True Light *will* be healed."

PART FIVE

The Blue Rose

CHAPTER TWENTY-NINE

Septkiés 27, 833: Seven Years Later

Beneath the dim blue and purple lights of the waning moons, they gathered, hidden among the tall trees of the concealing woods. Silence—save for the chirps of frogs and crickets—set heavily, as twenty men waited at Roslyn's sides.

Roslyn, crouching low, watched the nearby encampment—ten cylindrical green tents with conic roofs, some with awnings off their fronts. A few campfires burned in the trodden spaces in between. Most of the soldiers within the camp were but silhouettes, but occasionally, the moonlight or firelight would hit just right, allowing Roslyn to make out their emerald green tabards emblazoned with the symbol of Dayigo in yellow thread.

Two fighters from Port Lytel, crouching in their run, hurried from the camp and headed straight to Roslyn's position.

"Report," she whispered.

One of them leaned close. "Forty Dayigan soldiers, Commander, minimal alert, swords worn."

"How many captives?" she asked.

He shook his head. "We couldn't tell, Commander. They're locked in a cage. Maybe a dozen."

Roslyn nodded and motioned her men to gather near. "I can take out the entire camp at once," she kept her voice low, "but for an area this large, we'll need to draw a physical circle, an inch deep, around the encampment."

"How close to their camp, Commander?" a fighter asked.

"Close," she said. "The smaller the circle, the more effective with less psychic expenditure on my part."

Reaching out with both hands toward the camp, Roslyn circled her fingers in a wave.

A faint white circle formed on the ground a few feet from the perimeter, encircling the camp.

"That is our guide," Roslyn said. "Everyone, spread out and draw different sections. The entirety must be finished for me to cast my spell. Move quickly yet quietly, staying hidden as much as you can. Once we are detected—which I expect—'twill be much more difficult to finish our task."

Roslyn studied the camp for another moment before taking in a breath to steel her nerves. "Ready arms."

The Lytel rebels unsheathed their swords.

"Go."

The rebels wasted no time, spreading out around the camp and rushing inward to tackle various sections of the circle. Some planted their heels into the ground at the white circle, plowing out the soil, while others used their hands.

Roslyn found a short log that she stabbed into the woodland floor and dragged firmly.

As each fraction of the boundary reached its one-inch minimum depth, that area of the white circle changed to blue.

"You there," a soldier called from inside the camp. His voice rose with excitement, shouting, "We're under attack!"

Dayigan soldiers charged toward the Lytel fighters, and soon, the metallic ring of clashing swords rang out.

As many of the fighters as possible stayed on task—racing to complete the circle—but as more Dayigans charged them, more needed to leave the circle to fight or perish.

Sword raised, a soldier rushed toward Roslyn, but she cast out her hand and sent him hurtling into the camp. Stabbing her broken log into the white line, she frantically scuttled backward trying to gather pace toward completion.

A soldier stabbed a Lytel fighter through the gut, but Roslyn acted fast; jumping up, she cast her hand at the Dayigan—he flew back. She then rushed toward the injured fighter, raising her palm toward him and unleashing a torrent of blue energy that engulfed the man and healed him entirely.

He gave Roslyn a nod of gratitude before returning to battle.

Roslyn returned to drawing the circle, speeding her efforts.

All around her, she heard the impacts of swords and shouts of combat, but she remained on task. She needed it finished. The Dayigans greatly outnumbered the small band of Lytel fighters, and Roslyn knew her ragtag group wouldn't last much longer without her circle done.

Roslyn reached a section of the circle completed by someone else, already blue. She dashed to the next incomplete section. As she ran, one of her men was wounded by a Dayigan blade—a deep cut to the fighter's arm. With a wave, she sent the soldier flying backward, crashing into a tent. Another wave from Roslyn healed the fighter.

Finally, she connected all the sections; the entire circle appeared blue.

Two Dayigan soldiers, swords raised, rushed toward her.

She looked at the blue circle and clicked her fingers.

Nothing happened.

She ran, Dayigans in pursuit.

"There's still a piece missing," Roslyn shouted as she sprinted the perimeter as quickly as her feet would carry her.

All the while, she searched, but every fraction of the circle she saw shone blue.

The two Dayigans behind her gained ground. A third joined the chase.

Then she saw it—four inches remaining of the white guideline.

Roslyn skidded to a stop and whirled around to face the soldiers. With a flick of her wrist, they flew backward into their camp. Roslyn stabbed her fingers into the circle and clawed out the remaining piece.

Gasping for breath, she snapped her fingers once more, and this time, a wall of blue light erupted from the circle, surrounding the camp.

"Commander," a Lytel fighter called. "Some soldiers who were outside the circle flee towards the woods."

"After them," she commanded as she stood. "We cannot let them alert others."

Five of the Lytel fighters sped away in pursuit.

Thrusting both hands forward, Roslyn forced the wall of the circle to flow inward as a tight spiral, filling the camp as anesthetizing energy flowed through all trapped inside, knocking them unconscious to the ground.

Roslyn looked to see two men outside the circle fighting two of her own. She waved her hand, and the soldiers flew through the wall of light into the camp, passing out as they rolled across the ground.

She neared her fighters. "Search the perimeter," she said. "Assure that no more Dayigans remain outside the circle and assure none of our men are injured. Report back to me."

"Yes, Commander."

Returning to the circle, Roslyn extended her hand flat and slowly sliced through the wall. It dispelled as a brief swirling mist.

She stepped into the camp and soon located one of her own, sprawled senselessly on the ground. Placing her hand on his forehead, she spoke in a hushed murmur. "Awaken."

He stirred, blinking away sleep before groaning as he sat upright. "Forgive me, Commander. I couldn't leave the circle in time."

"'Tis perfectly all right." She helped him to his feet.

"The captives are this way, Commander."

Roslyn followed, her eyes surveying the unconscious soldiers strewn throughout the camp and waking any Lytel fighters she spotted along the way.

They arrived at a large cage that stood as a grid of branches secured together by ropes. Ten men and women were imprisoned within, their iron collars bound by thick ropes to a pole in the center. They, too, had been rendered unconscious by her spell.

"Key," Roslyn muttered to herself as she spun slowly, looking around.

The fighter began chopping at the cage with his sword, but Roslyn set her hand on his shoulder. "I would rather not have the structure fall on them."

"Of course, Commander." He lowered his sword.

She spotted a soldier who, by his fallen position, she assumed had been guarding the prisoners. She rushed to him, finding three iron keys fastened to his belt. Tossing them to her fighter, Roslyn commanded, "Unlock the captives."

"Commander," another fighter said as he ran up. "We've searched the camp. All soldiers have been neutralized. We have multiple men down from your spell, but no major injuries. We're performing first aid."

"Very good," she replied. "I'll revive our men soon. As for the Dayigans, the spell only has a one-hour duration, so we must act quickly. What of the soldiers who fled into the woods?"

"Permanently neutralized, Commander. But we secured a prisoner. He claims to have information that you'd find useful. About the villain Blastilv."

Roslyn nodded. "My thanks. I will go to him shortly."

She rushed into the cage to view the comatose captives, shackles now removed. The conditions were shockingly unsanitary, filled with the stench of piss and shit and decaying food. The people, too, were filthy, visibly starved, and dressed in rags.

The setting angered Roslyn—even if the cage had been a pen for dogs, it would have angered her, but these were people, *her people*, hated for no reason.

Roslyn moved to the closest captive and set her finger on his forehead. "Awaken."

She hurried to the next and did the same.

As she woke the last of the captives, the majority were sitting up on the dirt, all maintaining various degrees of disorientation.

"You're 'er, aren't you?" a man asked. "The Blue Rose."

"Some call me that, yes." She helped a woman to her feet.

"Praise be to Karulus," the woman said, as she stumbled weakly against Roslyn.

All the captives repeated a sickly, un-unified chorus of "Praise be to Karulus, spirit of truth, and of compassion."

To a Lytel fighter, Roslyn said, "The soldiers must have water here somewhere. Pray you, fetch it quickly and assure all here may drink."

"Yes, Commander." He dashed away.

Roslyn leaned the woman against the side of the cage and assured that she could hold herself upright. Roslyn then centered herself on the soon-to-be-freed people.

"You're all going to be fine. We've come to take all of you to Port Lytel."

"Thank Karulus," someone spoke up.

Roslyn continued. "There, we will allow you to rest and recover. We will also give you the choice to join the Veiled River, if you wish, and either stay at Lytel or sail the River to the Karulent Alliance, where our people may live normal lives free of persecution. Of course, if you wish to leave the Veiled River after you recover at Lytel, you retain that option too. No longer are you captives."

"Our thanks, Blue Rose," another man said. "You're a gift from the heavens."

Roslyn nodded. The title made her uncomfortable, as did the praise. She nearly reminded them that she was but a small part of the Veiled River, but she moved on. "Drink plenty of water," she instructed them instead. "My men will bring it to you shortly. We have a hard march spanning days ahead of us before we reach Lytel, so 'tis important you hydrate yourselves."

Roslyn stepped away, but realizing that was an odd note to end on, she added, "May God Karulus keep you well."

Then, turning to the fighter who'd told her of Dayigan's captive, she said, "Take me to the soldier with information on Blastilv."

—

In the wooded area just outside the camp, Roslyn and a Lytel fighter approached four other Lytel men standing in a loose circle around a Dayigan soldier.

The soldier cowered on the leaf-strewn ground, his legs nearly to his chest, as his wide, crazed eyes manically searched the surrounding area as he clawed at his knees.

Roslyn neared cautiously and started to speak.

"Get her away from me!" the soldier cried. His hand darted to his mouth, not so much biting his fingernails as clawing at his teeth. "She's one of them, ain't she? A witch. I seen her kind before, a man, though. He rotted . . ." He began clawing at his scalp. "He rotted the skin from their bones. Hundreds of innocent Dayigan men all around me, dying screaming, screaming, screaming!"

"I was told you have information about Blastilv."

He chuckled breathily, paused—staring with wide eyes— and chuckled more. "I know who you are. I seen a drawing. You're the one what wiped out his knights, ain't you?" He began quickly tapping the side of his head. "I know more 'an what people think I know. You're the Blue Witch. No more Knights Silthex now, are there?"

"Do you know Blastilv's location?" she questioned coolly, despite the mad scene before her.

"West. West, west." He gained an enormous smile. "They sent me west. They loaded us all up on a big ship in the holy city of Wendian and sent us to the untamed lands of the tree savages."

"The Drevite Nation?" she asked. "Was Blastilv there?"

"That's the place. They say Archbishop Blastilv led the Drevite Experiment, but I never laid eyes on him, meself. The commander give us our orders. Then the witch came. He was like a Demon above us with red light shining from his hands. And hundreds of good Dayigan men rotted whilst we retreated." He smelled the back of his hand. "I still smell it on my skin. The stench of the rot."

Roslyn set her fingers to her temples as she cradled her head for a moment. There seemed to be a kernel of truth in whatever he was spouting, but it was so twisted up in madness that it was difficult for her to determine what was real. She took a deep breath and looked at him again. "Can you tell me *when* this happened?"

"Long ago," he said. "Years and years and years ago. Or days ago."

"Can you tell me *what year*?"

"Eight thirty-one."

"Two years ago," Roslyn said to herself. "Where is Blastilv now?"

"I got away. I missed the ship, but I got away. But he found me. The witch found me. His cat... There was this giant dead cat. It sucked out me brain. So many nightmares. So real and horrible. The evil cat put chaos in me head. The Army just keeps me around for odd jobs now. I ain't good for much, says them, but I know more 'an what they think I know."

"'Tis all right." Roslyn crouched to his level. "I want to know what you know. What is the Drevite Experiment?" She reached out her hand consolingly toward his upper arm.

The man started screaming frantically as he pushed himself back across the ground. "Get her away from me! She's a witch. 'Tis him. He's found me again." He began to hyperventilate. "He's found me. Get him away from me. He'll rot off my skin!"

"Anesthetize," Roslyn said.

The man fell unconscious to the ground.

She stood and neared her fighters.

"Do you think his story is true, Commander?"

"In part. Perhaps. However, no one in centuries has wielded power on the level of the 'witch' he describes, much less a Drevite, but I do believe Blastilv must have led a military campaign in Drevite lands. It sounds as if the Dayigans fought a bloody battle. And they lost. 'Tis unlikely Blastilv remains two years after the fact. Even so, I will send word to the western arm of the Veiled River to investigate."

"And him?" The soldier glanced at the sleeping madman.

"Take him to the camp with the other soldiers. He'll awaken soon after them."

"If the beasts of the forest don't get them first," the fighter added.

"That is not our concern," Roslyn said. "Gather our people. We begin our march to Lytel forthwith."

CHAPTER THIRTY

A single flame flickered in the dark as it struggled atop the melted remnant of its soon-depleted taper candle. The white wax dripped down the cheap tin candlestick, pooling on the cavern floor. The tiny light did little against the surrounding dark, and Roslyn knew she hadn't much time before it snuffed out completely. Yet, she ignored it. Sitting on the ground with her legs crisscrossed and her hands on her knees, Roslyn stared at the small river running through the cave. Its water appeared black, though its minor peaks caught the candlelight. Its current was gentle as it babbled over its rocky bed.

"Relax," she whispered to herself. Roslyn set her fisted hand to her forehead. *"Relax,"* she ordered through clenched teeth. She needed this, to relax, not only for her mental well-being but also to recharge her inner magic. She needed to stay strong for her port.

Though all of Port Lytel was underground, this area conveyed it most clearly. The space between the river and the wall was narrow. Though Roslyn could stand, the craggy ceiling would be not quite a foot above her head if she were to do so. She could almost feel the hundred feet of rock above her pressing down. Many people loathed the area, complaining of a feeling of claustrophobia. To Roslyn, the small space offered refuge, a feeling of cool calm and protection. Everywhere else, *she* needed to be the fortress, protecting her people, yet here, the rocky walls were the fortress around her. Here, Roslyn could relax—normally.

She pressed her fisted hand against her forehead. "Relax," she said again, this time a desperate imploration. She even added please, as if her body might respond better to niceties.

"Commander," a voice sounded from the dark.

Roslyn faced upward, staring a frustrated moment at the rocky ceiling before she turned to see the silhouette of a man.

She recognized him—more by voice than form—as one of her fighters.

"Speak."

"Forgive me for disturbing you, Commander, but I have news that may raise your spirits."

"Did we find him? Blastilv?"

The silhouette faced downward. "No, Commander. But you have a visitor. From Reyigo. She says she is the widow of the priest who recruited you into the Azerent Mages."

"Cyneburga?" Roslyn whispered the name she hadn't spoken in years, and she couldn't help but smile around it. "Tell her I'll meet her in the chapel."

—

Roslyn entered the chapel area of Port Lytel to see Cyneburga, lost in thought, viewing the statues of Karulus. There were nine statues, each a little different, all over six feet tall and raised higher by their shared pedestal at the front of the chapel. Stone, metal, or wood—they each depicted a young man with blue skin and gold wings. The faces differed but were recognizable as the Azure Son of the Sun— some figures focusing on the God of the sea and water aspect, while others leaning more toward his healing.

Roslyn stepped forward. "They're beautiful, are they not?"

Cyneburga looked back at her and nodded. "Yes." She sighed. "But also . . . a little sad. Each one represents a fallen church. And judging by their quality, they're from churches much larger than our little Hunian parish."

"True. But I like to think, one day, they will stand before great congregations again."

Cyneburga nodded. There was a sadness about her that Roslyn had grown accustomed to seeing in most of their people, but in this figure from her youth—from before the dark times—in Cyneburga, the grief seemed wrong and struck to the heart. Against reason, a part of Roslyn expected her to be like the statues, frozen in a better time.

Instead, Cyneburga was older, in her late sixties or early seventies, now. Thinner. Faded. Unable to wear her church habit in the Dayigan Empire, she wore a drab gray dress that seemed fit for a poor fisher widow.

"I'm glad you could save them," Cyneburga said, adding a thin, forced smile, as if an afterthought. "We smuggled in some supplies for you and your passengers." She motioned to the cave-like entrance near the infirmary.

There, the first of a line of men Roslyn didn't recognize mixed with residents of the port to haul in barrels, burlap sacks, and crates.

Fidgeting her fingers and barely making eye contact, Cyneburga began walking toward the forming stacks in the main hall. "'Tis mostly food. Grains and dried meats. Some dried fruits. Herbs. *Barrels* of anything that could be pickled. There's some textiles and other items for you, too."

"It looks to be much more than our usual shipment from the Alliance," Roslyn said as they walked among the people hauling goods. She couldn't quite read the evasive woman, but decided to ignore it for now. "I'll begin rationing everything out to the other ports as soon as possible. On behalf of all Karulents in the Empire, I give you my thanks."

"Honestly, only a tiny part of the credit belongs to me directly. Everyone on the Alliance side of the Veiled River wants to support your efforts here. They talk about you, you know—the famed *Blue Rose*. They tell stories and sing songs of all you've accomplished. I admit, I can't listen to them all. I do worry for you, dear."

"'Tis but a silly nickname, nothing more. Idle tongues have created something of a legend around it."

"'Twould seem"—Cyneburga turned away—"you've become more of a soldier than a healer."

Roslyn glanced to the floor as she nodded. "I've become what our people needed me to become."

"Yes, and I'm certain your parents and Father Hanugfrie are watching you from Laqyigo and smiling with pride at the strong woman you've become. But . . ." She turned her fretful eyes to Roslyn's. "I do wonder what happened to the little girl who wished to be a healer."

"I am *still* a healer." A hint of defensiveness marked Roslyn's voice. She ran her hand over a soft bolt of wool fabric stacked atop a crate before she slowly walked toward an empty section of the large room.

They walked an additional few paces before Cyneburga leaned in and said, "Since you've taken command of this place, many have started calling it *Fort* Lytel." The words were spoken flatly, almost pleasantly, and Roslyn wasn't sure if they were meant to be an accusation. Roslyn decided not to take them as such but grew guarded.

"I've heard," Roslyn said and added a laugh. She'd always thought the play on words to be humorous, though Cyneburga didn't seem to share the joke. "The nickname has become so prevalent that many think it is the actual name. Nevertheless, I am certain that an aggressive stance with the Dayigans is the only way to end this civil war and allow our people to return home."

Cyneburga set the back of her hand to her mouth. "I know." She nodded. "I do. I really do, dear. But that was never the intent of the Veiled River. Or the intent of an Azerent Healer. The River was meant to help our people get to the Hyvile River and across it to the Karulent Alliance."

Roslyn stopped walking. Left wordless, she stared at Cyneburga. Though there'd been no anger in the elder woman's tone, there was no more ignoring the disapproval. Roslyn felt attacked in a way that no one else in the world could affect her, a childish hurt.

"I had to do what I did," Roslyn whispered. "You've been away from the Empire far too long to understand."

Cyneburga set her hand on Roslyn's. "Forgive me if it sounds as if I'm criticizing you, dear. You were right to do the things you've done. I'm just . . ." She squeezed her hand briefly. "I'm just worried about you, Rose." She released her hand. "You killed off the Silthex Knights. Your so-called 'Lytel Army' has attacked Dayigan fort after Dayigan fort."

"Rescue missions. And acts to destabilize the Empire."

"Roslyn, you're the most wanted woman—most wanted *person* of the largest Empire in the world."

"I've been number one on their list for years, and they've yet to catch me."

Cyneburga said nothing. She'd returned her pale fist to her mouth as she rubbed her index finger with her thumb.

"'Tis nice that you worry about me," Roslyn said, "but you have no cause. I am prepared for whatever end will come my way, and in the meantime, I will fight for our people and to

244 鯨 Jeremiah Cain

stop the Dayigans. You, too, are a sister of the Church, and you know, as well as I, that we must sometimes make sacrifices, even of ourselves, if it means helping our fellow man. That is truer now, in this time of turmoil, than it has ever been before." It was not the most assuring answer, Roslyn knew, but she wasn't about to stand before Cyneburga and try to convince her that the civil war was some sort of holiday.

"Things have escalated," Cyneburga said. "The Veiled River Commission wants you to leave the Dayigan Empire permanently and join the leadership north of the Hyvile."

"I—no. I cannot leave the—"

"They knew you'd resist," she said, cutting her off. "That's why they sent me here, to convince you. Roslyn, they're shutting down the entire Empire side of the Veiled River."

"But that *is* the Veiled River."

"We do a lot in the Karulent Alliance, as well. The countless refugees sent to us may not be in hiding there, but their journey is far from over. You would be a valued asset to our mission."

"My mission is *here*."

"Your mission is a success." Cyneburga sighed and then smiled. "The Veiled River was meant to get the Karulents out of the Dayigan Empire. And so it has done. Now, 'tis time to bring the port commanders and crews to the Alliance as well."

"I am pleased you came all this way, Cyneburga," Roslyn said firmly, "and if you would like to *visit* with me, I'd love to get reacquainted. However, I will not have this particular conversation. My work is here."

"The Veiled River has no *choice* in the matter, Roslyn!" Cyneburga burst in frustration. Afterward, she paused, composing herself.

Roslyn said nothing. Even such a minor outburst was uncharacteristic of Cyneburga—at least it was, years ago—and it threw Roslyn off guard.

At length, Cyneburga continued. "As I said, things have escalated. The Dayigans are putting pressure on the Alliance to end their support of the Veiled River. They're threatening war."

"They've threatened war with the Alliance for the last—"

"'Tis different this time." Cyneburga looked up, past Roslyn's shoulder.

Roslyn turned to see a man, a stranger, about ten years younger than herself—so, nearly thirty. His neat black hair hung just below his well-defined jawline and matched the trimmed goatee adorning his thin, deeply tanned face. He was lean and moderately well dressed—a thigh-length gray leather vest over an off-white shirt. He maintained a stiff, noble posture, yet his deep brown eyes showed uncertainty and a hint of sadness behind them, causing the posture to seem forced.

Approaching, he said, "What Sister Cyneburga is trying not to tell you is that the Dayigans are blaming *you*."

"Me?"

"I assure you," he said, "we—that is, the Veiled River Commission—are not blaming you for anything, and we see your actions as brave and necessary." He had a slight accent, most likely from the western edge of the Empire.

Roslyn eyed him for a moment. "And who, may I ask, is the bearer of this vexing news?"

"What are you asking?" the man asked.

"Your *name*. Who are you?" It could have been better stated, but her brain was tired.

"Right. Forgive me. I am Estéban, commander of Port Haven. It is one of the Alliance-side ports that receives the refugees your people send across the Hyvile."

"I'm familiar with Port Haven. And you said the Dayigans plan a war?"

"Yes. There are ancient treaties set between the Kingdom of Dayigo and the Kingdom of Reyigo, treatises that all who assume the respective crowns must vow to uphold. With Dayigo now the capital of the Dayigan Empire and Reyigo now at the helm of the Karulent Alliance, these treaties extend to all nations within the larger bodies. To put it briefly, the treaties state that the Dayigans and Reyigans cannot attack each other without a good reason."

"And I suppose I'm the reason."

He nodded. "Again, neither the Alliance nor the Commission sees any wrongdoing on your part. You are a heroine and will be honored as such—long overdue, from what I hear. But yes, when the Veiled River turned from just transporting our people to the Alliance to making calculated strikes on the Empire, it gave the Empire an excuse to break the treaties." Estéban paused and looked at her, perhaps gauging how she would take the news.

She restrained her composure, showing little sign of the storm brewing inside her. "Continue."

"The Empire is demanding that the Alliance cut all ties with any rebel factions operating in the Empire, currently or in the future. They must also stop accepting Dayigan refugees, stop shipping supplies here, and enforce laws to prohibit anyone else in the Alliance from violating the agreement."

"Those monsters. They're seeking reasons to attack the Alliance." Roslyn crossed her arms and clenched her teeth as she stared at the growing stacks of needed supplies. More than usual—with cause, she realized. "This is the last shipment of supplies."

"Yes," Estéban said.

Roslyn wanted to scream, or do something. She didn't. She felt as if the walls of her port cracked around her and the tons of rock above pressed down. That claustrophobic feeling people described in the small cave by the river now affected her, even in this vast chamber, as if the whole thing would soon crash down, burying them alive. Nevertheless, she kept her composure—as the leader of Port Lytel, as a lady of the Azerents.

Estéban's voice sounded distant as he said, "The Alliance is not the Empire. We are not as large as them, and more so, we do not have a unified army. It is something we are working on, but it will take time. While most kings in the Alliance stand with the Veiled River—and you—in spirit, they have no choice but to concede to this agreement. If not, every person in the allied nations, including the refugees we sent there, will be at risk."

Roslyn set her hand to her heart, feeling it pounding. "How long do we have?"

"The kings were able to delay signing the agreement by two months."

"It is not *nearly* enough time."

"'Tis all the time they could get us," Estéban said. "We've made a plan and should be able to get all the port crews out. We would like you to lead it. You've become the commonly accepted leader of the Dayigan side of the Veiled River. The other port commanders will listen to you."

"I haven't decided if I'm leaving yet."

"Roslyn," Cyneburga said. "You must. You'll be cut off otherwise."

"Either way," Roslyn conceded, "I'll lead the evacuation."

"Praise be to Karulus." Estéban sighed in relief, a long exhale that almost seemed exaggerated, but Roslyn could tell it was not. His rigidness washed away with the sigh, and she realized that it had truly been anxiety. He'd evidently feared that Roslyn wouldn't help him, or perhaps even hinder his efforts. Now, a pleasant smile formed within his dark goatee. He was an attractive man, Roslyn noted. She hadn't properly looked at him before.

"You said you have a plan," she said. "I'll need to know the details."

"Well, I am more the messenger than the deviser, though I did provide input. It is complicated, so I would like to say it as few times as possible. Is Port Commander Owen nearby? I can tell you both together. Assuming he agrees with it, he will be your second on this project."

"Commander Owen?" Roslyn shot him a perplexed look. "I assume he's in his own port, Port Dierne."

"Is he not in Lytel?" Now Estéban was confused, glancing about as if he might see him. "We sent a messenger ahead of us. The messenger and Commander Owen should have arrived in Lytel yesterday or the day before and given you a message to expect us."

"I received no such message. Your arrival was unexpected, and Owen is not here."

Estéban's smile faded as his features tensed again. Roslyn knew her own face surely echoed his composure. She turned to Cyneburga to see a silent dread.

"I must go to him," Roslyn said. She began a brisk walk, followed by Estéban and Cyneburga.

"I'm sure 'tis nothing." Estéban hurried to her side. "They will probably be here tomorrow."

"With respect, your optimism is born from your living in the Alliance. 'Tis not a luxury we have here." She stopped a Lytel fighter. "Gather a ten-man rescue unit. We leave in an hour."

"Yes, Commander." He hurried away.

"I'll go with you too," Estéban said. "But we should begin the evacuation as soon as possible. With your permission, my men can start the first phases without us."

Roslyn stopped, took a deep breath, and exhaled. She would have liked to have known the plan before implementing it. But time was short. "Do it." She felt as if she'd condemned the Veiled River to death with two words.

She turned to Cyneburga.

The elderly woman shook her head. "I'm not going to try to stop you from your rescue mission. I know there's no point. But do be safe, dear."

"I will." Roslyn took Cyneburga's hands in both of her own. "'Tis but a day and a half's journey. Whilst I'm gone, tell all of Port Lytel of the situation with the Dayigans."

Cyneburga nodded. "May God Karulus keep you well, dear."

"I'll return shortly, and we can catch up properly."

CHAPTER THIRTY-ONE

The large door was ajar before Roslyn carefully pushed it inward and slowly entered a short corridor, walled on either side by irregularly sized blocks of masoned gray stone. Estéban and ten of the Lytel fighters followed her to its end, entering into a small courtyard about twenty feet across and lined by the same stone walls.

Here, four flowerbeds filled the area, each edged in hedged boxwoods with a crossed path between them. A simple birdbath marked the center. It might have been relaxing at another time, but Roslyn knew better. She kept her guard up, searching every corner, doorway, and alcove. Though day, the overcast sky filled the space with murky shadows.

"This is nice here, yes?" Estéban said. "Whose is it?"

"Silence," Roslyn whispered. "This way."

She slowly stalked across the courtyard and opened a door carefully, peeking inside before entering a large room framed by the same masoned walls. Thirty-foot high rafters peaked above them while lattice-covered windows faced back into the courtyard. The opposite wall displayed four long banners, checked red and white and edged in gold. Long tables were set against three of the walls, while the fourth wall—paneled in dark wood—held a railed balcony meant as a stage for musicians or other acts of entertainment.

Roslyn crouched to a patch of pried-up, broken floorboards and touched a splintered beam.

She returned upright and whispered, "Someone was looking for priest holes." She motioned to other pried-up patches of floorboards. A bookcase was overturned, deformed by its impact with the floor, its contents scattered. "Fan out," Roslyn said, "and stay alert."

All but Roslyn and Estéban drew swords as the group moved in guardedly.

With Estéban just behind her, Roslyn passed a section of the paneled wall that had been smashed in, but with nothing of note behind.

"*Commander!*" a Lytel fighter shouted from outside.

Roslyn heard the clashing of swords before sprinting back into the courtyard.

There, two Dayigan soldiers were attacking the fighter who'd shouted. Before she could act, one of the soldiers thrust his blade deep into the fighter's stomach, eliciting a blood-curdling howl.

Halting, Roslyn set her hand before her face, palm outward, and clawed through the air. "Lacerations!" she screamed.

Five parallel lines of blue energy ripped savagely down one of the Dayigans' bodies, shredding his tabard, mail suit, and skin alike. The soldier staggered as he grabbed his lacerated chest in agony. Yet still, he held on to his sword firmly and refused to relent.

The other Dayigan barreled toward Roslyn. Undeterred, she sent a blast of force that slammed him against a courtyard wall. He slumped unconsciously to the ground.

"End him," Roslyn commanded Estéban.

"I—" Estéban's gaze darted from Roslyn to the injured soldier in horror.

Other Lytel fighters rushed in, heading straight to the soldiers.

The clawed soldier shook off the pain and fought on despite his wounds, sword clashing with another.

Roslyn cast her right hand at the Lytel fighter who'd been stabbed—collapsed to the ground as he grasped his stomach, blood flowing between his fingers. Blue light emanated from Roslyn's fingertips, surrounding him and rapidly healing all his injuries until only unblemished skin showed beneath the punctured tunic.

Finished, Roslyn turned to Estéban, who stared back at her with wide eyes filled with fear and judgment. His gaze wandered over to the two soldiers, both now dead by Lytel swords.

"They were Dayigans?" Estéban muttered, shock lacing his voice.

Roslyn nodded.

"I thought Dayigans wore red."

Her eyes returned to the soldier she'd thrown against the wall. His bloodied tabard bore, in yellow thread, the same symbol of soldiers of the past—the sun and two moons in a triangle above a downward-pointing triangle—yet it now emblazoned an emerald green tabard.

"That has not been true for years," Roslyn said somberly. "After the destruction of the Silthex, the Dayigans took on the Silthex color to honor them. And to remember."

"You mean remember to avenge their deaths," Estéban said. "We should have gotten you out of the Empire years ago."

She met his gaze, nearly replying, before turning away. "You four," Roslyn commanded, "check upstairs. You two, go right. You two, go left. Both of you check the rooms along the front wall. Estéban and I will go search the great hall and rear wall."

—

Estéban and Roslyn stepped cautiously into a plain, cluttered kitchen. The massive hearth glowed faintly with dying embers under a large cauldron of abandoned stew. The two bulky windows, barred in squares of iron, threw a faint light over the brick walls and brick floors, revealing a scene of destruction. One of the long prep tables had been overturned, casting pottery to shatter against the floor amid large wooden bowls and ruined vegetables.

Roslyn's solemn gaze swept to the body that lay beyond them, and Estéban rushed forward to assist.

"He is gone," Roslyn said coldly, her eyes never leaving the corpse.

Estéban halted a few steps away.

The man had been garbed in noble fabrics of red embroidered in gold, but they were now stained by his own blood which had poured through his hand—still remaining on his stomach—as his veins had emptied their former contents to dry stiffly against his skin. On the surrounding floor, red crusted the brick.

Roslyn took a breath and clasped her hands, touching them to her forehead. "May the Light guide you safely to Laqyigo."

"Astha'will-miabé," Estéban said. "Did you know him?"

Roslyn nodded. "Lord Athelric. He was a good man. A Déagrian, but an ally. This was his house, which he let us use as a port."

Estéban paused, searching for words before saying, "My condolences."

She sighed. "I should not have asked you to kill that soldier. You must understand, I cannot—"

"Kill. I know. You connect to the life force in each of your patients, lending a part of yourself to awaken their dormant ability to heal themselves. If you contaminate yourself with death, you'd lose the ability to connect with their life force, as you need to do."

Roslyn continued to stare at Lord Athelric. "You shouldn't know that much about our ways."

"I also know death pains Azerent Healers." He stepped closer beside her.

"Death pains everyone."

"Yes, but it affects you more than regular people."

Roslyn closed her eyes and took a breath. "I've killed before. Before I took my vows. For most, such a deed—even before their vows—would render them unable to use our sort of magic. The few at the Azerent College who knew of my action assured me that pursuing the path of a healer was a wasted effort for me. They encouraged me to become a mage instead. However, I *insisted* that God Karulus had called on me to be a *healer* and strove diligently in my work. I *needed* to be a healer, because . . ." She looked at Estéban. ". . . because I needed to *help* people—cure the sick and injured." She gazed at the dead lord. "To halt death in its tracks. Somehow, I was blessed to be able to still walk the path meant for me, even after my deed. Even so, I must live with that blood on my hands all my days."

"I would say your extra efforts were definitely not in vain."

"And yet," she said, "I continue to lose friends."

Silence lingered as she thought of Athelric, of all he had done for her people, even when it meant putting his own life at risk.

A Lytel fighter entered. "Commander, the house is secure. We found three dead passengers."

"Gather our fighters," Roslyn said. "We enter the port through the cellar."

—

She could smell death as she descended the rickety, creaking stairs into the dark cellar. Estéban followed just behind her with two of the fighters at his back.

At the base of the stairs, Roslyn held out her torch, casting flickering shadows across the dank walls of the disheveled pantry. Many of the food items had been thrown down from the shelves lining each wall. Roslyn proceeded over grain scattered across the floor from overturned baskets. Her footsteps crunched as she approached a shelving unit on the far side of the room, which had been pulled outward, showing a concealed door.

She passed through and entered a slightly larger chamber, illuminated by her torch. Three sets of old bunk beds were set against one of the block stone walls, and three more against the opposite, beside a toppled stack of crates. The furthest wall held a small chapel area.

Between Roslyn and the chapel lay three men and a woman—passengers who had lost their lives within this bloodied chamber. Their deaths had been brutal.

"Return to the pantry and stand watch," Roslyn said. "Estéban, remain."

"Yes, Commander." The fighters departed.

"This is where the people lived?" Estéban asked.

"In many ports, that would be the case. However, Lord Athelric let them live in the house." She circumvented the dead and neared the small chapel area. "This is where they prayed and hid in times of trouble."

More so than any other part of the house, everything in the chapel was wrecked or smashed or shattered. Some valuable items were missing altogether. She turned her eyes to God Karulus, painted on the wall behind the destroyed pulpit.

Deep strikes, as if from the angry wielding of a sword, cut deep into the painting of the blue God, passing through into the stone beyond.

Roslyn tenderly set her finger to one of the deep gashes, feeling the marred stone. "Swords are expensive"—she slowly ran her finger down the cruel wound in her God—"tools valued and often handed down from father to son. Yet, a Dayigan would risk destroying his for this senseless act of hatred. I just don't understand them." She turned back to Estéban.

He said nothing and only looked at the floor.

She bowed her head and clasped her hands at her breast. "Praise be to Karulus, spirit of truth, and of compassion. Watch over the people of Port Dierne, both the living and the dead. As thy will, may it be."

"Astha'will-miabé," Estéban said.

With a loud scraping of metal against stone, Roslyn lifted an iron stand from the rubble and set her torch within the thick rings at its peak.

"There were fifty people in this port," she said, "not including Commander Owen and Lord Athelric. One was a healer I trained myself and sent here. Yet there are not enough bodies to account for *nearly* that amount."

"Perhaps the rest escaped."

"Again, your misplaced optimism shows." She dusted part of a table with a brush of her hand. "I don't suppose you're used to this sort of thing in the Alliance."

"I've had my share of troubles."

"Even so. If a single survivor escaped, he would have made his way to Port Lytel. I must assume they were captured. And I must assume the Dayigans had a reason to capture them instead of killing them. Does the Dayigan Army know of the impending agreement between the Empire and Alliance?"

"I think they would have to."

"Then, they must anticipate our evacuation. They will torture our people into providing information that the Empire can use for one last strike against us."

"Do you think the captives will talk?"

Roslyn shook her head. "No. I trust them all. But I do think they will all be slowly tortured to death. Which is why I must find them and save them."

"We only have two months—"

"Do you *actually* plan to speak those next words?" Her words were cross as she cut him off. "Do you plan to stand here before our God and tell me we do not have the *time* to rescue nearly fifty people facing excruciating deaths at the hands of the Dayigans?"

He swallowed dryly and glanced down. "No. You are right. Of course, you're right. Forgive me."

"I will give you an escort to return you to Port Lytel. Oversee the evacuation, and I'll join you when I'm able." Roslyn looked upward, scanning the area. "There's . . ." She paused, sensing. ". . . someone here."

"A soldier?"

"Doubtful." She set her fingers to her temples. "'Tis a tiny flame of life force struggling on the verge of snuffing out."

She scanned the room. "There." She pointed to a messy pile of crates. "Help me move them."

Throwing the crates aside, they soon uncovered a little boy with tangles of dirty blue hair and grayish blue wings with touches of black and white resembling that of blue jay. Badly injured, the boy showed no sign of life other than the tiny spark Roslyn sensed clinging to his core.

"Clear the area," Roslyn said, "but try not to disturb the boy directly until I have made my assessment."

Estéban did as told and moved the boxes away from the child.

Roslyn kneeled at the boy's side. "The patient is an unresponsive Terovae male between the ages of five and eight with a deep laceration to his left dorsal bicep."

"What is a dorsal bicep?" Estéban grabbed another crate.

Roslyn motioned to the gash at the top of the boy's wing, making no attempt to hide her annoyance in answering what seemed clear.

"Saying it aloud helps me think and plan," she said. "He shows signs of a compound fracture to the right ulna and radius." She motioned to his swollen, discolored forearm. "And multiple contusions over most of his body consistent with . . ." She paused. ". . . boots."

"Boots?" With the crates clear, Estéban neared and crouched beside the boy.

Roslyn nodded solemnly. "Yes. It appears the boy tried to fly away, but was hindered by the low ceiling. A soldier cut his wing, causing him to fall on his arm, breaking it. Then the soldier, or soldiers, attempted to stomp him to death."

"He was probably crying," Estéban said, reaching his hand consolingly toward the boy but pulling back before contact. "The bastards were trying to shut him up."

Roslyn pushed back the wave of sadness at the thought. "I should be able to heal him. But I'll have to get his arm set first and open him up to repair internal damage."

"What do you need?"

"A lot. But none of it is here. I'll have to rely solely on magic, and older injuries are harder to heal." She looked Estéban in the eyes. "This location is known to the Dayigans, but we cannot move the boy. Talk to my men. One will escort you back to Lytel."

"No. No, I can help."

"Very well. We *will* save this boy."

—

Roslyn kept her hand planted on the stone wall, leaning her weight on it, slouching, panting slowly as she stared at the rough, vandalized painting of God Karulus. Her heavy eyes drifted down to stare at the floor.

"Are you all right?" Estéban asked, just behind her.

She weakly nodded her head, causing a wave of dizziness to throb down her body.

"You're pneuma depleted, aren't you?"

She shook her head. "No." She took a deep breath and pushed herself to stand aright before turning to him. She fell back against the wall. "Somewhat," she admitted. "I used more magic than I'd planned on treating the boy. As I said, wounds older than about ten minutes take more effort. Lingering on the edge of death had nearly drained him of all his vital pneuma, so I needed to restore it from myself. But I will recover."

"And him?"

She turned to look at the small figure lying still on a bottom bunk. "He, too, will recover."

She neared the boy. "I'd prefer not to move him, but we've been in a discovered port too long. You may need to carry him out." She turned to a Lytel fighter by the door. "Would you return to the well in the back garden and fetch more water? Be sure to take someone with you and stay on alert."

"Yes, Commander."

She sat on the bed. The boy was shirtless, revealing a scrawny body free of any injuries. His arm—before, broken and swollen—was whole. Roslyn took a moment. "His baseline vital pneuma is particularly strong. If it had not been so, I would have been unable to save him." He seemed so peaceful in his induced slumber, yet she knew he must have spent his entire life hiding from Dayigans, fearing capture. She hated to wake him.

Nevertheless, she set her hand on his forehead and leaned closer. "*Awaken*," she whispered.

The boy opened his eyes sleepily, blinking before he looked at her. "You're her," he yawned. "The Blue Rose."

Roslyn smiled graciously. "I am. And I've made you *all* better. Do you remember what happened?"

He looked away, facing the wall as he became visibly anxious.

"'Tis all right," she said. "We needn't talk about that, if you'd rather not. But we must leave this place soon. Can you sit up for me?"

He shifted around on the bunk until he took a slouched seat on the edge. His blue wings angled forward and inward to keep the bases from the thin mattress, yet to Roslyn, they resembled half of a protective cocoon. His legs dangled.

"Can you tell me your name?"

"Marcoulif."

"*Marcoulif*. That's a big name. Do people call you Marc?"

He nodded, facing the floor.

"Can you tell me how old you are, Marc?"

"Seven."

"That is a good age. I bet you're smart enough to tell me where we are."

He nodded sadly before mumbling, "Lord Athelric's house. He's a *good* Déagrian. He lets us go outside."

"Commander." The Lytel fighter she'd sent to the well had returned and stood by the door. "'Tis important we speak."

Roslyn nodded to the fighter and rubbed the boy's head. "You'll be all right, Marc."

She stood and approached the man at the door.

"We spotted Dayigan soldiers outside, Commander. At least two. They were watching the house. They were too far out to pursue, as we thought it best not to move too far from the house."

"An appropriate call. Gather the others. We leave as soon as possible."

Marc screamed and began crying out. "*Mummy!*"

Roslyn followed his eyes to the corpse of a winged woman lying against the edge of the room.

She rushed to Marc, grabbing him and embracing him in a tight hug, as she pressed his head into her shoulder so he could not see. She handed him over to Estéban, who carried him from the room.

Roslyn paused, looking for an extended moment at the dead woman. Another pointless, ruthless slaughter.

"May God Karulus be your advocate before the Lavender Lady. And deliver you safely to Laqyigo," Roslyn said. "I give you my word as an Azerent, your boy will be safe."

With that, Roslyn left the room.

CHAPTER THIRTY-TWO

Roslyn stood resolute in the entrance corridor leading from the courtyard, her ten fighters crowding behind her. Estéban stood among them, his shoulders bearing the weight of young Marc, now dressed in a drab gray tunic meant for a Human but ripped partway down the back to accommodate his wings. The boy's watery eyes were hollow, drained by the horrors they had witnessed.

With a heavy sigh, Roslyn pressed her fingers to her temple and closed her eyes, sensing the approaching danger. "There are many life forces out there," she said, her voice laced with unease. "I cannot determine their exact number, but I estimate at least a hundred. We are surrounded."

Lowering her hand, she opened her eyes and turned to face her comrades. "This house is no fortress," she said. "If we attempt to secure all entrances, we will only spread ourselves too thin while simply delaying the inevitable. Our only chance is to face this threat head-on and overcome it."

"But there are too many," Estéban protested. "We cannot go out there."

"We must," Roslyn replied firmly. "I understand your impulse to remain within these walls, but this is no passing storm. If we defend this house, we will only deplete ourselves whilst more soldiers gather. We cannot stay here forever, and the Dayigans will not leave. We leave now as a sprint or later as a limp. I choose now."

Estéban nodded grimly, unable to argue with her logic but clearly struggling with his own doubts and fears. As he turned away, Roslyn could see the anguish etched on his face—a reflection of what they all felt as they prepared to face their doom.

Roslyn looked past him to the boy on his back. "I need you to be brave for me, all right?" She set her hand on Marc's little arm around Estéban's shoulders. "We're about to see a lot of scary things, but we will keep you safe. I give you my word as an Azerent."

The little boy nodded, though his pale blue eyes stared cold.

Roslyn glanced at Estéban. The words were also meant for him, though she would have felt odd directly assuring a grown man that she would keep him safe from 'scary things.' Accordingly, he seemed somewhat comforted too.

She turned to the door, setting her hand on the latch. "When I run out, stay on me, and when I stop, stop near me."

Roslyn flung open the heavy door of the manor and raced into the open field, her allies close behind her. The rocky lawn, extending a hundred feet, offered little cover, but they sprinted toward the dense woods ahead. She knew it was their only chance for survival—a single chance to get this group that counted on her to refuge and possibly even escape.

Though fear threatened to consume her, she pushed it down and focused on their desperate run. She could sense the enemy closing in, but she could not yet see them. Her magical senses were vague, leaving her uncertain of who or what awaited them among the trees. All she knew was that they had to keep running, or face certain death.

With bloodcurdling shouts, twenty Dayigan soldiers—only a fraction of the number she sensed—burst from the woodline, their green tabards emblazoned with the symbol of their ruthless empire. Swords flashed in their hands as they charged towards Roslyn and her men. Other soldiers followed, forming a wide, approaching wall.

"Lytel, halt," Roslyn commanded.

She circled her hand three times above her head and shouted, "In the name of Karulus, I conjure protection from those who would do us harm." She pointed to the ground. "Anesthetize!"

A wall of marbled blue light sprang up around Roslyn and her men.

The soldiers slowed as they approached the circle, some stumbling back in confusion while others slammed into it, dropping unconscious as they passed its threshold.

"Finish them off," Roslyn commanded her Lytel fighters, pointing to the fallen enemies within the ring.

"Is that truly necessary, Commander?" Estéban asked as he set down the boy. It was more than a question; rather, an angry judgment.

Roslyn turned to face him. "You do not understand what it is like here," she said firmly. "The Dayigans will not stop until all of us are dead."

Estéban said nothing in response, but his expression spoke volumes.

Roslyn glanced at the Lytel fighters, who awaited clarification.

Estéban stepped toward her. "We must be better than they are."

"Leave the unconscious," she said. "But watch the perimeter. If any *conscious* soldiers make their way through, do not hesitate."

"Commander," a fighter called. "Above us."

Roslyn's eyes flicked upward to see four Dayigan Terovaes flying over the wall of light. With a swift movement of her hand, she extended the wall to curve higher and seal as a dome.

Undeterred, the Terovaes averted their paths, flying higher, but armed their bows and shot.

An arrow whizzed through the dome and past Roslyn's cheek while another struck a fighter in the chest.

She cast her hand toward the injured—blue light streaking from her palm to heal him.

The Terovaes shot again, but Roslyn was ready. With a wave of her hand, she stopped their arrows mid-air before swiping them away. Then, she cast both hands upward, this time at two of the winged archers themselves. She pulled them from the sky, through the roof of the dome, and set them unconscious on the ground.

The other two Terovaes quickly fled beyond her range.

"Pace your magic," said Estéban, sword raised as he kept one arm on the boy and his eyes on the perimeter. "You used a lot of it before."

"I know what I'm doing." A stone struck her back, causing her to call out in pain as she lunged forward, planting her hands on her knees. Despite the throbbing ache spreading through her body, she remained determined as she looked at the soldiers surrounding them.

Many of the Dayigans palmed stones, readying to throw.

In response, Roslyn let out a fierce scream and pushed her hands outward.

The dome expanded thirty feet in every direction, passing over the surrounding soldiers and rendering them unconscious. With a quarter of their enemies lying asleep within the dome, the others backed away, their courage having faltered—for now.

Roslyn slumped over in exhaustion, and Estéban rushed to her side.

"Are you all right?" he asked.

She nodded, out of breath and facing dirt.

"How long can you maintain this circle?"

She looked up, letting her fear show briefly before shaking her head. "You're right. 'Tis too soon," she said through pained breaths. "I haven't recovered from healing the boy."

She screamed, grabbing her forehead as a sharp pain ripped through her brain, sending her falling to her knees.

The entire dome wavered at once, fading to nearly nothing before returning as it was.

Again, Roslyn called out, clutching her forehead as the agony intensified.

The dome blinked out, gone.

Soldiers rushed toward the area.

Lytel fighters rushed to circle their commander as they readied to fight.

Struggling through pain, Roslyn concentrated with all of her might. The dome returned, smaller but strong, though the effort sent her to her hands and knees.

A handful of soldiers had managed their way past the smaller perimeter. Roslyn watched with blurred eyes as the Lytel fighters engaged with bloody force.

Estéban grabbed up the boy, holding him tight against his chest.

Every moment the dome remained up drained Roslyn further. She felt as if she bled out while her head was lashed with whips. But she knew she could not let the dome dispel or the men she led, along with the boy she saved, would die.

"Roslyn," Estéban's voice echoed through her. "Can you hear me?"

She opened her eyes but couldn't lift her head. She found herself lying on her side on the ground, though she did not recall falling. The Dayigan soldiers, who'd rushed into the dome, were dead, and the Lytel fighters braced for any others who might enter.

"Can you hear me?" Estéban tried again.

She tried to nod, to speak the word *yes*, but all she managed was to roll her heavy eyes toward him.

"You must break the circle. We have to surrender to them."

"No," she groaned. "I can't."

"I don't have to tell you what pneuma depletion can do to someone. We can surrender now—with you alive—or after you're dead. There is no other way out."

Her mind exhausted, Roslyn could barely think, and the sharp pain kept pulsing behind her eyes down the whole of her body. Either way—by her dispelling it or it dispelling on its own after she could no longer maintain it—the dome would soon dissolve.

"Go," Roslyn managed. "Negotiate terms. I'll drop the circle when I know my people will be unharmed."

Estéban jumped up and rushed to the edge.

CHAPTER THIRTY-THREE

Throughout the night, the ragged and exhausted Lytel unit trudged along a muddy path flanked by thick forest. Their hands and feet were bound in heavy shackles, connected by thick ropes that kept them in two lines. Hundreds of hateful soldiers marched alongside, weapons at the ready, their eyes fixed on the captives like starving wolves, eager for any excuse to unleash their violence upon them.

Roslyn, still weighed by the weariness of using so much magic, trudged along next to Estéban.

The boy walked in front of her, a position she'd chosen so she could keep an eye on him. Yet Marc seemed fine, too fine, too calm. It was the sort of apathetic calm that came from being too accustomed to this sort of thing—a defeated calm. Roslyn wondered if he imagined he might be rescued or if the seven-year-old had made peace with the fact that this path might lead to death.

"What castle is that?" Estéban asked.

Roslyn turned her eyes from the boy to the uphill path ahead. It led to a gate through old dark gray walls—natural rock left in place from the mountain range beyond, extended higher by mortaring more of the same drab stone. And within those walls stood an ancient, dark gray castle built into the mountainside, towering over its surroundings. Backlit by the rising sun, it cast long shadows over the land.

"This area," Roslyn said, "including the location of Port Dierne, is Isernstan—one of the many formerly independent nations that now comprises the Dayigan Empire. Although the kings are now subjects of the high king, they retain their titles. And castles. That is home to King Eadberht."

"Silence!" a soldier barked.

Roslyn complied, lowering her head as she walked.

Soon, they entered through the gate into the town within the walls. Shops and houses of dreary gray wood cramped the rocky landscape, squeezing much more into the walls than was most likely the original plan. The construction cared little for design and nothing for paint. The aged wood was left a dusty gray like the dusty stone around it. Most of the buildings touched the narrow main road, with their larger upper stories extending a few feet above it, adding to the confining feel of the area while lending to the sense that it could all topple inward.

Roslyn and her group, escorted by soldiers, continued along the uphill main road—paved in part, but mostly stony ground. It looked to be the widest of the streets, yet it offered only the width for two wagons to squeeze past one another. Trickles of wet filth ran down the street's edges. The side roads, squeezing between buildings, seemed meant for only foot traffic, and some included winding stairs.

Despite the restricted space, a growing number of townspeople squeezed against their shops and houses as they shouted out with vulgar animosity.

Roslyn tried to keep her head down and not meet the hateful gazes of the enraged people. There were too many soldiers crowded around the captives to allow the watchers to throw anything—that was a blessing, of sorts, Roslyn decided.

Yet their shouts were unhindered. The angry people called the Karulents wicked and yelled that God Déagar hated all like them. They demanded the captives return to where they came from—"We don't want you here!"—though where they thought the captives originated was unclear.

"Witches!"

"Savages."

"The True Light has no place for you!"

They demanded their deaths. "All others will perish."

Roslyn kept glancing at the boy in front of her.

Marc walked silently with his head down, shoulders slouched, and wings loose at his back.

At his age in this scenario, Roslyn would have been petrified with fear and would have cried out. Perhaps someone would've needed to lift her up so she could continue. Yet Marc showed nothing. Roslyn wanted him to scream; she wanted him to collapse; she wanted him to show some sign that the world had not already beaten everything out of him completely.

She didn't want him to be like her, not at such a young age.

The procession reached a small town plaza edged on three sides by angry townspeople and wooden shops. The fourth side held the castle, which was built into the side of the mountain from the same stone as the mountain itself. The castle might have been grand long ago, but it currently was in disrepair. Two towers had collapsed. A few old banners— tattered and blackened with mold—hung from high-up windows.

A raised stone walkway reached from the castle to end at a balcony about twenty feet above the plaza.

The soldiers stopped the prisoners in the center of the square to face the balcony, though the binding ropes forced the Karulents to remain in the same two columns they'd maintained on their march. The soldiers took a circular formation around them.

"Insurgents," a man called.

The crowded plaza hushed as Roslyn looked up to see a well-built, stiffly postured man standing on the balcony. His hands, sheathed in expensive gloves of fine leather, rested atop the stone railing. His neatly trimmed hair had nearly, but not entirely, transitioned to gray. His hateful eyes remained locked on Roslyn. From what she could see over the banister, he wore a nicer version of the Dayigan uniform—nicer material with nicer embroidery and stitching.

He reminded Roslyn of someone, both in form and manner. Recognition hit her. She gasped before she whispered to Estéban, "That's the man I killed."

"I would say he has recovered."

The unknown soldier who'd attacked her in her youth looked to be about fifty now. His eyes were cold, looking out above the captives.

"You're standing here today accused of high treason," the soldier projected his words, "of blasphemy and of witchcraft, of following the false path of Demigod Karulus and corrupting others to do the same thing, of murdering countless Dayigan soldiers, plus a lot of other charges that'd take too long to list here." He raised his gloved hands as he turned his eyes to the townspeople gathered at the edge of the square. "Righteous men and women of this moral town, I tell you this woman here, standing before you, is the whore of a witch called the *Blue Rose.*"

Gasps and whispers followed.

Yet, his words, meant to shame, strengthened Roslyn. Never had she heard the title that had been thrust upon her spoken so loudly and in such a public forum. The mythic

"Blue Rose" had always been a little more spectacular than Roslyn's actual self. To her, the persona was a version of herself that she could never quite live up to. Yet, here it was like an invocation, filling her. She stood taller as the haze of weariness faded.

The soldier on the balcony returned his eyes to Roslyn. "Do you deny you're her?"

"I do not," Roslyn spoke up proudly, her eyes meeting his. "I *am* the Blue Rose."

More gasps and more chatter sounded throughout the square. Her enemies' alarm only reminded her that she'd been doing *something* right.

Roslyn could see the anger filling the soldier's eyes, the same anger she'd seen as a teen when he'd tried to best her and failed. He wanted her to deny the identity, Roslyn knew. He wanted her to be the girl he'd grabbed and choked and tied to a bed. He wanted her to cry out and beg. Roslyn didn't. Every moment she stared him in the eyes seemed to drain away whatever power he imagined he had while delivering more to her.

"Was there anything else you wished to add?" Roslyn asked defiantly.

The soldier slammed his fist on the railing. "Lock them up with the others," he commanded. "We'll deal with the *witch* soon enough."

The soldiers converged on the captives, grabbing them by their arms.

"Wait," Roslyn shouted over the increasing noise. "I demand an audience with the king. I can give him what he wants."

The man on the balcony looked at her a moment, thinking. "Take them away."

CHAPTER THIRTY-FOUR

The door slammed shut, followed by keys rattling in the lock on the opposite side. Roslyn, along with her fellow captives, had been ushered into a large basement. Low, square vaults formed the ceiling, each supported by thick columns of filthy brick. It wasn't the worst dungeon Roslyn had visited, she noted, but she'd seen better. The thought made her wonder if she'd become something of a Dayigan dungeon connoisseur.

Amid the gloom of captivity, Roslyn recognized the people who were already scattered around the chamber as forlorn lumps: the passengers from Port Dierne. As she entered further in, a man Roslyn recognized as Coenric approached her with a swift walk.

"Master Healer," he said. "Thank Karulus you are here."

"And yet, I fear it is my fault *you* are here. 'Twas I who assigned you to Port Dierne."

"A blessing, Master Healer. These people, more than ever, need a healer trained by the great Blue Rose. And I am honored to use the knowledge you gifted me to ease their suffering in this horrid pit."

Roslyn smiled with pride. Coenric had blossomed into an accomplished healer under her tutelage, more so than she could have ever imagined when she first laid eyes on the shaky-handed boy who was near panic at her simply asking him to hold a crystal over Margaret while she reattached her soul.

"Are there any casualties?" Roslyn asked, beginning to amble among the haggard people slumped against the thick brick walls and columns.

"All are stable and ambulatory," he assured her. "Most wounds have been dressed, but I thought it prudent to reserve my remaining magic in case of further emergencies."

"An appropriate call," she said. "How long have you been down here?"

"Four days, Master Healer. Every so often a man appears—the Grand Inquisitor—who takes away a group of two or three of us, never to be seen again. Sadly, Commander Owen was one of the first taken. We fear he is interrogating them in order to find out the secrets of the Veiled River Commission."

"This Inquisitor, is he an older man wearing an expensive version of the Dayigan uniform?"

"Yes, Master Healer. That's him."

Roslyn's lips pressed into a thin line as she remembered the man from years ago. He'd gotten so much worse.

"I see you've brought Marc," Coenric continued. "We feared they'd killed him."

"They nearly did," she murmured. "We found his mother, but she . . ." Roslyn shook her head.

He glanced down. "Sadly, the Inquisitor has already taken his father."

Roslyn looked to the boy who clung to Estéban's hand as they wandered the basement in a slow, unhopeful search.

"And what of the other children?" Roslyn asked.

Coenric sighed heavily. "Taken. As per the Dayigan's usual. They'll be headed to orphanages to learn to work hard and fear Déagar."

Roslyn's gaze shifted slowly over the disheartened captives, their faces sunken with despair. Coenric had done what he could to tend to the most grievously wounded, but the people were in need of food and water. And hope.

She stepped toward their center and spoke, her voice echoing in the cellar. "I fear I bring you bad tidings, news that must be heard, nonetheless." Her words felt heavy as she continued her grim proclamation. "The Karulent Alliance has reached an agreement with the Dayigan Empire to sever all ties with the Veiled River. And without their support, the River will crumble. Thus, the Veiled River Commission is planning one mass exodus for all of our people who wish to leave the Empire. You are here today because it is not enough for us to leave. The Dayigans clearly plan to squeeze us for any information they can use to deliver a final bloody strike against us, even as we retreat. But I will not let that happen. No one else here will go to the Inquisitor's torture chamber. And all of you will return to Port Lytel. Where you go from there is up to you, but I assure you, you will have that choice to make. May Karulus keep you well."

Estéban, no longer with the boy, approached. "That is quite a lofty promise to make."

"I have a lofty scheme. Where is Marc?"

"We could not find his father, so he took a seat at the back of the room. He just sat down against the wall with his head bowed down. I think he thinks his father is dead, which he just..." Estéban shook his head. "...accepted. He says he wants to be alone."

"His father *is* dead," Coenric said despondently. "I'll go talk to him." He walked away.

"Poor boy," Estéban muttered.

Roslyn nodded.

"I was barely older than Marc when my own father was killed, while my parents struggled to get me and my brothers and sister out of the Empire," Estéban recounted somberly. "Back then there was no Veiled River, so the trip across the Empire was long and harsh and terribly frightening. Forgive me." He smiled sadly. "This place, the boy—it brings back too many memories. Why do I tell all this to the famed Blue Rose? I do not know."

"I'm not..." She breathed. "I'm Roslyn. Nothing more. Forgive me, it wasn't fair of me to assume your life had been easy simply because you reached the Alliance." Roslyn walked beside him through the cell. "What happened to your father?"

"In the Empire, with no ports to offer us rest, we hid where we could, often in unseemly places filled with criminals—of the aggressive kind. Our parents did what they needed to do to feed us, but death by starvation seemed just as imminent as death by soldiers. But it was the soldiers who finally killed my father." He looked away. "Those times... I've never been so scared in all my life."

"But you made it, at least. And..." she asked gently, "...your mother and siblings—did they?"

"Barely, but yes," he replied darkly. "But when my family finally reached the Hyvile River and secured passage across it, we reached another land that did not want us there. The Karulent Alliance had invited us to take refuge in their lands, but many of the common people grew angry that they must take in Dayigans. This is what they call us—Dayigans. Officially, we're Karulent Dayigans or Dayigan Refugees, but few bother with that in normal conversation. My arrival there was before the Veiled River intake ports were set up to welcome refugees and help us acclimate. I was no longer afraid for my life, and we no longer had to travel and hide, yet my mother . . . she started with nothing and needed to build us a home alongside the houses of those who did not want us there. I didn't want to be there either, truth be told."

Roslyn stopped and sighed. "I'd always thought this would be temporary."

He combed his fingers through his black hair, shaking his head sorrowfully as he continued, "That is what my mother kept telling me as a child: 'This is all temporary, Estéban. We will be able to return home soon.' She wasn't lying. She believed it, and I believed her. Every night, as a boy, I prayed that God Karulus would end the conflicts. Now . . .'"

"Now we're here." Roslyn glanced around at the broken people in the large cell. "When the Veiled River shuts down, there will be no one fighting for our people in the Empire, and no way for our people in the Alliance to ever return home. "No," she murmured softly, "not so temporary after all."

The lock in the door rattled. Roslyn began to move toward it, Estéban just behind her. Coenric also approached, followed by little Marc.

Roslyn stopped as the door of the cell swung open, hitting the wall behind it with a bang. Five soldiers charged in, one dashing for Marc, grabbing him, and holding a knife to his throat.

"Unhand him," Roslyn commanded.

The soldier from her past—the Inquisitor—descended the stairs just beyond the door. "The boy's just to make sure you cooperate." He entered. "Don't do anything stupid, and he'll remain unhurt." He stopped just inside the door.

Roslyn looked at Marc. "You'll be all right. I assure you."

The Inquisitor stood at attention. "May I present His Majesty, Eadberht, King of Isernstan."

The king descended from the stairs with a regal air, his garments befitting his title and displaying his wealth without the need of a crown. His shoulder-length hair, streaked with gray and brown, was matched by his thick beard covering most of his round face.

He fixed his gaze on Roslyn, who curtsied before him.

"So," the king began, "you claim to have *what I desire*. Speak then, madam. And do not waste my time with flowery words." His hand rested casually on his plump stomach. "What do I desire?"

Roslyn met his gaze with steely resolve. "Me."

"You?" the king scoffed.

"Yes. I will turn myself over to you if you agree to my terms."

"Unless my senses deceive me, madam, you are already in my custody."

"Am I?" Roslyn flicked two of her fingers, a minor motion, toward the soldier holding Marc.

The knife at Marc's throat flew away, out of the soldier's hand to clatter across the floor. Another slight motion from Roslyn sent the soldier himself flying backward into a wall.

A ring of blue light formed around Marc.

Roslyn maintained eye contact with the king all the while, even as the other soldiers drew their swords.

"Fucking hex-casting witch," the Inquisitor shouted. "I'll have you—"

"Stand down," the king commanded. "All of you."

Swords returned to scabbards.

"I could leave anytime I wish," Roslyn said. "And I could possibly get about half of my people out alive, as well. But that's not good enough." She crossed her arms. "I want them *all* released—safe and sound and unfollowed."

The king's eyes narrowed in thought as he scratched his bearded chin.

"Your Majesty," the Inquisitor spoke up, "you can't be considering this. These savages—"

"These *prisoners*," the king began, "other than the Blue Rose, mean nothing to the Empire." The king returned his eyes to Roslyn, his words somber. "In exchange for their safety, you would agree to remain in our custody, to stand trial, and to allow your sentence to be carried out?"

"Roslyn, you can't," Estéban said. "They will kill you."

"He's right," Coenric chimed in. "Our people need you."

Roslyn raised a hand to silence the commenters. "I would, Your Majesty. But I have one more condition. The soldiers took these people's children. They must be returned."

"*Sire,*" the Inquisitor said through teeth, "with respect, I remind you that His Highest Majesty, the high king, has declared Karulents not fit to raise children. They's murderers and fiends, and the high king's issued a general order to save as many of the children as we can from their savage path."

"Which is it?" the king asked Roslyn. "Are you a murderess or a fiend?"

"By Dayigan standards, I suppose a bit of both, Your Majesty."

"I see," he said. "The Empire has created enough orphans," the king dismissed. There was a bitterness in his tone, hinted at before but now apparent, and Roslyn wasn't quite sure what to make of it. "The children are in a nearby church awaiting transport. They will be returned. Roslyn, is it?"

"Yes, Your Majesty."

"Sister Roslyn of the Order of Azerents," the king began, "I vow by God Déagar, he who is Greatest of All, to return the children as you have requested and, afterwards, assemble a unit to escort them safely, along with these imprisoned here, outside of town whereat the unit will allow them the freedom to depart, unfollowed, to whatever destination the released Karulents choose."

The Inquisitor, clenching his fists at his sides, looked as if he might soon explode with rage but said nothing.

Roslyn felt relief wash over her—her people were safe. "My thanks, Your Majesty. And I, by the holy staff of God Karulus—spirit of truth, and of compassion—vow myself to your custody, Your Majesty, Eadberht, King of Isernstan. I vow to stand trial for my supposed crimes and to submit willingly to the punishment handed down to me."

"And I vow the same," Estéban injected as he jumped forward.

"No, you fool," Roslyn said, turning to him. "'Tis not your place."

"'Tis done," Estéban said. "I vow by Karulus to stay at your side. I will not leave you alone in this."

Roslyn closed her eyes and took a deep breath before turning to the other prisoners. "No one else is to make such a foolish gesture. If you wish to honor this moment, vow to live your lives well, as shining lights within the dark."

Roslyn returned to the king and nearly made some apology, but found him watching her. He seemed impressed, or at least intrigued.

"Your sacrifice is noble, Sister Roslyn," said the king.

"*Your Reverence*, actually, or *Master Healer*." She bowed her head slightly before adding, "Your Majesty."

"Of course, Your Reverence." The king nodded with a chuckle. "I will begin preparations at once."

"Can I have a moment to secure the prisoner, sire?" the Inquisitor asked. "Not that I don't trust the word of a lying Karulent whore."

"Do what you must," the king said, "but do not harm her or her people."

"As you command, sire."

The king exited up the stairs as the Inquisitor approached Roslyn.

"The rest of you, step back," he commanded, both to the other soldiers and the other prisoners.

Roslyn nodded to her people to comply.

Drawing Roslyn close to the wall, the Inquisitor began unbuckling a large leather satchel on his belt. "I'm guessing you remember me."

"Unfortunately, I do. I killed you."

"I'd say you failed," he said angrily and stopped fiddling with the satchel buckle.

"Clearly."

He turned his head to the side, stretching his neck as he pulled down the collar of his tabard.

He revealed a large scar on his neck, apparently from an old wound that had been sloppily burned to cauterize it.

A flash of hate flooded Roslyn as she stared, reliving the moment she'd slammed Jon's sword into this man's neck.

"Lucky for me," he said, returning his hands to the satchel buckle, "Lord Rothgar found me minutes after you left me for dead. He healed me by the holy might of God Déagar."

Her heart began to pound in her breast as her skin heated. "Rothgar knew you were alive when he sentenced my entire town to death for your—" Roslyn forced a breath. "It doesn't matter now." Despite her words, she clamped her teeth for a moment as she soaked in the bitter addition to her old wound. This revelation did not truly make the destruction of her town any worse, she told herself. It had been horrible a moment ago and was still just as horrible. Nevertheless, she found her fists clenched.

"Your town was lucky it were one of the firsts," the Inquisitor said through his teeth. "The later towns—after our Immolation Brigade was formed and we became organized—was purified much more complete."

Roslyn wanted to punch him in the face. She resisted.

"Put this on." He pulled a shackle from his satchel.

Roslyn took it into her hands, examining it. It was a cast iron collar formed of two, two-inch-wide half circles joined at a stiff hinge. Crusty soot was burned into the pitted metal, with parts showing the reddish-orange tint of old fire damage. The ends, where a lock would go, appeared to have been sawed off and replaced with newer iron along a rough seam.

"I vowed I would not escape," Roslyn said.

"Then you won't mind wearing that around your neck."

She glared at him, pausing before she slowly put the collar on and closed it.

From the same satchel, the Inquisitor produced a three-inch prism of pale green quartz, most likely prasiolite, and touched it to the collar.

The iron clicked twice and locked closed.

"I suppose you'll be chaining me to a wall now, as well," Roslyn said with little interest.

"No need."

Around the iron, symbols—including the Silthex Septenar—began to glow a subtle green. Roslyn gasped as she felt a sharp, though brief, pain.

"The collar's suppressing your evil magic," said the Inquisitor. "'Tis a gift from Archbishop Blastilv. He sent me out specific to find you. We know about the treaty between the Empire and the Alliance, and we know without the support of the Alliance, your band of unholy rebels'll try to flee our lands. Right? But you don't get that option, witch. The capture of these people, the slow torture and deaths at my hands . . ." He raised his thick fist toward her face. "That was all for you. Did you think we would ever let you get away after all you've done to us?"

"You're a monster." Roslyn slid her finger under the iron and tried to pull it apart.

"No, but I finally captured *my* monster. D'you know what it is like to live decades knowing I had someone in me grasp what would turn into such a wicked villain and I let her live?"

"I'm very much beginning to understand the feeling."

He grinned slightly. "I ain't the villain here, witch. I'm the good and holy one here. I'd stop trying to get that collar off if I was you. The witch that the Archbishop tested it on got it off, so he made some improvements on it. One, if you take it off without the key, 'twill set your head on fire."

Roslyn lowered her hands to her sides. "I'll keep that in mind."

He peered at her with obvious contempt. "I'll enjoy watching you burn, Roslyn." With that, he signaled to his men, and they departed.

CHAPTER THIRTY-FIVE

Roslyn sat on the floor of the castle basement and stared at the simple wooden door. She feared for those she'd sent out in hopes they'd find their way to Port Lytel—the half-starved men and women, the little boy. She knew her fighters would lead them and protect them, yet her thoughts and prayers lingered.

The basement seemed strangely large with no one but herself and Estéban remaining. Estéban paced the area, giving physical representation to the pacing within her mind.

"How do we know we can trust that ... *king*?" Estéban asked as he neared her. "For all we know, your people were—"

"I trust him." She continued to stare at the door. "But I don't trust the Inquisitor or the soldiers."

The key turned in the lock before the door creaked open. The king, alone, entered, letting the door stand wide behind him.

"Your Majesty?" Roslyn stood and approached.

"Your Reverence. I have personally come to inform you that your people, including the returned children, have been safely released a mile outside of town."

"My thanks, Your Majesty. Although, I am surprised you came yourself. And ..." She glanced through the door to the empty, shadowed stairwell. "... with no guards."

"Do I require guards?"

"No, Your Majesty." She bowed her head. "I suppose 'tis time for me to leave as well. For Dayigo."

"Not yet. The Grand Inquisitor has departed to procure your transportation. He will return for you in roughly four days."

She nodded, uneasy with the thought of traveling away with that man.

"I've had the servants prepare rooms for you and your . . ." The king motioned to Estéban. "They await you when you are ready."

"Will we not be staying here, sire?"

"If you like. But I see no purpose in locks against an Azerent who is bound here by her word. Until Inquisitor Swithun returns, you are guests in my home with the customary courtesies extended to you. Yet, you will not leave the castle."

"*Swithun*," Roslyn whispered, looking away. Just like that, unnamed no more. "You are too kind, Your Majesty."

"Yes. Supper will be served in your rooms in two hours." He turned and exited, leaving the door open behind him.

"Your Majesty, pray you, wait." She hurried after him, ascending the spiral of stairs to where he'd stopped midway.

"You throw kindness at me, sire, and then dash away forthwith."

"Manners. Nothing more." He turned to take another step upward.

"I think 'tis more than that. Forgive my jumping to conclusions, sire, but my remaining time in this world is short."

He stopped but continued to face away.

Roslyn took a step closer. "I think you're displeased with the ways of the Empire and the high king. I think you recognize that we Karulents are horribly mistreated. And I wonder how you, so clearly insightful, could have a lord sworn to you, residing not ten miles away, who kept a house full of Karulents without your knowing."

"Enough!" he shouted. "You have overstepped, Azerent." His words echoed in the stairwell. He calmed himself, facing her without looking at her directly. "As you said, your remaining life is short, and once you depart this castle, that time will be unpleasant. I suggest you cease your misguided endeavor, whatever you think it may be, and instead savor your brief visit here."

Roslyn looked at the stone steps. "My people could benefit from a kind man in your position."

"Good day, Your Reverence." He continued up the stairs.

—

Roslyn meandered alone in the castle bedroom, taking in the splendor of it all. It was a rather masculine form of grand—dark hardwood floor, stone walls bearing the stuffed heads of deer, and a few tapestries depicting war—yet she found it cozy, despite its size. The canopy bed was, of course, the focal point. Its hefty frame of beautifully carved oak displayed curtains of thick red velvet, pulled back with golden ties. An old trunk at its foot would have offered her storage if she'd brought anything to store. The large hearth stood empty and unneeded on the summer evening, while a few iron candelabras kept the room adequately lit.

Roslyn moved toward a round two-person table, complete with two chairs, which presented a nice supper for one—a brass plate overfilled with two golden brown pheasants, stewed cabbage, and a tear of bread, this beside a brass goblet and a pitcher of wine.

A knock sounded from the door.

"Enter," Roslyn called, stopping with her hand on the chair, yet standing.

Estéban parted the door before stepping through. In one hand, he held a brass plate copying the same food served to Roslyn. His other hand gripped a cup by its stem and a fork. "I thought we could eat together, if it pleases you."

"Gladly." She motioned to the other seat. "The table is meant for two."

Estéban set down his plate and cup and glanced around the area. "Your room is even nicer than mine."

"Is it? I've never been in such a place, even before the war."

"And this bed." Estéban neared it and pressed the soft mattress. "'Tis a shame we won't be able to enjoy it. That is . . ." He suddenly became awkward, stammering, "I mean, enjoy our separate beds. Separately."

Roslyn smiled before she took a seat at the small table. She again motioned a silent invitation to the opposite chair. "Do you not intend to sleep?"

"Not here." He sat down. "Despite all that the king tried to say to us, I'm certain we are carefully watched."

"The king trusts my word and with reason; I don't intend to break my vow."

"Your vow to a bunch of Déagrians who would see you dead without cause."

"My vow to God Karulus," she said firmly. Roslyn lifted the brass cup to her lips and took a sip of wine.

Estéban ate silently, using his hands to rip apart the pheasants while maintaining the glower of an angry child.

"I apologize," Roslyn said at length, "if you thought my agreeing to stay here was a deception. But it was the only way I could assure the safety of all the others who were captured.

However, your oath was barely an oath at all. The matter of its legitimacy is between you and God Karulus. If you wish to leave, I'll do nothing to stop you."

"I won't let you go through this on your own. You've done too much for our people." He shoved a forkful of cabbage into his mouth.

A grim smile tugged at her lips. "All of our people have made sacrifices. Even those who managed to flee to the Alliance, like you, have given up everything for our cause. You dedicated your entire lives to the Alliance-side ports of the Veiled River, welcoming our people."

He nodded as he swallowed. "It was what we had to do. My mother, my sister, and I worked tirelessly to build the very intake port I now command. But as you mentioned before, like me, you too hoped this would all be temporary. Even as I grew into my teens, I kept that hope alive. Yet home was a fading memory, and all my reason told me that nothing of it remained. By the time I became a man, the hope had faded, too."

She neared a fork to her mouth but paused. "It saddens me that you lost hope. I fear many of our people have done the same."

"I *did* lose hope, but no longer," he spoke with conviction. "As years passed, rumors spread of a fantastic woman fighting for our kind within the Dayigan Empire. *The Blue Rose*. And for a moment, I allowed myself to believe that maybe someday this suffering would come to an end."

"I hate to disappoint you, but those stories are nothing but exaggerations and fabrications, many of which, concocted by the Dayigan Army to rally their soldiers against me and the Veiled River. While I played a role in destroying the Silthex, the true heroine gave up her own life on that day."

"You are wrong," Estéban said. "Yes, I've heard the songs about the Blue Rose and the Silthex—I have even seen the puppet shows—but those are not the stories I refer to. As I said, for years, I've worked with refugees newly arrived in the Alliance. And for years, I've heard *firsthand* accounts of *you*. They told me how you had healed them or a loved one when they seemed certain to die. They told me how they were imprisoned, but you marched fighters into their internment camps and set them free. They told me how they were lost in hiding, yet *you* found them and led them to the Veiled River. *Year after year*, I heard countless stories of bravery and compassion about *you*, directly from the people you helped. Your actions gave them hope and restored mine, too. Our people need you, Roslyn. The world needs you. That is why you cannot march yourself into a fire, just because you swore an oath under duress."

His words left her with a warm glow in her heart. Though she tried to hide it, a smile of pride crossed her lips. It faded as she said, "You forget, the Veiled River will soon be no more. The people no longer need me."

"Roslyn—"

"Now, if you would please allow me some time alone, I'd like to spend the evening in silent prayer."

"Roslyn, I..." He looked at her for a moment. His dark brown eyes were akin to a puppy's in their sad stare. It seemed he had so much more to say, just on the tip of his tongue. Yet all he said was, "As you wish, Your Reverence," and departed.

CHAPTER THIRTY-SIX

Roslyn tried not to think of what was imminent. Most prisoners condemned to death only got a last meal, if they were lucky. Yet, she'd been granted four days in the life of a noble. To her, it seemed an insult to the king's gift to spend the time lamenting, not that she was the lamenting type. Too many years in battle had beaten away her tears—most of them.

No, she was the planning type. Normally, in a life-threatening situation, she'd be racking her brain to devise some way to make the situation not life threatening. Not now. There was no reason to. It was done. Carry on. There was a strange calmness to that.

Occasionally, her mind would wander to the evacuation of all the Veiled River complex from the Dayigan Empire, and she would think she needed to do this or that. But no, that wasn't her concern anymore. There was a strange calmness in that, too.

Or perhaps the calmness was truly numbness, as Roslyn forced herself not to think about the one thing so prevalent in her mind—the thing too large for her mind to hold, the thing that even the most base portions of her mind screamed she should avoid. Her own death. Sometimes, she felt so sick in the pit of her stomach that she thought she'd vomit. She didn't. She tried not to think of that, either.

Despite all this, the stay within the castle was actually quite lovely. The servants attended to all of her and Estéban's needs. She ate better food than she had ever eaten, bathed in a better tub with perfectly heated water, and slept in a better bed.

All the while, the servants did their best to limit conversation and eye contact. Whenever her eyes met theirs, Roslyn saw a mix of fear and hate. She was unaccustomed to Dayigans knowing her identity. In any other time or place, Roslyn would fear that these servants would turn her in to the authorities. Soldiers would rush into the castle, snatch her, and chain her. Ever since she'd left Hunia as a teenager, she'd feared capture and stayed on alert.

But now there was no reason to fear being captured; it was done, so the wary eyes of the servants didn't bother her. In some ways, their hateful glares were almost humorous in their pointlessness.

The king, too, tried his best to avoid Roslyn and with better success than the servants. The few times they crossed paths within the castle corridors, he kept his words brief and averted his eyes. Yet, his eyes didn't speak of hate, but sadness and perhaps shame. The few glances Roslyn shared with him reminded her that she was going to die.

Accordingly, Estéban was the one person Roslyn spent the majority of her waking hours with and with whom she shared the most conversations. At first, he made many attempts to steer their talks to serious matters, yet Roslyn promptly steered them away. Once she had made it clear by implication what topics she intended to avoid, their chats became lighthearted. They often shared laughter.

Tonight, Roslyn and Estéban ascended the tallest tower of the king's castle, a thin watchtower. Its trunk was little more than a spiral staircase within a cylindrical shell of stone blocks. Its highest floor contained a single room surrounded by large, window-height arches through its stone wall.

The space was empty, save for a desk and chair centered on the rough plank floor. The desk held only a few pages of blank paper, weighted by a stone, a pot of ink, and a quill. Roslyn imagined that someone must have found this to be a pleasant place to write his correspondences or, perhaps, more artistic writings.

She rapped her fingers on the desk as she passed. The tower did indeed have a splendid view.

With Estéban by her side, she neared one of the archways and stared out into the night. Within the quiet town below, a few windows flickered with subtle firelight. A single pedestrian carried a torch through the streets.

"It looks so peaceful," Roslyn said.

"Most likely our last peaceful night."

She nodded, keeping her eyes on the view.

"Forgive me," he said. "I know you don't like to—"

"'Tis fine. 'Tis nearly impossible to ignore at this point. This is our last night here." She looked at him. "You've been pleasant company. Although I do not approve of your volunteering yourself for execution, I'm glad you were here."

He turned to her, pausing before speaking. "I wish I . . ." He glanced away boyishly. "I wish I'd met you before all this."

She gave a gracious smile that turned sad. "As do I. But—" She breathed. "You need to leave. Tonight."

"We both need to leave."

"I swore myself to their custody, Estéban."

"As did I."

"What you said wasn't any kind of real oath. What did you say? Me too?" Roslyn pressed her fingertips to her forehead, pausing for a moment. She folded her hands and set them on the windowsill. "I don't want to fight with you. I've been fighting for too long, and I'm tired. Tired and uncertain if I've made any progress at all."

"You saved countless people."

"Perhaps." She returned her eyes to the tranquil town below. "But our war is over now. And we lost." Her hand moved to the side of her neck, to the iron collar. Her fingers drifted downward, and she began thumbing the silver chain of her necklace.

Staring at the torch of the wandering person below, she said, "They'll not let me leave the Empire, you know. Even if I tried. If I cross the Hyvile, they will pursue me into the Alliance. The Inquisitor all but told me so himself. I don't get to live a normal life after this. And if I try, more of our people will die."

Her words fell away to lingering silence.

Estéban, beside her, stared down into the town. "That square down there, where we first saw the Inquisitor, they shouted at us to go home. 'Go home.' 'Go home.' Where do they think that is? My mother kept alive the memories of our big house that we left behind. It had been in our family for generations."

"Are you a lord?"

He chuckled sadly. "No, not anymore. I was a child in that house, but the Alliance never felt like home. Just like the people here, they say the same thing: 'Go home.'"

"So the Dayigans hate us because we're Karulents and the Karulents hate us because we're Dayigans."

"My point is," he said, "we must *make* a home." He touched her arm and turned her to face him. "That might not have been the original goal of the Veiled River, but it is the new objective *you* gave it."

"Without the support and supplies from the Karulent Alliance, the Veiled River will crumble. You know this, which is why we're getting our people out."

"I *thought* that. But meeting you in person ... Rose, you will find a way to keep the River alive. You have to. If our people leave the Empire, the Empire will only grow stronger. In time, they *will* expand into the Alliance, too."

Roslyn walked away from the window, only a few steps with no actual destination. She pulled her necklace from beneath her blouse and gazed at the pendent—a steel ring topped with a blue-painted rose.

Estéban approached. "What is that?"

"Home," she said sadly. "My lost home. My lost life. 'Tis like your large boyhood house—another life, full of lost possibilities, reduced to faded memories." She pulled the necklace over her collar and head and from beneath her blond hair.

"When I was eighteen," she recounted with melancholic words that stung to speak aloud, "a wonderful boy—Jon—proposed we marry." She gazed at the ring in her palm. "I've never been so happy. I loved him. So much. It seemed we were on this wondrous path that would take us to this blissful life. We had it all planned out." She shook her head, biting her lip a moment before she took a deep breath and released it slowly, shakily. "That Inquisitor—Swithun—killed him. No reason. No warning. Everything just shattered by random hate." A tear ran down her cheek. "Swithun just showed up one day like a storm, and ..." Roslyn sniffed and set her hand to her forehead. "'Twas a long time ago."

"But you still love him."

Roslyn nodded. "Yes. But not in the same way as before. He died so young and never aged in my memories. It might sound silly, but in many ways, I almost feel motherly towards him now. I mourn him as a sweet boy who died so young and so pointlessly. And, too, I mourn his would-be bride, who was destroyed." She gained a sad, reminiscent smile. "She was so sweet. Barely a care in the world. Unprepared."

"You are still a sweet rose."

She sighed. "I'm not sure *what* I am at this point. A healer. A soldier. Roslyn. The Blue Rose. What does the world want from me?"

"What do you want to be?"

Roslyn looked at Estéban, into his deep brown eyes. "I want to be at home. I want to stop fighting. But I don't know how that's possible. If we stop fighting, what happens? The little we've accomplished regresses."

"Which is why you must *live*."

"Don't you understand, Estéban? *I can't do it anymore!*" she shouted in frustration, but calmed. "I promise our people these dark days will pass, but I am *lying*. I no longer see any path forward—any end to this. I'm just surviving every day, and I am *tired*." She wiped her face with her hand. "Our people need a new champion. One with hope."

Silence fell for a moment as Estéban faced downward. Finally, he extended a consoling touch to her arm. She neared, circling him in a tight hug, as she set her head on his chest.

"This is no longer my fight," she whispered. "But you must leave this place. Please."

"I will not leave you." He squeezed her tighter. "I can't."

"Your chivalry is foolish." She pulled away and stepped back. "And frustrating." She grew angry as she said, "Do you think they'll march us hand in hand into the fire? When the Inquisitor's men return tomorrow, they'll divide us forthwith. They will most likely burn you to death right down there"—

she motioned through the arch—"as a spectacle for those same people who shouted, 'Go home.' And I'll be shipped off to Dayigo to meet the same fate, just as alone as if you left now."

Estéban said nothing as he, broken, stared at her. He seemed half-scolded, half lost in the visions of the fate she'd described.

She hadn't meant to be so harsh with him, but she needed him to listen.

"M'lady," a woman said from the top of the stairs. She was one of the castle servants, but Roslyn didn't know her name.

Roslyn, wiping her eyes and forcing a polite smile, approached. "I'm not a lady."

"If it pleases you, I'd rather not call a Karulent, *Your Reverence*."

Roslyn stopped as her smile dropped and her eyes narrowed. She wasn't in the mood for this right now. "Lady is quite all right," Roslyn said with bitter politeness. "Or Your Unholy Witchiness is fine, too."

The servant pursed her lips, no doubt biting her tongue to avoid the reply she wished to make. "His Majesty would like to see you. I'll take you to him."

—

The servant led Roslyn a winding distance through narrow corridors until they reached an arched door. The servant directed Roslyn inside.

Roslyn looked to her for answers, to which she gave none.

"Go on, then," the woman said. She'd been cross with Roslyn since they left the tower and reaching the destination hadn't changed that.

Roslyn nodded. She entered.

The servant closed the door behind her.

The room was small—small for the castle, though nearly the size of the house Roslyn grew up in—and dimly lit by candles set in brass holders throughout. It was what one might call a study or a small library. Two tall shelving units set side by side on one wall and were filled with books. As a scholar and Azerent, Roslyn had seen far grander collections, but little girl her would have been amazed. Indeed, it was more books than most people would see in their lifetime— about fifty. A part of her wished to investigate, but it wasn't the time.

Instead, she turned her eyes to King Eadberht. He stood rigidly near the opposite wall, his hands locked behind his back, which was toward her. He stared at a portrait in a beautifully carved frame of an old king—a relative, no doubt— displayed over a grand fireplace.

Not turning Roslyn's way, he asked, "Enjoying your stay?"

"His Majesty has been most kind."

"*Most kind.*" There was a crestfallen thought in his repeating the words. "I fear you must not have had many occasions to compliment the kindness of Dayigans."

It was nothing Roslyn thought she should answer; thus, silence set for a beat.

"'Twas my father's decision to join the Empire—that's him there." He pointed to the painting. "It was before the actual war on Karulents, but there were signs as to where the Empire would go. Nevertheless, it seemed the best path to recover from the Blue Sickness."

"Karulent kings also joined the Empire," Roslyn consoled, "during the initial years."

He nodded as he turned to face her. "Only to have their titles and lands stripped away," he said. "And oftentimes their lives as well."

He verbalized Roslyn's own thoughts, though she had not dared speak them aloud.

"Are you old enough to remember the time before the Empire?" he asked.

"Vaguely. I was a young teenager. A young woman when the civil war began."

"Before the Empire, it was rather fashionable to have your kind employed in wealthy houses. The Church frowned on it, of course, but Azerent Master Healers were in short supply, high demand, and thus quite costly to retain. A status symbol few could afford. Our family's healer delivered me from my mother's womb and attended to my boyhood illnesses and injuries. Kind, kind old man. This was his area." Eadberht lifted his arms to present the space. "Half apothecary, half infirmary."

Roslyn glanced back at the books on the shelves.

"Those weren't his," the king said. "Most everything of his in here was declared heretical and burnt—along with him— in the town square."

The news wasn't shocking, but it saddened Roslyn. She glanced down. "With respect, sire, you would do better to seek an Azerent *priest* if you wish confession."

"There is no absolution for me, Your Reverence. As a king in the Dayigan Empire, I've . . ." He sighed. "You were correct in saying that I knew Athelric kept a Veiled River port in his home. At least, I suspected and turned a blind eye to it. He was my brother, you see. I don't expect you knew that."

"I did not, Your Majesty. He was a good man."

"Yes. Athelric was a good man, but careless in hiding his secret. When the army discovered the port, I did nothing to save him or those people for fear I'd share their fate."

"Could you have stopped it?"

"Who knows? Most likely not. What I do know is that you did more for the remaining people of Athelric's port than I did for my brother, even when you knew the Empire would kill you for it."

"Through prayer and contemplation, I have made peace with my fate."

King Eadberht folded his hands at his stomach. Whatever he meant to say next, he hesitated, glancing down before saying, "You do not know your fate." His words held a foreboding tone. "Not all of it. What they intend to do to you . . ." He shook his head. "The horror of it has kept me sleepless every night since the Inquisitor's departure."

"What do you mean?"

"Where is your companion?" The king looked back toward the door. "I'd meant for the servant to bring you both."

"Pray you, what do you know of my fate?"

That hesitation again. Finally, he said, "I will tell you both, together. You will need the comfort of a friend at your side."

Roslyn's entire body tensed near to the point of shaking. She squeezed her hands together at her waist. But she controlled herself and nodded. "He's in the highest tower, Your Majesty."

"I will meet you there."

CHAPTER THIRTY-SEVEN

Roslyn returned to the tower ahead of the king—he'd needed to sort out a few things but assured her he'd be there "shortly." She found the delay maddening but conceded without complaint.

Estéban, she now saw, stood before one of the large archways and looked out over the darkened town. Hearing her footsteps, he turned to her. He gave a smile at first, but his expression shifted to concern as he saw her.

Slouched, Roslyn kept her shaking hand on her aching forehead. She had no idea what the king wished to tell her—countless scenarios rushed through her brain—but as she was already worked to her limit to hold herself together, the prospect of further bad news left her shattered. The king knew she'd already prepared herself to be burned at the stake—what could be worse?

"Are you all right?"

"I don't know." She couldn't quite catch her breath. "I'm trying, Estéban, trying to press on, but . . ."

He neared and wrapped his arms around her, pulling her tight in an extended hug. Roslyn set her head on his chest and felt his consoling warmth. He asked no other questions, and she gave no other answers. Instead, they basked in fretful silence.

The king entered up the stairs. "Forgive me. I needed to ensure that none of the guards or servants were nearby."

Roslyn stepped back from Estéban and gained a rigid posture as she contained her emotions—a composed lady of the

Church. "'Tis quite all right, Your Majesty. You said you had news."

He nodded. "I am afraid so. Inquisitor Swithun is working for the former Grand Master of the Knights Silthex, Blastilv, Archbishop of Klikate."

"I am aware, sire."

The king glanced downward, hesitating. "'Twould seem the Archbishop, with leave from Patriarch Krasil, has no intention of martyring the Blue Rose. He would rather make an example out of you." He paused again. "Perhaps you would do well to take the hand of your companion. Or take a seat."

"I'm fine, sire. In what way will he make me an example?"

Eadberht folded his hands on his stomach. "I confess I know not the details. Shortly after you vowed to stay in exchange for your people's freedom, I overheard whispers between the Inquisitor and one of his men. Imagine," he scoffed, "me, the King of Isernstan, needing to *eavesdrop* on soldiers in my very own castle."

"Your Majesty, please." She took Estéban's hand. "What will they do to me?"

"Of course." He nodded. "From what I understand, Archbishop Blastilv has devised a means to strip you entirely of your free will. Rather, they are very near to refining such a means. They mentioned a setback. For now, they intend to transport you to a place the Inquisitor only called 'the abbey.' There, you will be incarcerated until their method is perfected. Afterwards—with your volition entirely suppressed—you will serve directly under Blastilv as his mindless puppet. The Inquisitor mentioned a few vulgar actions he would have you perform, but I'd like to think they are not part of Blastilv's actual intent."

Her face went blank. "They wouldn't," she whispered, barely able to speak. She folded her arms across her stomach, her composure fading fast. "'A fate far worse than death.' That's how Blastilv described what he tried to do to me when he tried to lock me in stone. Now this."

"I am afraid the transportation that Inquisitor Swithun left to procure is one of the golden mirrors. It will take you straight to the tallest tower of Fidelumair Palace, where another mirror will take you to this unknown abbey. It could be anywhere on the continent of Bikia."

"Unthinkable," Roslyn whispered. She searched for the nearest chair—at the desk at the room's center—and hurried to it, taking a seat.

Estéban followed and laid his hand on her shoulder. She gripped his hand.

"How is such a thing even possible?" Estéban asked. "Removing your freewill?"

"Some sort of powerful mind control, I would guess," Roslyn said, facing downward. She grabbed the iron shackle around her neck. She felt hot and trapped. Her breathing hastened.

The king nodded. "That is my guess, as well."

"That settles the debate," Estéban said. "You cannot let yourself be transformed into some thrall for a Déagrian Archbishop. It doesn't matter what you vowed to their twisted church."

"The vow was to me, actually," the king said.

"Whatever the case," Estéban said, "this news changes things. Killing you is one thing, but this . . ."

"I know," Roslyn said. "At least, I think I know. I'm not sure what to do. 'Tis about more than a vow, though I take such things quite seriously." She took a deep breath and released it. "If I flee, they will hunt me down and torture others to find me."

"True, they might," Eadberht said. "However, the Empire has no shortage of manufactured reasons to torture and kill Karulents." He stepped a few paces away. "For some time, I have suspected that the Church and the Empire were off course. But you . . ." He looked at Roslyn. "You truly are a genuinely good person." He stated it less as a compliment than as a sad realization that troubled him. "The world is in terribly short supply of good people these days. Therefore, I must remind you, Your Reverence, this is not your choice. Did you not vow yourself to *my* custody and vow you would stand trial and accept the sentence handed down to you?"

"I did, sire."

"Very well. Stand up."

She glanced at Estéban before standing from the chair.

"As King of Isernstan, I am prepared to deliver your trial myself. Right now. I've heard all I need to hear. On the various charges of insurrection against the Holy Dayigan Empire and the Church of Déagar, I find you irrefutably and overwhelmingly *guilty*."

"How can you say that?" Estéban objected.

"How can I not? She's nearly given me a complete confession." He paused for a moment. "I sentence you . . . to *life*—life in service of the Karulent people and to the True Light at large, by which you will do whatever is in your power to return our lands to the proper path from which we have so greatly strayed."

Despite his serious tone, Roslyn grinned at the sentence. "Your Majesty is most magnanimous. I give you my thanks."

"'Tis mankind who owes you *our* thanks, Your Reverence. You've proven to me that the Blue Rose is the only one who can restore our lands."

"I'm not the—"

"You are. You can. You will," the king said. "You must."

Roslyn nodded.

He looked at Estéban. "You also vowed yourself to me, didn't you . . ."

"Estéban, sire. Yes, I did."

"Right. I sentence you to be her assistant and keep her alive. Not an easy task, I'd imagine."

"I will do my best, sire."

"Now"—the king gave a firm nod—"there's still the matter of getting you out of the castle. The Dayigan Army has done away with individual coats of arms and regularly shuffles its garrison units from town to town throughout the Empire. The soldiers assigned as my castle guards and town guards follow my orders because the Army tells them they must. However, their only true loyalty is to the Army itself and the high king. I cannot order them to let you leave." He sat at the desk and grabbed a blank page of browned paper. "However, I can draw you a route that should—"

"'Tis not enough," Roslyn spoke up. "Forgive me, Your Majesty, but it is not enough to send us on our way and be done with us."

"Roslyn," Estéban touched her shoulder as if to soothe or silence her. She brushed his hand aside as she stepped toward the king.

Estéban walked away.

Eadberht had lifted the quill within his fingertips, but now he lowered it to the desk before looking at Roslyn. "I do not *appreciate* your asking for more when I have already done *far* more for you than any other Déagrian would have."

"And I appreciate that, truly, sire. Most Dayigans would have left us down in that dungeon to await that horrible sentence. However, you aren't most Dayigans." She crouched to his seated position. "You see what is wrong in the Empire. A man with that insight and in your position . . ."

"This is not my fight. I empathize with the plight of you and your people, but I cannot help you further. I am a Déagrian, not a Karulent."

"This *is* your fight," Roslyn said, *"because* you are a Déagrian. No longer is empathy for our plight enough, not with how corrupted both *your* empire and *your* church have become. When Pontiff Krasil came into power in eight hundred and eight, he inherited a church decimated by the Great Pestilence. He filled all those empty positions with people of his choosing, people who believed what *he* thought they should believe and people who hated what *he* thought they should hate. For nearly as long, the high king has awarded titles and lands under the same twisted qualifications. Thus, the plague of hatred infecting both the Déagrians and Dayigans is now firmly rooted in all levels of church and state. Caring—although good—is not enough to fix the darkness twisting your institutions from the inside. You must actively stand with us, not only for *our* sake, but also to save what is left of yourselves."

The king took a long breath and looked at her for a moment. He chuckled. "You're quite the impressive woman, Your Reverence." He lifted the quill and leaned over the page.

"Not to interrupt you," Estéban said, "but we have a more immediate threat." He faced one of the large arches open to the night.

Walking toward the stone portal, Roslyn saw torches lining the main road through the woods and moving toward the town. Once nearer, she could see the shadowed figures holding the dim lights: soldiers, about two hundred. She set her hand on the stone sill of the archway, her heart pounding as her eyes stayed locked on them.

"They're early," Roslyn said, holding a shaky calm. Her hand jumped to her neck, and she ran her thumb along the rough iron of her collar. "So, this is the end."

Estéban grabbed her shoulders and turned her to face him. "This is *not* the end, not for you," he said, staring into her eyes. "You are the *Blue Rose*, a title you earned by . . ." He smiled. "By being generally amazing. You will find a way."

"My magic is bound, Estéban."

"You will find a way."

Roslyn gazed into his deep brown eyes before placing her hand on his cheek. She neared his lips with hers, pausing before she kissed him gently, briefly. "I will not let you die," she whispered. She pulled away, leaving him pleasantly shocked with a dopey grin.

"Your Majesty," Roslyn said as she approached the king. "Do you have any means to remove the shackle from my neck?"

"Unfortunately, no. From what I understand, the one way to remove it without killing you is by the key in Inquisitor Swithun's possession. Take this." He presented a page of paper.

Roslyn scanned it to see it topped with the header, *"Targets for Assassination"* in hastened script. Two columns of names followed below.

She shot the king a quizzical glance. "You wish me to kill these people?"

"No, no. The title is but a quickly devised ruse to perplex anyone who might discover it. You are correct; the time for inaction has passed. In truth, there was never such a time. I will help the Veiled River in any way I can, but I must do so clandestinely. Otherwise, the high king will strip my title and give it to another, thus voiding any benefit the River might receive from my position."

"Roslyn," Estéban said. "We must go."

"And the list?" Roslyn asked the king.

"You've proven yourself to be quite the persuasive speaker, Your Reverence. I believe others might be persuaded to join your cause, but they will require a fair amount of convincing. I cannot so much as broach the topic with them myself for fear of exposure and prosecution if I am wrong—not that they would speak to me if I did, for fear of the same. But you . . ." He nodded encouragingly. "Start with my name on the list and then skip four lines. The next name is a potential ally. Continue the pattern, and you'll have seven names."

Roslyn read the list. "There are at least two kings on here with kingdoms larger than your own."

"*Three*. It will not be easy to convince them to turn against the Empire, but I have confidence in your abilities."

"Are you so certain I can survive the night?"

"You must. No one else can bring these names together."

In near shock, Roslyn's eyes lingered on the page as she absorbed the magnitude of what it represented. "This could change . . ." She looked at the king. ". . . everything." Her heart pounded. "With these allies"—she smiled breathlessly—"we could truly destabilize the Empire."

"Rose," Estéban called anxiously from an archway at the edge of the room. "They are entering the town gate." He dashed to her. "We must go."

"He's right," Eadberht said. "The potential of the list is contingent on your survival. *Go.* May the Light guide you through the Dark."

CHAPTER THIRTY-EIGHT

The fire atop her torch roared, its flames barely clinging to the paraffin-soaked jute as Roslyn rushed down the narrow, stone hall.

"This way," she said to Estéban as the two cornered an intersection.

Her thoughts lingered on the list folded within the leather purse on her belt. Her hand kept finding its way to the purse, touching it every so often to ensure that it hadn't somehow fallen off. Its potential value was still sinking in. Her mind rushed with possibilities as quickly as her feet rushed down the hall. King Eadberht had given her seven names. If she could secure their support, how many more names would *they* give her? And them. She touched the purse on her belt.

"This way," Roslyn said, as they turned another corner.

She didn't know if she was prepared to start and coordinate a rebellion of Déagrian royals and nobles. The idea was absurd, she thought. Yet King Eadberht seemed to think she'd succeed—this, of course, based on the few days he'd known her. Granted, she'd become the de facto leader of the Empire side of the Veiled River and had done well. She touched the purse on her belt—still there. *How did this happen?* How did she, some girl from a little layover town who dreamed of being a healer, end up being the one who would need to stop the largest empire in the world? She wanted to scream. At the same time, Roslyn maintained a growing excitement—albeit twisted up in a knot of anxiety. If she could do this, even to a minor degree, they could funnel supplies into the Veiled River from Dayigan sources to replace those lost from their disconnection with the Alliance.

If she could do this, a large majority of the Karulents in the Empire could stay in the Empire. Roslyn touched the purse on her belt. If she could make this successful, the resulting resistance could pose a real internal threat to the entire Empire.

She stopped running, throwing her arm in front of Estéban to stop him as well.

Up ahead, a soldier stood where the narrow corridor opened up into a large room. He froze, watching the Karulents. He crossed his hand across his stomach to circle the grip of his sword. Despite his emerald green tabard displaying the symbol of Dayigo, he wasn't one of the Swithun's men. Instead, Roslyn recognized him as one of the castle guards but knew the difference was slight.

"That is the door," she whispered to Estéban.

It was a simple wooden door just up the hall, closer to Roslyn and Estéban than to the guard, though not by much.

"Run," Roslyn said, and she and Estéban bolted toward the door—but also toward the soldier.

The soldier, drawing his sword, charged them. "The prisoner is escaping!" he shouted to someone at his rear.

Roslyn and Estéban reached the door first, threw it open, and leaped inside. Roslyn slammed the door in the soldier's face and slammed down a wooden beam across the door, securing it into iron mounts on either side.

The banging outside the door began at once—powerful strikes, as if a boot against the wood. She scanned the small room. Its only content was a small round table atop a circular rug.

"That door won't keep them out long," Estéban said.

"King Eadberht said there was a trap door. It must be under the table."

As Estéban rushed to the table, Roslyn opened the leather pouch on her belt, removed the folded page, and unfolded it.

"Is everything all right?" Estéban, with the table moved, kneeled to the rug.

"Yes. I know 'tis silly, but I . . . I just need to see it."

"'Tis not 'silly' at all." He rolled the rug, revealing a door cut into the plank floor. "That list is the path of hope you were looking for." He grabbed the iron ring of the trap door and yanked it upward with a grunt. "At least it *can* be, in *your* hands."

Roslyn nodded and refolded the page, returning it to the pouch. She hurried to the passage and positioned herself to begin down the ladder.

The door of the room cracked against the impact of steady kicking.

"We must hurry." She descended.

—

Roslyn lifted her torch as, behind her, Estéban climbed down the ladder. The flickering light showed a tunnel just higher than her height. The width was not quite enough for three people to walk side by side. Thick horizontal logs crossed the ceiling, holding it aloft, yet the aged, unmaintained trusses bowed under their heavy burden. A few sections of the walls had been reinforced with blackened, moldy bricks, yet those sections, too, were heavily cracked and bricks lay scattered on the floor.

A rat squeaked as it fled the light, splashing down the trickle of water that meandered the tunnel's center.

"Underground again." Roslyn pushed back a grouping of dangling roots.

Estéban kicked the ladder, rattling it within the iron brackets that mounted it to the ceiling. He kicked again, firmly. The third kick brought down the ladder, the brackets, and one of the bricks framing the trap door above. The pieces clattered to the slimy floor.

"If we come to a point where only one of us can survive," Estéban said, "you must *promise* me you will not hesitate to go on without me. You are the only one who can unite the names on that list."

Roslyn looked at him for a moment. "That missing ladder won't stop them. We must run."

Down the tight, winding tunnel, they ran. Heart pounding and hand clutching the handle of her torch, Roslyn feared the entire world depended on her running as fast as possible. Her other hand touched the leather pouch on her belt. It was still there, she assured herself—the hope for her people. Estéban ducked under a log truss that had fallen diagonally from ceiling to floor. Roslyn was right behind him. She glanced back.

Over two dozen torches rushed toward the two, though their distance remained considerable.

Estéban held a sword; Roslyn looked at it, knowing how pointless the single weapon would fare if they were caught.

Perhaps Estéban saw her looking. He offered an uncertain nod. "We will be all right." He dashed down the next span of the passage.

A bend in the tunnel blocked the sight of those behind them while delivering them to a fork.

"Which way now?" Estéban asked.

"The king made the list instead of the map. And said nothing of this."

Much of the tunnel crumbled in disrepair, but the tunnel to the left, particularly so.

Anxiously, Roslyn looked back; the sight of the soldiers was blocked. She touched the pouch. "To the right," she guessed.

Without further pause, they ran. The route was not fifty feet before they found the tunnel collapsed and impassible.

Estéban struck the wall of rubble with his sword—an angered impulse more than an attempt to cut through.

A few large rocks tumbled down, clicking and splashing on the floor.

"How far back are the soldiers?" he asked.

"Surely, not as far as I'd like. But we have no choice but to turn around and beat them to the intersection."

"Karulus help us."

His words reminded her of her stolen magic. Roslyn touched the iron collar around her neck.

They ran.

Running from the soldiers had already filled Roslyn with adrenalized anxiety. Now, running toward them caused her body to tense so rigidly that she felt as if her muscles might snap. She stared unblinkingly ahead, waiting for that dreaded moment when the torches of the hunters would come into view. Not yet—*thank Karulus for that.* She ran faster. They needed to reach the intersection before the soldiers or their way would be blocked.

Roslyn nearly wept with joy when they reached the fork in the tunnel. She nearly melted in relief. But the victory was brief. She looked down the originating tunnel to see how much ground the soldiers had gained, but the bend blocked all sight of them. They could be just beyond it, and she would be unaware.

They hurried into the severely dilapidated lefthand tunnel and twisted around fallen rock and curtains of roots. The air was stale and smelled of old mud and mushrooms. The roof was lower, causing them to crouch. Still, they knew they could not let the mounting obstacles slow them.

The soldiers, Roslyn knew, would not need to choose left or right at the fork. They could divide their force and take both paths at once. Half would still be enough to capture Roslyn and Estéban, kill them, or whatever the soldiers' intent.

Roslyn touched the pouch on her belt. She had to survive to unite the names on the list, to keep her people in the Empire, and to destabilize the Empire. The frustration of the ordeal swelled a need in her chest to scream. She kept silent, even as her need to go faster collided with her frustrating need to slow and navigate the obstacles of the broken passageway. The route became tighter, closing in around them. Still, they pressed on as quickly as they could manage.

Like rats, they crawled over and under rocks. The few glances back that Roslyn allowed herself offered nothing to determine how far away the pursuing soldiers followed.

Roslyn and Estéban climbed over a mound of rocky rubble, squeezing between it and the ceiling, and jumped down to a significantly more open section of the tunnel.

This area, for a span of twenty feet, had a stone floor with only a few cracks along its length. Brick walls supported a rounded vault overhead.

Roslyn breathed as she touched the old blackened brick. "This must be from the Trasilvokan Empire—the Dark Light empire that predated the Dayigans by centuries. They ran the muck from their cities in passages underground."

Estéban, also catching his breath, returned to the crumbled section of tunnel from which they'd come, to the thick logs framing it as support. He touched his sword to a vertical log against the wall, pulled back, and delivered a firm chop with his blade. He pulled again and readied another strike.

"What are you doing?" Roslyn asked.

He chopped again. "If I take out this support, it should be enough to cause the unstable tunnel to collapse on the Dayigans."

"No."

He pulled back his sword. "The stone section will protect us from the collapse."

Roslyn set her hand on his arm and turned him to face her. "Only a few days ago, I asked you to deliver a quick death to *one* Dayigan, and you were aghast. Now you would do *this—crush* a dozen men?"

"This is different, Rose. I cannot let them take you."

She set her hand on his cheek—rough with black stubble—and gazed into his dark brown eyes. "The Dayigans have taken something from me," Roslyn said, "part of my very soul as a Karulent." She slid her hand down his neck to his chest, feeling his pounding heartbeat through her fingertips. "I will not let them do the same to you."

"But your survival," he said. "The alliance of those names on that list . . ." He breathed. "Rose, it is the only hope our people have."

She turned away, casting her eyes at the floor of the Trasilvokan section of the tunnel. Roslyn stared, thinking. Yet, before she could respond, something caught her attention.

Where the floor met the brick wall, a small arch stood, just large enough for the two of them to squeeze through, one at a time.

Roslyn rushed to it and squatted down before placing her torch into the tiny entrance.

Though the rocky, wet area beyond was no taller than the arch's peak, it widened out significantly, just past the wall.

"We must go this way," she said. "The soldiers will not expect us to deviate from the path."

"Are you sure we can fit there?"

Roslyn looked past him. The blackness of the tunnel had begun to fade with amber light. She could hear the faint clinking and scuffling of the pursuers navigating the many obstacles of the decrepit tunnel.

"Quickly," she whispered, waving him to herself.

Estéban glanced back before rushing her way and crouching.

Torch in hand, Roslyn reached as far as she could into the tiny portal and set down the light behind the wall.

"You go first," Estéban whispered. "If the soldiers arrive before we are both in, I'll lead them away down the tunnel."

Roslyn nodded and lay flat on her stomach, her head at the small archway. With no time to ready herself, she planted her forearms on the stone under her and dragged herself forward, arm over arm, knees pushing one by one to grind into stone. Steadily, she inched forward and began to squeeze through the archway.

Just past the threshold, the ground turned from rough stone to slimy gravel. She could feel the abrasions forming and worsening on her forearms and knees, yet she pressed on, planting her stinging limbs firmly into the rocky ground and dragging herself farther forward into the cramped space.

With her upper body through the archway, Roslyn was horribly aware of how exposed her legs were in the main tunnel. She could no longer see Estéban. She had no idea where the Dayigan soldiers were. She half expected someone to grab her feet at any moment. As quickly as she could manage, she continued through wet filth.

With her entire body finally through the portal, she began the struggle to slide herself around so that her head faced the archway.

Estéban had opted to enter feet first, and Roslyn received a muddy boot to the face before she slid back, closer to the torch behind her.

She grabbed his waist and pulled, hastening his entrance. He struggled as his broader shoulders scraped through the archway. Roslyn wrapped her arms around his stomach, pulling as hard as she could. The soldiers must be close, she guessed, but she had no way to know. They could be watching Estéban now as she yanked him in. If they saw him, he would die in her arms.

At last, he was beyond the archway. They relaxed slightly, face to face and inches apart.

"Forgive my closeness," he said. "I . . ."

"'Tis fine." She paused, looking at his handsome face in the firelight, and rolled to face away.

Roslyn grabbed the torch and rolled the flames into a trickle of muddy water, extinguishing it with plumes of thick smoke.

In absolute darkness, Roslyn scooted herself backward to press her body against Estéban's. She wrapped his arm around her and held his hand, lacing her fingers between his.

They waited.

Silence.

With every elongated moment, Roslyn's body grew tenser. She barely breathed, fearing that the slight sound of inhalation and exhalation from her fretful lungs might draw attention to her position.

Boots slapped the stone floor.

Roslyn flinched, tensing more within Estéban's arms. A soldier had no doubt jumped from the rocky mound that marked the start of the brief brick section of the tunnel. Other footfalls followed.

The vaulted brick tunnel section lit up with increasing torches as the soldiers gathered to await those who still navigated the previous obstacles. Roslyn could see the brown boots, the bottoms of black trousers, and the bases of emerald green tabards, but she was unable to get a proper count of how many men gathered a few feet from her face. She assumed it was half of the original group she'd estimated as two dozen; this based on the assumption that the other half would have taken the other fork in the tunnel leading to the dead end. It was all speculation. Whatever the number, the increasing light and increasing boots with their heavy steps filled her with a growing dread.

A soldier commanded his men to hurry. "We will not let the Blue Rose escape."

Within the small tunnel where they hid, Roslyn squeezed Estéban's hand tighter. Surely, one of the soldiers would see the small archway, she feared. Surely, one would think to search it. Her heart thundered in her chest.

Finally, after what felt like an eternity of terror, the footsteps faded and darkness returned. They were gone. It was then that Roslyn allowed herself to relax, a shaky breath escaping her lips. She turned to face Estéban, finding solace in his arms.

In the pitch-blackness, their bodies pressed together as if trying to merge, touch melting away her anxiety. Hesitating at first, their mouths met in a gentle kiss, fueled by fear and longing. It had been so very long since she had felt such desire, such passion.

As they clung to each other in the filth and muck of the tunnel floor, Roslyn knew she could never let go. But the reality of their dire situation soon pulled them apart, leaving only the bitter taste of longing on her lips.

"We cannot return to the main tunnel," panting, she whispered into his stubbled cheek, "or we'll be between the two Dayigan groups. We'll need to crawl through this small passage and hope it leads somewhere."

CHAPTER THIRTY-NINE

From a hole within the tangled roots of a birch tree, Estéban emerged, planting his palms on either side of the rim as he pushed himself up and climbed out. He reached his hand down through the same hole, firmly grabbing Roslyn's hand to help in her ascent.

"My belt is caught," she said, struggling to wiggle free.

Estéban grabbed her other hand, tugging firmly.

Finally, Roslyn was delivered from the ground to thick woods under a night sky. A welcome breeze brushed her face. She heard a stream and found it flowing just behind the tree.

"We made it," Estéban said with a smiling sigh.

"Get down," Roslyn said. "We're not—so to speak—out of the woods yet. The soldiers could be anywhere."

Estéban crouched, drawing his sword and watching the area.

Roslyn set her hand to the pouch on her belt, checking—"'Tis gone," she whispered, her heart skipping a beat before she looked back toward the tunnel. "The pouch holding the list."

Estéban looked at the hole from which they'd emerged. "It must have come off when your belt got caught. I'll go back for it."

She breathed and nodded. "My thanks."

Estéban, in a crouching trot, hurried to the hole and entered.

Roslyn scanned her surroundings, searching for any pursuers. The area around her was sparsely wooded but open with few shrubberies, and the moons overhead gave more light than she would have liked. Nevertheless, not twenty feet away, the woods grew thick. She was exposed, with no clear sight into the nearby woods. Anyone could be there.

Staying low, Roslyn stepped forward.

"Stop where you are," a man's voice sounded from the shadows of the woodline. Inquisitor Swithun emerged, his hand raised to chest level and cupped upward, holding something.

Roslyn froze, eyes darting as she plotted an escape while trying to determine who else might be with him.

"I was starting to think this fucking thing might be broke," Swithun said. "You're half a mile from the tunnel's exit and there's no way you could've got past the soldiers stationed there. But here you are." With a lowering of his hand, the item in his palm moved between his fingertips, which he raised to display for Roslyn's benefit.

It was a three-inch, glowing, pale green crystal that she recognized as the key to the iron collar around her neck.

"'Tis a tracker," Swithun said. He pointed it away from her—causing it to darken—and then back toward her—causing it to relight. "Since you're probably planning to run off, you should know that it can also cause you a lot of *pain* through your collar."

"Of course." Roslyn smiled bitterly as she stood upright. "Another anti-magic Dayigan who is also a caster. I suppose you are now a Silthex knight."

His eyes narrowed. "I ain't no fucking caster. I'm just using something made by someone what had a special dispensation from the Church to make it. And there ain't no Silthex left." His voice lowered with anger. "The few of us what weren't there for your massacre have moved on from the Order. But *we remember what you did.*" He clamped the crystal in his fist.

Pain shot from the collar like fire around her neck, causing her to cry out and grasp at the iron in desperation as she fell to her knees.

But Swithun did not falter, his grip on the crystal only tightening as he stepped forward. "Did you watch me holy brothers screaming in pain? When you was burning 'em alive?"

The pain grew more intense, throbbing down her body. "'Twas not my intention to do that to them," she choked out, her fingers clawing desperately at the collar. "But I do not mourn them. Blastilv needed to be stopped."

Swithun's lip curled in disgust as he loosened his grip on the crystal he held. The pain lessened, but Roslyn could still feel the lingering effects of his cruel magic.

"D'you think you've stopped the Archbishop?" Swithun scoffed. "Right now, his experiments in the west promise us a force far more formidable than the Silthex you murdered."

"The Drevite Experiment?"

"How do you know about that?"

Roslyn straightened herself, chin up. "I know all about Blastilv's wicked scheme."

He looked at her for a moment, gears turning. "Do you? Well, I guess I can talk all about it then, can't I, since you know everything already?" He laughed. "Do you think I'm an idiot?"

"I'm certain you'd rather me not answer that."

He again angrily clenched the gem in his fist.

She cried out as a short agony ripped through her, and she lunged forward, grabbing the collar with both hands.

"The Drevite Experiment," Swithun said, "is nothing you need to know about, right. Not yet. But you'll know all about it soon enough. For now, me men will come here, drag you to a hole, slam the door shut, and lock you away 'til the Archbishop's good and ready for you. See, burning you's not enough for what you done. The Archbishop's devised a nice little *special* torture for you." He clearly meant his words to be news to her, and he gave a domineering stare as he awaited her reaction.

Roslyn gave none. Instead, she again postured herself as tall as she could on her knees, chin up, and met his gaze with calm. "Your men are not nearby," she spoke up louder than she needed for the few feet between him and her. "I assume you did not want them to witness your use of a magic crystal to find me."

"I promise you, witch, my men are close enough. And the pain the collar has brought you so far is just a little taste of the agony you'll feel if you don't come with me without resisting."

"Half a mile away, you said." Roslyn kept her eyes on Swithun, resisting her urge to search the area. "That's where you said your men guarded the tunnel's end." She knew Estéban was close. The anticipation swelled within her as she waited.

"Stand up," Swithun commanded.

Roslyn began to comply as slowly as she could, feigning some sort of stiffness in her body. It seemed reasonable, she decided, that the collar would have left her aching.

"Stand up, witch. I don't have all night."

Then Roslyn saw him, sword in hand: Estéban. He crept from the treeline behind Swithun. Steadily, he approached, careful not so much as to crinkle a leaf underfoot.

"Stand up, *now!*" Swithun shouted.

Roslyn braced her hand on her knee, pushing herself up.

Swithun grabbed her arm and yanked her up before raising his hand to strike. For a moment, Roslyn was a teenage girl in the Hunian church tower, panicked. No, she thought—she was not her anymore. She punched Swithun in the face.

With the soldier distracted, Estéban lunged forward, his movements silent and quick. In one swift motion, he plunged his blade into Swithun's gut.

Eyes wide in pain, the Inquisitor groaned before collapsing to the ground. He curled to his side, arm grasping against the blood flowing from his stomach.

"The Archbishop'll find you," he said through bloody teeth.

"I invite Blastilv to find me," Roslyn said, staring down at him. "I've searched for him for years. Where is the crystal to unlock this collar?"

Swithun gripped his gore-soaked fist tighter.

Pain shot through her neck, but it was mild and brief.

Roslyn crouched to the dying soldier. "Unlock this collar, and I give you my word I will save you."

"Why should I believe you?" Swithun growled.

"Because I have no reason to lie," she said. "To be blunt, you'll be dead in minutes if I don't, and as I am a Master Azerent Healer who did quite well in my studies in Vilana—before your people destroyed the city—I am certain I will have no trouble whatsoever, using the crystal myself after I pry it from your dead fingers."

"Why—" He choked. "Why would you save me?"

"Because I am a healer." Roslyn sighed. "Despite what you and your army have forced me to become, all I ever wanted to do was to help people be free of pain and sickness. This time, whilst I awaited execution, has allowed me to reflect. For years, I have viewed the Déagrians *as* the sickness. That's what I yelled at the Silthex: 'You are the disease, and I am the healer,' and I thought myself quite clever at the time. In truth, you are the *sick*. And for the sake of the True Light, I must help your people, as well as my own. A part of you knows your path is wrong. You saw it once, long ago, in Hunia. I know you did. You questioned your twisted church. Father Hanugfrie told me you came to him seeking answers."

Swithun looked up at her with heavy eyes. After a contemplative pause, he lifted his shaking hand, holding the key as far as he could manage.

Roslyn leaned down, meeting him halfway as she touched the lock of the collar to the crystal.

His hand fell limply to the ground.

The collar fell open. She grabbed it and tossed it behind her. She rolled the Inquisitor onto his back.

"*Remain awake,*" Roslyn whispered, "*yet feel no pain.*" She positioned her hand flat a few inches above his chest. "Can you understand me?"

He nodded weakly.

Her palm began to glow blue. "You're going to be all right, Swithun. Nex has begun to encroach into your vital pneuma—that is, death energy is encroaching into your core life force—but I am halting its progression."

She took the crystal key from his bloody hand and handed it to Estéban. "Use your sword to draw a circle on the ground around us. Make it as close to exact as you can manage free-hand."

"Yes, Commander." He hurried to the task.

"I want you to listen, Swithun, and understand our magic. Thus, I must heal you slower than normal, explaining, but you will feel no pain." Roslyn placed her hand on the emerald green fabric of his tabard, over his heart. "When the Holy Mother, Titaness Lágeya, first created mankind long ago, she gave those first people perfect bodies able to heal any injury that might befall them—no matter how dire. Death, old age, disease—these, too, were no concern of these first people. However, when the Dark Light corrupted mankind, their bodies were also corrupted, and our ancestors' ability to heal was tremendously lessened. Yet the full extent of Lágeya's gift lies dormant in us all, even now."

She moved her finger in a slow circle around his heart. "Now, with the power and wisdom of the True Light God Karulus, I use the pneuma of my soul to awaken, temporarily, this primordial gift from Lágeya. I empower your body to heal itself, as it was meant to do."

The circle Roslyn drew glowed blue through his tabard, with rays of white shining outward across his chest.

"Yet even with this ancient gift awakened," she said as she moved her hand above the gore-crusted hole into the flesh of his stomach, "it is not as it was in the first of the ancestors. And so I must guide it, lest your body heal itself incorrectly."

Roslyn closed her eyes. "In the Aetherial Plane, I create a replica of your body formed of lines of blue light. I can see your injury—not only what is visible on the surface but also what is within. Your chain mail slowed the sword, but you have a four-inch-deep puncture, which has caused tissue and organ damage, including a perforated liver, as well as severe internal hemorrhaging. With my mind, I manipulate the affected region of the aetherial replica of your body, restoring what was damaged, and your actual body follows the movement of the replica. With your tissues in their proper place, I guide your body to heal. And then I move outwards, repeating, and further outwards, repeating. Until finally, I reach the surface."

The surface of the wound glowed blue as the skin closed together and fused with no sign that a sword had ever entered.

"Currently," Roslyn said, "the bonds I have created are fragile and liable to break apart if you were to move. But I have ensured that even the tiniest capillary is in its proper placement. And so, I call upon that ancient gift I spoke of before." She set her left hand over his heart as she moved her other hand in a large circle a foot over his body. "Praise Titaness Lágeya, Mother of the Gods and creator of man. Praises to the Gods true to her—praise God Karulus, praise God Déagar, praise Goddess Larissa, praise Lady Ashatra. Restore this man to health. Refill his arteries, so his pneuma may flow steadily with his blood."

Swithun's vascular system glowed white through his skin.

"Restore him, O True Light powers, and make him whole again. As is your will, so may it be."

Roslyn looked at the scar on his neck, where the wound she had inflicted long ago had been sealed under a severe burn. She remembered the anger she'd felt when she had inflicted it. She'd wanted to kill him. She'd believed she had for years. With a breath, she let it go.

"I forgive my enemy," she whispered, "not for his sake but for my own, that I might vanquish the anger I've held far too long."

She touched her fingers to the scar. It glowed blue as it faded with the healing of both the surface and the damage below. And the scar was no more.

She bowed her head and lowered her arms to her sides. "It is done."

Inquisitor Swithun sat up slightly and looked at her, wordlessly and confusedly. He pushed two fingers through the hole in his bloody tabard and rubbed the skin where the injury had been.

"My hope," Roslyn said, "is that you can understand—at least in part—that our magic is not wicked. That *we* are not wicked. That is why I shared details of our methods unknown to anyone outside the Order of Azerents. We strive to restore the gifts Lágeya meant for all of us to have, gifts stolen from us by the Dark Light. And we do so within the magnificent path of the True Light."

Swithun seemed lost in thought or shock. He kept his hand on his healed stomach.

Roslyn stood, walking a few paces away to join Estéban, who watched.

"*Thirty million,*" Swithun growled behind her. "That's how many people your Blue Sickness murdered, including me wife and little boy."

Roslyn stopped, but did not look back.

"If you think your blasphemous talking would stop me from wiping out every single one of you wicked Karulents from the face of Perdinok, you are a fool." He jumped up, snatching a dagger from his belt.

Roslyn clicked her fingers.

Blue light shone up from the circle Estéban had drawn around the Inquisitor. It remained a translucent, marbled wall.

"No," she said calmly. "I am no fool. Only hopeful." She turned to him. "The wall will remain for three hours. I advise you to wait. If you cross it, you will enter a psychically in-duced coma for three days. However, how you choose to proceed is your decision. Either way, I am done with you."

She grabbed the iron collar from the ground, nodded to Estéban, and they walked away.

Once Roslyn and Estéban had gone some distance, she stopped and turned to him.

"Most of the soldiers are gathered half a mile away, presumably at the exit of the tunnel. There's another large group further to our left, and a few pairs patrol the woods. Now that my ability to track life forces is restored, we can avoid them."

Estéban looked back at Swithun—sitting on the ground with his arms crossed and looking rather furious with life.

"It was good what you tried to do for that man."

She nodded. "His reaction was disappointing, but not surprising."

"Thus, the circle."

She smiled. "Thus, the circle. But I have better things to think about than him. I have news, wondrous news that I dared not speak aloud before, for fear someone might snatch it away."

Estéban grinned curiously. "Truly? And what is this news?"

Roslyn's smile grew larger, shining brighter than any smile she'd shown in years. "The king of Freoldreor is on the list of potential allies."

"Freoldreor?"

"Freoldreor is the kingdom that holds the town of Hunia." Roslyn sighed contentedly. "My home."

PART SIX

The Encroaching Chaos

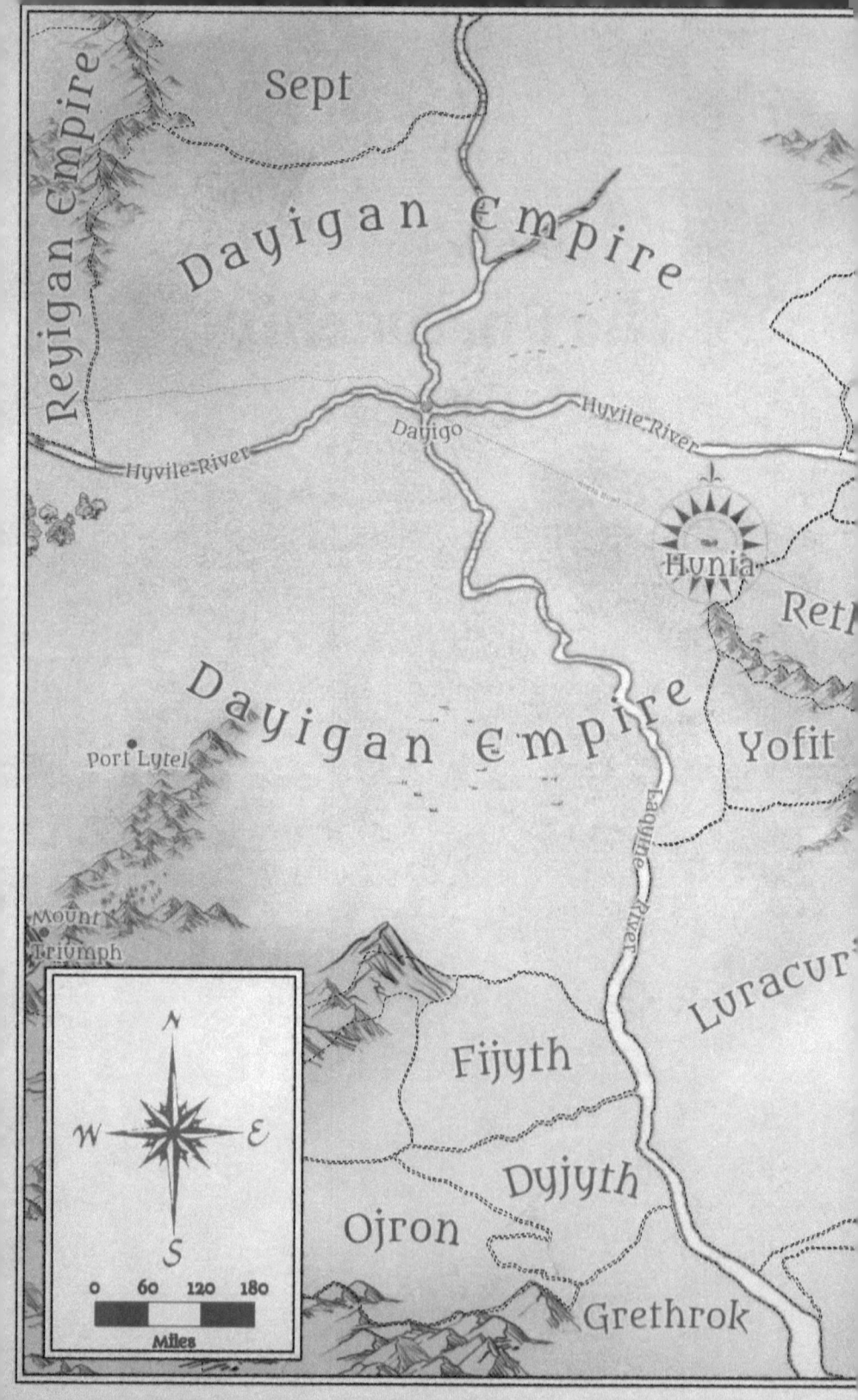

CHAPTER FORTY

Duodeki 21, 839: Six Years Later

After the long and arduous journey, the irregular cobblestones of the wide road were harsh beneath the wooden soles of her gray shoes. Her dress, an equally drab gray, hung heavily on her tired shoulders. Her body was sore, and the winter chill did nothing to help it. Her brown leather bodice was too tight. Her long blond hair was limp and tangled. Nevertheless, Roslyn was happy to be home.

Eight soldiers marched on either side of her in two lines on either side of the road. Their tabards were gray, each with a large circle embroidered in white, filling the front above the belt. No color, no crest—the army of the Resistance.

They continued their march down the wide road lined with wattle-and-daub houses and shops. A few dirt side roads led slightly beyond the shops, stopping at the ten-foot walls of sharpened vertical logs that formed an irregular pentagon around the town. The addition of the walls had given the entire town a different feel—more confining—one Roslyn still hadn't fully gotten used to.

Residents hurried outside to join the growing number of townspeople edging the cobbled road. Excitement filled the bystanders as they watched. Some lifted their children on their shoulders to better see the small parade.

Roslyn stopped. "Ambassadorial unit," she spoke up, "fall out. I will be fine from here."

"Should we join the soldiers at the perimeter, Ambassador?" one asked.

Roslyn glanced at the wooden guard tower beside where the road met the edge of town—it was one of five towers now in place. "No," she said. "Inform the garrison commander that I've given you the rest of the day off. We've had a long journey."

"Yes, Ambassador. Our thanks." The soldiers dispersed.

Roslyn glimpsed the old mill with the ox trudging around the grinding stone inside. A part of her half-expected Nell—the miller's wife from when she was a child—to run out. But no, she'd been dead for decades. She smiled sadly at the memory of Nell.

As Roslyn continued into town, people greeted her warmly. "Good morrow, Ambassador," a woman said with a smile as she passed by.

"Blue Rose! Welcome back," a local man called as he waved from a wooden stall selling thin gray blankets.

They were not the original residents of Hunia, of course. Almost all were from the various ports of the now-defunct Veiled River. But over the last few years, they'd made this place as much their home as Roslyn's as they worked to restore the long-abandoned town.

Roslyn stopped at the wishing pool in the center of the street and stared at the inn. Despite similar plank walls and a thatched roof, it was not quite like the original, yet it stood upon its ashes. Smoke billowed from its stone chimney. No matter how many times she passed the new inn, it still unnerved her somewhat. She never entered. She wouldn't have had it rebuilt at all, but it fulfilled a vital need.

At times, at night, Roslyn could still hear the screams of the burning Hunians lost twenty-seven years ago.

She continued, passing to a two-story shop a few doors down. A wooden beam protruded outward over the door. From it, two short lengths of chain held a wooden sign. It displayed a mortar with a pestle extending above its rim.

She entered.

—

The shop was a welcome respite from the biting winds and bitter cold outside. Roslyn shut the heavy door behind her, shutting out the world and its troubles for just a moment. The air inside was thick with the heady scent of herbs and incense. Shelves upon shelves were packed tightly with potions, salves, and tonics, all promising miraculous cures and remedies. A sturdy worktable stood to her right, stained with all manner of ingredients and tools. A small hearth burned brightly, casting flickering shadows across the room and illuminating an empty cauldron hanging above it. But Roslyn's attention was drawn to the man standing in the back corner, his back turned to her as he meticulously arranged jars on a shelf—Estéban.

"Excuse me," Roslyn said. "Have you anything to help me gain my husband's attention?"

He turned, producing a large smile as he approached. "I do not think anyone as fair as you would have troubles in that regard. Welcome home."

"*Home.*" She glanced down with a sad smile. "'Tis still strange to hear. 'Tis particularly strange after returning from such a long trip away. Hunia has become a unique bubble of comfort in an otherwise turbulent land."

Estéban's eyes wandered for a moment, as if he was looking for a response. He found none. Instead, he took her hand and squeezed it. "Your hand is freezing," he said, before wrapping his arms around her.

She snuggled in his welcomed warmth. "Forgive my woeful words." She laughed. "I am simply pleased to return. The shop appears to be doing well."

He rubbed her shoulders briskly. "A few potions and balms are out of stock, but nothing you need to rush to replenish. However, there are few itchy residents who'll be happy to see their healer returned—although not as happy as I am to see my *wife* returned." He kissed her lips. "How was your trip?"

"*Achingly* boring, in truth." She set her head on his chest. "Nothing but an assortment of tired old royals and tired old nobles sitting around tired old tables negotiating and bickering ad nauseam about who should have more power when each of them has plenty already."

"I'm blessed to have skipped it."

"You truly are, indeed, my love. But . . ." She stepped back and lit up with growing excitement. "We have made much progress. Another kingdom is leaving the Dayigan Empire to join us. That would put the Resistant Nations at twelve kingdoms."

"Amazing, though not surprising," he said. "I know well that my Rose is an excellent negotiator." He gave her a peck on the lips. "And the Empire has yet to offer *any* retaliation?"

The question removed Roslyn's smile. "None as yet." She turned to the nearest shelf and began straightening a row of small blue cloth pouches, each topped with a drawstring tied in a bow.

"Forgive me," he said. "I didn't mean to bring up bitter subjects."

She stopped her straightening but let her hand rest on the pouches. "I know retaliation is imminent. And I know our town we built here could be easily wiped out." She sighed.

"The stronger the Resistance grows, the stronger our defenses grow, along with our army, but also our potential as a target. We cannot guess when the Empire will attack, but, hopefully . . . we will be strong enough by then."

"Hopefully, later than sooner."

Roslyn turned to him. "We suspect the Empire delays out of fear of ramifications from its own people. For them to attack the Resistance—that is, to attack fellow Déagrian nations that have chosen to leave their Empire—is to send a *clear* message that membership in the Empire is not a choice. Kings like to believe that they act of their own volition, thus taking that away could cause more nations to leave the Empire simply on principle, causing it to ultimately unravel completely."

"You've given that speech before."

"More often than I would like." She smiled. "The reality is, despite how powerful the Dayigan Empire has become, it is only thirty years old, and a lot of its infrastructure is precariously held together by yarn and twine hastily woven by the Church of Déagar via fear of a plague that has long passed."

"Too bad they have no problem using their yarn and twine to attack *Karulent* nations," Estéban said bitterly. "They declared war on the Alliance, even after they signed a treaty."

"On who?" Roslyn asked playfully.

"What?"

Her smile returned, though slight. "You referred to the *Karulent Alliance* when it has been the *Reyigan Empire* for years."

"You know what I am saying. The Dayigans signed a treaty not to declare war on the *Reyigans* if they stopped supporting the Veiled River. We shut down the River. The Dayigans attacked them anyway. My sister almost died in that first attack." He paused before muttering, "A bastardly move."

Roslyn straightened a row of bottles that were already straight beforehand.

Estéban stepped close behind her and wrapped his arms around her waist. "I suppose you've had your fill of this sort of talk while you were away."

"More than my fill, in truth. Now, I'd like to close up shop early, go upstairs, bathe, and relax. I extend the invitation to you on all counts."

"Who am I to refuse the invitation of the great Ambassador of the Resistant Nations?" He kissed the side of her neck. "However, 'tis important you talk to our son first."

"Is something wrong?" She turned to face him.

"No, nothing like that. He has been preparing himself for your return all week. He's in the church."

CHAPTER FORTY-ONE

Roslyn climbed the seven steps of the parish church and entered the large blue doors.

Inside, at the base of the bell tower, a small room held little more than a wooden font, like an immense wooden chalice, centered on the room. The font was original, yet it no longer displayed varnished wood. It had needed to be painted sapphire blue to cover restoration patches and obscene graffiti. The rest of the room bore a coat of thick white paint.

Roslyn dipped her hand into the holy water within the font and prayed a silent prayer, purifying herself so she could enter the nave of the church. Despite all her efforts to walk the path of God Karulus as best as she could, a part of her always doubted her actions any time she stood in this place, hand in blessed water. *Am I truly worthy of stepping foot into the house of Karulus?*

She finished her prayer and continued through another set of doors.

As Roslyn entered the church proper, she saw, centered on the empty gray tile floor, a thirteen-year-old boy. He kneeled—his head bowed with chin-length blue hair hanging forward, his eyes closed, and his blue wings folded at his back. He kept his hands clasped at his chest.

Roslyn approached quietly and stopped a few feet behind him as she looked up—toward the front edge of the vast room—at the icon of God Karulus. Votive candles in blue glass cups atop a stepped rack twinkled at his feet. The statue was a beautiful stone representation rescued from a great cathedral, much nicer than the wooden one that had been here before, although Roslyn missed the former, a lost friend.

Without looking up, the boy said, "You're home earlier than I expected. I'd hoped for more time to prepare."

"Prepare for what?"

He jumped up and excitedly turned to her. "I'm ready to become an Azerent, Mother."

"I see. And how have you reached that conclusion?"

"I've been a novice since I was eleven, and I think I've made a lot of progress in the last two and a half years—under the tutelage of the famed Blue Rose."

Roslyn smiled graciously. "I'd really rather people did not call me that, especially my son. It makes me sound like something mythic."

"Yes, Mother. But I *have* made much progress, and I think I'm ready to join the Order properly."

Roslyn thought for a moment, not so much debating his readiness—he truly had made significant progress—but reflecting on how fast he was growing up. It seemed just yesterday that Marc had come into her life as a little boy of seven. Now he was already a young man.

"If that is what you wish, you'll need to make a formal request," Roslyn said with a grin, "to me. And I will need to make a formal evaluation to determine if you are right for me to take on as an official apprentice."

He stood straight, shoulders back, wings tight, and arms to his side. "Your Reverence, Grand Healer Roslyn, I Marcoulif, son of Estéban, formally request you to initiate me into the Order of Azerents as an apprentice healer under your guidance."

Roslyn looked him up and down. The thirteen-year-old had an unremarkable face framed by blue hair with black lowlights—nicely trimmed just past his jaw in a style intentionally identical to Estéban's. His pale blue eyes often alternated from icy to innocent. Innocent now. His grayish-blue wings held touches of black and white, much like a blue jay's. A bit skinny, even for a Terovae, but not unhealthy—Roslyn had kept him fed as best as she could. He'd always stayed a bit pale, as he preferred to spend more days reading than playing outside. Estéban had tried to train him in swordsmanship, but he'd never shown much interest.

"I would like to examine your pneuma," Roslyn said. "Is that all right?"

He nodded excitedly. "Definitely. I've been working particularly hard to strengthen it whilst you've been gone."

She touched two of her fingers to the center of his forehead. A cord of white light appeared down his center, with seven larger points of white down the cord. It appeared strong.

Roslyn stepped back and set her hands flat together. She pulled them apart, and the boy became engulfed in a painless blue fire that spread about four feet around him.

Marc looked in all directions. "Will I learn to do that? See souls?"

"We cannot truly see the soul. I've created a visual representation that I, admittedly, copied from those who trained me. But yes, in time, I'll teach you to do the same."

"Mine is blue now, because I'm an Azerent Novice?"

"I see it as blue, yes. Yours actually extends quite farther than when I checked it two years ago, and it was strong then. Do you remember what this outer portion is called?"

"*Coronal pneuma*," he said. "'Tis the power used to perform magic."

"Correct. You have a good amount. Remember, there is no distinct division between it and the *vital* pneuma that powers one's vital organs. So you must be very careful not to use too much magic or you will become very sick and possibly die. If you run low, you must stop what you are doing and take the time to meditate and connect yourself to the *Mystical Body*—the spiritual song of all Karulents throughout the lands. It will restore you"

He nodded with a child's forced seriousness. "I'll be careful, Mother."

Roslyn felt her cheeks tighten in the start of a proud smile, but she subdued it, maintaining her objectivity.

"Further in," Roslyn continued, "in a section I have not visualized, is a layer called *nex*, or death energy. When you see this layer encroach upon a patient's pneuma, it means they are dying. Nex powers the soul after it leaves the body. And finally, in the core of your soul, there is set an orb of Light from the Plane of Light. This is your true self—the self you must discover as an Azerent."

His eyes widened in amazement. "How do I do that, Mother?"

Roslyn waved her hand and the representation of his soul vanished. She smiled somewhat slyly. "I'm still learning that myself. To be in the Order is to be on a continuous journey of knowledge and self-discovery."

Marc's smile widened, and Roslyn could tell that his mind surged with possibilities. She remembered how excited she'd become after a similar conversation with Father Hanugfrie many years ago.

No longer able to contain it, Roslyn beamed with pride. "Marcoulif, as an Azerent Novice, you have consistently excelled in your training and have continued to impress me.

After examining your coronal pneuma, I have found that you have levels substantially higher than the requirement to enter the Order."

She could tell Marc was straining every muscle to resist jumping up and down, and she couldn't help but note the irony that, in this formal moment, her young man neared reverting to a little boy. Something she easily forgave.

"Thus," Roslyn continued, "with these factors combined, I happily grant you my full recommendation for initiation into the Order of Azerents."

Marc bounded at her and wrapped his arms around her in a hug.

"My thanks, Mother. I mean, Grand Healer. Is it wrong that I wish my birth parents were here to see this?"

"No." Roslyn returned the hug. "Not at all. I pray that God Karulus affords them the opportunity to view this moment from beyond. And, if they watch, I know they'll be as proud of you as I."

"I will not disappoint you. Or them."

"Of that, I am certain. I will contact the Order forthwith."

—

Below the Hunian parish church, in the small alchemic laboratory once belonging to Father Hanugfrie, Roslyn sat in a wooden chair and polished a large silver bowl.

The new parish priest was no Azerent; thus, he'd given Roslyn this space to use whenever she needed it. Here, she felt a closeness to Father Hanugfrie. And to Mother Cyneburga. It would have been nice, she mused, if they were still alive to see Marc's initiation.

She'd modified the space somewhat. The walls were now plastered white and smooth. On the west wall hung a large square of velvet showing the Azerent Seal—a large, white, five-pointed star with a five-petaled, stylized periwinkle nearly filling the star's interior. In the center of the flower was a pentagon holding an eye with a blue pupil.

Old tables and shelves lined the north wall. The tables held an assortment of bulbous glassware and other items for alchemic research and creation—currently empty and neatly stored. An array of herbs, too rare to keep in her shop, hung upside down from a rack above. Centered on the wall above the table, she'd set and mortared gold-painted stones as a Septenar—the crossed number seven.

Against the east wall, bookcases displayed a few books— not as many as she'd have liked. Between them, more tables waited empty as workspaces. Centered above them on a wooden plaque, a purple-handled dagger pointed down.

The south wall held copper lamps, both hung from three thin chains. Their flames were steady in the windless room. Beside them, the wooden door was closed.

Roslyn stopped polishing as she saw her reflection. Within her shoulder-length hair, she could see strands of gray dulling the blond. Her skin wasn't wrinkled, but looked older in a way she could not quite name. Her eyes looked tired. Roslyn remembered when she thought forty-five was old. She didn't feel old. Perhaps sometimes.

Roslyn stood and set the silver bowl on the floor beneath the Azerent Seal. From a table, she took a clay pitcher of water and poured it into the bowl, filling it. She sat cross-legged before the bowl and set her hands palm upward on her knees.

She closed her eyes.

In her mind, Roslyn remained in the room, but it was empty and the walls were glossy black and edged in blue light. In the room, she could see herself, depicted in blue, sitting before the bowl.

Water flowed down the wall in front of her.

To her right, the wall turned craggy black.

Fog wafted up the wall behind her.

To her left, the wall burned.

The bowl was there but black, and the Roslyn in the room reached out a finger and ran it along the rim, creating a blue circle of light.

"Come to me," she whispered.

Roslyn opened her eyes. She waited.

After a few minutes, an image formed. A Terovae man, in translucent shades of blue, hovered above the silver bowl. He sat cross-legged, his hands on his knees and eyes closed. He looked about sixty and wore a long, loose habit.

"Supreme Hierophant," Roslyn said with a respectful bow of her head. "I hadn't expected you to answer my call yourself. I only wished to seek approval for a new initiate to the Order. 'Tis my son, Marcoulif, who comes with my full endorsement."

"A wondrous occasion," he said. "Yet, sadly, we have a more pressing matter."

He stood up—above the bowl—and waved for Roslyn to stand as well.

She bowed her head and stood.

"But first," he said, "how are you, my child? It must be difficult in the Resistant Nations?"

With a long sigh, Roslyn nodded. "It is, Your Holiness. But we are making progress. Our army has shut down many internment camps throughout the Empire and has processed the former captives into the Resistance. We have neutralized strategic imperial forts, deweaponizing them and sending their arms and armor to the Reyigan Empire. We have gained *many* allies amongst Déagrians, themselves, and helped them realize that the twisted path of the Empire is not the path of God Déagar. I am hopeful, Your Holiness."

The Supreme Hierophant nodded solemnly. "It pains me," he said, "that I should ask a sister of the Church of her well-being, and she should answer like a soldier."

"I assure you, Your Holiness, our work is vital. However, I no longer participate in military actions. I serve as an ambassador. A dozen kings pulled their kingdoms from the Empire, all of whom I met with personally. The Dayigan Empire heads towards destabilization."

"Your secular work is indeed important, child," he said. "However, I fear you neglect your spiritual work. Such is true for all Dayigan Azerents—what few of you who remain—but you, in particular . . ." He sighed. "You have *such gifts* in the esoteric arts. You should be here in the Inner Circle."

"I am honored, Your Holiness," Roslyn said. "Truly. But, with all respect, I cannot leave the Resistance. Our people need me here."

He nodded. "I know," he said sadly. "It is the quandary we pray about every day. Do we sacrifice our future to save our present? And yet, our present continues to dim. Whilst I would prefer you to teach a course at the Azerent College in Reyigo, it pleases me to know you are, at least, taking on an apprentice. If he comes with a referral from the Blue Rose, nothing else needs to be said on the matter. You have our leave to perform the initiation ritual and allow him to take vows."

"My heartfelt thanks, Your Holiness. I believe very strongly he will do quite well and go far within the Order."

"Excellent. The Order will need strong members in the coming days." He paused, folding his hands at his waist. "Chaos energy is seeping into the world of Perdinok."

"Chaos, Your Holiness? But how?"

"The Inner Circle is at a loss," he said. "We consulted the stars, the Guardians, and performed all manner of scrying and experimentation. All we can determine is that the issue is growing worse. We believe *you* can find the answers we seek. However, you will require an assistant. We suggest you take Coenric, but the choice is yours. You must leave as quickly as possible."

"Unfortunately, Coenric is miles away, as is every other Azerent. As you said, we are very few here."

"I see." He cleared his throat. "Then, I fear our new initiate will need to test himself far more quickly than most."

—

Worry weighed Roslyn as she ascended a cramped, dark staircase that led directly into a stone wall. Her thoughts lingered on the Supreme Hierophant's words.

She set her hand on the rough stone, pausing for a moment with a concentrated thought. The solid stone, while looking no different, became like mist into which her hand sunk through. She walked through, entering the office that had belonged to Father Hanugfrie years ago. None of the furnishings were the same as when it was his, but the desk—which she now stood behind—was in the same spot. The shelves were placed similarly. It still felt like his office to her, and that comforted her.

Marc paced near the door while biting his fingernails. He stopped when he saw his mother. "What did they say?"

"You should not be in the priest's study, Marc."

"I asked his permission. Did the Inner Circle approve me to join?"

Roslyn paused, glancing downward.

Marc melted, looking as if he would cry. "They said no? But—"

"Forgive me," she said, forcing a smile. "I do not wish to cast a cloud of gloom over your happy occasion—*our* happy occasion. They said *yes*—more than yes. I spoke directly to the Supreme Hierophant of Light, and he said we must postpone the ritual to a more opportune time, yet he has given you leave to join without it. You *are* an Azerent Initiate. Right now."

Marc gained a large smile as his eyes lit up, but the joy faded quickly. "But there's something wrong, isn't there?"

Roslyn nodded. "Something complicated. The Inner Circle has given me a dangerous mission of grave importance." She paused. "And I require the assistance of another Azerent."

"But there aren't any other Azerents in Hunia." Marc paused. "Oh. Of course." He stood straight and gave a curt nod. "Of course, Grand Healer."

Roslyn's eyes ached as if they would tear up, but she continued, "'Tis well above your grade, so I'm giving you a choice. I will, of course, protect you as best as I am able, but we will face forces I've never encountered before." She felt sick in her stomach, putting such a choice on her son—a large part of her wanted him to refuse—but these were desperate times.

"We must evoke a Harpy," Roslyn continued gravely, "a deadly creature from the Plane of Chaos, and press it to give us vital information."

Marc swallowed dryly and nodded. His pale blue eyes glazed cold. Life had given the boy the ability to accept horrors with detached resignation. Accordingly, he said, "'Twill be an honor to assist you, Grand Healer."

CHAPTER FORTY-TWO

In the back of her apothecary, Roslyn stood in the doorway of a small closet. Inside, a broom was set against the wall, and wooden shelves held large jars of various materials needed to create items for the shop. Her attention, however, was on the doorway itself. The right jamb had been opened—opposite the hinges and the open door—revealing the inner section of the frame.

Rods of gold, five inches long and the thickness of her thumb, ran end to end inside the doorframe—truly, the rods ran inside all sides of the frame, including the floor, yet only those in the open side were exposed. One of the rods, missing from the column and instead in her hand, left a five-inch gap to which she crouched as she worked the rod back into place.

Roslyn tapped the rod carefully with a small hammer.

Estéban entered the shop, crossed to the closet, and watched her. "I gathered ten men, as you requested. They are all former Lytel fighters. They're preparing now and will meet us here soon."

Finished, the rod firmly in place, Roslyn stood. "They'll need to be in plain clothes."

"I told them."

"My thanks. You can close up the frame now."

He nodded. "Yes, surgeon, closing up the patient."

He grabbed a long board leaned against the wall outside the closet, a hammer from the floor, and some nails beside the hammer. He centered the board inside the frame, which fit perfectly from threshold to peak and covered the column of gold rods. "Will it work now?" He began hammering.

"It always worked," Roslyn said. "*Technically*. However, the Azerent who made it could only give the door a one-mile range. We are currently over six hundred miles from Port Lytel, so—needless to say—it took a lot of time and effort on my part to make the ends of the portal connect. It was actually a rather interesting project. The Gellic Nation to the northeast has made significant advances in interplanarmuralis tunnels, which is a similar, though much less advanced, technology."

"Is it so?" he mumbled around nails between his lips as he hammered.

"It is. And the Order of Azerents has been able to get some of their research from secondhand sources, which I was able to study and use. But, of course, Gellic magic is Faery-based, and this door—created from a Déagrian Corridor Mirror—is divine magic."

"Of course."

"I know you're only having a laugh, but 'tis truly fascinating. Goddess Larissa and God Déagar forged the Corridor Mirrors themselves. In that regard, this is more similar to a Tridulan octolisk, which was crafted by the Dark Light deities, Goddess Gliéska and God Zeanázel. But True Light-derived magic and Dark Light-derived magic are very different, and neither set of Gods exactly wrote notes on how they built their portals." She smiled.

He took the last nail from his lips. "You've completely lost me now." He crouched to hammer the lowest nails. "But I'm glad to see you so excited about something."

"You needn't truly know all that. 'Tis just interesting. To me."

Estéban, finished, turned to her. "But will it work?"

She sighed. "In truth, I wasn't prepared to test it yet. But we need to use it now. 'Tis important we move quickly."

"You still haven't told me where we're moving quickly *to*. Or why."

She glanced downward and nodded. "Only Marc and I may know the details. You know that. But I'll give more information once everyone gathers."

Roslyn closed the door to the closet and kept her hand on the handle while she concentrated. "Lytel," she whispered, and the latch shimmered around her hand. She opened the door.

The closet was no longer seen. Instead, there was a four-foot span, on all sides, of light in all the colors of the rainbow—wavering and twisting around one another like fire, yet more akin to a turbulent, vaporous fluid than flames. Beyond the short tunnel of light was another doorframe leading to a natural tunnel of rock.

"The spatial compression is not quite where I'd like it to be," she said. "There shouldn't be a gap. But squishing six hundred and seventy miles into four feet... I can live with that for now."

Estéban nodded. "I'm sure we can jump over the gap."

"That would be unwise. It is raw interplanar energy. If any part of you inadvertently touched it, that part would be obliterated." She looked around the shop and spotted a bench. "Ah. A perfect bridge."

Roslyn carefully extended the bench through the doorway as Estéban gave her a hand. When they set it down, one leg was in the shop and the other was miles away in the tunnel leading to Port Lytel.

She gave a satisfied nod, accompanied by a smile. "It appears we're ready to go."

—

"Spread out," Roslyn said, as she held her torch high. The cavernous main room of Port Lytel seemed so much more cave-like when lit by only the few torches held by Roslyn and her group. "You five, stay nearby," she continued. "You five, check the route ahead."

The ten soldiers, all in plain clothes, drew swords. Half formed a large, moving circle around Roslyn, Estéban, and Marc. The other half hurried to the large exit tunnel past where the infirmary used to be.

"Are we expecting trouble, Mother?" Marc asked.

"'Tis better to err on the side of caution. Lytel has been empty for years. Someone could have gotten in, despite the entrance being locked."

A layer of dust covered everything, and Roslyn's path took her through the occasional massive spiderweb. Luckily, no large spiders accompanied the web—at least not as far as she could see.

She stepped down the two steps into the chapel area and fondly remembered the day she and Estéban were married here—one of the many memories that made her feel a sadness for this place, fallen to such dilapidation. Silt masked the floor, but her footprints revealed the checkered tiles of blue and gray. All the icons of Karulus were gone—sent to better homes—leaving the front of the chapel area strangely bare. A part of Roslyn wanted to apologize to the entire port—*forgive me for abandoning you after you were our home for so long.*

She continued through the chapel, stepped two steps up, and made her way toward the infirmary. A lump formed in her throat, even as she knew how silly it was to mourn it. There was nothing left to call an infirmary—just a naturally carved alcove with a now out-of-place tile floor.

Estéban placed his hand on her shoulder. "Do you miss it?"

"'Twas my home for ten years, the last three of which I spent with you and Marc as we started our family. But no." She forced a somber smile. "No, our time in hiding is finished."

One of the soldiers returned from the tunnel and hurried to Roslyn. "The exit tunnel's clear, Commander. I mean, Ambassador."

"In truth, this is no ambassadorial mission, either." She spoke up so all the men gathering around her could hear. "As you know, this is an Azerent mission; thus, I cannot share the details of why we travel to our destination. However, I can say that the latter half of our trek will take us through Dayigan-controlled lands. We venture to a point near Mount Triumph."

"The old Silthex lair?" a soldier asked.

"Near there, yes. Your task is to get Marcoulif and me to the mountain. Yet, only the two of us may ascend to its peak. If we do not return, you are not to investigate, but are simply to return to Hunia via the portal here, without us."

Marc faced the floor—that silent resignation of his again.

"Rose," Estéban spoke up, "you—"

She cut him off with a look before addressing him directly. "I will do all I can to keep him safe. You know that. And, you know, if I were to put him in any danger at all, the task must be absolutely necessary."

Estéban nodded. He glanced at his son. "Be safe."

"We will, Father."

"Move out," Roslyn commanded.

CHAPTER FORTY-THREE

After a long week of hiking through freezing woods and rocky paths, the group from Hunia made camp on a snow-covered gradual slope at the base of a mountain spire.

Beside the crackling fire, Roslyn stared at the ominous mountain. It looked to her like the tooth of a crocodile, though what kind of crocodile had a twenty-thousand-foot tooth was a frightening thought.

Behind her, Roslyn heard footsteps crunching in the snow. She turned to see Estéban.

"We got the supplies," he said. "Gaderian says hello."

"Gaderian?"

"The former port commander in the town. He said you have met. A Terovae."

"Ah, yes. Ages ago and very briefly. Under a spoon shop, if I recall. Can you believe that was the year Marc was born?"

Estéban chuckled. "They make pottery vases now as a front for a resistance safe house. He wished you a happy New Year's Eve. 'Tis the 30th of Duodeki."

"It is, isn't it? I'd completely forgotten." She glanced down. "The forties. I thought we'd be long finished with this by now."

He sighed. "You are worried." He slid his gloved hands onto Roslyn's shoulders and began to rub.

She nodded.

"You'll get us through this," he said. "You always do."

Roslyn kissed his glove.

"At least it has stairs," he added.

Roslyn looked at where he'd mentioned. They'd made camp right at the base, and she could see up the steps carved into the rock. The steps angled steeply before they curved around.

"They're most likely Trasilvokan," Roslyn said, "the empire that ruled these lands long before the Dayigan Empire. That means they're at least eight and a half centuries old, and I doubt anyone has maintained them."

"Definitely not the locals," Estéban said. "They won't go near this place. They say 'tis cursed and haunted by evil spirits."

"I should hope so," Roslyn said. "I've come to speak with them."

—

Roslyn clacked her wooden staff against the icy step and climbed a bit further. Using a staff made her feel a bit like an old wizard in a faerytale—which, she conceded, was not far off—but now, an hour into the upward hike, the staff had become priceless to her. She ached down to her frozen bones, and the cloud-hidden sun did nothing against the frosty wind.

Estéban and two other men were right behind her, all with similar staffs and similar thick, snow-sprinkled, gray cloaks. They all seemed just as frozen and miserable as Roslyn.

Marc, however, was about thirty feet up, sitting precariously on the edge of a cliff. His legs swung back and forth over a dizzying plummet, as if nothing more than a child in a too-big chair. The sight would have horrified Roslyn if he were Human. It still looked a little unsettling. To add to this, he wore no cloak—just his same backless tunic—and had assured her the cold didn't bother him.

As Roslyn passed Marc, he looked up at her with a carefree, boyish smile. Evidently, he was having a lovely day.

Marc said, "It must be really hard going through life without wings."

Roslyn was certain he attempted to commiserate, but it sounded like a boast. "It is today." She continued past.

Another gust of icy wind blasted over her.

"What's that?" Marc asked as he pointed.

Roslyn stopped and immediately regretted it, knowing she'd have to start again. She looked where the boy pointed.

Within the craggy range beyond the steps, Roslyn saw a circular wall of jagged peaks. Inside, the rock was blackened.

"The remnants of Mount Triumph," she said. "It is where the king of the Vatelam, Fersivolíel, stood when he threw the Demons into the Plane of Chaos. Afterwards, the mountain collapsed and swallowed him up."

"Where you defeated the Silthex?"

Roslyn stared, remembering the horrors she'd faced there. "Yes."

Marc jumped up, nearing her to whisper, "Is that why the Harpies are here?"

"The two are most likely related," she said.

"I don't really know what they are," Marc confessed with shame. He looked downward, over the edge.

"Forgive me. I should have said." She turned to Estéban. "Could you give us some space, please?"

There was a hint of worry in Estéban. He covered it with a chuckle. "Secret Azerent talks, yes?"

"Yes," Roslyn said. "It won't be long."

"Come on, men."

The other Hunians moved some distance up the steps.

Roslyn returned to Marc and spoke quietly, saying, "The Harpies are called the Hounds of Ignísekhet. After people die, some souls are deemed too wicked to remain in za and fall into their domain. Déagrians—and admittedly most Karulents—would have us believe that most of mankind is damned. Though it is true most go to za, we Azerents—through study and communication with extraworldly sources—have learnt that za is not a place of torment. Yet, there is such a place. The dire sentence is extremely rare and earned only by those who nearly all of mankind, regardless of religion or lack thereof, would consider truly vile."

She looked down at the rocky land far below. "In the Hall of Truth, where the Lavender Lady judges the dead, she condemns these indisputably evil souls to the custody of the Harpies. And the Harpies take them to the Plane of Chaos, to the Nightmare Realm ruled by the Archdemoness of Wrath, Ignísekhet. There, Ignísekhet and her Harpies force the damned to relive the vilest moments of their lives, often through the eyes of their victims. This, the Deep Nightmare, is everlasting in constant, vivid loops."

Marc's eyes went cold as he digested the words. "Then the Harpies are... good?" he asked. "If they punish the truly evil."

"They are complicated," Roslyn said. "They serve an important role in the grand scheme, but they delight in tormenting the damned. If given the chance, they would lead the whole of mankind into damnation, just so they could have more toys for their twisted games."

"Will they..." Marc began, his fear showing. He swallowed. "Will they try to take us to the Nightmare Realm?"

Roslyn looked at the boy as she paused—too long of a pause, she knew. She should have lied and given a firm and comforting *no*. He was just thirteen, and Roslyn knew she'd already scared him. However, he was also an Azerent. The best she could say was, "Hopefully not."

Marc nodded, taking the ambiguous answer. "'Tis important, what we're doing," he said coldly. "The entire world of Perdinok needs us to succeed."

Roslyn nodded. "Very true."

A freezing wind cut across them, and Marc folded his arms across his chest and shivered.

"Are you sure you aren't cold?" Roslyn asked.

"In truth, Mother, I am quite uncomfortable. Terovaes are more resilient to cold, but not mountaintop-in-the-dead-of-winter resilient." He smiled. "But I cannot wear a Human cloak."

Roslyn sighed. "I know you've had a rough life, Marc, but you mustn't repress everything, not even things like that. If you're cold, you must say you're cold."

"Yes, Mother." He paused, looking at Roslyn with sad blue eyes. "In truth, too, I . . ." He hesitated. "I'm scared, Mother."

She set her gloved hand on his upper arm. "That only means you understand. However, it is not too late for you to turn back. If I must go alone—"

"No. I will go."

She nodded. "I give you my word. I will watch over you. And the Guardians will watch over us both."

"Guardians?"

"Beings of pure light. Each person in the entire world has his own personal Guardian watching over him. Yours will protect you. As will mine. And, as an Azerent, you will eventually learn to speak to yours directly."

Marc gained a perplexed smile as he drifted into thought.

Roslyn resumed her hike but called back, "I've packed you a nice, thick robe—a Terovae robe with two slits down the back to allow your wings. And a belt to hold it in place. They are in the bag you carry."

Roslyn turned to the men further up the mountain. "We continue upwards."

CHAPTER FORTY-FOUR

O nly Roslyn and Marc ascended the last of the stairs. They rounded to a flat peak about twenty feet in diameter. Roslyn had reminded the others to stay back and not to come, no matter what they saw or heard. "This," she'd said, "is an Azerent matter."

At least two feet of snow covered everything, but upon their entry, a wave of fire emanated out from the center, melting away the icy cover, yet leaving Roslyn and Marc unharmed.

The fire revealed a nine-foot wide circular stone platform two steps higher than the surrounding area. Carved into its surface, around its edge, was a circle. Moving inward, a spiral of many words in what looked to be Gellic runes—assumedly names—formed three more circles. A final circle closed the area with the names.

Within this, four large hexagrams marked the four cardinal directions: west, north, east, and south. Within each point of the stars was a letter of the name of the Holy Mother—L Á G E Y A. The number seven marked the center of the hexagram. Finally, in the very center of the platform was a large square of red marble.

Outside of the platform, four black marble pillars, each with a pentagonal base, marked the four intercardinal directions: northwest, northeast, southwest, and southeast. These pillars were nine feet tall, and atop each, a brass bowl held fire.

"What is all this?" Marc, amazed, asked in a whisper. His eyes were wide as he looked warily around the monument.

Instead of answering, Roslyn walked around the circular platform, scanning its precise carving.

She came to a second, smaller platform two feet from the first and two feet higher. This was triangular, pointing away from the first, and a circular obsidian mirror filled most of its surface. In the triangle's corners were the letters: NY JIN ITON.

"'Tis goetic," Roslyn whispered in uneasy awe. "It is not something we normally use."

"I don't understand."

"Of course. Forgive me," Roslyn said. "As far as ritual magic goes, we Azerents almost exclusively use *theurgic* magic; that is, we call upon benevolent beings and *ask* for help. In goetic magic, a mage essentially traps a malevolent being and demands its help. To put it very basically."

"Dark Light magic?"

"Not necessarily. The founder of the Azerents perfected the goetic ritual. Yet, it has fallen out of practice in the Order. Nevertheless, we came here with a goetic purpose. I actually expected to find a dark shrine, but this . . ." She looked around. "This almost looks Azerent."

"It doesn't feel Azerent." Marc rubbed his arm.

She nodded. She felt it, too, an ambient evil energy that permeated the area, stronger than the cold or the wind. It was a pressure against her body, particularly her breast, causing her breathing to labor.

"We should begin," Roslyn said. "I'll need you to—"

Thunder sounded, echoing with such volume that Roslyn, a grown woman, felt the need to snap her hands to her head and duck.

The sky filled with black clouds—properly black, not dark gray. They blocked out the sun.

"Hurry!" Roslyn shouted to Marc. "Get to the red square in the center of the circle."

"What's happening?"

"I don't know," she said. "We must begin the ritual at once."

Marc nodded and ran up the steps to the circle.

Roslyn took a moment to look at the triangular platform.

Above the obsidian circle, a mass of black particles formed. Its currents were quick and erratic, with streaks of crimson light darting and twisting within.

Roslyn dashed toward the circle.

When Marc crossed the spiral of names, they and the circles edging them lit up in yellow light. They shone upward as a wall. It rose three feet before fading transparent.

Roslyn slapped her hands on the unseen part of the wall. It felt hot. "Marc," she called, "you must let me in!"

"I"—he looked around, panicked—"I don't know how."

Roslyn looked back at the ominous mass of blackness forming above the triangle.

It grew larger and more solid.

Roslyn ran to the side of the circle opposite the triangle and motioned Marc her way.

"I need you to cut a door through the circle," she said with urgent calm. "Do you have a dagger?"

"No. I have nothing."

"'Tis all right," she encouraged. "Hold your hand flat with your fingers together—imagine it is a blade."

Marc complied, though his hand shook.

Roslyn looked past him.

Whatever was forming above the triangle now appeared to be three whatevers.

She kept her calm.

"Now," Roslyn said, "I need you to chop downwards through the wall of the circle and envision it cutting apart like a wall of cloth. Envision an entrance forming."

Marc closed his eyes as he lifted his hand. He chopped his hand downward. But instead of cutting the wall, his fingers hit it. He recoiled as he called out.

"It didn't work," Marc said, cradling his fingers.

Roslyn looked again at the triangle.

Three figures had formed. Each had the body of a Human-breasted vulture and the head of a woman—though hideous with sharp teeth. The eyes were crimson voids in cracked sockets.

"'Tis too late," Roslyn said to Marc. "Get in the red square."

"I can't leave you out there unprotected."

"Go! I'll be fine. The triangle will contain them."

The Harpy at the front of the other two, this one slightly larger, spoke with a harsh, cronish voice, saying, "I feel such anger in you, girl." Her words held dark delight. "So much want of vengeance."

Roslyn took a deep breath, gathering herself. She walked around the circle, nearing the creatures while keeping a distance. Standing resolutely, she faced the Harpies.

With a commanding shout, Roslyn called out, "In the Holy name of God Karulus, holder of the Sapphire Ib, I compel you to answer my questions."

"Who are you, girl," the largest Harpy asked, "to demand actions of us?"

"I am a grand healer of the Order of Azerents, those who follow the teachings of King Azerhad."

"Ooooo," the Harpy mocked as she turned to another, "an *Azerent grand healer*. So impressive. 'Tis a pity though, truly, that King Azerhad never taught his followers to stand *within* a protective circle, not beside it."

The Harpies cackled wildly.

"No," the same Harpy continued. "I see no healer here. I see an *angry little girl* who wants to hurt those who hurt her."

"You are wrong," Roslyn said firmly. "I've come for information. Nothing more."

The Harpies began cackling again as they flapped their wings and hopped about in delight.

"What is his name?" the Harpy asked. "I can almost hear it in the wind."

"I don't know what you mean," Roslyn said. "The Order has sent me here to—"

"Jon," the Harpy shrieked. All three repeated it, all three squawking his name over and over like crazed chickens. "Jon. Jon. Jon. Jon."

"Stop it!" Roslyn shouted. "Don't you *dare* say his name?"

The Harpies stopped and silence fell, though they leered.

Rage rushed through Roslyn's veins and pounded in her heart. She clenched her teeth and clenched her fists as she glared at the Harpies.

"Infinite apologies," the largest Harpy said. The three long-clawed fingers atop her wing moved to her breast as she bowed her head in a parody of regret. "It must feel so very wretched to lose your love—so young, so sweet. The two of you would have had a happy, giggly little Karulus-worshiping life together, wouldn't you have? Even now, after all these years, you can still see the shop he planned to build you."

"I have that now."

"'Tis not the same, is it, though your new husband does try. It can never be the same, because the girl you were *died watching everybody burn.*"

In a flash, Roslyn suddenly stood frozen in the wishing pool outside the old Hunian inn. It burned before her eyes. She could see it, feel the heat, hear the people screaming, smell the smoke as if she were truly there again. In a flash, she returned.

"Ah," a Harpy said, "but you have lost so much more. Your father, to a plague they blame you for. Your friends, your subordinates. I understand why you want your enemies to pay."

Roslyn snapped her shaking hand to her forehead, cradling it as she slouched forward. "You know nothing about me. I fight for justice and the freedom of my people."

"Oh," the Harpy hissed, "and we mustn't forget about poor Margaret. Did you keep your vow to her? Did you *end the plague of hatred infecting our lands*? We can help you, if you allow us to."

Roslyn again held her head high and stood resolutely. "In the name of Karulus, holder of the Sapphire Ib, Sentry of the West, I compel you, tell me why Chaos is flooding into our plane."

"What has your blue God done for you as they stole your world away?" the largest Harpy asked. "They stole your son's world too. He's never said what he witnessed, what vile things he watched those soldiers do to his mother before they slit her throat."

Roslyn looked back toward Marc.

His emotions, always so hidden, showed clear as he collapsed to his knees, jaw clenched, icy eyes glossed with tears. He snapped his shaking arm across his eyes and turned away.

"Can you protect him?" another Harpy asked. "You *are* strong."

"We can make you stronger," said another.

The first said, "With us, you could be a mighty force of vengeance ripping through all who have harmed you and those you love. The Dayigan Empire could fall by your hands." She fisted her claw.

"The Empire is already destabilizing," Roslyn maintained, "in part by my efforts. It will *already* fall."

The Harpies started cackling.

"She doesn't know," one said.

"Of course she doesn't know," said the first. "The fate is so wrapped up in Chaos that the Azerents are blind to it."

"Stop shrieking and cackling," Roslyn shouted, "and tell me what you mean."

The largest Harpy grinned a horror of sharpened teeth as she said, "Everything you built—your little town, your little family—the Déagrians will take it *all away*. Your efforts are for naught, Azerent."

Roslyn's breaths hastened as her hands flexed as fists to her sides.

"Did we make you angry?" a Harpy asked.

"We wouldn't want that," another said. "Especially not now, when your child is dying."

Roslyn turned to Marc.

He was pale and hunched over, with his hands on his knees.

Roslyn hurried to the edge of the circle. "Marc," she called. "Can you hear me?" She pounded on the unseen wall.

"He is strong for his age, isn't he?" the largest Harpy said. "But this is a *powerful* set of circles. And they require a lot of energy to hold them. Though only partially powered by him, it seems he will soon be drained to death."

"Marc," Roslyn pleaded. "Please respond."

Roslyn pushed herself against the wall, trying to break through, yet it was like a stone.

"Another unavenged death," another harpy said. "The Déagrians have so much to pay for."

A Harpy hissed, "They say death from pneuma depletion is *agonizing*."

"Marc!" Roslyn screamed.

He fell over to his side.

CHAPTER FORTY-FIVE

Roslyn set her hand on the invisible wall of the circle and watched helplessly as Marc lay in its center.

He was alive, but she could see his soul dimming in his body as the circle drained him. He wouldn't last much longer.

"Forgive me," Roslyn whispered. "I thought I could protect you." She closed her eyes as a tear rolled down her cheek. "This is my fault."

"You've seen much death," the largest of the three Harpies said, her voice shrill. "The Empire has taken so much from you. 'Tis right you should make them pay."

"I am a healer," she maintained with a shaky voice. She stared at Marc.

Roslyn set her forehead on the warm, unseen wall. "I am not whatever vengeance-seeker you are trying to make me out to be. I just want to help people."

"Is it so?" the harpy asked.

Roslyn jerked as she gasped in pain. Crimson flashed before her eyes.

She found herself standing near a wooded rocky hill with a dirt road curving around it. At the road's edge, the ground dropped gradually. There, at a distance, she found herself again—another Roslyn.

The other Roslyn lay on her stomach behind a rocky mound as she stared intently at the road. Four men lay at her sides, also watching. Others were spread out behind various other concealments.

"Where are we?" asked a young man's voice behind the on-looking Roslyn.

Roslyn turned back. It was Jon, her love from so long ago. Eighteen looked so much younger to her now. He wore the old-style Dayigan tabard—red with amber thread depicting the Dayigan symbol. He looked like a child in a costume, and it pained Roslyn to remember how young he'd been when he died.

She looked away. "You are horrible to take that form."

"Jon's death," he said, "was the genesis of your vengeance. The moment that propelled you here. Again, where are we?"

Roslyn sighed before looking at the other her, crouched beside the road. "I believe it is the spring before I met Estéban and Marc," she said. "Port Lytel received intelligence that a Dayigan convoy was making its way to a nearby fort. This is the point where it would be the least guarded."

"A rescue mission?" Jon asked. "Are you, perhaps, saving some poor kidnapped Karulents?"

"No," Roslyn whispered with a hint of shame.

Four Dayigan soldiers approached in a staggered formation on either side of the road. From here, Roslyn could see their uniforms, the emerald green tabards embroidered with the same amber Dayigan symbol as Jon's.

Behind them, three horse-drawn wagons clattered down the road. Six more soldiers marched on either side, four more behind.

There were twenty soldiers, not counting the men driving the wagons. They were twice as many as the waiting Port Lytel fighters.

The Roslyn hiding by the road glanced up the way to a Lytel fighter holding ropes. She raised her hand slowly, waiting to signal.

The wagons continued, passing so close in front of her that the dust they stirred up wafted around her in clouds.

Roslyn dropped her hand.

The fighter released the ropes.

A large tree, fitted with many spikes, fell and smashed through the lead soldiers as it slammed down to block the road.

The lead horses reared up, whinnying in fright.

Lytel fighters, swords drawn and shouting, rushed onto the road.

Soldiers grappled for their swords, drawing quickly.

The two sides clashed.

Roslyn stood up but did not charge. Instead, she thrust her hands toward the first wagon driver. He lifted from his seat, hovering a moment, and dropped to the ground. Second driver: the same. Third driver: the same.

A Lytel fighter cried out as a soldier ran his blade through his shoulder.

Roslyn rushed toward him, casting her hand toward the assailant. The soldier flew back against a wagon.

She hurried to examine the injury. "It missed your heart," she said. "You'll be fine."

A soldier charged her, but Roslyn cast her hand toward him.

"Anesthetize!" she shouted.

The soldier tumbled to the ground.

Roslyn set her hand above the fighter's injury. Blue light glowed from her palm, healing the injury completely.

The fighter rolled his shoulder. "My thanks, Commander."

"Go," she said.

He leaped up and ran back into the fight.

Another Lytel fighter called out, as he took the blade of a sword. Jumping up, Roslyn ran to him.

The Roslyn who watched from a distance saw the forest blur and streak, like water washing over paint.

"You've become quite the soldier," Jon said.

She nodded sadly. "I've had to adapt to what the world required of me. However, I've now taken on a diplomatic role."

The surrounding woods reformed. Now, the Roslyn within the event walked in front of a line of nine Dayigan soldiers. Each was on his knees beside the wagons. Their hands were tied behind their backs.

The dead were laid out, uncovered and gruesome, beside the road.

"What do we have?" Roslyn called to one of her men in the back of a wagon.

He looked into a crate a moment more before responding. "Our sources were right, Commander. 'Tis Gellic swords, the best I've seen. I count about thirty per crate. Three crates per cart."

Roslyn turned to the nearest soldier. "We thank the Dayigan Empire for your fine contribution to our defense efforts. We'll assure these weapons make their way to Veiled River fighters throughout the Empire."

"Fucking whore," the soldier growled, struggling at the ropes. "You won't get away with this. We know who you are, the *Blue Witch*."

"Saying *witch* like it is an insult doesn't make it one," she said. "'Tis just inaccurate."

"Whatever you are, you'll pay for what you've done."

"What *we've* done?" Roslyn asked angrily. "The Dayigans have taken *everything* from us. And you keep taking and taking."

He spit at her. "Your people murdered millions of men, women, and children with your Blue Sickness."

"Lies!" she screamed. She punched him in the face.

Jon laughed as he watched the scene from a distance.

The current Roslyn stared at her past self, as her past self stared vacantly at her fist.

"I should not have done that," Roslyn said to Jon. "But it doesn't prove whatever you're trying to prove. That was the me before I met Estéban and Marc. They helped me remember my true calling."

"I never knew Azerents smuggled stolen weapons," Jon said.

"It is necessary."

The woods darkened away until she and Jon stood in empty blackness.

"What became of the Dayigan soldiers?" Jon asked.

"We tied them to trees some distance from the road," Roslyn said. "But before you start, once we were at a safe distance, we sent word to a nearby fort of their location, which is much more than—" Roslyn stopped herself.

"More than they deserve?" Jon gained an enormous smile. "Yes, I agree. I would have left them there."

Roslyn breathed. "That is not who I am," she maintained.

"Is it not? Shortly before you met your life-changing husband and son, you left an entire encampment of Déagrian soldiers unconscious in the woods."

Another scene formed around them—night in the woods just beside a small collection of Dayigan tents. Again, Roslyn saw herself, this time standing over a soldier—a mad soldier, she remembered. Her past self had rendered him asleep.

The Roslyn of the past spoke to one of the five surrounding Lytel fighters, saying, "Take him to the camp with the other soldiers. He'll awaken soon after them."

"If the beasts of the forest don't get them first," said a fighter.

"That is not our concern," Roslyn said. "Gather our people. We begin our march to Lytel forthwith."

The scene faded, and again Roslyn and Jon stood in total blackness.

"If you mean to assert I'm driven by vengeance, you are wrong. Even then, I was driven by a desire to help my people."

"Even so," Jon said, "wolves found those soldiers. They ate them, screaming and alive, whilst the other soldiers were just awake enough to watch and wait in horror whilst unable to move. What say you, Azerent? Not your concern?"

Roslyn said nothing. She crossed her arms and stared with stern eyes.

"It was a lie, anyway. I have no idea if they were eaten." Jon maintained that eerie smile. "And who were you *helping* when you tried to kill the man who killed Jon? Swithun. Should I show you those moments?" Still, he smiled as his stomach burst open with a gaping wound spilling thick blood down his tabard.

"Please," she gasped. "Please, don't."

"All right." He grinned. "I don't need to. You remember well what it was like to grab that sword and furiously hack into the flesh of the man who killed your love." He casually ran his fingers through the blood flowing from him. "You tried to tell people, even yourself, it was necessary. Self-defense." He smeared blood across his face and laughed. "It wasn't."

"I did not kill him."

"You tried. In a beautiful explosion of pure retribution, you tried."

Roslyn only looked away. She wanted to say something in her defense, but there was nothing to say. He was right.

"I do not judge you for your actions," he said. "On the contrary, we can help you if you allow us to. You have so many reasons to rightfully justify your wrath. We can help you overcome the limitations of the Azerents. We can forge you into a powerful sorceress, unrestrained, able to rip through the Dayigan Army with a might unseen in ages."

"No!" Roslyn shouted. "I'm not what you think I am. *Get away from me!*"

She cast her hands toward Jon, and he flew backward until he faded into the blackness.

—

Roslyn woke beside the protective circle. Marc remained inside, dying.

A noise attracted her attention. She turned to her left.

The largest Harpy now stood just beside her.

CHAPTER FORTY-SIX

The Harpy lunged to grab Roslyn with the three clawed fingers atop her wings. Roslyn dodged, rolling on her back—a pain on the steps to the circle. Roslyn thrust her hands forward.

The Harpy did not fly back, but neither could she move forward.

Roslyn concentrated with all of her will, trying to push the creature away. The Azerent's might became a thick ray of blue that the Harpy struggled against. The creature's mouth opened wide with dagger teeth as her wings thrashed wildly toward Roslyn.

"You are a fool, girl!" the Harpy shrieked. "You do not have the will to fight a Harpy. Give up and stop wasting our time."

"You are but an extraplanar projection of yourself."

"Do you think that matters?" the Harpy cackled. "Even as a projection, I'm still more powerful than you."

The Harpy strained against Roslyn's magic, pushing forward.

With a painful grunt, Roslyn focused her concentration. The rays of blue glowed brighter, shoving the Harpy backward, though only by three feet.

"Very strong, girl," the Harpy said. "Still, when my sisters free themselves, we will rip out your soul, and the boy's, and drag you to the Nightmare Realm."

Roslyn looked at the other Harpies.

They clawed and bit at the invisible walls of the triangle that held them.

"Marc," Roslyn called.

The boy lay on his side, unmoving. His face was flat against the red marble square. Eyes closed. Nose bleeding. Mouth open and drooling.

"Marc, I know 'tis difficult," Roslyn said, "but I need you to fight. The Order is counting on us."

His bloodshot eyes opened weakly, but he didn't move.

The Harpy lunged forward.

Roslyn cast a stronger force to hold her in place.

Roslyn gasped as a sharp pain stabbed above her right temple.

"Marc, I need to know if you can hear and understand me."

His head moved ever so slightly in a nod against the stone.

"All right. You're doing very well. I need you to listen. Though you did not *cast* the circle, it is *your* circle. It is an extension of *your* will, a part of you. You must *feel* the circle, know it. Do you understand?"

He shook his head weakly against the stone.

The Harpy gained ground, and the others clawed frantically at their confinement.

"Marc," Roslyn called. "You must concentrate. You are an Azerent. You can do this. The circle has a vibration linked to you. You must gain control of it."

The Harpy swiped at Roslyn, claws cutting her upper arm in three deep gashes.

Roslyn jumped away, holding her arm as it healed. She ran and evaded.

The Harpy was quick, shrieking as it flew at her.

Roslyn cast out her hands, capturing the thing again in rays of blue.

Roslyn looked at Marc. His eyes were again closed. Was he fighting in his mind, or had he given up? She couldn't tell.

The Harpy cackled. "You're proving to be entertaining, girl. But I know you can't keep this up much longer. We will have you both."

She was right, Roslyn knew. She could feel her power weakening, but she had no choice but to press on.

Then, Roslyn saw a thin vein of blue light snake its way slowly up the circle's wall. It was a trivial thing, barely noticeable, but Roslyn knew it must be Marc.

More veins formed, all thin and faint, but spread out along the entire perimeter, stretching far up into the unseen section.

"Good job, Marc," Roslyn whispered.

With greater resolve, she pushed ahead and stepped forward, while nudging the Harpy back with blue light. It was like forcing a cart of boulders with her bare hands, but she knew she must move the Harpy back into the triangle.

Roslyn cried out in pain.

"Running out of magic, deary?" the Harpy asked. "They say dying from pneuma depletion is agonizing. I cannot wait to watch!"

Marc grunted weakly and jerked in pain. He coughed blood to ooze from his mouth.

"To watch twice over," the Harpy added gleefully.

Black began to twist around the blue within the circle's wall. Death energy was encroaching.

Roslyn stopped, though she maintained her force against the Harpy.

"Marc," she called. "Can you still hear me?"

No reaction.

"Marc, I need you to keep going a little bit longer for me, all right?" The words to the hurt boy pained Roslyn to speak, and her voice cracked around them. "You're attuned with the circle. That's wonderful. The circle has a lot more energy than what you put into it. I need you to pull some of that energy into yourself. Just from the circle, not from the triangle. Do you understand?"

"'Tis too late for the boy," the Harpy said. "He's as good as dead. And you'll soon be, too. Yet, our offer still stands. Die here in agony or become a mighty sorceress, ripping down your enemies. *We know what you are.*"

"What I am is *angry*," Roslyn screamed as she cast a greater force against the Harpy. "And I'm tired of being angry, and I'm tired of fighting *battle* after *battle*, year after year, for nothing more than the meager goal of normalcy." The light from her hands grew brighter with greater force. "All I wanted was a simple life with my sweet husband in our little house, with our children and my shop. But they *took* it. And I built it again, yet they threaten to *take* it again. They keep *taking* and *taking*. And yes . . ." She breathed. "Yes, sometimes I am driven by vengeance, but that is *not* who I am. I want peace between the Karulents and the Déagrians. *That* is what I fight for. And we will achieve it."

Thunder accompanied yellow lightning as it shot inward from all sides of the circle, striking Marc. He screamed as it lifted him, arched horizontally, his arms and wings outstretched.

Roslyn pushed harder against the Harpy, shoving her backward, closer to the triangle.

The creature of Chaos fought frantically against the Azerent, as the hideous sisters behind her fought to rip through their cage.

"You're growing weak, too," Roslyn said through clenched teeth. "Your name is beginning to show."

On the Harpy's forehead, letters of fire burned: E . . . K . . . D . . . I . . . The Harpy shrieked.

In a commanding voice, Roslyn shouted, "Hear me, Titaness Lágeya, the Holy Mother. Hear me, Titan Jerah, the all-seeing sun. Hear me, God Karulus, the spirit of truth and compassion. Hear me, Ashatra, the Lavender Lady. By all the names I've said, I constrain you, Harpy Ekdikasis. Return to the triangle *at once*, and do not leave until I command it."

The Harpy screamed as she flew backward onto the obsidian mirror within the triangle.

Roslyn looked back at Marc.

In the center of the circle, the boy kneeled, though it was not a weakened stance. With one knee on the red marble and the other up with his hands folded atop it, he looked like he was ready to leap. His blue wings spread wide. He stared forward.

"Drop the circle," Roslyn commanded Marc. "Concentrate all the energies on enforcing the triangle."

He glared at the Harpies. "Yes, Grand Healer."

Marc touched five fingers to the red stone at his feet. The wall of the surrounding circle shattered and faded downward.

The wall of the triangular platform grew stronger, becoming visible, like glass, as did the inner wall around the black circle that filled the triangle.

"What did you accomplish?" the Harpy, Ekdikasis, hissed. "You've only put us back how we started. The boy will be drained again. We will be free again. And now, now there is no circle to protect him."

Unmoved, Roslyn said, "Then I better act quickly." She turned and hurried up the steps of the circle. She passed its threshold without issue.

"Are you all right?" she asked Marc.

He nodded as he stood. "I think so. I think my Guardian was with me. I'm really hungry now, though." He touched his stomach.

"I won't be much longer. Just concentrate on keeping the confinement walls up. Can you do that?"

"Yes, Grand Healer."

Roslyn turned toward the Harpies and took a strong, well-postured stance. In clear, loud words, she said, "Behold, O Harpy Ekdikasis, I stand before you, armed in strength by the divine rulers of the True Light. In their might, I hold no fear. In their might, I command you: answer my demands with clarity and obedience."

Ekdikasis hissed as she lowered her head. Her face scowled around hate-filled, crimson eyes. "Speak, Azerent. I cannot disobey."

Roslyn continued, saying, "By the True Light rulers, I command you, Ekdikasis, to answer truthfully. Why is Chaos seeping into our world?"

The Harpy groaned. "During the time you call the first calendar," she recounted, "the stone warrior, Fersivolíel, created a portal from the world of Perdinok, in the Physical Plane, to Trasilon, in the Plane of Chaos. 'Twas right there, above Mount Triumph." She stiffly looked up.

The sky above still held pitch-black clouds. They flashed with occasional streaks of crimson.

"Afterwards," Ekdikasis resumed, "he evoked every Demon and their spawns and threw them through. The True Light Gods—God Déagar, God Karulus, and Goddess Larissa—then combined their magics to create three gates to seal the portal shut. Yet they never anticipated how *idiotic* their worshipers would become."

The three Harpies began cackling and hopping about as they flapped their wings.

"Calm yourself and continue your answer," Roslyn commanded. "What do you mean?"

Ekdikasis again looked toward her, sharp teeth grinning wide. "'Tis the war, you fool," she said. "The war within the True Light—between the Déagrians and the Karulents. It has weakened the gates that seal the interplanar portal."

The three shrieked in high-pitched guffaws.

"And as if that were not enough," Ekdikasis said through laughter, "the fool Blastilv—*who we know you know well*—has used the same hand that created the portal to make a weapon of his own.

"With her creation, just over two weeks ago," Ekdikasis continued, "the first gateway to Perdinok has opened!"

"What weapon?" Roslyn asked. "We destroyed the body of Fersivolíel."

"Not all of it, my dear." Ekdikasis lifted her wing, stretching out her three clawed fingers. A disk of crimson mist formed, and within it, an image:

A priest in a green robe held down a naked, struggling, white-winged girl before a statue of God Déagar. Beside them, Blastilv shouted out an incantation. Green lightning shot from the armored hand of Déagar, striking the girl's eyes.

The image swirled away.

"The hand remains," Ekdikasis said. "And with it, Blastilv will soon ravage the lands. You thought the Dayigan Empire neared collapse? No, no, no. Its might has not even begun. And its wrath will open your world up to all who inhabit Chaos."

"I don't understand. Why would Blastilv, even as vile as he is, unleash the inhabitants of Chaos?"

"'Tis Blastilv who doesn't understand." She smiled sharpened teeth. "In his hate-fueled quest to build an army, he dabbles with forces far, far, far beyond his control. Weakening the interplanar wall is a . . . hapless minor mishap."

"*Oopsy*," another Harpy called out with a laugh. "I didn't mean to destroy the planet. *Déagar forgive me*."

The three began another bout of raucous laughter.

"I wonder," Ekdikasis said, nearly choking on her twisted glee, "will Chaos destroy your world, or will Blastilv's army? Only time will tell."

Roslyn's hands flexed as fists. "How do I stop it?" she demanded.

Ekdikasis ceased her laughter. "I've told you that already. Let us strengthen you into a sorceress. Be our chosen vessel in the mortal realm."

"That will never happen," Roslyn said firmly.

"Very well," Ekdikasis said. "The prince and the whore will birth the line that births the Bloodheir. Hate's wrathful fire will birth the Firechild. *They* will end the Dayigan Empire. That is all I know."

"Where do I—"

Marc called out in pain as he bowed forward, grabbing his head.

Roslyn looked toward him, fearing for him.

He nodded, groaning, "Keep going."

"How do I find them? The Bloodheir and the Firechild?"

"They aren't born yet," the Harpy shrieked merrily. "Who knows if they ever will be? Your world might be ripped apart by then. The future's always changing, you know."

Roslyn paused, digesting the bleak words.

She again stood strong, lifting her arms upward. "Heed, O Harpy Ekdikasis and your sisters beside you. As you have fulfilled my reasons for summoning you here, I grant you leave to depart. Return directly to the Plane of Chaos whence you came. Do so in peace, with no harm to anyone or anything here or on your path. Go, I say, in the name of Karulus, his Holy Mother, and his wife, who is the Queen of the Dead."

Blackness shone up from the obsidian mirror beneath the Harpies and twisted them with shadow arms. The arms pulled the Harpies down, and they were gone.

Roslyn stared as the walls of the triangle faded.

"Praise be to Karulus," she whispered, "spirit of truth, and of compassion. You are our God and our savior. Heal our hearts, although we are wicked, and by your light, guide us safely to Laqyigo. By your waters, wash this place clean of any wickedness that remains. Make it again pure and purify us who have touched wickedness. As thy will, may it be."

Marc approached Roslyn. He looked pale and shaken, but all right. He asked, "Why did the Harpies think you'd become a dark sorceress?"

She sighed and glanced downward. "I fear they know I've lost myself."

"But," he grew uncomfortable, "isn't knowing yourself one of the most important parts of being an Azerent?"

Roslyn nodded sadly. "'Tis difficult to explain to someone so young. Sometimes, even when we are genuinely trying to find and be who we truly are, the world forces us to be something else."

Marc nodded. "I do understand, Mother. More than I wish I did." His innocent blue eyes glanced downward.

Roslyn forced a thin smile. "But you said you were hungry. Go ahead and fly down to the camp. Our fighters there will find you something. I'll walk down with the others."

"Yes, Mother." Cheerlessly, he turned to walk away.

"Wait," Roslyn said. "Forgive me. I told you wrong."

He paused and looked back.

"Sometimes," she said, "we *let* the world change us into something we're not. I will not let that happen."

Marc nodded. "I will help you, Mother, if you want me to."

She chuckled lightly through a slight grin. "That would be very nice of you, Marc. Now, go on. I'm sure you must be starving."

He nodded and ran toward the cliff. Spreading his wings, he jumped over the edge.

Roslyn looked upward, toward the sky above the broken Mount Triumph. The first gateway to Perdinok had opened.

The location looked no different from any normal sky.

Continue at

JEREMIAHCAIN.COM